3

"A first-rate tonic . . . an odd but compelling mixture, in almost equal parts, of Star Trek, Cordwainer Smith, and . . . culture studies. . . . This is his best job so far in giving us a fully textured planetary society. . . . Coppel keeps our interest, and delivers another satisfying, swashbuckling finale."
—*Locus*

"Told from both the cats' and the humans' perspectives, this is a humanized *Tailchaser's Song* in space. Recommended."
—*Library Journal*

"Coppel, who is best known for his espionage thrillers (*The Apocalypse Brigade,* etc.), has been publishing SF steadily sinced 1947. With that deep experience, he can't help but spin a tale that . . . will engage readers with its easygoing style and suitably soap-operatic scale."
—*Publishers Weekly*

D0557505

Tor Books by Alfred Coppel

THE GOLDENWING CYCLE

Glory
Glory's War
Glory's People

GLORY'S PEOPLE

•

Alfred Coppel

A TOM DOHERTY ASSOCIATES BOOK
NEW YORK

For Virginia Kidd and Gene Wolfe.

NOTE: If you purchased this book without a cover you should be aware
that this book is stolen property. It was reported as "unsold and destroyed"
to the publisher, and neither the author nor the publisher has received any
payment for this "stripped book."

This is a work of fiction. All the characters and events portrayed in this
book are either products of the author's imagination or are used
fictitiously.

GLORY'S PEOPLE

Copyright © 1996 by Alfred Coppel

All rights reserved, including the right to reproduce this book, or portions
thereof, in any form.

Cover art by David Mattingly

Edited by David G. Hartwell

A Tor Book
Published by Tom Doherty Associates, Inc.
175 Fifth Avenue
New York, NY 10010

Tor Books on the World Wide Web:
http://www.tor.com

Tor® is a registered trademark of Tom Doherty Associates, Inc.

ISBN: 0-812-52395-4
Library of Congress Card Catalog Number: 95-53749

First edition: June 1996
First mass market edition: July 1997

Printed in the United States of America

0 9 8 7 6 5 4 3 2 1

And what rough beast, its hour come round at last,
   Slouches toward Bethlehem to be born?
                                    —William Butler Yeats
                                       "The Second Coming"

PROLOGUE:

WHAT ROUGH BEAST?

•

SETI's begging signals were heard long ago.

Before the Jihad, Earth's Hubble Telescope imaged a bulge of energy a thousand light-years long and half a thousand wide as it burst from a dark disk in an elliptical galaxy in the Virgo Cluster. Ecstatic Terrestrial astronomers theorized that they had identified a black hole, three billion times the mass of the sun.

At the turn of the Twenty-Second Century, in an interval between the religious wars, a second, smaller, but equally intense, phenomenon is imaged by the Lunar Observatory near Tau Vulpecula. Again the astronomers hypothesize that they are observing the birth of a black hole—nearby, a mere three thousand light-years from Earth.

But this time the theorists are wrong. What they see is the opening of a Gateway and a transit. There is something new amid the galaxies of the Local Group.

The Intruder is implacable, a predator, a creature of an environment where there is neither space nor time. It finds in this young universe an endless well of life and energy, free for the taking. It assumes the aspect of Red Sprites to suck dry the planetary storms common on the planets of Tau Vulpecula. And it listens to the faint outbound signals from SETI, a program, a fad long ago abandoned.

By the Earth year 2200, the Intruder has depopulated the aquatic planets of the Virgo Cluster and is moving toward the source of the SETI transmissions. For many years it has drifted *across interstellar distances at an Einsteinian pace. But it can move much faster—as fast as it wishes, for it knows nothing of time or distance.*

By the time the Third Millennium is half done, Earth's great Goldenwings have populated the planets of the Near Stars.

The intruder has discovered the narcotic effect of powerful emotions, powerful fears. It now hunts beings who can travel at only near-relativistic speed in a construct of gossamer webs and skylar wings.

It stalks Glory.

PART I

•

A samurai with no group and no horse is not a samurai at all.

—YAMAMOTO TSUNETOMO, *HAGAKURE*

1

YEDO

.

Goldenwing Syndic Duncan Kr awoke from an oppressive dream. The room sensors reacted to his waking and increased the illumination in the chamber to a soft glow. From beyond the electronic door there came the softly feminine syllables of a newsreader describing, in classical Japanese, yesterday's ceremonial events.

Duncan, a tall and angular man too large for the bed in which he had spent the night, swung his bare feet to the elegantly tatami-matted floor and drew in several breaths of the heavy, richly scented air. His recently acquired (and out of date) Japanese limited his understanding, but he surmised that the newsreader was informing her listeners about the extraordinary arrival in the Tau Ceti System. She used the New General Catalog astronomical name instead of the local *Amaterasu*—the Sun Goddess. Probably as a gesture of politeness toward *Glory*'s people. The girl assured her viewers that the visit of the syndics to Planet Yamato, long awaited and fortuitously coinciding with the approach from the south of the Cherry Blossom Front, would not be a disappointment to the citizens of the city of Yedo.

Duncan heard a sharp clap of command as Amaya turned off the holo projector in her room. *Glory*'s Sailing Master was already up and exercising in her part of the suite. Their hosts had expected Amaya to share Duncan's bed and they had been embarrassed when Duncan explained that Amaya was neither his wife nor his concubine, and that Broni Ehrengraf, the other human female aboard the orbiting ship, would not be making the shuttle flight down to Yedo.

The domain patriarchs of the welcoming committee (there had been no women in the formal delegation), had rather sheepishly apologized. "It has always been our understanding that Wired Starmen live in delightful promiscuity, Kr-san. Have we been misinformed?"

Apparently, Duncan discovered, the Wired Starmen of Goldenwing *Hachiman,* the ship that had deposited the first clan of colonists on Yamato, had indeed been delightfully promiscuous. Yamato's great chronicle of the voyage from Earth—the *Monogatari no Hachiman*—was a seething tale of battles, sexual and dynastic conflicts and misadventures. After reading the *Monogatari* sent to *Glory* by radio, Duncan found himself wondering how that first load of colonists had survived the adventure.

The legend was bloody and, given the customary ethics of Goldenwing syndics, unusual to say the least. The chronicle described a number of occasions when colonists were awakened from cold-sleep to serve the needs of the samurai syndics who sailed *Hachiman.* On Yamato there were still many descendants of the children begotten in space by the *Hachiman* syndics.

The *Hachiman* had been unusual in that it made three voyages between Yamato and Earth before vanishing into legend and the vastness of Deep Space.

Duncan and his crew—Amaya, Broni Ehrengraf, Damon Ng, Buele the prodigy, and Neurocybersurgeon Dietr Krieg—had had seven months of uptime to receive, decode and study the broadcasts from Yamato. Amaya, a Centauri feminist, and Broni Ehrengraf, the descendant of Afrikaner Voertrekkers, had found the sexual history described by the descendants of Yamato's First Arrivers a chronicle of hilariously boastful tall tales. But Dietr Krieg refused to be dubious. "Not all syndics are as Spartan as we," he said slyly, "and not everyone has had the benefit of your ball-breaker upbringing, Sailing Master."

Dietr delighted in reminding Anya Amaya that she had been sold by the New Earth Eugenics Authority to the Goldenwing *Glory* syndicate precisely because she had been unwilling (actually she had been unable) to produce female offspring through the strict New Earth protocol of in vitro fertilization. Dietr, with rough syndic humor, claimed to attribute Anya's sterility to her feminist upbringing.

"Someday, Duncan," Amaya often said, "I am going to kill or castrate that Kraut son of a bitch."

Duncan stood and walked to the shoji screen covering the transparent wall. He slid the wood-and-paper construct aside and stood looking down through perfectly clear glass at the city of Yedo. Like a reincarnation of the ancient Japanese capital built by Tokugawa Ieyasu, Yedo was a city of many tiled roofs, walled courtyards and sand gardens. The old mingled with the very new in what *Glory*'s computer described as "the Japanese style."

The ryokan in which he and Amaya had been housed soared a thousand meters above the streets of Yedo—a city that covered the low coastal hills on which the First Arrivers and their multitude of clansmen and retainers had, over centuries of local time, built their Domain capital.

The sky was clouded and a warm rain was falling. It was early spring in Yamato's equatorial zone. Duncan could see no fewer than four squalls on the broad, copper-tinged ocean to the southeast. Lightning, like threads of gold, streaked the shadowy cloud towers and danced like faerie fire over the surface of the sea.

To the north lay the Fuji Mountains, a massively broad-shouldered range with perpetually snow-covered heights. It was in the Fujis that Yamato most resembled the ancient Homeland. Great coniferous forests of iron-hard wood from the Fujis provided the planet with most of its building material—a resource that made the Domain of Honshu the wealthiest on the planet.

On Yamato the Domains took the names of the continental islands that comprised their territory. The Japanese had fought civil wars for a thousand years on the home planet. They had no intention of continuing that tradition on Yamato. Land distribution was made soon after Lander's Day more than a millennium and a half ago, and the distribution remained in effect to the present. Honshu was the family domain of the Minamoto clan. The other continental islands were ruled by other ancient clans. Of particular interest to Duncan was Kai, governed by the Yoshi, an ambitious family of entrepreneurial newcomers (who had arrived on Yamato aboard Goldenwing *Musashi* years after the original settlers debarked from the *Hachiman*). Hokkaido was ruled by the Genji, impoverished descendants of a blue-blooded family whose holdings were covered with ice for nine of the thirteen Yamatan year months.

Duncan looked for his clothes and failed to find them. In the wardrobe, instead, were a half-dozen replicas of his skinsuit, the ordinary shipboard attire when syndics were not naked. The skinsuits were all tailored in beautiful silk fabrics. A number of overgarments, created in the manner of the ceremonial samurai surcoats worn by the "industrial class" Japanese of Yedo, hung beside the skinsuits.

The Yamatans, who wore gray jumpsuits when not indulging in ceremonial splendor, had been careful to provide their visitors with syndics' skinsuits and not Yamatan apparel. It was apparent that the Yamatans were observant and meticulous people. Their hosts seemed determined to treat the Wired Ones among them with great politeness and generosity.

Today he and Anya would meet the senior daimyo, Minamoto no Kami, the ninety-year-old ruler of Yamato, now celebrating his sixtieth year as Shogun. Their guide and sponsor was a young man less than one-third the Shogun's age, the daimyo's nephew, according to *Glory*'s database. Minamoto Kantaro was Lord Mayor of Yedo and clearly a politician favored by the ruler. He was also a man of considerable sophistication. He was going to need it, Duncan thought.

As Duncan stepped through the portal field into the *ofuro*, his presence triggered a flood of steaming water into the sunken tub and a holograph of a young girl dressed in a translucent kimono in the center of the tiled shower area. She smiled and bowed, asking, in charmingly accented spacial Anglic, if he required her services as assistant in his bath.

Before he could reply, the girl's attention was caught by Amaya stepping through the force-field, dressed only in sweat.

"*I* will bathe the Master and Commander, thank you," Amaya said, deliberately reverting to the old and traditional title used by syndics to refer to their Captains.

The holograph of the *ofuro* girl smiled, bowed and vanished.

"Now you have confused our hosts," Duncan Kr said. "They already think you are my concubine."

"I am broadening their chauvinist horizons," Amaya said, stepping gingerly into the hot bath. She lowered herself into the water, laid back her head to wet her thick, dark hair, and found a seat under water.

"This is pure heaven," she said. "I had no idea people actually lived like this."

Duncan stepped into the steaming bath and breathed in the slightly salty scent of the water. On Yamato all water was laden with mineral salts. He crossed the deep pool with a single stroke and returned to take a seat next to Anya Amaya.

"What are you thinking, Duncan?" Amaya asked.

He smiled. "It is rather like microgravity."

She stretched, drew a deep breath and allowed her body to float. Her breasts surfaced like rising islands. She ran a fingertip over her nipples. They rose and hardened. Duncan wondered if their hosts were watching—learning, as was said to be their way, by observation. Judging from the *Monogatari*, there was little the folk of Yamato needed to be taught about sex.

"Get out," Amaya said.

"What?"

"Get out and I'll soap you. What's the Earth aphorism Dietr is so fond of? When in Rome . . . that one."

Duncan rose obediently from the bath. Captain he might be, but like all the men of *Glory*, he tended to defer to Amaya in matters of pleasure. In order to distance herself from her coldly feminist upbringing, Anya had made a study of pleasing herself by pleasing men. Duncan guessed that the Yamatans would approve of that.

He sat on a tile stool beside the steaming *ofuro* while Anya covered him with faintly sea-smelling soap. The Sailing Master was wonderfully skilled at male-female contact.

When she had done and had washed the soap off his angular body with a cool spray, she took his place on the stool and let him wash her in turn. Amaya's body was that of a trained and conditioned athlete. Her feminine parts were small and responsive.

"Enough," Duncan said.

Amaya sighed. "Yes, Master and Commander."

They returned to the tub for a final dip and then rose to stand in the air-dryers until their skins glowed.

In the bedroom, Duncan selected a silken skinsuit. It was sea blue and worked with almost invisible silver threads. "Have you something like this in your room, Sailing Master?" he asked.

"Much grander," Amaya said as her naked backside vanished though the force-field into her part of the suite.

In minutes she was back, in a scarlet skinsuit with an over-kimono of scarlet and gold silk. She had caught her hair in a long chignon with a golden comb. Rare metals were not rare on Yamato, Duncan thought. That, at least, was a promising development.

"Come look at this," Duncan said, and led the way to the window wall facing north. He opened a panel, exposing a keyboard. He used the keyboard to produce an image of the night sky of Yamato on the window.

The constellations of this portion of Near Space were familiar. Despite the eleven light-years between Amaterasu and Sol, the skies were Earthlike. Sirius A dominated the deep sky and Orion the Hunter looked much the same as he looked from Earth. The two ringed gas giants of Tau Ceti's outer system, Toshie and Honda, named for ancient Tokugawa vassals, were still in the dark blue sky. Stars and planets often shone in daylight on Yamato, easily overcoming the dim light of the yellow G8 star the natives called Amaterasu.

"Kantaro-san gave me a key to the scanner," Duncan said.

"To what purpose, Duncan?" Amaya had a tendency to distrust men. It was bred into her Centauri genes.

"I suspect he may know why we have come."

"How remarkable. Zen understanding a mere few parsecs from the Land of the Dragonfly."

"Don't sneer at these people, Anya. They've come closer than anyone in space to lightspeed travel. *You* remember why we are here."

"Yes, Captain."

"Look." Duncan manipulated the keyboard to recall the eleventh hour of full dark last night, a time when none of Yamato's three moons was in the sky. A bright point of light swept across the sky.

"There. Did you follow it?"

"It was *Glory*?"

"Yes. But did you notice the Trojan points?"

Amaya frowned at the projected image. "Run it again."

Duncan repeated the display. At the moment when *Glory*'s tiny image could be framed in the center of the observing field, he froze the image. "There. Leading and trailing. What do you see?"

A hundred twenty degrees ahead and a hundred twenty degrees behind *Glory* could be seen dim points of light.

"Yes. Satellites?"

"Warships, I think. There are several in synchronous orbit as well. These people are frightened."

"Not of us, surely."

"I don't know yet. But I am encouraged."

"Oh. God, Duncan," Amaya said tremulously. "Must we return to that so soon?"

Duncan laid his hands on her silken shoulders. "Have we a choice, Anya?"

The truth was, he thought, that all the crew was in what the psychiatrists called denial. The memory of the battle they and the people from the Twin Planets had fought both with and against one another, and finally, terrifyingly, against the force they had come to think of as "the Terror," lived just below the level of human perception.

Did *Glory*'s cats, Mira's pride, feel the same way? On the voyage from Ross 248 to Tau Ceti the cats had been secretive and withdrawn—occupied, Amaya said, with cats' business. Duncan hoped with all his being that the beasts were not withdrawing from their human partners. Without them, the Terror could burst from nowhere, ready to devour souls. He used the religious term deliberately, in a reversion to his childhood on the dour Calvinist seaworld of Thalassa.

"We have come for help, Anya. And to give warning."

Amaya ran a hand over the beautiful silk brocade she wore. "If only we could forget, Duncan. If only we could live like this."

Duncan put his hand on her head, fingers resting on the drogue socket that marked her completely and forever as a Wired Starman and a Goldenwing syndic.

"I know," Amaya whispered. "I know."

Duncan extinguished the visual interface on the window wall. "Then let's be diplomats, Sailing Master," he said.

Amaya looked through the wall at the mountainous northern horizon. There had been nothing like the Fuji range on New Earth. As the first of the colony worlds NE had repeated most of the mistakes made by the collectivist states of Earth, levelling mountains, relocating rivers, changing the weather, regimenting the people. The result had been tragic. Life on New Earth was regimented, constrained, an ultimate expression of the ancient war between the genders. The first expeditions to the bleak new world had been heavily staffed by angry women and "sensitized" men. A crash program of artificial aids to procreation had resulted in men being relegated to sperm producers. The gender experiments had not prospered. Finally, in extremis, the power to rule had been surrendered to the militant feminists who remodeled NE's government into a school for survival without joy or pleasure.

How will my homeworld meet the Terror when it comes, Amaya wondered. *Should I even care?*

I must, she thought.

Duncan said, "Ready? We have a schedule to keep."

"Lead, Master and Commander," she said.

2

AN ORBIT OF YAMATO

•

Glory passed in low orbit over Yamato's Inland Sea, so called by the Yamatan colonists because it was separated from the Great Ocean by the coastlines of the planet's three continental islands. It was a sea far more vast than the Japanese Inland Sea of Earth from which it drew its name. Everything was on a larger scale on Planet Yamato. The seas were larger and emptier, the islands were near continents, mountainous and varied. Yet the planet, being less dense, massed only eighty-seven percent Earth normal.

Yamato had been discovered by a Japanese probe in the decade of the Jihad, and migration had been planned well in advance of the full horror that exploded from the mountains of Asia Minor. The colonists of Yamato prided themselves on their historic—and fortunate—foresight.

Whether the legends of the *Monogatari no Hachiman* were true or not, the fact was that three voyages of the *Hachiman* succeeded in populating the island-continents Honshu, Kyushu, and Takeda. A thousand years after Lander's Day, the population of Yamato stood at 200,000,000. By any standard, Yamato was one of the more successful colonies of Earth's Age of the Exodus.

On Kyushu the colonists had concentrated their heavy manufacturing and their flourishing space program. Once each seventh orbit, the *Gloria Coelis* overflew the Kyushu City spaceport. It was there that Anya and Duncan had been requested to land their sled. From the spaceport they had then been flown, rather ostentatiously in Cybersurgeon Dietr Krieg's opinion, by the Yamatans to the planetary capital, Yedo. It was a sophisticated display, and intended to be so. A show, Krieg thought, designed to impress the people of the *Gloria Coelis.*

It had succeeded. But *Glory,* herself, impressed the colonists far more. The last call of the *Hachiman* had taken place six hundred planetary years ago, and save for old tri-d photographic images and many beautiful (but inaccurate) screens and paintings, there had been nothing to prepare the people of Yamato for the reality of the ancient artifact now orbiting their world.

The vast ship glistened in the warm light of the G8 star. Her skylar sails were furled on her twenty-kilometer spars, exposing her monofilament rigging to throw spears of light with each change in the angle of the soft light from Amaterasu.

It pleased Yamatan sensibilities that seen from Earth, their sun was a part of the constellation Cetus, or in their language, *Kujira,* the Whale. Two of Yamato's three moons, Oda and Toyotomi, were white. Tokugawa's methane atmosphere shone with a creamy yellow light. With their pelagic primary, they seemed suitable companions for the beautiful Goldenwing that had brought hundreds of thousands of aesthetically trained Yamatans onto their rooftops in a festival mood.

Already celebrating the approaching Cherry Blossom Front moving north on Honshu, the folk of Yamato had greeted the arrival of *Glory* with street theater, Noh performances and origami festivals. Orbiting Yamato once each ninety-eight minutes, *Glory* displayed herself differently on each successive pass.

Her hull was of woven monomolecular fabric stretched over a titanium frame as fragile and delicate as the skeleton of a bird. The observation domes of her "weather" decks glittered like great diamonds in the yellow light of Amaterasu. There were dozens of smaller transparencies in the ship's thousand upper compartments, placed under the nine masts so that the Wired Starmen could observe the sails and the work of the "monkeys"—the cybernetic organisms who performed the more dangerous tasks in the rig. These transparencies flashed diamantine in the shifting light.

Mizzens and foremasts extended ten kilometers from deck to topmast, mainmasts twice that. At the moment, the hove-to ship was being conned by the junior syndics: the Astroprogrammer,

Broni Ehrengraf; Damon Ng, the Rigger; and the one-time Supernumerary and present Theoretical Mathematician, young Buele. Broni and Buele had joined the ship in the Luyten Stars.

Damon Ng, the present watch-keeper, had initialized the cameras on board to make images for the *Sailing Directions*. Wired sailors never lost an opportunity to add to the *Directions*.

Dietr Krieg, the Cybersurgeon, was unoccupied by duties to the ship. While in orbit, Dietr became Supernumerary, and neither he nor the cats of Mira's pride—no one knew precisely how many there were—had specific duties to perform. This gave the physician time to return to his endless attempts to communicate directly with Mira.

At this moment Dietr was engaged in a task that both consumed and distressed him, and had ever since he had surgically altered the matriarch of *Glory*'s pride, connecting her (for good or ill) to the mainframe computer.

Mira, the ten-year-old queen, sat still as an Egyptian statue on the Cybersurgeon's worktable. She did this willingly, but somehow with an attitude that expressed weary contempt for Dietr and his inability to communicate with her kind in any meaningful way.

The radio link Dietr had installed in the cat's small skull showed only in the hair-thin antenna that made wireless linkage between animal and ship's computer possible. Nine shiptime years had passed since Krieg performed the surgery. In that time he had repeated the procedure on many of Mira's kittens. Until he had discovered, thanks to Buele and much to his own chagrin, that the electronic link was no longer vital. Somehow, whether by accident or design, Mira's offspring had developed the ability to communicate with *Glory* without further physical intervention by the surgeon.

Mira and her pride would have been, Dietr often thought, a Terrestrial animal-breeder's nightmare. Her first litter had resulted from an artificial insemination performed by the Cybersurgeon on his first voyage aboard *Glory*. The newer members of her pride were the result of random matings among siblings and, in some cases, matings with Mira herself.

Dietr puzzled over the variety that resulted from so small a gene pool, and he puzzled even more over the strange capabilities of the pride. How did Mira succeed in passing to her off-spring the faculties Dietr Krieg thought he alone had the ability to bestow? And why did a ten-year-old queen, who should have been showing the signs of advancing feline middle age, have the physique of a cat just rounding into full maturity? How long would Mira and her kittens live?

More profound questions remained to be answered. How did Mira and her pride sense the presence of what the syndics of the *Gloria Coelis* had come to know, chillingly, as the Terror? How did the cats sense—no, it was more precise than that—how did they *perceive* the force, whatever it was, that had taken life so savagely during the ill-considered attempt to hijack *Glory* by the bitter people of Nimrud? Without the cats, *Glory*'s syndics would be dead—along with their would-be conquerors—and the *Gloria Coelis* would be a splintered, scattered wreck drifting between the stars.

Dietr regarded the cat attentively. There had been a time when Mira and her responses to the doctor's "modification" would have been simply exhibits in Dietr Krieg's medical collection. Dietr was aboard the Goldenwing not because he had ever had a calling to become a Wired Starman, but because the time dilation of near-lightspeed gave a man of science the ability to spread—to elongate—his normal span of years, sampling the science of many worlds.

It had not worked exactly that way. Dietr had sampled many colonial sciences, but few had been the equal of the Terrestrial science he had left light-years and centuries behind. During his tenure as medical syndic aboard *Glory,* the ship's wake extended from Sol to Aldrin to the Wolf Stars to Barnard's Star to Epsilon Indi to Voerster in the Luyten Stars to Ross 248. Nowhere had he found the medical miracles he had been seeking. Instead he had performed them.

He stared at Mira, who stared back. "And I don't know how I did it," he said aloud. "Why won't you speak to me?"

Mira's tail gave a single lash. Somehow he knew that was a message of understanding. Not a caring message. He had been around *Glory*'s pride long enough to know they cared nothing for human ambitions. Theirs was a far more basic world. Perhaps the word was *natural*. Whatever it was, it lay out there beyond Dietr's human capabilities.

"You have taught me humility, you little monster," he said. "Who would have imagined it?" The Cybersurgeon was not a humble man.

He used to joke with Duncan, who had a far closer bond with Mira and her get than Dietr, that since he had made Mira what she was, the queen should at least be grateful. Duncan usually replied with some variation on the question: "First you had better discover exactly what she is, don't you think?"

As Master and Commander of Goldenwing *Gloria Coelis,* Duncan needed to know. To a human in Deep Space it was a need as vital as air. If the Terror had a purpose, Duncan believed, it was to *consume* life. Or perhaps, Dietr thought, it was to teach humankind that it does not belong out here, light-years from Earth.

Mira arched her back and growled in disagreement; her tail went expressively erect.

"Damn you, Mira, you *do* read me. Why can't *I* understand *you*?" He pulled the drogue from his skull and flung it at the rewinding receptacle. Mira stretched, pulled at the fabric of the table with her foreclaws, and trilled at him. He had a fleeting impression of Buele, the so-called idiot savant from Voerster, exchanging—information?—with the cat. With many of the cats.

Mira leaped from the table to the wall nearest the open valve into the plenum. With another, and dismissive, flick of her tail, she was gone.

Dietr sat staring at the spot the animal had abandoned. It was near to impossible to conduct reasonable experimental science with an animal who had free will and sentience equal to that of a human being.

But by God, he thought suddenly. *I did read her for a moment. And without the drogue. Was that a breakthrough?* It was humbling that the most brilliant medical student ever at Heidelberg now orbited a Japanese planet eleven light-years from Earth, ready to beg for help, and consumed with jealousy of an adolescent *lumpen* from a world of quarreling Afrikaners—because the lowborn boy could communicate with a colony of near-to-feral cats and the brilliant medic could not. Where was the justice in that?

With a sigh, he re-stowed his data-collecting gear. Useless, most of it, he thought dourly. He stowed it neatly because that was his habit. When he had done, he headed for the plenum himself. A view of the beautiful planet below the Goldenwing made one feel more important, more *competent*.

The terminator lay briefly on 123 degrees west longitude before sweeping onward across the vast expanse of the Inland Sea. Between 120 west and 160 east only scattered small islands, the tops of ancient seamounts risen from the deep sea, broke the surface of the ocean.

A deepening twilight lay on the western coast of Honshu, the largest of the Yamatan islands and the domain of the Minamoto family, whose daimyo was also the first daimyo of all Planet Yamato. From the *Gloria Coelis*, orbiting inverted at a height of 239 kilometers, the city of Yedo shone like a pile of gemstones. Thin beads of light extended to the north, south, and east—roads and outlying towns and villages binding Yedo to the smaller communities scattered in profusion across the island-continent. Over the Fuji Mountains and covering most of the eastern coast, a pattern of spring storms formed complex circular cloud formations that were occasionally illuminated by flashes of violet lightning.

Broni Ehrengraf, confined to the microgravity aboard *Glory* by the limitations of an artificial heart, floated on her back in the still air of the vast ob-deck. Like Duncan Kr, she was enchanted by the spatial views through the transparent carapace.

On Broni's bosom rested one of Mira's large sons, a black tomcat whom Broni had named Clavius, in honor of a beached Starman whom she had known and honored on her homeworld of Voerster. Whenever she played her balichord, she remembered Black Clavius.

Broni was a Voertrekkersdatter, daughter of a planetary ruler, the Voertrekker-praesident of Voerster. Her birth had destined her for a loveless political marriage, and her rheumatic heart had condemned her to an early death. The arrival of the *Gloria Coelis* at Voerster had changed all that—and a great many other things as well.

Damon Ng, the Rigger, recently relieved on watch by Buele, appeared beside Broni out of the dimness below.

"Another seaworld," Damon said. "Duncan must be pleased."

Their commander's affinity for oceans was the subject of many conversations among the junior Starmen aboard *Glory*.

In silent companionship the young man and young woman watched the apparent movement of the planet above their heads. The terminator slipped past the western coast of the island-continent of Kyushu. The lights of coastal towns and villages grew dim as the planet rotated and *Glory* moved on. The deep darkness of night lay on the face of a largely empty planetary ocean.

At the horizon the syndics could see the burgeoning glow of Moon Hideyoshi. It burst from the sea and climbed precipitously toward the zenith.

The planet's satellites were named for the three warlords who unified ancient Japan: Oda Nobunaga, the rustic daimyo (of whom the people of Old Japan had said: "He grew the rice"), Toyotomi Hideyoshi, the peasant general ("He made the paste") and Tokugawa Ieyasu, the warrior aristocrat ("He ate the cake"). Minamoto no Kami, the ninety-year-old Shogun of Yamato, was descended from the same stock as the legendary Tokugawa.

The first moon to rise from the sea was the nearest, a mere 260,000 kilometers from Yamato. Moon Oda, at 1,700,000 kilometers mean distance, would rise more slowly. And Ieyasu, the largest and most distant at 2,500,000 kilometers, would rise more slowly still to flood the sea with yellow light. Hideyoshi, thought Broni, like the peasant he was, had leapt into the sky to begin his race for the far horizon.

Damon, who came from a tree-canopied world where the sky was seldom seen, was always impressed by swiftly moving celestial objects. "How fast it is," he said.

"He, Damon. How fast *he* is. Yamatan colonists speak of celestial objects as masculine. Duncan says we are to get it right. Small things are important to colonists. Duncan says we must be correct." To take the edge off her Afrikaner tendency to haughtiness, Broni said, "I have been studying with *Glory*. Do you know why they named him for Hideyoshi?" She took care to pronounce the name correctly, accenting the next to last syllable as *Glory*'s computer assured her the Yamatans did. She repeated the parable of the rice cakes.

"Tokugawa Ieyasu's family ruled ancient Japan as Shoguns for more than three hundred years," she finished approvingly.

As the daughter of a ruler and politician, Broni Ehrengraf appreciated the difficulty of the achievement.

"Weird people," the Rigger murmured.

The two young syndics were silent as *Glory* moved swiftly through the night sky of Yamato. Hideyoshi silvered the sea and made a spangled path across the water. A coastline appeared below. "What is that?" Damon asked. Damon had qualities, but being an attentive student of *Glory*'s lessons was not one of them.

"Kai. It is ruled by a family who claims to be descended from Takeda Shingen, the Mountain Lord," Broni said. "There is a legend that Shingen was killed during a siege of one of Tokugawa's castles because he returned to the same spot every night to hear an enemy soldier play the flute. I rather like that story. I think I like Takeda Shingen, too."

"And Oda? You *are* going to tell me about Oda, aren't you?" Damon said with a grin.

"You should know these things," Broni said primly. The cat on her breast gave a low trill of agreement.

"Oda was a great warrior but a very bad man. He died of overconfidence. That's what *Glory* says. Of overconfidence, and full of arrows, on top of a burning temple."

"I hope that's not an omen for us," Damon said with one of the sudden mood switches for which he was famous aboard Goldenwing *Glory*.

Glory's orbital track crossed Yamato's equator and dipped into the southern hemisphere. In the dark before the approaching dawn terminator could be seen a half dozen of the artificial satellites in orbit around Yamato. Beyond, despite the glow of dawn on the horizon, the starfields were bright. On Yamato the stars shone in daylight. Amaterasu provided only half the illumination of Sol at Earth.

At latitude $-18°$ *Glory* passed over a scattering of small, empty islands. Like much of the sea-girt land on the planet, they were volcanic. At $-43°$ *Glory* passed from night into day high above still more empty ocean. To the south the syndics could now see the edges of the Southern Ice Cap that reached in this season to latitude 40 south.

On Yamato, a planet not greatly changed from the Pangaea

stage, the poles were covered by caps that could reach, in winter, almost to 50 south. Cold Oda now rode high in the lightening sky.

The water below averaged a depth of nine thousand meters. The dark seas beneath the polar caps were the nurseries for the myriad sea diatoms that were the only indigenous sea life on Yamato. The fish-eating Terrestrial Japanese who had settled on Yamato had swiftly developed a taste for the microscopic plants of their sea. They were not precisely fish, but the colonists of Yamato ate them with relish. As far as anyone knew, an intelligent animal had never been found in the seas of Yamato, nor was one likely to be. The chances were, *Glory* declared, should such an animal exist, it would be eaten without remorse.

Glory's orbit carried her north again, across a wilderness of stormy southern ocean. She recrossed the equator at longitude ten west and overflew the island-continent of Honshu to the shores of the Inland Sea. As the *Gloria Coelis* passed once again over the coast of Ieyasu, the city of Yedo below was awakening.

Dietr Krieg appeared in the ob-deck. He had brought with him a handheld video receiver. On the tiny screen the Wired Starmen could watch the appearance of Duncan and Amaya on the plaza before their luxurious guest quarters in one of Yedo's tallest ryokans.

The streets, even at this early hour, were jammed with cheering people. Many waved paper flags bearing a sea-creature that they imagined to be the national insignia of Thalassa—for Duncan Kr—and silhouettes of big-breasted women in aggressive New Earther stances for Anya Amaya.

"*Glory* has been informing their planetary database about us, I see," Dietr Krieg said thoughtfully. "I wonder if that is such a good idea."

"Why should you wonder that?" Broni asked.

"Middle-aged suspicion, I suppose," the Cybersurgeon murmured. "What people don't know they can't use against you."

"It looks to me as though the people of Yedo are very pleased to have Starmen on their world," Damon Ng said.

"I'm sure," Dietr said drily. "But will they be so happy when Duncan asks the hard question, I wonder."

"Will they be afraid, Dietr?" Broni asked.

"They would be fools if they were not," the Cybersurgeon said.

At that moment a thread of ruby light streaked across the tiny screen. It originated somewhere in the mass of people gathered to see the offworlders. It terminated in the breast of an official standing next to Duncan Kr. The man fell, his chest vaporized by the heat of the beam.

"*My God . . .*" Broni's voice was thick with shock.

A human shield of police had formed around Duncan and Amaya, and armed men began frantically clearing the square in front of the ryokan.

Dietr took command.

"All right, children," he snapped. "Back to the bridge. Let's get this ship ready for Deep Space. Duncan must have asked the question. I think we've just had an answer."

3

A DEATH IN YEDO

•

The most casual and unintended movement had shifted Duncan's position in the group in front of the ryokan. There was a red flash and he felt the heat of a laser bolt as it burned past his cheek and exploded the torso of the city official behind him. The smell of ozone mingled with that of seared flesh, and Duncan felt the sting of sizzling hot droplets of blood on his face.

Duncan caught Anya by the shoulders and shoved her to the ground. The forecourt of the high-rise ryokan that had been, only a moment ago, crowded elbow to elbow by ranked Yedoans was now a swirling mass of frightened people, some running, some lying on the ground sheltering behind their fellows. Official Yedo had become a terrified mob. What agency could create such fear?

Duncan became aware that a cordon of yellow-clad domain policemen, weapons out, had formed around him and Anya.

A policeman shouted, "He's wearing a nullgrav harness!"

Another ruby laser bolt cut down a line of Domain lawmen. Duncan stood, ignoring the orders from his cordon of police to stay down. Across the forecourt there was violent activity. Details were impossible to see. Minamoto Kantaro, gorgeously attired in a samurai's court dress, appeared with an incongruously modern energy weapon in his hand. "Take shelter, Kr-san," he shouted. "We have a ninja!" To his police, he shouted, "Don't let him live! Kill him and guard the *gaijin*!"

Across the square, a figure burst upward from the throng. It was a man dressed in black and wearing a backpack under the shreds of a formal kimono. In all the worlds Duncan had visited, only the Twin Planets of Ross 248 and Yamato possessed personal antigravity units.

The man rose into the air, but people clung to his legs, overburdening the lifting power of the backpack. With no hesitation whatever the ninja put his lazegun under his own chin and pressed the firing control. His head dissolved into an elongated cloud of steaming, bloody froth. Hissing fragments showered the crowd.

Startled, those holding his legs released their grip and he shot skyward, leaving a trail of bloody red vapor behind his headless body.

Minamoto Kantaro shouted for more police. "And get an air patrol after him! Get him down!"

The police were swiftly restoring order. Duncan put an arm around Amaya and asked, "All right?"

"He was aiming at you. He was trying to murder you." The Sailing Master was more outraged than frightened.

"Enough, Anya," Duncan said softly.

Minamoto Kantaro stood before Duncan and made a deep bow. "I am dishonored, Kr-san. I am steeped in humiliation."

Duncan regarded the young man thoughtfully. *Glory*'s database informed him that ninjas were an essential part of Japanese history and culture. It also warned that if a ninja's attack failed for any reason, a second and third might be expected.

Still bowing with head low, palms on his knees, Minamoto Kantaro said, "Yamato is shamed, Kr-san. *I* am shamed."

"Politics is an unruly business, Kantaro-san," Duncan said. "Please. Let us hear nothing more about it. If you cannot grant me this request, then *I* shall be dishonored for having brought trouble to Yamato."

A trio of yellow police tilt-rotors swept over the recovering crowd in pursuit of the soaring corpse.

Kantaro-san straightened and said, "My obligation will be decided by my daimyo. Whatever is decided, it will not reflect your honor or the honor of your ship."

Anya Amaya moved to speak but Duncan signalled her silence subvocally. *"Let it go for now."*

Aloud, he said, "How high will the nullgrav carry him, Kantaro-san?"

"It depends on the efficiency of the unit and the amount of fuel it carries, Kr-san," Minamoto said. "Customarily we only use them in space, and then to create gravity rather than nullify it. We dislike free-fall." His dark eyes glittered. "He has had a bitter death. Failure will forever shame his memory."

"But *I* honor him for it," Duncan said drily.

A police official drew Minamoto Kantaro aside for a moment. Amaya took the opportunity to whisper to Duncan, "Might he commit seppuku, Duncan?"

"Only if his daimyo commands it."

"Perhaps he should. You might have been killed. You very nearly were."

"Ritual suicide is not commonly practiced on Thalassa, Anya."

"I knew men of some societies did such things on the homeworld," she said. "I wondered if all men carried their foolish traditions into space with them." Amaya tended to make harsh judgments on males. It was part of her feminist upbringing.

Before more could be said, the mayor rejoined them and said, "Where there is one ninja there are sometimes more, Kr-san. We will go to the Shogun's garden now. A tilt-rotor is waiting for us on the ryokan roof." He turned to an aide and said, "Find that body. I want what is left of it."

The ten-meter tilt-rotor was handsomely—but austerely—equipped. Duncan could discern nothing to set it apart from the aircraft that had carried him and Anya Amaya from the spaceport, yet it was one of the squadron reserved for the personal use of the Shogun and his staff. Each of the dozen seats was fitted with an impressive console containing the controls for outside video-imagers, cellular com devices, and other services not immediately apparent.

Kantaro-san had spent the first five minutes of the flight with the pilots. He now returned to attend to the comfort of his guests. Duncan found the way in which he dealt with the incident of the ninja in Yedo fascinating. Clearly, he was upset. The incident, as severe as it had been, had implications for the young samurai that Duncan found difficult to grasp. Yet if he were ever to prevail upon the colonists of Yamato to do what no colonists had ever done—seek out a threat and offer battle—he would have to interpret the complexities of the system of duties and obligations that governed life in the Tau Ceti System.

Kantaro-san, an opulent figure in brocaded silk *hakama* and kimono, still managed to look like a warrior, Duncan noted. *Glory*'s crash course on Yamato and its people emphasized that Yamatan society mimicked that of feudal Japan. There was an antique cast to life on Yamato that suggested a psychological return to ancient Japan—the Japan unified after the Battle of Sekigahara. The Minamoto Tokugawa Ieyasu established his clan hegemony that foggy day in 1603 and for 264 years nothing had changed until Japan was opened under the guns of an American naval squadron.

Clearly the Minamotos of Planet Yamato had resolved to do at least as well as their ancestor, Ieyasu. To descend, as *Glory* had, on such a society bearing a call to war was not going to attract friends. The ninja's attack was practical proof of that.

When the mayor had settled himself in his seat and turned it to face the syndics, Duncan asked, "May I ask some questions, Kantaro-san?"

The Yamatan's face was round, unlined. His heavy lids with their pronounced epicanthic folds shielded eyes black as fuligin. Standing, Duncan would tower over the Mayor of Yedo, as would Anya. Yet Minamoto Kantaro was a figure of power. Duncan, descendant of Gael fishermen living on a world of rock and sea, understood that Kantaro-san's presence was the result of forty generations of selective breeding. *Glory*'s database contained descriptions of the almost fanatic lengths to which Yamatans went to ensure the purity of the gene pool of their Great Houses.

Kantaro regarded Duncan distantly. Duncan had already noted the tendency of Yamatan eyes to empty when one asked inopportune questions. "About the ninja?"

"And other things."

"Ah." Kantaro-san steepled his supple fingers and looked out the window of the tilt-rotor. "It is the *tonno*'s place, not mine, to exchange ideas directly with you."

Duncan noted the use of the Japanese word for "lord." Every nuance held meaning when dealing with people as complex as the colonists of Yamato. Under the circumstances, Minamoto Kantaro was saying politely, it was Minamoto no Kami, the daimyo of Ieyasu and the chosen Shogun of Yamato, who would deal with the outsider.

Minamoto no Kami, Duncan amended mentally, *or no one.*

"Still," Duncan persisted. "Is the Ninja Order as strong on Planet Yamato as it once was in Japan?"

"What does your ship's database tell you?"

"It suggests that it is, Kantaro-san."

"Your database is correct, Kr-san. Here the Master of the Order takes the name of Tsunetomo—the author of the *Hagakure*—the book by which samurai try to live. The Order is secret and not political."

Duncan's heavy brows arched skeptically.

"It is so, Kr-san. On Yamato we say that the Ninja Order is the sword arm, not the brain."

"Killers work for pay and not out of political conviction?"

"We do not regard ninjas merely as killers, Kr-san. But yes, the agents of the Order are blades in the wars of ideas."

What a remarkable way of seeing the world, Duncan thought. And how bloody risky it made life for a stranger on Planet Yamato. But there was no point in carrying on this conversation now. "You said something earlier that interests me, Kantaro-san. About Yamatans disliking free fall. I find that unusual for a spacefaring race."

The Yamatan shrugged. "Perhaps it is because so many of our ancestors experienced cold-sleep for only part of the voyage from the home planet. Now most who leave the planet's surface do so wearing grav units. They are expensive, but very good."

And their concentration of gravity control might account for their advanced state in the development of mass-depletion propulsion, Duncan thought. A fascinating, paradoxical people.

The tilt-rotor's flight was carrying them from the coastal hills upon which Yedo stood, across a wide, lowland valley, toward the foothills of the Fuji Mountains.

From what appeared to be about fifteen hundred meters' altitude, the valley below could be seen clearly—an intricate pattern of waterways and paddies. Dappled yellow sunlight glinted as the aircraft's sun-angle changed. It was as though the field below were sending golden arrows after the interloper. Duncan's empathic sense made the impression powerful. The land seemed to be warning off the machine flying above it.

Duncan glanced at Anya to see if she was getting the same psychic message. But the New Earther was staring out the window at the wetlands below. Water in such quantity was unknown on New Earth.

Kantaro said, "I took note of your interest in the valley, Kr-san. Do you know what crops are being raised down there?"

"It appears to be rice, Kantaro-san."

"It is rice. Now, rice grows poorly on Yamato. The conditions are not favorable," Kantaro-san said. "But rice is of mystical importance to Japanese, Kr-san. Did you know that it was once a medium of exchange on the Home Islands? One *koku* of rice was the amount needed to feed one warrior for one year. The daimyo who owned a crop of a million *koku* had at his command, in effect, an army of a million men." He gestured to the land below. "That rice could be genetically reengineered into a crop more suited to the ecosystem of Yamato. This has been proven a number of times over the last millennium in the agricartel laboratories. The engineered rice is designed to the Yamatan taste and indistinguishable from the rice you see growing down there. It may even be more savory. But I would not know. I have never eaten any of the rice growing in those paddies. Nor have any of the secular inhabitants of the Four Domains. The rice grown with such difficulty in those paddies below is rice reserved for the temples and monasteries. I have no idea what the bonzes and monks do with it. For the most part, they eat what the rest of us eat— cereal grains and meat from the descendants of offworld food animals. Yet rice, specifically *that* rice you see in the paddies below, rice grown with great labor, is the food of our ancestors. It is *rice*. True rice." He smiled grimly. "What, you may ask, has rice drawn from the alien mud of Yamato to do with the ninja who tried to assassinate you?"

"I begin to understand, Kantaro-san. The *way* of living is more important than the *fact* of living."

"Yes, Kr-san," Minamoto Kantaro said. "The *Hagakure*, the book by which we try to live, is called the Way of the Samurai. We live by symbols, Kr-san. You will have already noticed that we dress conservatively for our day-to-day lives. But let there be an occasion or a festival—and we have hundreds of festivals, Kr-san—you see how we love our ancient finery. Symbols, tradition. For example, when the rice crop fails—and it fails often in this climate—it is taken as a warning from the mystical powers. From the animist spirits said to live in the stars, from the *kamis* of rock and river and mountain. From the Sun Goddess. Even from the Buddha. We have always had many faiths, we Japanese. Yet they are one. We united them. We do things in an ancient way on Yamato; we cling to our traditions—whether they are good traditions or bad." He caressed the golden pommel of the *wakizashi* short sword in his scarlet sash. "We often wear the two swords of the samurai. Despite our technical sophistication, we do other things as archaic. It is our way." He paused. "But we are also a practical people. Thus, sometimes, Kr-san, when we can, we influence the gods by spoiling a rice crop—or employing a ninja." He fell silent.

"You are gifted as a teacher, Kantaro-san," Duncan said. "I shall remember your words."

"I suggest that you do, Kr-san."

Anya Amaya was following the conversation closely now. "How many daimyos know why we are here?"

"You are here to summon us to war, Amaya-san. All the daimyos know." Kantaro-san hid his hands in his kimono sleeves. "But the daimyos wonder if you know what you are asking."

"We fought the Terror in the Ross System, Kantaro-san," Amaya said. "We know."

"And the point is," Duncan said quietly, "that *you* know, as well, Kantaro-san."

Minamoto Kantaro looked uncomfortable. "We have lost spacecraft," he said. "But the daimyos are divided."

"How is that possible?" demanded Anya. "The threat is real."

"Perhaps we are being warned not to venture into Deep Space, Amaya-san. It is our way to consider all the possibilities."

"What does the Shogun know?" Duncan asked. The question was blunt, too blunt for these archaic Japanese, but the Terror was real, and it drew nearer each day. *Glory*'s syndics felt it like a chill in their bones.

Minamoto Kantaro said, "He knows that we have lost spacecraft. Some tests of the mass-depletion engine have not gone well. So long as our spacecraft move slowly and remain close to Amaterasu, flights are uneventful. Some of the older daimyos believe the Sun Goddess protects them."

Amaya snorted in derision. Duncan warned her with a glance.

Kantaro shrugged in apparent agreement. "But as the speed of our ships increases and their range extends, events not necessarily to Yamato's advantage take place."

Duncan heard in the Lord Mayor of Yedo's words the echo of the Great Rescript, which had ended the last great war the Japanese fought on Earth. Japan had lost two cities to atomic attack, and a hundred more to conventional bombing. Her navy was on the bottom of the sea and her people starving. At this point the Emperor had written that the war must end because "events had not necessarily developed to Japan's advantage."

"I see," Duncan said. "And suddenly we appear."

Minamoto Kantaro remained eloquently silent.

So the government of the Four Domains knew that something was killing their new, experimental lightspeed ships. The ninja's attack indicated plainly enough that powerful Yamatans connected *Glory*'s arrival from Deep Space and the loss of their own mass-depletion-powered ships.

They see us as in flight, pursued by a superior force, Duncan thought. *Not a situation calculated to endear us to the people of Planet Yamato.*

Kantaro-san said, "There are many secret societies on Yamato. Their names would mean nothing to you, and hardly more to me. Their activities have always been limited to family feuds and clan disputes. Until now. The bolt fired at you was political. The lord Minamoto must decide what is to be done."

Duncan said, "There is nothing political about *Glory*'s call in Yamato, Kantaro-san."

"Here, Kr-san, survival is political." His hand rested on the cord-braided hilt of his *wakizashi,* a short sword that was clearly sharp as an old-fashioned razor. Duncan Kr studied his host's unlined face intently. The syndic's empathic power brought him to the edge of understanding. But not farther. Duncan was a Caucasian. Before his people colonized Thalassa they had accumulated the experience of three thousand years of Western history in their genes. In Minamoto Kantaro's heredity was twice that number of years dominated by east Asia's intricate ethos. The psychological infrastructures upon which the personalities of the two men depended were, literally, worlds apart. Close observation and study, Duncan thought, might bring understanding of a sort, but would it bring the empathy without which a human defense of Near Space might be impossible? Planet Yamato lay like an unaware gatekeeper, at risk on a strange and terrifying frontier.

Perhaps, Duncan thought, regarding his host shrewdly, *this feudal man might become an ally.* But what of the daimyo of Ieyasu—the chosen Shogun of this world? Without his approval *Glory* herself might never leave orbit.

Duncan watched the looming mountains thoughtfully. He was about to deal with the ruler of the only colony in Near Space able to build the spaceships that would eventually retire the Goldenwings. The mass-depletion engine under development in the spaceship yards of Kai used tachyons in a new and radical way. Duncan lacked the engineering expertise to understand the concept fully, but Yamatan broadcasts claimed to have achieved speeds comparable to those reached by Goldenwings. The idea both saddened Duncan and gave him hope. Such engines, fully developed, would put an end to the Age of Sail. But those same engines might give humankind a fighting chance against the Terror lurking the dark of Deep Space. It depended on his meeting with an old autocrat in a mountain garden.

4

THE SHOGUN'S GARDEN

•

As the tilt-rotor made its way north toward the Fuji Mountains, the Sailing Master noted with fascination the odd way in which even in daylight, the stars could be seen in the band of deep azure sky at the horizon. All else was tinged by Amaterasu's coppery light. Amaya had some psychological difficulty discarding the astronomical nomenclature she had learned as a child for the more fanciful names adopted by colonists. Subconsciously, she scorned the Yamatan's choice of their Shinto Sun Goddess's name for the star she had always known as Tau Ceti. She knew this as a failing in her character—God knew Duncan had pointed it out often enough in their travels across the sky—and she repeatedly promised herself to do better, to learn tolerance. But since such a change of heart would have been a denial of all the hard-core feminist ideals she had been taught on New Earth, she suspected that any real change would be a long time coming.

As a penance, she forced herself to view the sky with Yamatan eyes.

Rising in the east was Orion, the quadrilateral of stars known here as Ryoshi, the Hunter. Low on the horizon, the sky had the aspect of night. Nearer the zenith, the coppery G8 light of Tau Ceti managed to overbear the stars. But Yamato's swift trio of moons bounded the ecliptic plane like signposts. Tokugawa, the gas body, was at this moment displaying the single, thin ring that would swiftly disappear for a day as the viewing angle changed. The sky of Amaterasu's single terrestrial planet was a constantly changing enchantment, Amaya thought grudgingly. She could not help the swift thought that her own life might have been very different if New Earth, the First Colony, had been a kinder world. But no, it had been biology—her own—not planetary topography, that had caused her to be sold to the syndics of the *Gloria Coelis*. Unable to produce female offspring by the politically correct in vitro method, she had been offered a choice between a sex change and assignment to the permanent labor force or immediate sale to the syndics at that moment fortuitously present in the Proxima Centauri System. New Earth was perennially strapped for the hard currency of Goldenwing syndic goodwill, and Amaya had no love of physical labor, so her choice was ordained. "In the stars," Dietr Krieg liked to say. At first terrified, she came to treasure the memory of the day she boarded *Glory* and was socketed.

She had been listening to the conversation between Minamoto Kantaro and Duncan. It had been terse and laden with meaning until a few moments ago, when it became apparent that Kantaro-san had said all of substance he was authorized to say. From that point on the talk became fitful and Amaya lost interest.

She regarded Duncan covertly, as she often did. The Master and Commander was a man of hidden depths, but the intimacy among Wired Starmen allowed her to know him well. Much of what she knew was physical, but not all.

Starmen tended to have unusual—even bleak—childhoods. Her own among the cadres of New Earth's feminist hegemony was similar to most. Dietr was a product of Earth, the homeworld, and it was significant that his only comments about his early days were statements of his delight at being recruited as Neurocybersurgeon of the *Glory*. Damon Ng had been a frightened child in the branches of the treeworld of Nixon, bred to an impressive number of phobias that he was only now, after nearly a dozen shiptime years in space, beginning to shed. And Broni and Buele were, by any standard Anya Amaya would accept, refugees from a deeply troubled world consumed with ancient racial problems.

That left Duncan, and he was both the most interesting and the most baffling of the lot. He had been found on Search by the last of the former generation of syndics who had brought *Glory* out from Earth. The practice of Search was rare now among Goldenwing syndics. It had once been the only way of selecting young recruits to man the sailing starships. The Searchers looked for physical skills and stamina, that was a given. But they also sought empathy, a quality that was as difficult to define in Starmen as it was to find among colonists. By recruiting Duncan the old ones had achieved a triumph. Under his command, the Wired Ones of *Glory*'s crew combined with their ship to form a remarkable entity. And this entity had, in the last years, been strangely enhanced by the cat Mira and her progeny. There were now a dozen cats capable of connecting with *Glory* by interfacing with the ship's computer.

And I feel incomplete here, away from my fellow syndics, Anya Amaya thought. *Duncan is my strength.* In a cold, shuddering mental wind, the reality of the Terror seemed to brush her mind with pallid fire. . . .

Duncan turned to look at her. Empathically linked to her Commander, Anya felt a protective presence ready to defend her—to the death if need be. The psychic signature of the Master and Commander of the *Gloria Coelis,* once a fisherboy of Thalassa in the Wolf Stars.

He regarded her soberly and then returned to his murmured conversation with Minamoto Kantaro. In the years that Anya Amaya had served as Sailing Master aboard Duncan's ship, she had never been able to truly fathom his depths. But she loved him, as only a syndic could. Mother, sister, lover, wife, companion. Wired Ones developed powerful ties.

Under the tilt-rotor's wing, the landscape shifted, became rocky foothills darkly green with proto-conifers, the mountains alive with flame yellow lichens. Golden sunlight glinted on a hidden lake. A river tumbled through a narrow canyon glittering like a torrent of amber as it pushed and crowded its way between shoulders of rock toward the paddies and man-made marshes in the valley. From this altitude one could see far out to sea. There were no islands on this stretch of coast, only rocky cliffs and surf. In the distance ahead lay the misty granite tower of Mount Kagu, where Goldenwing *Hachiman*'s shuttles were said to have deposited the First Landers.

Amaya, both enchanted and made uncomfortable by the traditional Yamatan garb she wore, found herself wondering about the man they were soon to encounter. Minamoto no Kami had been Shogun of the Four Domains for many more downtime years than Amaya had been alive, yet his grandparents had been young when she was born on New Earth. Such anomalies were functions of the Einsteinian time dilation that governed the lives of Wired Starmen. If what Duncan and young Damon Ng believed about the technology under development here on Planet Yamato was true, then there was a chance that star-voyaging at speeds denied by Einstein might become possible. Amaya hadn't the technical knowledge to understand mass-depletion technology—few did—but Duncan believed that the depletion engine might make it possible to reduce the time of flight between stars to zero rather than years, bypassing the Time Dilation Effect entirely.

To the stars *instantaneously.*

Anya Amaya closed her eyes and tried to imagine what sort of society would arise from such a technological revolution. From here to Proxima in a heartbeat. From Proxima to Luyten in two. Witchcraft. Black magic. The ability to match the speed of the Terror. She shivered. What lay ahead for humankind? Faster-than-light speeds and hunting-cat partners for all warriors? A great change was in store for humankind. The war for the stars was beginning.

There were no certainties on Planet Yamato, but a near miss by a lazegun bolt tended to organize the mind swiftly and very well, Anya Amaya thought.

Kantaro-san said, "Look there, to the north, Amaya-san. In the shadow of Mount Kagu. The Shogun's garden."

It was a good bit more than a garden, Amaya thought. Under a canopy of imported Terrestrial pines, sequoias and cypress trees growing proudly amid the Yamatan conifers, lay a ten-hectare parkland of sand and rock gardens dotted with graceful structures of native wood roofed with colorful tiles. From time to time a ray of yellow sunlight would glint from the placid surface of a carefully sited pond or lake. Reflections painted the water's surfaces: clouds in black and bronze; pale, copper yellow sky at the zenith; starry, dark sky at the horizon. It was a man-made environment of stunning beauty. The Yamatan botanists had made it grow from the soil of Planet Yamato. An enormously difficult task.

Her face must have shown how the scene moved her, because

Kantaro-san said quietly, "Shoguns of the Four Domains have nurtured this great garden for a half a thousand years, Amaya-san. And for centuries before that they dreamed of it."

The tilt-rotor circled and descended to two hundred meters. At that altitude it hovered. Anya was empath enough to feel that it was being scanned by sophisticated eyes, both human and electronic.

"Security check," she said.

Kantaro-san's eyebrows lifted. "I had heard that Wired Starmen listened to the wind," he said with a thin smile. "I had not expected to have the legend confirmed so quickly."

Duncan was watching the Yamatan with shrewd interest. "Do you 'listen to the wind' as well, Kantaro-san?"

The Mayor of Yedo shook his head ruefully. "Nothing so grand, Kr-san. I know the routine, that's all."

The aircraft began again to descend. It sank softly to the ground between stands of thirty-meter *Sequoia sempervirens,* ancient imports from Earth brought to the Tau Ceti system aboard the *Hachiman.* Duncan looked about for the residence of the Shogun. From the air he had seen a number of wooden mansions suited to be the residences of a planetary ruler. But here, in the redwood grove where the tilt-rotor had landed, he could see only a small structure of burnished woods and paper shojis with a roof of tiles and retroussé overhangs. He recognized the style from images in *Glory*'s database. It was a *chashitsu,* a setting for the *chano yo,* the traditional tea ceremony. There were no security forces in evidence, no servants or retainers at all save a single slender boy in traditional dress of a samurai page standing like a carving before the low door to the teahouse.

Duncan spoke to Kantaro-san in the most tactful tone he could manage. "How seriously has the ninja affected your situation with the Shogun? Forgive me for asking, but we need you to speak for us with the daimyo."

Minamoto Kantaro said somberly, "My influence was diminished this morning." His dark eyes fixed on Amaya and his expression softened. "But the Shogun is easily moved by handsome young women, and if Amaya-san smiles on me, so may the daimyo."

Anya looked at Duncan in perplexity. Duncan read what she

was thinking: *The daimyo is ninety. In real years. Have the Yamatans discovered a fountain of youth?*

Minamoto Kantaro stood and indicated the open door of the tilt-rotor. The page had presented himself in a manner so formal that he made an honor guard of one as the syndics stepped to the lichen-covered soil.

The air smelled of pine and recent rain. Duncan could not remember ever having stood in so still and so engaging a place. Wind sighed in the high branches of the *sempervirens*. Beyond lay the sea and the vast copper and blue of Planet Yamato's early spring sky. Duncan was reminded of the high, silent cliffs of Thalassa, many meters above the spuming surf that shattered silently on the rocks far below.

There was a torii gate hung with bleached hemp guarding the path to the teahouse. Seen from nearby, the elegant little structure seemed a part of the silent forest.

"The Lord of Ieyasu built this with his own hands," Minamoto Kantaro said, indicating the teahouse.

"The daimyo has built handsomely," Duncan said.

The page bowed and mutely led the way to a low, meter-high door in the paper-and-wood-frame wall of the building. Inside, the *chashitsu* would be spare, stark in design. A small room with wood-and-paper walls and a stone hearth in the center. Next to the hearth would be the tools of the *chano yo:* the drinking bowls, the teapot, the tea brush. Steaming hot water and towels. The entry, on hands and knees, was meant to teach humility, and the sparse surroundings were intended to remind one that *makoto*—sincerity and simplicity—was to be desired above all things in life.

Yet, if the building and its owner followed ancient tradition, the tea utensils would be of fabulous antiquity and value, probably artifacts brought from the Home Islands on Earth. Far-travelling syndics aboard other Goldenwings said that the old ways were no longer venerated on Earth, but in this colony, at least, Zen discipline and Shinto devotion lived on.

The page, still in total silence, slid open the low door. Kantaro-san indicated that Amaya should enter first. Anya dropped to her knees to pass through the low portal. Duncan and Minamoto Kantaro followed. The boy page resumed his vigil astride the path.

* * *

Inside, a handsome old man, dressed in opulent simplicity, knelt before the hearth, the utensils of the tea ceremony to hand. The ceremony might contain an element of humility, Duncan thought, but humility among planetary rulers was a relative thing.

Minamoto no Kami, Shogun of Yamato and daimyo of the Domain of Ieyasu, wore a caftan and kimono woven of black silk and golden thread. On his left breast was embroidered the circle containing the three hollyhock leaves of the Tokugawa clan, on the right the solid orange-gold disk that claimed the old man's descent from the Sun Goddess Amaterasu.

Minamoto-sama's face was crisscrossed with the web of fine lines to be expected in the visage of a man nearly a hundred Earth-standard years old. But the eyes were brilliant and alert and the hands, exposed within the deep sleeves of the ornate imperial kimono, were lean and strong.

"Welcome to my garden, Honored Syndics," Minamoto no Kami said. "We will drink tea together and meditate on the blessings of peace. . . ." His black eyes seemed to pierce Duncan like obsidian blades. "Then," the Shogun said, "we will speak of other things."

5

THE DAIMYO OF IEYASU

•

The tea ceremony was long and intricate. Duncan found it calming. How traditional was the ceremony as conducted on Planet Yamato? Duncan wondered. Japan was eleven light-years distant.

The Starmen watched the old daimyo brew the green tea, whip it to a steaming froth with the bamboo tea brush, then pour it into the beautiful bowls, handing first one to Anya Amaya, then another to Duncan Kr.

It was to the Sailing Master that Minamoto no Kami addressed his most cordial conversation. Anya had studied the accounts of Yamatan customs found in *Glory*'s database: On Planet Yamato women could be purchased. All colonies valued women, most for their reproductive function—but that was far from the only reason. No colony of Earth could afford to disdain women and their founding function on the colony worlds. Despite all the eugenic experimentation indulged in since the Jihad, the woman remained the keeper of humankind's future—in space or on the worlds of Near Space. On Yamato, the ancient art of the geisha lived on.

Kantaro-san's comment about Minamoto no Kami's susceptibility to women seemed true enough. Anya had that effect on men. The Shogun's admiration was open. Anya hoped that the Shogun would make no bid to "buy her contract," as the Yamatan phrase went.

Glory's syndicate had bought Anya Amaya, because it was the way of doing things on New Earth. But Anya was no longer for sale. A Goldenwing syndicate might buy a woman, but it would never sell one.

The skull-socket of a Starman bestows certain responsibilities, Duncan Kr thought sardonically, *else I might have sold myself to the Elmi of Voerster.*

When the tea drinking was done, Minamoto cleansed the containers and placed them gently and reverently in the alcove where they rested next to an arrangement of bamboo fronds—cut carefully from the descendants of Terrestrial plants. *Where does one world end and its descendant begin?* Duncan wondered. *If we defend a world do we defend our history?*

The delicate, segmented stalks of bamboo were displayed in a slender ceramic vase that might have been created to hold them. The blue-and-russet glaze seemed to glow from within with a light of its own. Like much that Duncan had seen on Yamato, the vase was simple and beautiful. Was Yamatan engineering as successful and as pure?

The quality of the ceramic tea utensils, Duncan noted, had been different from the vase—rougher, more ancient, yet in their way, as lovely. The tea set was probably a family treasure beyond price. At one point after the tea ceremony the daimyo had explained with some pride that the utensils had come from Earth on *Hachiman*'s second voyage. They had once been the property of the now-extinct imperial family of Terrestrial Japan.

Minamoto no Kami knelt on the tatami with his *katana* and *wakizashi*—the samurai's *daisho*—at his side. The ancient swords were the work of the armorer Momoyama, and had been used by a Minamoto at the Battle of Sekigahara in the year 1600. The weapons were polished and dusted with talcum, the blades unadorned with engraving in the battle-wise style of Momoyama. Even in this modern environment, they seemed suitable weapons for this rather splendid old man.

"Speak to me of this war you seek, syndic-san," the Shogun said. "To judge from this morning's business, it appears others know more of it than I, and have strong feelings about it."

The statement was direct and un-Japanese. Duncan had expected something quite different. This demand for information could have come from a fur-fish boat captain on Planet Thalassa. Duncan needed to remind himself that Minamoto no Kami was not, after all, a daimyo of Japan's feudal era, but a ruler of Yamato's Second Millennium.

Before politics dominated his life, he said, he had been a practicing xenobiologist with considerable experience in space. "I may look like a samurai painted on a war fan," he had said with a barely perceptible smile. "No doubt Minamoto Kantaro has emphasized what an old-fashioned man I am. That is true. But I am under no illusions that the date is sixteen hundred. Or that politics have grown simpler since then."

"Warning taken, Shogun," Duncan said.

"One of the skills required in the exercise of power, Starman, is the ability to distinguish between truth and wish."

"A skill I suspect you have mastered, Shogun," Duncan said.

"No one ever masters it, syndic-san. But one's percentage of success rises over time. And I am old." He spoke with a steely ring in his fragile voice. "I have learned which of my wishes I have a right to see fulfilled. One of these is to be told the truth."

"I did not bring *Glory* to Yamato to tell lies, Shogun," Duncan said evenly. "It is not a syndic's way. And it isn't mine."

"Good," the old man said. "You appear to be a man who heeds warnings."

"When I can, Shogun."

The Shogun glanced at Kantaro. "It is not like an assassin of the Ninja Order to fail, nephew. How did it happen?"

"He must have misjudged the temper of the crowd in front of the ryokan, *tono.*"

How calmly they discuss our near-miss, Duncan thought. Whatever else they were, they were certainly pragmatics. The task was to interpret events, and so be prepared.

The daimyo turned back to Duncan. "Be warned. The Order does not take failure lightly, syndic-san."

Duncan shrugged, his light eyes cool. "Karma, Lord Shogun," he said.

Minamoto no Kami nodded approval of Duncan's reply. "Tell me about the war you seek," he said.

"We seek no war. We have made a discovery, that is all."

"A disquieting discovery."

"Yes."

"Enough to bring you here without hope of gain."

Glory had warned that the colonists on Yamato were highly

evolved capitalists. Their asteroid subcolonies were treated as independent states, free to exercise all their commercial and entrepreneurial skills, even on the inhabitants of the home planet.

"That is so, Shogun," Duncan said. "Unless one chooses to assign a cash value to life, liberty, human survival . . ."

"I am being chided, I see," the Shogun said. "Well. I asked, you answered. One sometimes does, syndic-san. You do well to remind me," the Shogun said. He looked at Anya curiously. "You have spoken very little, Anya-san. Have you nothing to add to what your daimyo says?"

"Only my agreement, Shogun," Amaya said in her selfassured way. "Despite what happened in front of the ryokan this morning."

"Or because of it. I understand," the old man said.

The Lord Mayor of Yedo flushed. He was not accustomed to hearing the most exalted official on his world spoken to so—most particularly, not by a woman. He began a protest, but the Shogun interrupted him.

"*Iie,* Kantaro-san," the Shogun cautioned. "Our guests must feel free to speak plainly. We did not serve them well in Yedo today."

Kantaro's face became an instant mask. Duncan was reminded of *Glory*'s warning that the price of failure could be very high on Planet Yamato. The Shogun could issue harsh orders. Seppuku was common on Planet Yamato.

"The battle has only begun, Shogun," Duncan said. "We are still searching for friends to share the burden." Including a live and functioning Minamoto Kantaro, who would be well worth recruiting into *Glory*'s fight against the Terror.

The old man regarded Duncan intently. "I wonder if you are not too frank to prosper on Planet Yamato," he said.

Anya Amaya said quietly, "Shouldn't we be open with one another, Shogun? There may be difficult times ahead. Wouldn't we do well to remember that we are all Earth's children?"

The old man said, "We have been separated for a very long time, Anya-san. We may have grown too far apart to share the burdens."

"Or spoils?"

The megacapitalist steel glinted in the old man's eyes.

"*Carefully, Anya,*" Duncan subvocalized. He felt her bridle, and then she said, "Whether we share or not, it will come and we must face it. I think we would do better as allies and partners."

"Even if we die, Anya-san?" the Shogun asked in a voice like a stiletto blade probing.

"Even then, Shogun."

The old man smiled thinly at Duncan. "Are all your women made of steel, syndic-san?"

"They tend to be, Shogun," Duncan said.

Minamoto no Kami said, "So this is what one learns in Centaurus." The women's colony of New Earth in the Proxima Centaurus System had been established before *Hachiman* had departed for Tau Ceti. The Japanese of Earth had violently ejected the feminist recruiters who came to their islands seeking converts. Some had been killed. *Perhaps it is a human trait,* Duncan thought, *that our quarrels and troubles outlive our civilizations.*

"I don't know, Shogun," Anya said. "But when New Earth's time comes, I hope they will remember they are human beings before they are women."

"*When* it comes?" the old man asked.

"When, Shogun, yes."

The Shogun looked at Anya approvingly. "A samurai's answer, Anya-san." He turned to Duncan. "Now tell me of your enemies, Starman. Describe them."

"I have never seen them, or it," Duncan said. "I have only seen the men they have killed."

"An invisible adversary, Kr-san?"

"There are colors the human eye cannot see, sounds the human ear cannot hear."

"That is not reassuring," the old daimyo said.

Duncan shrugged. "There are nonhuman Terrestrials aboard *Glory*. Our partners. They first sensed the Terror at a great distance."

"Your partners? You mean your cats?"

"Yes, Shogun."

The daimyo's gaze shifted to Minamoto Kantaro for confirmation. "*Neko?* Truly?"

"I have not seen them, Shogun. But I am told they have remarkable powers," Kantaro said.

Duncan had given Kantaro a detailed description of *Glory*'s pride of cats. He had no idea whether or not the Yamatan believed him.

"Can you demonstrate the skills of your animals?" the Shogun asked. Minamoto no Kami was not *only* a skeptic. As a xenobiologist he was at least apt to be open to the idea that species other than human had abilities men did not. *Mira's pride would be a revelation to the daimyo of Honshu—of all Yamato, actually,* Duncan thought. But, of course, there was no way fully to demonstrate the animals' abilities to one who could not Wire to *Glory*'s computer.

The Shogun said to Duncan, "I keep cats. As pets. They do not breed well on Planet Yamato, but those that do are companion animals, nothing more. We claim no supernatural powers for them."

Duncan said, "With respect, Minamoto-sama. There is nothing supernatural about our animals. They were born and have lived all their lives in Deep Space. The environment has changed them. And our Cybersurgeon has given them implants that allow them to interface with *Glory*'s computer. What Starmen do with drogues and sockets, the cats do by radio-link. The results have been—surprising."

Duncan felt Amaya thinking and subvocalizing sardonically: *"That is an understatement only a Thalassan could make, Duncan."*

"Remarkable," the daimyo said drily. Clearly he was far from convinced. But someone on Yamato was, Duncan thought. Convinced enough to send an assassin. The urge to hide from the unpleasant and the dangerous was, apparently, still universal among men.

The Shogun said, "We humans have criticized ourselves for millennia for being unable to establish reasonable interspecies relationships. You have succeeded where so many others have failed?"

"You are losing him, Duncan," Anya subvocalized.

"A few small successes, Shogun," Duncan said. "But those successes have kept us alive. I believe our adversary is attracted by Terrestrial emotions. Enraged by them. I don't know why. At the moment I don't care. I think your new technology has taken Yamatans out far enough to draw attacks."

"Emotions? Feelings? I think that a strange provocation, Kr-san."

The old man was fishing for knowledge, Duncan thought. And the Yamatans *had* suffered losses caused by the Terror. He was certain of it. "Fear," he said. "Any emotions might be dangerous. But fear is the common element in our encounters. I think I, personally, drew it down on my ship when I strayed too great a distance from *Glory* in a sled. I was afraid—and it *knew*. It fed on my emotions."

"This is what you bring us, Starman?"

"With regret, Shogun." Duncan realized it was not the style on Yamato to give a short, simple answer. But if the Yamatans were ever to work with the syndics of Goldenwing *Glory*, some changes in their ways would have to be made. The thing *Glory*'s people and the warriors of Nimrud and Nineveh had fought to a temporary standstill in the Ross Stars was unlikely to stop hunting Man now. It had a taste for death.

Duncan wondered, *Are the colonists of Yamato capable of meeting the challenge* Glory *brought?* He regarded the old daimyo steadily. The wars fought by the Shogun's ancestors had not been conducted with tea ceremonies and Zen meditations. Like all mankind's wars, they had been hard, bloody and savage.

"Kr-san, let us speak without ceremony," the Shogun said.

"Please do, Minamoto-sama."

The Shogun's eyes flicked to Amaya and back to Duncan. "Do you wish to excuse your woman?"

Amaya flushed but maintained silence. *Glory*'s data bank had much to say about the interpersonal relations of the men and women who came into space from Earth's Japan.

"No, Daimyo. I do not," Duncan said. "Amaya is my Sailing Master, my second-in-command."

"As you wish. First allow me to instruct the Mayor of Yedo." The Shogun spoke rapidly to Kantaro in an ancient Japanese dialect. The younger man, on his knees, bowed low with his knuckles touching the tatami. Then he moved to the entry, slid the door panel aside, and departed.

Duncan felt a flash of anxiety. "Daimyo," he said. "The happening before the ryokan in Yedo was probably unavoidable. I would regret if our presence in your Domain of Honshu became the cause of any administrative trouble." *I wish I could say,* Duncan thought, *that the worst thing that could happen would be to have Yamatan society turned upside down to uncover some plot or other against the* gaijin—the foreigners. That was not the way to win allies in a very losable war.

The Shogun's old eyes turned frigid. "Let me be the judge of that, Kr-san. Let Japanese problems be solved with Japanese methods." The statement was remarkable for the use of the word *Japanese*. The ethnic name for the people of Planet Yamato was almost never used. When it was, the intention was extreme emphasis and separation from the rest of human society. It was a clear warning that said: *Keep out. This concerns only us, not the* gaijin.

The old man smiled grimly. "Don't expect ritual disembowelments, honored syndic. Such things are seldom done here among our people, and never by the enlightened."

"I am relieved to hear it, Shogun."

"I have instructed my nephew to, among other things, make contact with your vessel and inform your people that you are safe and well." The old man looked at Anya and essayed a barely perceptible smile. "Does that meet with your approval, Sailing Master?"

"We are in your house, Shogun," Anya said, guided by her Hispanic ancestors. "We rely on your wisdom."

The Shogun's smile broadened. "Very good, Sailing Master. Well said. Spoken like a Japanese."

Duncan was thinking that this encounter was becoming more and more like a wandering *ronin*'s reception in some castle in the feudal Home Islands of two millennia ago.

"Kantaro has spoken to me about your battle at the Twin Planets," the Shogun said. "Tell me now. All that you can remember."

"It was scarcely a battle, Shogun," Duncan said. "It was at the most a skirmish."

"One that, without the cats, you would have lost?"

"I believe so."

"Say on, Kr-san. Old men love war stories."

Duncan felt a surge of impatience. The daimyo's elliptical manner grew exasperating. Anya gave Duncan a covert look of caution. It was fitting that she, who came from the most rigid social order represented aboard *Glory*, should best understand the old Shogun.

But Duncan could not help replying, "Isn't it more fitting to speak of that which is to come rather than that which has been, Shogun?"

"We have fought battles as well, Starman. And lost them, too. The people who sent the ninja are frightened. They think we can hide. I do not. But first let us be certain we fight the same enemy."

6

A SWIFT KILLING

•

Higashi Ichiro, Commander of the test ship MD-23, was tremendously pleased with the performance of his craft and three-man crew. The handling of the mass-depletion engine had been all that the engineers and research physicists back on Yamato could have wished, and Masao Kendo, the Specialist in Astrogation, now confirmed that the MD-23 had jumped a full 278,000,000 kilometers in an interval too small for the craft's chronometer to record. There had been no perceptible acceleration and no apparent passage of time. The event was mind-boggling. Ichiro had been warned that actually doing the impossible was unsettling, to say the least. But the reality left him and his crewmates speechless.

Ichiro felt disoriented. He had read of the time dilation experienced by Goldenwing Starmen as their ships approached lightspeed. This was time dilation multiplied by infinity. In the Near Away time did not exist. No Yamatan physicist understood it, but such was the medium through which mass-depletion devices moved.

Now, however, MD-23's mass-depletion engine was drained of power. The return journey to Yamato would be powered by reaction engines and would take months.

And, unnerved or not, Ichiro couldn't prevent the burst of joy in his chest when Masao-san confirmed that MD-23 had actually completed its first flight into and through the Near Away.

With this test flight, the fleet of Yamatan ships capable of attaining more than lightspeed numbered eleven. Of the eighteen constructed on Moon Hideyoshi, seven had failed to return from test journeys. That was frightening, but a samurai understood that a nation was advanced by the self-sacrifice of its people.

MD-23 had been fuelled correctly with sufficient capacity to emerge from the Near Away on the far side of Amaterasu, in the satellite system of the gas giant Toshie—which now filled a substantial part of the sky visible in MD-23's navigational screen. What the engineers called the Law of Inertial Mass Depletion had functioned exactly as the techs had predicted it would. The ship had emerged into normal space near to, but not dangerously within, the vast gravity well of Planet Toshie, and still within a tedious but manageable distance from Yamato in normal space. Ichiro had never before been so far from home, and the sight of the huge yellow planet ringed with cloud belts was overpowering.

Ichiro was no physicist. He understood the principles of inertial-depletion flight imperfectly. This ignorance he shared with his fellow astronauts.

He had been taught that the engine was powered in the environment of the Near Away by the tachyons storming out of the white hole at the galaxy's center. Goldenwings, Ichiro knew, were powered by the same tachyons, but their capture of tachyons with skylar sails was primitive compared with the processes within the tokamak at the heart of the MD propulsion unit.

Goldenwings used tachyon pressure on square kilometers of golden skylar sails to drive their great tonnage in the same way the winds had driven the clipper ships across Earth's vast oceans. Since tachyons exceeded lightspeed only by a small fraction, the sailing ships could never actually surpass lightspeed. The Near Away remained forever out of reach. Like all sublight matter and particles, the Goldenwings were subject to all Einsteinian time-dilation effects.

The mass-depletion engines operated with a complexity orders of magnitude greater than the Goldenwing sailplans. Tachyons were captured by the engine and stripped of inertia. The resultant power was channelled to the plasma rings that were the most obvious physical feature of MD ships. In flight the vessels were ringed with plasma that glowed like St. Elmo's fire. The MD rings converted the tachyons' inertia into delta-V, driving the ship into and through the analog of normal space the Yamatan builders called the Near Away.

In that "place," analogs of distance and direction existed, but an analog of time did not. Entry and exit from the Near Away were simultaneous; direction and distance were controlled (or so the crews hoped and believed) by the amount of inertial mass depleted by each jump. The results were stunning. A voyage that would take a nuclear rocket-powered spacecraft years to complete would take a Goldenwing months of shiptime (and decades of "nondilated" downtime). But an MD-powered spacecraft, destroying its own inertia as it went, took *no* time.

To the visionaries on Yamato, the new technology offered instantaneous travel throughout the galaxy—and even extragalactic voyages seemed within reach. The dreams were unlimited.

The first problem to arise for the MD engineers was the endurance of the engines. A voyage of three hundred light-days totally depleted the largest tokamak's inertial mass–destroying capability, leaving the spacecraft stranded months, or even years, from planetfall in ordinary space.

From Tau Ceti, to the nearest star, Epsilon Eridani, was a mere 5.4 light-years—a voyage of months in a Goldenwing, but quite unreachable through the Near Away because an MD ship would burst helplessly out of the Near Away a light-year and a third from its launch point, tokamak drained of power, marooned between the stars. The Near Away eliminated time, but in normal space distance remained, real and demanding.

There were "to-come" MD ships in the design computers, ships capable of carrying two or even more of the massive MD engines to be used serially. But an MD tokamak functioning in the vicinity of another destroyed the passive engine's ability to generate the necessary plasmas. Unless shielded with impossibly dense barriers, an MD engine, when carried within the inertialess field created by another MD engine, swiftly became useless.

The problems would be solved, all Yamato's space engineers agreed with that. What no one could be sure about was *when*.

For the moment, in order not to exceed the Point of No Return, Yamato's Near Away craft were limited to a journey through the Near Away of less than 300,000,000 kilometers. Enough to reach the orbit of ringed Toshie, Amaterasu's inner gas giant, but no more. Higashi Ichiro and his experimental ship floated in normal space at the end of Planet Yamato's reach.

Whatever the unsolved technical problems, Ichiro thought, Yamatan physicists' and engineers' genius had brought them across the system faster than light could make the journey.

Shorter flights were routinely made now, but this great leap forward was a triumph.

Ichiro-san spoke into his com-set to Alto Yamashiro, the ship's Communicator. "Dispatch the yes signal to home base, Alto-san. The numbers confirm that the MD-23 is fully operational."

It would take the message a hundred and eighty minutes to cross the Amaterasu system. Radio emissions operated under Einsteinian laws. Ichiro had no doubt that soon messages would travel through the Near Away instantaneously.

Ichiro forced himself to suppress his excitement and turn to his other duties. All computer readings had to be stored on bubbles and then transmitted to Moon Hideyoshi. It was an ironclad rule that since the last disappearance of an experimental Near Away craft, flight records had to be transmitted to base after each stage of a transit. Should an accident occur, only the machine and the men—replaceable items—and not totally unique flight data would be lost. Records fuelled the MD project.

Some of the experimental pilots complained that the engineers valued their precious data more than they did the MD crews. But in this Ichiro Higashi came down on the side of the engineers. The ships were the future. Not only of Yamato, but of spacefaring humankind. Test information was priceless because the inertial-mass-depletion engine would make Yamato the foremost planet in the galaxy, and soon MD-powered Near Away vessels would leave the Amaterasu System for *truly* deep space, that great dark ocean heretofore the exclusive venue of the majestic Goldenwings. Ichiro intended to be aboard one of those pioneering MD ships.

"Alto-san, send the flight-recorder records first," he ordered.

"Shouldn't we send the engine scans before anything else, Ichiro?"

Ichiro tried briefly—and ineffectively—to suppress his quick surge of fury. Ever since he, Ichiro, had taken Miyako-san, Alto's cousin, to be his concubine, his subordinate had begun to put himself forward. This was common among Yamatans, and it was universally castigated. But the rigidity of society on Planet Yamato assured that any ambitious man would take whatever advantage he could derive from his circumstances. Alto Yamashiro was more than ordinarily ambitious and, because of his pretty cousin's new status, he chose this moment to challenge his senior officer's authority.

Alto-san was no fool. The challenge was mild and carefully contrived. Whether or not the engine scans preceded the astrogational numbers in the radio message to Moon Hideyoshi was unimportant. The careful rebellion was calculated to cause the commander of MD-23 to consider the opinions of someone who was, almost, an in-law.

But the Commo Officer miscalculated. Commander Higashi was, at the moment, on an emotional high. For a year and a half, since a minor contretemps with a superior on Hideyoshi, the young man had been deeply worried about his advancement in the Exploration Corps. Alto's argumentativeness—at the moment he was engaged in a prolix explication of why it would be more suitable that the astro numbers be sent before the rest of the message—seemed an outright provocation.

In point of fact, the dispute was meaningless. Aboard a happier ship than MD-23, it would not be taking place.

But Ichiro, suddenly red-faced and explosive, began shouting at his junior officer. Alto-san, taken aback by the flash of fury, chose to shout back. The two officers found themselves face to face in a particularly acrimonious, escalating quarrel.

Masao Kendo, the Astrogation Specialist, attempted to intervene. "Commander—Alto-san—This is not seemly, sirs. I beg you to control your tempers. We are too close to Toshie to allow our attention to wander into trivialities."

Kendo's use of the word *trivialities* exacerbated the Commander's already aroused bad temper. Ichiro's rages were famous on Moon Hideyoshi, and on this auspicious occasion he allowed his stormy nature to rage free.

But the storm was brief. Brief and horrible. Before the horrified eyes of his subordinates, Higashi Ichiro seemed suddenly to be caught up in an invisible tornado of force. An ordinary bad-tempered, arm-waving tirade typical of his age and class changed violently into a spastic, wrenching dance. His right arm was flung about with such ferocity that the crew of MD-23 heard the ulna crack like a dry twig. Angry words were supplanted by a scream of anguish as his inner organs were squeezed and torn with ripping force. Blood spewed from his open mouth and his blinded eyes extruded from their sockets as the internal pressure in his skull was doubled, then doubled again. In the microgravity, his grotesque dance was executed with such ferocity that he left a thick, bloody smear on the overhead before being flung into space through an inexplicably twisted bulkhead.

The crewmen of MD-23 had only moments to take in the horror of Ichiro Higashi's destruction before the tensions twisting the small spacecraft ripped it apart, spilling the crew, unarmored, into space.

Though there was no human eye nearby to see it happen, the wreckage of MD-23 spun into a tight orbit around a darkness that was blacker than black, a tiny Gateway into the Near Away.

It was never so near, nor so far away.

On the island of Kai, in a planetary observatory atop a mountain called Suribachi, a Junior Astronomer stared in disbelief at a monitor as Planet Yamato's largest telescope recorded the destruction of MD-23 and the death of its crew.

7

SHOCK WAVES

·

Aboard *Glory* the destruction of the MD-23 was captured by a surveillance camera atop the port mizzenmast. This camera, ordinarily used to monitor the condition of the upper five kilometers of the spar, was activated by the FTL flash of tachyon power released across the Tau Ceti Star System by the forcible opening of the Gateway from the Near Away.

When inertial-mass-depletion-powered Yamatan craft transited between the Near Away and normal space, their size and low power created openings that were small, less than a thousand meters in diameter, and the Gateways were not held open for any measurable time. But the disturbance caused by the Gateway that devoured MD-23 was emotionally familiar to *Glory*'s crew members, who'd encountered it before in the Ross Stars.

Glory's monkeys, confined for refurbishment and safety while in orbit around Planet Yamato, were frantically disturbed by the power of the distant Gateway's forcible distortion of normal space.

In the battle *Glory* had fought in the Ross System, a monkey had been slaughtered by a soldier of the boarding party from Ross 248 Beta. Now, months of shiptime later, the monkeys were still deeply disturbed by what had happened. Since *Glory*'s commissioning in orbit around Earth's Moon, no cyberbeast had ever died, and any who met with an accident had been swiftly repaired. Death is a human concept. The chimp-descended monkeys had been shocked by the demise of one of their number. The cats knew this. Their closeness to the human syndics had given them a grasp of what it meant to cease living. But neither Mira nor any of the other members of the pride had yet conveyed to the Starmen the import of what had happened to the monkeys at Ross 248.

Glory's mainframe had detected both the anxiety and fear the monkeys were feeling. Yet sophisticated as it was, *Glory*'s computer was still only a machine. It had taken no action about the monkeys so long as they performed their duties safely and correctly. Now the impulse that swept through Near Space from the Gateway that had opened across the system agitated the monkeys. *Glory* tranquilized the small cyberbeasts and saved the information in memory, but she did not alert the syndics, being fully occupied with more serious possible danger to the ship.

Dietr Krieg, even though the least empathic of the Starmen, nevertheless was able to recognize the emotional signature of the wave of rage that swept across the inner Tau Ceti System. The Cybersurgeon felt the others' emotional surge.

Warned by the attack on Duncan and Anya on the surface, *Glory*'s people had been preparing the ship for a precipitous departure. Attempts to contact Duncan and Anya by radio had failed. Almost immediately after the ninja's attempt—witnessed by all aboard *Glory* on the Yamato Planetary Television Net— there had been an immediate Loss of Signal from Duncan's and Anya's communicators. The phenomenon of LOS was as old as orbital flight. Only on planets ringed by relay satellites could it be avoided when the sending transmitter vanished over the horizon. On Yamato the problem was not a lack of relay satellites; Planet Yamato had them to excess. But the satellites did not transmit or receive in the radio bands used by the personal com devices of the Goldenwing's crewmen.

Demands sent by the syndics downworld had not immediately produced the geographical coordinates of the Master and Sailing Master's location. The *gaijin*'s exact whereabouts was classified because it was also the location of Minamoto no Kami, the planetary daimyo. By ancient tradition the Shogun's location was a state secret. Shoguns were prime targets for assassins. Except when public duties made it impossible, the Shogun's whereabouts was kept secret from the ninjas who operated freely on

Planet Yamato. Often the attempt at secrecy failed. In the last five hundred years only one hundred Shoguns had died of natural causes.

After a dozen increasingly concerned demands for information, *Glory*'s syndics were coldly informed that a certain dignified patience was the approved demeanor for visitors to Planet Yamato. "We will soon make contact with your officers," the Planetary Security Net told the anxious syndics. "They are safe and well protected."

Broni Voerster, though excited and upset by what she had seen on the planetary telecast, was nevertheless determined that when Duncan returned aboard he would have nothing whatever to complain of regarding her performance of duty. At this moment she lay in her pod, Wired to *Glory*, composing the basic astroprogram for *Glory*'s retreat from the Tau Ceti Star System, maneuver by maneuver.

When the MD-23 was destroyed within the gravimetric confines of Tau Ceti's gravity well, Broni had received a jolt of malevolent psycho-empathic energy that made her cry out and pull the drogue from her head. She lay nude in the gel, bathed in a surge of stinging inertia-stripped tachyons. From her shoulders to her knees she felt the pulses from across the system. By this time she was syndic enough to reconnect to *Glory* swiftly and ask that the ship compute the exact location of the Gateway that had caused the surge. That was the first thing Duncan would want to know.

Mira's image of the open Gateway was part rathole and part dragon's lair. She had never seen either a rat or a dragon, but she recognized the vast, searching, hungry malevolence. Not only was the knowledge imprinted in her DNA and present in the lessons learned in purrs from her surrogate mother, the great-queen-who-was-not-alive, but Mira herself had sensed it before. Many times. And she had stalked it time and again, through that night without space or time.

All this she had passed on to her offspring, so that when the young cats indulged in their savage play, it was not dead or wounded animals they brought as offerings to Mira and to the syndics, but images of creatures from Glory's vast database:

reptiles, chimerae, phantasms. Recently these images had been reinforced by the memories of the fight at Ross 248 Beta, amplified by kittenish nightmares of teeth and claws and empty eyes burning with a loathing of life.

The cat floated in free-fall on the ob-deck. Above her the pelagic image of Yamato rolled swiftly by, a gleaming copper-tinged panorama of sea and cloud. Beyond it, far beyond, on the far side of Tau Ceti, the Gateway burned an instant and then was gone, closed, leaving only the star-shot sky of Near Space.

Mira uttered a trilling call for her brood to assemble. She knew, beyond any doubt, that there would soon be a hunt and a battle, and that there was work for her and hers to do. But where was the dominant tom? She raised her small head to see more clearly the planet Glory *orbited. There, she thought, the dominant tom is there and we are here to face the dragon without him. And though she could not possibly reach him with her call, she began to yowl.*

Buele, working in one of the vast holds where the landing sleds and shuttles were stored, sensed Mira's furious cries. Immediately he abandoned his task of preparing a shuttle for descent to the planet and settled into the lotus position (a move taught him by the skeptical but open-minded Cybersurgeon). It took the boy no more than four seconds to establish contact with *Glory's* mainframe. Through the computer, Buele reached out to make mental contact with Mira.

"Angry rejection. You are not what I want."

He made a mental effort to push into the rapport between cat and computer.

"Stay away! You are not the dominant tom." Threat. Image of teeth and claws.

"Mira! You know me. Hear me. Tell the pride to prepare for hunting. It is what the dominant tom would say to you if he were here."

"Sullen disbelief." Feline skepticism. Of which there is no greater.

"Hear me, Mira. Hear me. I am one of you."

"You are not."

Buele sensed a wish to disengage. He was in danger of losing his contact with the small queen. He cast about for help and found

Damon Ng. The Rigger had detected the cyberorganisms' distress and he had hurried to the Monkey House, where he was now fully engaged. Buele cast his search farther afield, found Broni.

"Help me, Sister Broni!"

"Buele? Is that you? You aren't Wired. How have you reached me?"

"Never mind, Sister Broni. Help me with Mira."

Mira snarled her exasperation. Cats did not respond well to being forced to pay attention when they chose not to do so. Both Buele and Broni felt the small queen's anger. It was far greater than her size.

Broni and Buele together addressed the cat: *"Pay attention, Mira. Hear what we say."*

Buele once again took control. His thoughts were sharply defined, honed and as sharply delivered as the strokes of a weapon. *"Mira. Tell the others. Either we hunt It or It will hunt us. Tell them, little mother."*

Mira: *"Call the dominant tom. Do it now. He will know what to do."*

Broni: *"We cannot."*

Buele (interrupting): *"We can. We will. But we can't wait for his return to prepare."* The boy and girl felt Mira's reluctance. There was a moment when her decision rested on such intangibles as the scent of her offspring in *Glory*'s internal atmosphere, the familiar sound of ancient machinery maintaining the life-supporting systems, the trust she had begun to develop in syndics other than the dominant tom. Buele and the girl on the bridge heard her calling her pride. It was a feral, emotional cry. Though they could not smell the air in Mira's vicinity, somehow both human girl and boy knew it was filled with pheromones.

They heard echoes throughout the vast ship as all the cats replied to the summons.

"Buele," Broni sent through the computer net. "What's happening?"

Though un-Wired, the boy heard Broni clearly.

Then Mira said, with shocking clarity: *Call Duncan.*

Duncan, Buele thought. *She called him Duncan.*

The net among *Glory*'s syndics—among *all* her syndics—was forming.

Buele looked around the dark, mainly empty, hold in bewildered wonderment.

Under his touch, in sight of his inner eyes, *Glory* was becoming a thing that had never existed before in all the universe. Powerful forces were gathering, using *Glory* as a matrix.

Buele felt himself bathed in icy sweat. It was a frightening thing to become part of an angry god.

Dietr Krieg, Wired to the com panel in the bridge, felt a shift in the forces around him. It was peculiarly comforting, as though he were being gently but firmly guided into a slot, a position he could—and must—fill until Duncan was once more aboard.

The Cybersurgeon was a man with little empathic Talent. He had served *Glory* for years by substituting intellect and curiosity for the empathic ability so prized among Goldenwing syndics. What he offered was accepted; he had always sensed that this was so, but now, at this moment, he felt an upwelling of love and gratitude for the whole into which he had, over the course of years and parsecs, been integrated.

Glory spoke through the drogue: *"I have located Duncan and Anya. The coordinates are in the communications console. Use the Yamatan com-net and tell Duncan that a Yamatan spacecraft was just destroyed and that others will be unless he can bring them aboard."*

Dietr was shocked. Not by what the Goldenwing's computer had just told him—he had expected that—but by the fact that *Glory* had spoken *to him directly* on a subject not related to his medical specialty. Shock gave way to pride and then to a strong desire to be worthy of *Glory*'s trust.

He began the procedures that realigned the communications antennae. *Glory* was capable of performing the task more quickly and efficiently than any one of the syndics aboard, but Dietr remembered one of Duncan's dicta: Never lose your humanity. Dietr also remembered the terrible encounter in the Ross System. An important part of one's humanity was the ability to feel fear. It had kept early Man alive on the open savannahs of Africa. It might keep *Glory*'s syndics alive here, under the Tau Ceti sun.

In the tube outside the bridge, Mira and three of her sons met and, despite their high anxiety, exchanged feline greetings, rit-

*ually sniffing one anothers' pheromones. Mira's brood did not
yet think in abstract concepts. Their mentation was direct, without embellishments. But the concept of fear was a universal to
all species originating on Earth, and among Mira's kind fear was
always accompanied by anger. Mira was angry now. The dominant tom called Duncan was somewhere in that light that could
be seen through the transparent overheads, and he belonged
with his pride, with the great-queen-who-is-not-alive, with the
others of his kind, and most importantly with Mira and her offspring. He should be here, preparing to fight. But since he was
not, Mira's augmented mind sullenly accepted a substitute.*

*The surrogate was not the-tom-who-cuts or the young-queen
or the tom-who-speaks-to-the-frightened-things-in-the-rigging
(Mira's view of her world was expanding at a rapid pace as she
approached full maturity, but it remained ailurocentric). The
surrogate had to be the annoying young tom who irritated Mira
and her brood by addressing them in their "speech"—a speech
he would always know imperfectly because he lacked a supple
body, vibrissae, scent glands and a proper tail, the use of which
assets were vital to total expression in the language of the Folk.
(Mira had slipped easily into thinking of her kind as "the Folk,"
meaning the true people.)*

*Mira had accepted that Buele must stand in for Duncan. She
could sense him still demanding her attention. With a swift switch
of her slender tail and a trilled command, Mira marshaled her
young hunters and prepared to fight the dragon.*

8

TSUNETOMO

•

Minamoto Kantaro left the *chashitsu* as he had entered it, submissively on his knees. He did not stand erect until the teahouse was hidden from view among the garden trees. Where the path left the clearing and curved into a grove of Earth sequoias, he paused and brushed the stones and needles from his ornate court-dress.

Many of Kantaro's peers—samurai all—would have scorned his caution, but Minamoto no Kami was not only the elected Shogun of Planet Yamato, he was also the hereditary daimyo of the Domain of Honshu and Kantaro's uncle and clan lord. If that were not enough, there was a genuine affection between the two men.

When the colonists for Tau Ceti left Earth, they had been forced to abandon much. But ancient traditions had been brought to the new lands by Goldenwing *Hachiman. Gimu* and *giri,* the concept of obligations to nation and family that for two thousand Earth years had been the heart of *bushido,* were, if anything, stronger on Planet Yamato than they had ever been on Earth. Under the Tau Ceti sun the complexities and contradictions of Japanese life not only survived—they throve.

Hachiman's journey had been organized by Japanese who sought to revive the historic past. Like their ancestors under the Tokugawa Shoguns, Yamatans had isolated themselves. They had reconstituted the old religions, the animist Shinto and the self-disciplining Zen Buddhism. These faiths did not deal in absolutes. One died and was reborn, but not into some fantasmic paradise—not at all. One was reborn into the real, physical world. This freedom from paradise allowed Yamatans to deal with each day pragmatically.

Like their Terrestrial ancestors, the Japanese of Tau Ceti, despite their obsession with loyalty and obedience, could shift allegiances in a heartbeat. Many of ancient Japan's civil wars had been decided in this way, by a sudden change in the loyalty of a daimyo—in the language of pre-Jihad, technical Earth, by a paradigm shift.

Minamoto Kantaro was experiencing such a paradigm shift. He was close to convincing himself that the failure of a ninja before the ryokan in Yedo—an extremely rare event—might be a signal of guidance from Amaterasu, the Sun Goddess.

For near to a thousand Terrestrial years the people of Planet Yamato had lived undisturbed in isolation eleven light-years from Earth. The unexpected arrival of *Gloria Coelis* raised strange ghosts from the Japanese past.

Long ago, the black ships of Commodore Perry's naval squadron had appeared at the entrance to Yedo Wan and demanded that Japan open itself to the *gaijin*. There were Yamatans who still regarded that long-ago event as the beginning of the road that led to the destruction of Japanese culture and civilization. Great cities were burned in bitter wars, and eventually Japan was nearly obliterated by the Muslim Jihad.

The mayor of Yedo was a young man in whom modernity and a reverence for the past were constantly at war. He had watched with chauvinistic pride the breakthroughs in FTL research. The genius of Yamatan scientists appealed enormously to his Zen samurai sensibilities, but success had brought mystery—even dread. Kantaro was, like most of his class, an isolationist. If asked, he would have said that it "was in the genes." The unexplained disappearance of inertial-mass-depletion-engine-powered spacecraft had affected him in the same manner it had affected many of the more senior daimyos, and the unexpected appearance of *Glory* stimulated ancestral fears.

Kantaro sensed a presence as he strode through the Shogun's garden toward the command post of the shogunal guard. The appearance of the *gaijin* ship, the Mayor of Yedo thought, was forcing decisions all over the planet. Decisions that no one, save possibly his uncle, the Shogun, wanted to make.

The redwood grove covered the seaward side of a long, narrow plateau. Through the great forest Kantaro could see the exposed shallows, the planetary ocean, ruddy gray, streaked with the coppery sheen it sometimes acquired when Amaterasu was high.

At the moment the sea beyond the tidal flats was calm and smooth as a tabletop. In less than an hour it would be roiled by tides raised by the swift passage of the smallest and nearest of Yamato's satellites. At the moment, in the dark band below the coppery sky, Moon Hideyoshi showed only a thin crescent as it rose from the sea.

What were the MD scientists about up there? Kantaro wondered. Were the scientists making any attempt to discover why the ships of which they had grown so proud were vanishing? Or were they, in the manner of good Yamatans, allowing the ruling samurai to solve the mystery in their own way?

Kantaro paused beside a particularly massive *Sequoia giganteum* and paused to regard the scene before him. The contemplation of nature—called "viewing"—was an artistic discipline of the samurai class, and here at the edge of the Shogun's garden there was much to contemplate. Sheer cliffs, striated with sandstone, granite, and basalt, plunged down to the sea. The tidal flats were exposed by the gravitational pull of Moon Tokugawa, out of sight now behind the trees. Several hectares of shallow seabottom normally concealed by water were exposed. The underwater plants and corals glistened in the ruddy sunlight of Amaterasu.

Before the tide would rise again, Tokugawa and Hideyoshi together would expose twenty kilometers of seabottom. Beyond the low, receding edge of the sea, coppery swirls in the water reflected the coppery weather patterns in the sky. Clouds were seldom white on Planet Yamato.

Kantaro detected the soft whirring noise of a tilt-rotor patrolling between Mount Kagu and the sea. Had the police found the corpse of the ninja? Kantaro wondered. Depending on how well fuelled the antigravity pack the man wore was, his headless corpse could have fallen into the sea a dozen or more kilometers downwind by now, or it could have risen into the jetstream that kept Yamato's atmosphere in constant motion. If the former, well and good. The Four Islands spanned two dozen degrees of longitude; all else was water. Though finding a ninja's corpse wearing a nullgrav unit might cause many questions to be asked. A nullgrav unit was worth the ransom of a fief.

But if the harness were heavily fuelled, the inept killer might now be on his way to Moon Hideyoshi or points far beyond. Kantaro sincerely hoped so.

He stepped clear of the forest and stood for a moment at the edge of the precipice. To the north Mount Kagu rose like a ghost of Fujiyama from the copper-tinged stratus clouds around the mountain's base.

Kantaro recalled a haiku written aeons ago by the poet Taruhito about another Mount Kagu, on the homeworld:

> The mists of spring
> Hang on Mount Kagu,
> The hill that fell from the skies.

Was it so? he wondered. Did the original mountain fall into the Land of the Dragonfly from the skies? From heaven? What dark power in his heart had chosen this particular haiku to be remembered at this moment?

"The 'mists of spring' were very different on Earth," a low voice said behind him.

Kantaro was startled. But the silent approach was warning enough to make him turn very slowly.

A man, masked and all in black, said, "It is written in the *Monogatari no Hachiman* that the mists of Earth are pale gray and white. Here they are the color of the furnishings on my *katana*."

Minamoto Kantaro took swift notice that the black-gloved hands were on the black-lacquered sheath of the man's sword. It was a *katana* of great antiquity, surely brought from Earth aboard *Hachiman*. The man before him was Tsunetomo, the Grand Master of Ninjas. It could be no other. The Ninja Order on Yamato was ever present, yet secret. Ninjas lived by the wisdom of the *Hagakure*, the Book of the Samurai. Apart, but always nearby, always ready. Kantaro did not ask how Tsunetomo had come this far into the Shogun's garden, alone and unapprehended.

The hired ninja had failed to kill Duncan Kr in Yedo, and as swiftly as this the Master appeared—ready to retrieve the failure with his own far superior killing skills. This was the way of the ninja. Once having been aimed at a victim, they did not stop until death.

"It would be best," Kantaro said, dry-mouthed, "if no further action were taken against the *gaijin* here, Tsunetomo-san."

"The choice of place and time is yours, Minamoto-san," the ninja said. "Within limits." The dark, basilisk's eyes left Kantaro's face for a moment and looked out over the sea. "How beautiful is Yamato," he said. "A treasure to be cherished and guarded."

Kantaro felt the words like the flick of a lash. He had been uncertain about killing the *gaijin*. They were, after all, almost sacred persons. Who could know what the *kami* of their great vessel might do to those who shed the blood of Wired Starmen?

But the daimyos, meeting secretly without Minamoto no Kami, had taken the decision, and Kantaro had been moved to join them. What was it the first Tsunetomo wrote in the *Hagakure*? "In the Way of the Samurai, one needs neither loyalty nor devotion, but simply to become desperate in the Way. Loyalty and devotion are themselves within desperation."

The words of the *Hagakure* were familiar to all Yamatan samurai. The *meaning* of the words only the ninja understood.

"It was karma that your warrior failed, Master," Minamoto Kantaro said. "The Shogun is of the opinion that we should listen to the syndics until we learn what we face."

The Master Ninja's hand rested on the hilt of his *katana*. His eyes took on the look of a zealot. "Where are you going, Lord Mayor?" he asked.

He whispers like an oracle, Kantaro thought. "I have just now been sent to assemble the daimyos."

"A decision has already been made." The Ninja Master continued to speak in that otherworldly voice. Ninjas were priests and monks of a terrible sort.

Kantaro's palms began to sweat. To have acquiesced to a public assassination of a stranger was not beyond the pale of behavior for a daimyo of Planet Yamato. Politics, after all, was a risky calling. But to agree now to the cold-blooded murder of a man with whom the Shogun was negotiating in the Shogun's own teahouse was another matter. Despite what the *Hagakure* said, loyalty *did* matter. In other places the first Tsunetomo wrote glowingly of loyalty.

I am not so depraved a samurai that I can ignore it, Minamoto Kantaro thought. But to draw his sword against a ninja—against *this* ninja, the most skilled on Planet Yamato—was an act of seppuku.

Though he could not see the other man's mouth, Kantaro knew somehow that he was smiling. Grimly, no doubt. The way Death smiled.

Tsunetomo bowed. "As I have said, Minamoto-san. Time and place are yours to select. Within reason."

He turned with a swift grace that was almost inhuman. In a stride he was in the shadow of the giant trees. In two he had vanished.

Kantaro flexed his aching hands. He closed his eyes and then opened them, looking again at the vast emptiness of the planetary sea stretching away to the west. Moon Hideyoshi had risen fifteen degrees into the western sky and his crescent was now nearly lost in the ruddy light of Amaterasu.

Kantaro had forgotten to ask the Master what had happened to the failed assassin's body. He flushed. It would have been presumptuous to remind the Master of the failure again.

Kantaro began again to walk toward the guardpost where communications equipment could connect him with anyplace on the Four Islands. As he walked, his geta sank into the soft, loamy soil and Yamato seemed to bestow a gentle caress. The scent of pine and native flowers was almost unbearably sweet and poignant.

What a wonderful thing it is to be alive, the Mayor of Yedo thought, breathing deeply the thin, cool air of his native world.

To the north, though the trees, Kantaro could make out the steep slopes of Mount Kagu, "the hill that fell from the skies."

When he was a child, studying the ancient poetry, his master told his students that Mount Kagu's beauty was a gift from the sky gods. He thought of that often.

As he walked through the conifers his personal com pinged with the Shogun's personal code.

"Kantaro," he said.

Minamoto no Kami's voice was steely. "Another MD ship has just been lost," he said. "We are running out of time. Order the daimyos to assemble in Yedo by midmorning. There will be a council aboard the syndics' Goldenwing."

It was like a blow. The Goldenwing and her people were taking over the life of Yamato. *The hill that fell from the skies.*

Goddess, he thought, looking toward the invisible ship in orbit, *how many gifts from the sky can Yamato take?*

9

A SMALL MUTINY

•

The message from Duncan and Anya reached *Glory* at the moment Damon Ng was facing the first cyborg rebellion in the history of star-sailing.

In conformity with the ukase given him by Acting Captain Dietr Krieg (the young Starman always thought of the Cyber-surgeon's commands in such florid terms), Damon had issued the computer inputs needed to alert the monkeys and set them in motion.

The young man's empathy warned him that Dietr's command to work should probably not have been issued so abruptly in this time and place. Dietr was a fine medic, but as a bridge officer he left much to be desired.

Though no one was certain of the reason, every Starman knew that monkeys behaved oddly in deep-gravity wells. In addition to this fact of a Starman's life, *Glory*'s syndics well knew that the thousand cyborgs aboard had been deeply shocked by the deliberate attack of the Nimrudite boarders with whom *Glory* had had to contend in the Ross Stars.

Nimrudite attackers had blundered into the Monkey House, panicked, and lasered the harmless creatures where they reclined in the power racks, killing one and injuring others. The entire monkey contingent had been aghast. On some Goldenwings monkeys were denied free choice and worked to death at only the most primitive, labor-intensive tasks. They were, in fact, called monkeys because their tasks were those relegated to the "deck apes" on the transoceanic racers of ancient Earth.

But on *Glory* monkeys were treated differently. Duncan insisted that their semisentience be respected and their safety considered. Deaths among *Glory*'s monkeys had been unknown since Duncan had assumed the rank of Master and Commander.

The encounter with the Nimrudite pirates had changed all that. The critters had seen human beings at war with one another, and a monkey had died at the hands of a human invader. The monkeys had been shocked. It was a measure of *Glory*'s monkeys' loyalty that despite a gratuitous act of murder, the small cyborgs had continued to perform their assignments nominally on the voyage from Ross 248.

But the psychic disturbance that reverberated through the Amaterasu System when the portal from the Near Away opened finished what the killing at Nimrud had begun. It totally immobilized the half-chimp, half-computer constructs without whom no Goldenwing could be sailed.

A frustrated and dismayed Dietr Krieg had a psychiatric term for the condition. It was *fugue*. Not knowing what else to do, he had despatched Damon to the Monkey House to deal with the problem. It was Damon who dealt most intimately with the monkeys, so it must be he who could persuade the critters to return to work. The trouble was that the monkeys were not human beings, and argument and persuasion were not likely to have any effect on them.

Suited for space, Damon floated in the light gravity of the Monkey House. He was baffled by his charges' behavior, by their refusal to move, to communicate, or even to acknowledge his presence among them. He sensed that they were terrified and required leadership. But leadership was not the young Rigger's strong suit.

Damon drifted in the central bay, looking down the long, dark rows of power-racks, each holding a silent monkey. He could feel them looking at him. God knew what their thoughts were. If cybernetic organisms thought.

The notion had a sting like that of the punishing stiletto blades carried by the aristocrats of his forested homeworld. After six years under the command of Duncan Kr, it was an unacceptable thought. Of *course* cybernetic organisms thought. What else was

Glory but a vast cyborg? And her thoughts were vastly more profound than those of any aboard her.

"Damon, do you read me?"

Thank God, he thought. *Duncan.* *"I read you, Captain. Do you see what is happening aboard?"*

"Well enough, boy. Don't try to force the situation. We will deal with them when we have to."

"It will be difficult to get under weigh without monkeys, Duncan."

"Dietr, belay the order to prepare to leave orbit."

"Aye, Captain." There was enormous relief in the Cybersurgeon's sending.

"Make ready to take aboard a scientific and political delegation, Dietr. I have come to an agreement with the Shogun. Damon, you will have to hangar a squadron of small spacecraft. Can you manage it without the monkeys?"

"Yes, Captain. Broni and Buele can help." Damon sent. *"Mass-depletion-powered ships, Captain?"*

"Yes."

Damon could not resist asking, *"Are they as fast as the rumors say?"*

Dietr interceded testily. *"What does that matter right now? Captain, the Planetary News Net is saying something about an accident in space. We felt something—ah, familiar. Is it what we suspected it was?"*

"Yes."

Damon sent, *"It's what frightened the monkeys. I am sure of it."*

"It frightened the Yamatans, too. At just the right time."

"Is this meeting going to be political or scientific, Duncan?" The surgeon's communications were tightly controlled, drained, insofar as possible, of emotional content.

"It will be a gathering. That is all I can say without guessing. Yamato has a unique political structure. There are no real nations, only clans and families. We have to convince the daimyos to go outside."

Aboard *Glory* there was silence. Then Broni's sending came through fresh and clear: *"The Yamatans surely understand we must fight together."*

All could sense Duncan's regard for Eliana Ehrengraf's daughter. "*I hope so, Broni. I do sincerely hope so. But there is self-interest, too. They* have *spent a century developing mass-depletion power. They have a reason to resist being confined in Near Space. Damon, in addition to six MD ships the Shogun's barge will be coming aboard. I want you and Buele to meet us at a thousand kilometers and guide us in. Make certain that Glory is her most impressive. Open an ob-deck for the visitors and make their quarters as comfortable as possible. They think we are archaic. Be prepared to make them think otherwise.*" Duncan addressed them all. "*Be Wired as often as you can, and keep checking with* Glory. *I don't want any misunderstandings.*"

"*Aye, Captain.*"

"*You felt the event in space,*" Duncan sent. "*What was it like aboard?*"

Dietr said, "*It sent the monkeys into fugue.*"

"*Very likely. Start considering how you are going to bring them out of it.*"

Everyone aboard *Glory* had felt the burning death of the Ya-matans aboard the distant spacecraft. The syndics had recognized the threat instantly. But only Duncan thought ahead.

There was a flare of feral anger that shook both Dietr and Damon. It was directed at Duncan, but it was carelessly directed and enormously demanding. Though it was not couched in human words its meaning was heatedly clear. A translation into human language would be as plain as it was angry: "*Why are you not here with the Folk where you belong, defending what you must defend?*" There followed an unmistakable demand that Duncan return at once to the lair.

"*Ah, Mira,*" he sent. "*Very soon now.*"

The cat was not placated. Mira had a strong sense of Terrestrial, mammalian distribution of duties. At this time the proper place for the dominant tom was with the Folk and the great-queen-who-was-not-alive. That was the way of life.

"*She is very upset, Duncan,*" Dietr said. "*All the cats are.*"

Damon said, "*I think she can communicate with the monkeys.*"

"*I hope so,*" Duncan sent. "*Someone will have to or* Glory *will never leave this system.*"

Dietr's comment was devoid of his usual bravado. "*Lieber*

Gott, Master and Commander, I was never really cut out to be a warrior."

"You're warrior enough, Dietr," Duncan said.

Every living thing aboard and in the loop received an emanation of power from the Goldenwing and her Captain. To Damon it was like an infusion of pure courage. He hoped that it was the same for the others. *If we fail now,* Damon thought, *we have come as far in space as men ever will. . . .*

He felt Mira and her pride making themselves large, ruffs and guard-hairs erect and extended, ready for battle, and he had a small but potent epiphany. *"They call themselves the Folk."*

Buele interceded powerfully. *"You should think of them that way, Damon. It pleases them."* Damon had never received so clear a sending from a fellow syndic. Not even from Duncan.

Buele meant the cats, of course. How could he know what the animals felt and how was he able to state it in such simple, human—no, *Terrestrial*—terms?

"In ten orbits, then," Duncan sent, preparing to break contact. The message was clearly for Dietr Krieg, and the Cybersurgeon acknowledged it—and the shift of responsibility—willingly.

"Aye, Captain," he sent.

Ten orbits was nine hours eight minutes Standard, Damon thought. What he had learned from *Glory's* database about the splendid Yamatans had rather intimidated him. But, the exchange with Buele reminded him, even out here, they were all children of the Earth. *That is the most important truth of all our lives,* he thought.

Broni Ehrengraf, at her Astroprogrammer's post on the bridge, listened to the nuances she detected in Duncan's sending. With his customary intuitiveness, he had picked up the feelings of tension that flowed from the ship. It was more than a simple horror of recalling the fight in the Ross Stars. It was the enervating fear that despite anything that could be done, failure and horrible death lay at *Glory's* end.

Broni's carelessly held religious beliefs had always taught that the universe lay balanced between the powers of good and evil. Kaffir preachers on her homeworld sang of Armageddon, the Final Battle at the end of the world. Such matters had always seemed quaint to the daughter of the Voertrekkerpraesident of

Planet Voerster. But *Glory*'s encounters with the Terror changed that. Her religious training had been too cursory to provide comfort, but her personal experience at Ross 248 was a real memory and it terrified her.

Now the Terror had struck again—across the Amaterasu System, to be sure, but what did time and distance matter?

Duncan's personal command was like the touch of his hand. *"Broni,"* he sent. *"You are our resident aristocrat. That makes you chief of protocol. In ten orbits the daimyos are visiting in state, or as much state as they can manage aboard their MD ships. Have* Glory *brief you on what they will expect. Will you do that, please?"*

Somehow, Duncan's manner was bantering, and Broni knew the Captain was smiling. She sensed that the others aboard, Damon, Buele and Cybersurgeon Krieg, responded to it and to one another. It seemed to warm the air they breathed. Now Damon and Buele were exchanging sendings about either the cats or the monkeys. She could not be sure which. But the particulars didn't matter. Tension had diminished aboard *Glory*.

What a beautiful man you are, Duncan Kr, she thought.

The thought was unshielded and there came instant, sardonic comments from the other syndics aboard. She accepted them without comment. She had what she wanted: a swift, unguarded flash of warmth and affection from Duncan.

And perched on the curve of Broni's pod, Mira regarded young human female with the intent, inscrutable stare that only the Folk can manage.

10

ABOARD THE *DRAGONFLY*

•

The bridge of the Shogun's barge, *Dragonfly,* a reaction-powered craft of ten meters' beam, was crowded with Yamatan clansmen dressed for space in colorful pressure suits over which they wore their traditional finery. Duncan had explained in some detail that EVA gear would not be needed since the barge and the MD craft accompanying it would all be accommodated in one of *Glory*'s multiplicity of empty holds. But plainly the Yamatans had only a vague notion of the dimensions of the vessel they would soon be boarding and fully expected to walk her unprotected decks.

It appeared to be a quirk of the colonial man to forget the nature of the ships that had carried his ancestors into Near Space. Pictorial evidence abounded, but the ships were overbearing. There was a reluctance among Earth's children to acknowledge the vastness of the ancient technology.

The result was that colonials almost always suffered culture shock when they approached a Goldenwing. The reality of *Glory* and her sisters was stunning to men and women who had spent their lives either downworld or, at most, in low orbit.

The *Dragonfly* was decorated for the occasion with flags bearing the *mon* of the Minamotos, their silk held extended by frames in the airless void. The barge was a substantial ship used by the Shoguns of Yamato primarily for inspections and planetary surveys from orbit. As spacecraft went, the *Dragonfly* went slowly. It was a ceremonial craft, gilded and decorated like the ships that once had sailed the seas around the Japanese Home Islands on

Earth. The sled Damon and Anya had ridden downworld from *Glory* was stowed (with some difficulty) in the belly of *Dragonfly*. The barge's Captain, a gray-haired samurai named Honda, the head of a clan that had served the Minamotos for two hundred years, had been cautioned to keep a sharp lookout for the small craft that had been launched from the Goldenwing to guide *Dragonfly* and the accompanying flotilla of MD ships to rendezvous with *Glory*.

Anya Amaya, uncomfortable but resplendent in a brocaded kimono (a gift from the Shogun she was assured she must accept) stood with Minamoto Kantaro and several other shogunal court notables (whose names she had great difficulty pronouncing or even remembering) near the forward-facing quartz windows. *Dragonfly* was still laboring into orbit, struggling to match the orbital parameters sent down from *Glory*. The effort created a low gravity and a disorienting pitch to all onboard movement.

From where Amaya stood she could see two of the MD craft accompanying *Dragonfly*. To Amaya the experimental light-speed ships were unprepossessing. If anyone had ever told the New Earth woman that she had the aesthetic sensibilities of an artist, she would have scorned the notion. Centauri colonists were known for their hard-rock feminism, political intolerance and a well-developed taste for severity in all things. Amaya's nurturing had been as austere as any New Earther's, and she had been sold to *Glory*'s syndicate because she had denied the Population Authority's right to artificially inseminate her. In the absence of a Goldenwing fortuitously in orbit, her punishment could have been far worse. Nothing in Amaya's early life as a New Earth clone had nurtured aesthetic appreciation. But life aboard *Glory* had remade her. At this moment the beautiful kimono she wore seduced her (comfort was another matter—as was wearing finery over space gear), as other fine or beautiful things often did now.

The bronze-colored clouds below her pleased her innate sense of color, and she awaited with pleasure the moment when *Glory*, in all her splendor, would appear above the advancing planetary horizon.

Anya regarded Kantaro-san's handsome face and wondered what his reaction would be to his first true sight of a Goldenwing in space. Not an image, but the real thing. For that matter, how would the Shogun react? In the Ross Stars, *Glory* had awed the bitter folk of Nimrud and had made them a trifle less formidable. But for that, the intervention of the Terror might have finished them all while they were fighting among themselves. She shivered at the memory.

"Are you uncomfortable, Amaya-san?" Minamoto Kantaro showed his concern for Amaya with some reticence. Women were valued but not highly ranked on Yamato. "Females are often affected by null gravity."

Amaya, her Centauri prickliness aroused, said, "I have spent the last six years in space, Daimyo." In fact, the opulence of the salon aboard the Shogun's barge rather dismayed her. Its classic Japanese elegance attracted her, and she disapproved of the attraction. There was still much New Earther in *Glory's* Sailing Master. "It takes a great deal more than null gravity to upset me," she said primly. She knew she must restrain herself from marching into a feminist confrontation with the Lord of Yedo.

Anya stood with her eyes fixed on the distant horizon of the planet below. The vast stretches of empty, copper-colored sea moved swiftly beneath the climbing *Dragonfly* and her MD consorts. Directly ahead of the flotilla, all of Yamato's natural satellites hung in one of their frequent conjunctions. Hideyoshi, smallest and brightest of the moons, and the scientific base that produced the MD ships accompanying *Dragonfly,* had only just risen from the planetary ocean. Above it, Nobunaga, the mining-colony moon, reflected with the color of rusting iron.

Above the smaller pair, the methane yellow and baleful disk of Tokugawa dominated the celestial zenith. It was surrounded with a halo of stars and the soft luminescence of Amaterasu's zodiacal light. Many of the constellations familiar to Earth's night sky could be seen here, only slightly distorted by distance. There were others, named by the Yamatans, that no native of Earth would recognize: the Shark, Amaterasu's Comb, the Crucified Warrior. At the zenith shone the bright beacon of Alpha Carinae, known on Yamato as Ryukotsu—the Keel of Argo—and to *Glory's* syndics as Canopus, 165 light-years from Yamato, an impossible distance even for *Glory's* far-reaching wings.

For a moment Amaya allowed herself to think what space travelling might become if the ugly little ships accompanying them were the precursors of true hyperlight flight. The idea both thrilled and repelled her. Human reach would be unlimited, but mankind had a way of cheapening whatever became easy.

Perhaps, she thought, that was the purpose allotted the Terror in the great plan of the Universe. She grimaced. It was a thought more suited to her dour Thalassan Captain than to a woman of New Earth.

The *Dragonfly*'s compartment was filled with magnificently clad—and armed—daimyos. Each lord of a Domain had with him a dozen retainers, all dressed in the manner of a Sixteenth-Century feudal-clan court. There had to be five hundred kilograms of archaic, useless, beautifully wrought weaponry in the barge's salon. What odd people the Yamatans were, Amaya thought, modern in almost every sense of the word, skilled in technology beyond any other colonials, yet still choosing to costume themselves for special occasions as did their ancestors of nearly two millennia ago.

How human, she thought.

And then she smiled again, secretly, thinking that the phrase was better suited to the small, feral mind of Mira, *Glory*'s cat.

Shogun Minamoto no Kami left the group of daimyos around Duncan and appeared at Anya's side. "Does my spacecraft please you, Anya-san?"

"She is quite beautiful, Minamoto-sama," Anya said as tactfully as she could manage. The ship's salon was actually reminiscent of the teahouses she had studied in *Glory*'s database on the inward journey from the Ross Stars. The room was panelled in real wood and there were brocaded tatami on the floor. Anya Amaya did not truly approve. Elsewhere in the vessel the flight crew worked in titanium compartments lined with flight instruments and gear, but here one stood in a Sixteenth-Century Japanese manor.

It was perplexing—and oddly touching. *But take care not to sentimentalize these people, Amaya,* she warned herself. *They are not what they seem to be.* "I have never seen a spacecraft quite like it," she said neutrally.

A veiled smile crossed the old man's lips. "Are you certain there are no Japanese among your ancestors, Anya-san? You have our gift of saying nothing most gracefully." He glanced pointedly at Kantaro. It was an unmistakable command to withdraw. The younger man did so, with a formal bow.

"Try to forget what you have learned aboard your far-travelling ship of diplomacy," the Shogun said. "I believe you to be intuitive, Anya-san. Perhaps it is that quality you Wired Ones call empathy. Whatever it may be, I ask you to put it at my service." He inclined his head at the daimyos gathered in suspicious groups at the forward end of the salon. "The lords of Kai and Hokkaido. With them are the leaders of the *daibatsu*—do you know that word?"

"It is what you call the industrialists, *tono*."

Minamoto acknowledged the use of the word for "lord" with an almost imperceptible nod. "They are a good bit more than that, Anya-san. On Yamato, the *daibatsu* is ancient history that people say no longer exists. Yet they are powerful men and they are suspicious of you and Kr-san. Their research departments have brought the mass-depletion engine to the point where short voyages at hyperlight speeds are possible. They suspect that as Goldenwing syndics you have good reasons either to take the technology for yourselves or to destroy it. They are not convinced there is a threat—out there." He looked somberly at the stars beyond the aligned moons. "With Kai and Hokkaido we have the worst of antiquity and modern times. Kai is arrogant and Hokkaido is impoverished. Lord Yoshi imagines he is a genuine Takeda, and Lord Genji sits on his frozen island hoarding his bloodlines and guarding his poor treasury. They both would profit by your failure at Yamato."

"We did not come to steal," Anya said.

"*I* believe that, Anya-san," the Shogun said. "But there should be no misunderstanding. Our MD ships represent a huge investment by the *daibatsu*."

"Whereas, Shogun, we syndics risk only our lives, our ship, and the future of man in space," Anya said icily.

"I do not blame you for resenting our caution, Anya-san. But we have always been a careful people. Please understand us. It is a great concession that our ruling caste has agreed to this conference aboard your Goldenwing."

"I have studied your history, *tono*," Anya Amaya said. "Our definition of caution is apparently not the same as yours. Unless the Yamatan word also carries with it the inference of 'self-interested.' "

The Shogun remained silent, his attention fixed on the visible stars.

"Tell the *daibatsu*, Shogun, that we Starmen have seen the enemy close by. It attacked us because we drew near to its preserves. It attacks your MD vessels because you are crossing a border. The two acts are alike. They vary only in degree. But the stakes are the same for us all. Tell your merchant lords that, Shogun."

"Is that what your empathic sense tells you is the best course, Anya-san?"

"It is what my *every* sense tells me, Shogun. There is really no other choice."

"Surrender?"

Several of the nearer daimyos were now listening to the conversation between their Shogun and the *gaijin* woman. *It is just as well,* Anya thought. *Duncan might give these people an illusion of escape. I will not.*

"There is no surrender, *tono*." She looked at the circle of faces that now surrounded them. "Only annihilation."

Duncan had joined the group at the salon window. Instinctively, the Yamatans looked to him for masculine confirmation.

"What my Sailing Master tells you is true," he said. "You have had your own reports of the disturbance when something from the Near Away swallowed still another of your spacecraft."

A daimyo of Kyushu said, "We are by no means certain that some*thing* from the Near Away is responsible for our losses. Even if we concede that what you say is true, *gaijin*-sama. We have yet to hear what can be done about it."

Duncan appreciated the adroitness of the Yamatan's use of the term *gaijin-sama*. The Starmen were being called intruders and outsiders, but politely, in terms customarily reserved for lords of substantial domains and leaders of clans.

"The Terror—we use that term for lack of a better, since we know so little about it—the Terror appears to be attracted by strong emotions," Duncan said. "*Glory*'s Cybersurgeon thinks we might someday be able to avoid it by shielding our emotions. I find that doubtful. We cannot learn to hide again—as we once did on the savannahs long ago. Not out here, Shogun. We are a starfaring species and we will be so until we go extinct. Which might be soon, Shogun. That is why we are in Amaterasu space.

Your scientists have forced the door to open a bit more. The door-keeper sees us even more clearly."

"To speak of any natural phenomenon as 'the Terror,' *gaijin-sama*, seems—medieval," Lord Yoshi, the daimyo of Takeda, said with lofty distaste. The incongruity of such a statement from a man dressed as a Sixteenth-Century samurai seemed not to have occurred to the Yamatans.

It was a fine point, Duncan thought, but the time to address the matter was not now. Duncan wondered which of the assembled nobles was responsible for the ninja attack in Yedo. The act spoke volumes about Yamatan attitudes. It appeared that the *daibatsu* thought the Wired Ones were a bigger threat than any mysterious force that struck out of nowhere.

Duncan said, "We speak of the Terror, Lords. You, of course, will speak of it in whatever terms seem suitable to you. But you *must* speak of it. The faster and the farther you travel, the more surely you will attract the enemy." His gray eyes were level and steady. "We theorize that the Terror may not even live in the universe we know, or whether or not the physical laws we know apply to it. My suspicion is that they do not. I am not cosmologist enough to know. For that we ask your help. Your scientists are among the best of the colonials. But it can be deflected—our ship deflected it in the Ross Stars by beginning the process of putting all living things aboard into cold-sleep."

"You ordered that, Kr-san?"

"Yes, Minamoto-sama."

Duncan had the strong feeling that Minamoto no Kami and most of the rulers assembled in *Dragonfly*'s salon approved. These were people, after all, to whom the act of seppuku was noble.

Duncan said, "I may be wrong in saying that it *seeks*—anything. We are certain of only one thing. It has an enormous power to kill, and I believe that anything that kills wantonly can *be* killed." He looked at the members of the gathering evenly. "You have learned to duplicate one of its powers. You can open a Gateway. Now we must go through that Gateway."

A daimyo of Kyushu, old and crusty in his manner, said, "It seems rather like an executioner discovering rope and offering it to lower us all into hell."

"Not quite," Anya interjected. "No one is offering Yamato

rope, My Lords. Something quite different. See."

At that moment *Glory* had appeared above the planet's horizon and began its climb toward the zenith. It was a stunning sight, and as the seconds passed and *Dragonfly*'s orbit began to synchronize with *Glory*'s, the view became dazzling.

Glory aligned nearly perfectly with Yamato's natural satellites. The effect was breathtaking. At first the Goldenwing seemed to hover over the disk of Moon Tokugawa, her furled wings ready to embrace the distant satellite. Above Tokugawa Hideyoshi and Nobunaga reflected the coppery light of Tau Ceti like mirrors of hammered bronze.

The decreasing distance between *Glory* and *Dragonfly* began to put the scene into scale, but no changes in perspective could detract from *Glory*'s fantastic dominance. Her skylar was almost entirely furled save for the steadying jibs and spanker, relatively small, but brilliant, scalene triangles of ruddy golden light at bow and stern.

At the moment *Glory* flew in a vertical orientation to the planet below, so that the twenty kilometers of deck and masts was seen from far above, yet clearly in the airlessness of space, and surrounded with the zodiacal glow of her incredibly dense and complex monofilament rigging. In this attitude, *Glory* resembled a mythic creature. Anya felt the strong surge of satisfaction from Duncan. Her empathic sense assured her that this was precisely what Duncan wanted—that the nobles of Yamato should see *Glory* as not only beautiful, but formidable.

"My ship, Daimyos," Duncan Kr said. "Within the hour I shall be honored to welcome you aboard her."

11

THE SMALL QUEEN, THE YOUNG QUEEN

•

Mira crouched on the young human queen's nest, eyes fixed on the holograph displayed in the still air of the heart-of-the-lair. Inside the container, the young tom the human folk called Clavius groomed his elevated hind leg as Mira had taught him in kittenhood. It was a gesture Duncan spoke of as playing the cello—whatever a cello might be. But this was not the time for playing or grooming.

Clavius was not as clever as Mira would wish, but he was quicker than any of the other members of the pride, male or female. He was as clever as most of the humans in all that mattered, swift and strong, and inevitably given to tomcat vanity. We still have much to learn, Mira thought, knowing that the great-queen-who-is-not-alive was listening.

The other Folk were stationed throughout the length and breadth of the great queen; each had, at Mira's instruction, established a territory over which they were enjoined by the great queen to watch. New humans were coming aboard and Mira remembered too well what had happened the last time strangers had been allowed within the world.

As her cognitive skills increased Mira began to think of the great queen as both a being and a world. This seeming contradiction did not disturb her. The Folk lived with contradictions—had done for thousands of years. It was a normal part of coexisting with human beings.

The great queen had warned Mira not to allow her natural territoriality to cause conflicts. It was important that the strangers *should not be distracted from whatever it was the dominant tom, Duncan, wished them to do.*

Mira remembered that long ago, when she was not so well schooled by the world, she had been both frightened and enraged by the thing she sensed in the vast darkness around the great queen. To the small cat quantitative distinctions were unimportant. Measurements simply did not matter. Any distance she could not leap was simply large. But it was not empty. She had known that from the moment she had awakened sharing her thoughts with the great queen on the table of he-who-cuts. She had perceived the Outside as a great room in which a savage thing hunted for anything alive. According to the great queen, humans believed that cats killed for pleasure. This was untrue. Cats reveled in the hunt, but they took no pleasure in the taking of life. The space surrounding them, even on the homeworld, was so enormous and so cold and empty that only life warmed it.

Yet menacing Mira's world was a thing that killed for pleasure, and she had reacted to the threat as the Folk had been reacting since time began—with arched back, bared teeth and extended claws.

Duncan, the dominant tom, had sensed this at once. He was a creature of powerful perceptions and empathy. There were times, Mira thought, when she could imagine Duncan clad in fur, a yowling tom with a beautiful voice and ferocious scent. In time she learned to accept the impossibility of her sexual fantasy, but she would forever consider it with a powerful and savage pleasure. Duncan became effectively a member of Mira's disciplined pride, which was a new thing among the Folk.

The other cats accepted Duncan because he was large and powerful—but also because Mira was matriarch, and set the standards. With their mother's milk, her offspring learned to defer to and accept hierarchy. The individual who did not know his place must fight for better. If he lost he was in danger of becoming an outcast. It was the Folk's way of life. Mira's patterns and abilities were bred into her blood and bone by ten thousand feline generations. Her new skills were only a gift from the great-queen-who-is-not-alive.

Mira was not yet totally at ease with human concepts such as "generations." But the great queen's algorithms had been written by human beings, and she had begun imprinting Mira the in-

stant she filed and saved the information that he-who-cuts had finished his work on Mira.

About this, the small queen made some judgments. Mira's natural value system and Glory's were almost identical. Both were at home with yes-or-no, go-or-no-go decisions. Glory did nothing to Mira to change her feline ways. Cats' decisions seemed maddeningly deliberate to humans. And so they were. But once made they were instant and arbitrary, like a computer's.

As leader of the pride, Mira decided for all. There was no appeal. There were many cats in the pride and some were larger and stronger than she. But Mira ruled. She was the queen, ready to enforce her choices with tooth and claw. Fortunately, the great-queen-who-is-not-alive was programmed to reject life-and-death conflict and seldom permitted it, even among the human folk.

Mira trilled a message to Clavius to cease his preening and pay attention to the view displayed by the holograph. He complied, understanding only a fraction of the information the great queen was supplying. Mira unsheathed her foreclaws in irritation and then retracted them. It was only now, after much teaching by the great queen, that she understood that she had the ability to be patient.

Clavius would learn, as would the others. Without knowledge, courage, shrewdness and, above all, an unfeline forbearance, the learning of the great queen, the courage of the humans and the wisdom of the Folk—all would vanish into emptiness.

Mira launched herself across the bridge to land, claws extended, on the fabric strips Duncan had caused to be placed everywhere around the great queen's interior for the convenience of the Folk. From this new vantage point above the holograph Mira could identify the shuttle carrying the young queen, Broni, and the two sleds carrying the often frightened tom, Damon, and the persistent one, Buele.

It was Buele who seemed determined to become part of the pride. It was impossible, but Mira found she did not resent it as she once did. It made her aware that under the guidance of the great-queen-who-is-not-alive she, and all the Folk, were changing.

For a moment she allowed herself a flash of motherly satisfaction. Her offspring were, usually, a source of pleasure to her. There

*was Clavius, of course. Her particular favorite. In leisure moments
she still groomed him as though he were a kitten, licking his ruff
and broad head until the fur shone. Then there was Big, who was
half again as broad as Clavius, a prodigious leaper and athlete
with a regrettable—but forgivable—tendency to bully his siblings.
Then there were Tail, Gem, Shadow, White Paw, and Stripes.
Among the females, all of whom had inherited Mira's small stature
and graceful conformation, were Marissa, Beauty, Windstar, and
Trekker. All names bestowed by the young queen, Broni. Names
from her homeworld, Mira surmised from what the great queen
said. Not all the pride had names. Naming was a human thing, one
to which Mira was only now becoming accustomed. With or without names, Mira knew exactly where each member of the Folk was
at any given moment and what he or she was doing.*

*Right now they were patrolling the vast cavern Broni and
Damon had prepared for the accommodation of the strangers
who were at this moment drawing near the great queen.*

*Mira felt the waves of half-electronic, half-neurological fear
emanating from the Monkey House. The foolish critters were
clinging to their sanctuary because they, too, felt the approach
of human strangers.*

*Monkeys were inedible and they were too programmed to pose
a threat to anyone. Yet in the Ross Stars, foolish men had cal-
lously killed one of the innocuous cyborgs. Perhaps, Mira
thought, when matters were not so stressful, she would communicate with the foolish creatures. They had no true language of
trills and cries, not even one of words like the humans. But perhaps she could manage.*

After the human visitors were seen and judged.

*She watched the sleds maneuvering to intercept the cloud of
sparks that was rising from the curved lake of sunlight below.
Mira had on rare occasion been a passenger on one of the small
vehicles the great queen carried. At first she had not known exactly what was happening to her, but with the great queen's all-
knowing assistance, Mira began to interpret the information
that flowed continuously through the tiny wire protruding from
her skull.*

*She did not remember when, exactly, it was (cats were not
great creators of time ladders) that she began to interpret what*

*the human-folk were thinking. They were not always drogued,
and at such times reading them was difficult. But when they, like
she, were connected to the great-queen-who-is-not-alive, their
mental images came through with great clarity.*

*Being with Duncan sometimes gave her solitary moments by
a foggy gray sea and a chill, pebbled shore. At such times Mira
would float in the null gravity, eyes unfocused, while nearby
Duncan's mind would create pictures and strange, human-folk
sounds:* The sea of faith was once, too, at the full, and round
Earth's shore lay like the folds of a bright girdle furled—*Mira
received clear images from the dominant tom's strongly empathic mind. She understood them on a deep, inchoate, but
powerful level. Clearly the human words moved him deeply
with images of his homeworld.* I . . . hear its long, withdrawing
roar . . . retreating to the breath of the night wind . . . *Memories
stirred in her awakened mind. Not of the sea, but of the dark
savannahs her ancestors had known—*

*Mira, born in space, saw the image of "the world" in Duncan's
mind. It was not the homeworld that gave his kind and hers life.
Earth was a world Duncan had never actually seen. The true
provenance of his mental image was another place, a place of
rock and sea very like the place where the night wind blew down
the vast edges drear and naked shingles of the world, but colder
still and more distant. At such times Mira lay in air, transfixed by
the richness of the images that flashed through her small brain.*

*Her ability to share Duncan's dream became a source of sen-
sual pleasure to her. Here, within the great-queen-who-is-not-
alive, joys were shared. She understood that all things happened
because other things happened. To accomplish this breakthrough
she had to make connections that went beyond those customarily made by her species. She even had begun to realize that her
own young offspring were not so swift of mind as she because,
though he meant to be, he-who-cuts was not infallible.*

*The cats were learning, as were the great queen's human-folk.
But Mira was filled with anxiety. Though she did not yet grasp
the true concept of time, she sensed that there was little left. The
hungry beast waited just beyond the darkness.*

Broni, alone in one of the larger shuttles, could hear Buele's
vocalizations clearly over the radio-link. The boy was talking to

a cat, probably the one called Big, who was his favorite companion. Buele had a habit of carrying Big with him when he flew one of the enclosed sleds. Duncan did not appear to mind. He even accepted the absurd notion of Buele's that eventually Buele would teach Big to fly a sled.

Broni was concentrating on the navigational holograph she was using to pilot the shuttle. She wanted her performance to be perfect, but Buele's babble was distracting. She was fond of her uncle's former potboy and tolerant of his peculiar notions, but this was *not* the time to be discussing the human concept of hell with one of the cats.

The Yamatan ships were all in sight and closing on *Glory*'s orbit in preparation for landing aboard, and Duncan had entrusted Broni and Damon and Buele with the task of guiding the colonists in safely. A botched landing could seriously damage *Glory*—a possibility Broni did not even care to contemplate. Like all the Wired Ones, she was fiercely protective of the great Goldenwing.

But Buele rambled on: *"It should interest you, Big, this idea all humans have of 'hell.' I don't suppose cats have any such myths. You wouldn't tell me if you did, would you? But have you considered the possibility that there really is a hell and that it lies in what the Yamatans call the Near Away? The devil might be real. He could be that thing that tried to kill us in the Ross Stars. Isn't that of interest to you people, Big? You don't mind if I say 'you people,' do you? I mean it as a compliment—"*

Damon's voice: *"For God's sake, Buele, pack it in, will you? The colonists' ships are approaching orbit."*

"I see them, Brother Damon. Just stay with me if you don't."

Broni suppressed an impulse to giggle. It took some doing to become accustomed to Buele's innocent bluntness. But he had innate skills and abilities that had been recognized even on their homeworld of Voerster. She remembered clearly how he had helped Healer Tiegen and the Captain of the dirigible *Volkenreiter* to a safe landing during that terrible storm near the Shieldwall. Probably if it hadn't been for Buele, neither he nor she would have lived to become syndics.

But the way he did things and the things he said. She rolled her eyes momentarily away from the holograph and swiftly back again. Buele was, as the Cybersurgeon said, quite a piece of work.

Damon was replying angrily to Buele. Telling him that he could see perfectly well, thank you, and needed no assistance flying his sled to the rendezvous point.

Cybersurgeon Dietr from *Glory*'s bridge deck: *"Less talk, if you please. Duncan and Amaya are probably listening while you embarrass them."*

Never, thought Broni. Duncan would never be embarrassed by things the younger Starmen said or did. He seemed to trust them completely, with a confidence-building self-assurance. It was probably part of his Captain's persona, but Broni (and Buele, too, she suspected) would rather die than cause him concern.

With a flourish, she matched orbits with the advancing fleet of small spaceships. The shuttle was the leader of the welcoming formation, and Buele and Damon would have to match their actions to hers. That should keep the former Astronomer-Select's potboy out of trouble for an hour or two. Of all the syndics aboard, Broni had the most empathic ability to pilot small craft. Her skill was not greater than Anya Amaya's, she admitted. But it was certainly no less. Women seemed to have an innate talent for conning small spacecraft.

As the three auxiliaries from the Goldenwing drew to within a hundred kilometers of the Yamatan flotilla, Broni smiled with delight. The Yamatan mass-depletion ships were small, but they were slender as swallows with solar-cell wings not too unlike, at this distance, the wings that *Glory* spread. Tiny by comparison, but brave, Broni thought, the instincts of a Voersterian noblewoman showing through the decorum of a young female syndic about to meet the males of a fanatically paternalistic colonial society.

It had taken Broni the better part of a shiptime year to take to syndic ways. She still felt more at ease in a skinsuit, which was what she wore now. A grand skinsuit it was, too. Vibrant with embroidery and appliqués of the constellations of Near Space picked out in gold and silver. Dietr Krieg had encouraged her to don finery. "It will not do to let these colonials outshine us, Broni *liebchen*. Use the replicators—let *Glory* outfit you like a princess."

Broni ignored the temptation of reminding the Terrestrial that she *was,* in point of fact, a princess. Or as near as made no difference. On Voerster a Voertrekkersdatter was almost royal.

At fifty kilometers Broni could make out the ornate decorations on the Shogun's barge. It was an odd combination of Yamatan spacecraft and ancient Japanese junk. Its solar cells resembled closely the battened sails she had seen in *Glory*'s database, and the hull was decorated with dragons and demons with scales of brilliant gold that burned in the rose-colored sunlight of Tau Ceti.

Buele and Damon had closed in on either side of the shuttle she piloted, and Broni was satisfied with the precision of their station-keeping. Duncan would notice. So would Amaya, but unlike Duncan, she would make cutting remarks if all was not done perfectly.

Recently Broni had begun to feel a certain rivalry with the Centauri woman. She was troubled by it, but whenever Amaya and Duncan went off alone together, for whatever purpose, Broni felt twinges of jealousy. Dietr explained the reason for this, though Broni would have much preferred that he did not. But that was the Terrestrial's way. He was capable of remarkable sympathy and understanding, but it was always from *without.* Dietr Krieg was the least empathic of all *Glory*'s syndics. Too much brain and too little heart, Broni thought, with an understanding beyond her years.

Clustered protectively around the Shogun's barge, the experimental MD ships looked delicate and fragile. They might be, thought Broni, but they carried within them a technology that might well mean the end of the Goldenwings. The thought made her shiver with distaste. At a hundred kilometers behind the shuttle and its accompanying sleds, *Glory* was still a dazzling sight. Broni never saw the great ship without a thrill of joy and pleasure. The thought that one day she might never sail again, that she might spend eternity orbiting some minor planet light-years out from the worlds she helped colonize and supply and repopulate, was more than could be borne without melancholy.

"I love you, Great Ship," she thought. *"You are my life."*

That was an actual as well as a figurative truth. The artificial heart beneath Broni's budding breasts would not keep her alive in a true-gravity well. Broni and *Glory* would live and die together.

12

THE MEPHITIC CHAMELEON

•

Minoru Ishida, a man sometimes known as Tsunetomo and at other times simply as "Master," stood with a group of low-ranking samurai near a vision port thoughtfully regarding the spacecraft the Shogun's barge was overtaking.

Ishida, who did not at all resemble the black, menacing figure encountered by Minamoto Kantaro in the Shogun's garden only a day ago, was dressed in the modest garb of a *ronin* probationer in the ranks of Clan Takeda of Kai. Takeda outfitted his retainers with simple gray and brown silk. They were discouraged from wearing gold or silver ornaments, a simple prohibition to enforce because the Daimyo Yoshi of Kai paid the lowest wages in all Yamato. Lower, even, than the penurious Lord Genji of Hokkaido. Like all present save the Starmen, Ishida wore a grav unit beneath his *hakama* and kimono. The costly units belonged to the clans. Few samurai ever accumulated the price of such a device, but they were glad for the use of them, for dignity's sake. None of the daimyo were willing to face the syndics on their home ground without the perceived advantage of being able to plant their feet firmly. The spectacle of a hundred or more Yamatan lords and their samurai floating helplessly about in free-fall was not to be tolerated. Ishida found this sardonically amusing. Like all ninja, he had been disciplined in nullgrav martial arts.

Minoru Ishida had changed his appearance from a warrior of darkness into an undistinguished man of middle age, overweight and heavy-lidded from soft living. The personal retainers of the

Yamatan daimyos often took on the characteristics of their Masters, and the Lord of Kai was slow-moving and pompous. Only Ishida's eyes peering sharply out of a puffy face warned the onlooker that this was not an ordinary man. A close examination of his weapons carried the same message. The *katana* and *wakizashi* of his *daisho* were new, not family heirlooms, made of the best gray Yamatan steel, harder and sharper than any weapons ever forged by the swordmasters of ancient Japan.

In addition to the traditional *daisho* carried by a samurai, Ishida had secreted about his person a set of six throwing stars, a wire garrote, and a selection of knives. He needed none of these tools of his trade. At the request of the *daibatsu*, the government-industrial combine, he had dispatched dozens bare-handed. Ninja used the old-style weapons only when the death needed to be *correct*.

The guardian animal of the ninjas was the mephitic chameleon, a breed native to the islands on the homeworld. Despite the fact that no such animal existed on Planet Yamato, the *kami* was well chosen, a powerful symbol of death and duplicity.

Ishida stood staring in apparent stupidity out of a port. To his companions he was simply the ex-*ronin* Ishida, a dull, aging man hired to do menial tasks for the higher-ranking members of Lord Yoshi's retinue.

After the failure in the center of Yedo City, Ishida had assumed the killing task himself as a matter of honor. There was no more proficient killer on Planet Yamato, and so the Wired One was as good as dead.

But not before time. The original task had been merely to kill the *gaijin* in front of the people of Yedo. But it had got beyond that now. The Ninja Society might benefit vastly from the knowledge that could be had from the Starmen. One close look at their enormous starship could not fail to impress. Ishida had been prepared for that. But the Goldenwing's sheer mass daunted even the Master of Yamatan Ninja. He had never seen a craft of sea, air or space one-hundredth the size of the *Gloria Coelis*. It was true that mere size was no fair measure of the treasures the vast craft might contain, but having taken the trouble to view the starship through the twenty-meter telescope on Moon Hideyoshi, some few of the daimyos, the ones who had originally contracted for the ninja to liquidate the foreigner, now expressed a willingness to allow some delay in destroying the stranger. Not that it really mattered. In any case, the Ninja Society's decision to murder the Starman was now immutable. All that remained to be decided was when and under what circumstances. And these choices were Tsunetomo's to make.

Minamoto Kantaro was in the same compartment of the *Dragonfly* as Ishida, but though he had looked squarely at the ninja a dozen times, he had failed to recognize the man who had so contemptuously declined to kill him in his uncle's garden. Members of the ninja caste on Yamato were skilled in many things. The art of assuming characteristics not one's own was child's play for the ninja Tsunetomo.

"Gods," a young Oda retainer breathed in awe to Kantaro. "The thing is *enormous.*"

"But beautiful," said a companion. "Have you ever seen anything so grand?" The retainers crowded at the viewport pressed one another to get a better view.

At forty kilometers, the sun angle had changed so that the ruddy light of Amaterasu was refracted through *Glory*'s rigging of translucent monofilament. The effect was breathtaking. The vast ship seemed to glow with jewelled fire. The fretwork on bow and stern (the work of *Glory*'s first crew of syndics, who whiled away the long months of the first mission tamping gold leaf into the creases and crevices of the Goldenwing's long, curving shearline) made a pattern of golden fire dancing along the hull with each change of angle and aspect. The Yamatans, trained since infancy to respond to exhibitions of aesthetic beauty, murmured with pleasure.

Ishida allowed his attention to shift from the Goldenwing to the high-ranking daimyos who stood above the deck on a steel mezzanine with the Shogun and the members of his personal security detachment. The ninja's hand vanished into a bolse to fondle a throwing star. Fondling death-dealing artifacts gave Ishida much pleasure.

Great ninjas before him had made Yamatan history by assassinating Shoguns. For Ishida, the temptation to make history was always present, he thought ruefully, withdrawing his empty hand. When all this was done, he thought, he must have a long retreat in the mountains of Hokkaido. Solitude always healed the psychological wounds he inflicted upon himself in the course of performing his dark duties.

The male *gaijin* stood at the port with Minamoto Kantaro. He was a tall, melancholy man with deep, far-seeing blue eyes. He would bear watching, Ishida thought. And he would be best killed by stealth. He had the look of an experienced warrior. Who knew what battles he had fought, or where. He was explaining something about the Goldenwing to Minamoto. The retainers pressed near to hear what he had to say.

The ninja looked away and back at the golden apparition that was now rapidly filling space. The thing was, as the awestruck samurai had said with such feeling, simply enormous. Amidships, it had a midship beam of almost a quarter kilometer, yet it was so long it seemed slender and graceful as a bird. Ishida wondered how it would look with golden skylar spread from the thousands of yards crossing its ten-kilometer-tall masts.

Three small craft, glittering like diamond chips in the roseate light of Amaterasu, had taken stations around the Shogun's barge. One was a shuttle comparable in size to the MD ships accompanying the *Dragonfly;* the others were sketches of spacecraft, one fitted with a bubble, the other no more than an open frame, both with simple reaction engines working. The *gaijin* called them sleds. Ishida wondered at the primitive technology they represented.

The Yamatan ships assumed a line-astern formation, apparently in response to some orders from the craft from the Goldenwing. In a long arc, all approached the starship's stern, where a huge hatch was in the process of opening, displaying a cavernous interior lit with illumination that matched exactly the shade and color of Amaterasu. If the Starmen had contrived that as a courtesy to their visitors, it was neatly done, Ishida thought. Familiar light-tones and intensities would be calculated to make the colonists feel more comfortable and at ease in surroundings that were, assuredly, stranger than any Yamatans had experienced since the days of their transit aboard Goldenwing *Hachiman.*

Ishida watched as the range closed. With each meter travelled the starship appeared to expand until it seemed that it would fill all the sky. Could it possibly be true, Ishida wondered, that such a construct was crewed by six people? Perhaps a reevaluation of the technology he was so recently tempted to disparage was in order.

Attended by its flotilla of MD ships, *Dragonfly* approached the looming stern of the Goldenwing. The opening now was displayed in its true dimensions. From one side of the open hatch to the other was two-thirds of a kilometer, perhaps even more. The fittings that Ishida could see were posts and strakes of what appeared to be titanium—a metal used sparingly in Yamato because of its rarity and cost. The opening easily accommodated *Dragonfly*, whose pilot carefully followed the foreign shuttlecraft into the huge interior.

The passengers had fallen into a hushed silence. Not one of them had ever been inside a human construct of this size. Even the temple of Hachiman in the necropolis of Kyoto on Kyushu was not so large as this single great space within the Goldenwing. *They call her "Glory of Heaven,"* Ishida thought. *She is well named. But she is made of fragile titanium bones and monofilament fabric. Her sails must be as delicate as an insect's wing. To murder her Master could very well bring about her destruction.*

He smiled a secret smile. *That* would be a ninja act of murder that would cause Yamatans still a thousand years unborn to shudder with terror.

13

THESE ARE SAMURAI?

•

The great stern hatch descended soundlessly in the hard vacuum, blotting out the shining, coppery image of Yamato, and beyond, the brilliant disks of the nearer moons, Hideyoshi and Nobunaga.

Dragonfly and the MD spacecraft occupied only a fraction of the deck space within *Glory*'s vast hangar. The fabric bulkheads curved inward with the air pressure elsewhere within the ship, but as the great hatch closed, atmosphere began swiftly to build within the compartment.

Warned to stay within their vessels until a safe environment was established, the Yamatans pressed against the ports of their ships, staring at their surroundings with undisguised awe.

Broni, delighting in her speed-learned Japanese, broadcast instructions over the shuttle's communications net. She hoped that Duncan was paying close attention and appreciating how much effort she had made to become instantly proficient in the language of Yamato, and how much information she had absorbed through her still-new neural drogue.

"If you will please be so kind as to stay within your ships until the atmosphere in the compartment is fully established. Syndic Kr-san will tell you when it is safe to debark."

The use of the archaic word *debark* appealed to Broni. Even on Voerster, where two-thirds of the planet was ocean, such ancient expressions relating to ships and the sea were seldom used. But Duncan, a native of pelagic Thalassa, would appreciate the appropriateness of her phrasing.

The hangar illumination rose as the hatch descended and closed. *Glory* had duplicated the light of morning on Yamato. In the distance, holographic forests of Terrestrial pines lent a feeling of open, mountainous country.

Damon Ng, dismounting from his sled, stood respectfully before the still-latched hatch in *Dragonfly*'s belly. The Shogun's barge was equipped with large and antique gravity controllers designed fifty planetary years before for the comfort of the then Shogun. They were being used now to keep the mass of the ship suspended three meters above the woven monofilament deck.

The Goldenwing sailors created a sense of wonder by the size and purpose of their great ship, but the Yamatans were a proud people, a people secure in their scientific and technological skill. There were things about which they could feel superior to the Starmen. It had surprised many aboard *Dragonfly* that the syndics made no effort to create and manipulate gravity. And it pleased them that there were technological accomplishments they, the Yamatans, had achieved that the Starmen had not.

Damon Ng, standing now with unlatched helmet and gripping the deck beneath him with Velcro soles of his boots, was as impressed as the Yamatans could have wished with the spectacle before him of their massive ship hovering above the hangar deck as steadily as if it were anchored with mooring and spring lines.

He spoke into his com unit: *"The atmosphere is now breathable, honored sirs. You may open your hatches and debark."*

The hatches of the barge dilated, extruded handsomely decorated ladders. The Yamatans began to descend. Their silk clothing, kimonos and *hakamas* finely embroidered with gold and silver dragons and mythical designs, rustled as they moved. Damon made a great effort to retain an impassive face, but on Nixon, the wooded forest world where he was born, no one, no matter how wealthy or highborn, wore such magnificent clothing.

Warriors wearing two swords thrust through their blood-red sashes descended to the softly giving deck of the hangar bay. The grav units they wore were state-of-the-art devices fitted closely to the wearer, but they still marred the line of the Yamatans' sartorial magnificence with their bulk. Nor were the armed men accustomed to wearing the grav harnesses. The samurais' movements were not exactly what they would have been on the surface of the planet below. They moved like men burdened. Damon wondered why they should so handicap and trouble themselves, but Broni had explained that the Yamatans were too "dignified" to endure zero-G. Theirs was a society of ancient proprieties.

As the samurai reached the deck, Damon realized that they wore stylized, lacquered armor over their magnificence. The thin-gauge steel pieces were decorated with fine macramé in brilliant colors, each article of armor secured to the next with cords of bright colors. The helmets on their heads were inlaid with gold and silver designs, and each displayed a crest—the device, or *mon,* of the individual warrior's clan. The effect was one of barbaric splendor.

Damon also noted that each man wore a laze pistol in his sash. *Ceremonial guards they may be,* the Rigger thought, *but they do not rely on antique swords to protect their Shogun.*

That individual descended to *Glory*'s deck with perfect dignity. He was less fully armored than the fifteen or so samurai who had preceded him, but his clothing was even more sumptuous. The silk he wore was a black of deepest night worked with diamond stars in the constellations seen, not from Yamato, but from ancient Earth, the homeland.

Damon had to remind himself that these were people who, in the ordinary course of working days, wore outfits similar to the skinsuits the Starmen favored—though not so revealing. This was clearly an occasion of tremendous ceremonial importance.

Yamatans continued to debark from the barge and from the small MD ships moored nearby. A circle formed around Damon and the Shogun. The Rigger wondered if this were proper, he being a junior member of the Goldenwing's crew. But it was not like Duncan to object. Duncan wondered what his forebears (most of them time-dilated years dead by now) would think of the agoraphobic countryman they had consigned so willingly to the service of the Wired Ones standing in conversation with the glittering rulers of Planet Yamato.

Damon bowed deeply, as *Glory*'s database had taught that he should, and said in Yamatan Japanese, "Welcome aboard *Gloria Coelis,* Minamoto-sama. I am Damon Ng, Starman." He indicated the movement in the gathering crowd where Broni was approaching. With just a touch of vainglory, he added, "And this is Starman Broni Voerster, formerly Voertrekkersdatter of Planet

Voerster and now a member of this syndicate."

"Well done, Damon." Duncan Kr stood below the *Dragonfly*'s open hatch. "Well done, Broni."

Damon's eyes widened. Duncan wore a skinsuit of an opulence never before seen aboard *Glory*. As did Anya, who materialized beside him. Yamato, thought the Rigger, must be a world of fabulous wealth. He had heard the childhood stories, of course, that on Earth the Japanese had paved the streets of their capital, Kyoto, with golden bricks. He had doubted such tales until now.

Minoru Ishida, surrounded by the detachment of Clan Takeda samurai and stepping with the awkward precision of a man wearing a gravity harness, moved away from the anchored spacecraft toward a valve opening in a distant, arching wall of monofilament fabric.

The entire Yamatan contingent, over one hundred strong, travelled like a ceremonial procession across the vast hangar deck toward what the young syndics had announced as private accommodations for the Shogun and his many escorts. Ishida knew Minamoto no Kami well enough to know that he allowed all this pageantry because it was part and parcel of the business of governing the powered classes of Planet Yamato. The nearer one came to authority, Ishida thought sardonically, the farther back in time one had to reach for the ceremonials and rituals of the people.

In his persona of Tsunetomo, the Master Ninja had become perhaps the planet's greatest authority on the mythic past of the Japanese colonists whose descendants now populated the Amaterasu System. Outsiders—*gaijin*—might have difficulty understanding a people who lived their ordinary lives in business dress and surrounded by every convenience a sophisticated technology could provide, yet performed their government functions dressed like characters in a Noh play. Outsiders would almost certainly imagine that such people were primitive at heart, rather than the reverse, which was the actuality.

The business of governing the colony established by Goldenwing *Hachiman* under the Tau Ceti sun was as complicated and as sensitive as ruling the Home Islands on Earth had ever been. Yamatans did not take to strangers, and tended to look down upon them (even such strangers as the Starman syndics who had long ago planted the people on Planet Yamato). The colonists had long since ceased to think of themselves as colonists. Their ties to the homeworld were mythic, psychological, and not at all physical.

The islands on Earth whence these people had come were in the seismic region known as the Ring of Fire, a circle of great faults surrounding the largest ocean on the homeworld. They were repeatedly subjected to catastrophic earthquakes. Yet in antiquity the ancestors of these folk had been known to pridefully reject aid from *gaijin* in times of disaster. While cities burned and thousands died, the offers of help from "outside" were refused.

Tsunetomo understood this, and the reason for it. Ethnic isolation had produced a closed culture. It remained closed even light-years from the islands that spawned it.

Now another catastrophe threatened. Tsunetomo-Ishida did not for one moment doubt that the threat was real. The cosmos, after all, was a place of darkness and danger. But the offer of help from strangers from beyond the near stars was worse than any threat from the Near Away. One danger promised only war and destruction. The other promised change.

Duncan, walking carefully in his unfamiliar Velcro slippers, considered that so far, at least, the conclave had begun well. *Glory*'s database was somewhat out of date. A Goldenwing's situation made that ever likely. But it had prepared both Anya and himself for the odd quirks of the Yamatan sense of dignity.

He had refused out of hand Minamoto Kantaro's offer of gravity packs. The very notion of such a thing had set Anya Amaya's eyes to rolling in a feminist outburst of opinion about Yamatan social ethics. Duncan had promised her that once all were safely accommodated aboard *Glory,* all the syndics would be free to return to their normal free-fall behavior. It seemed probable that at such a time the Shogun and Kantaro would be able to remind the daimyos (most of whom had never been offworld) that the Starmen had their own ways, and their own ideas of dignity and that their ability to be at ease in zero-G was no *waza*—no trick, no mere performance.

"Forgive me, Kr-san," Kantaro said when they embarked on the *Dragonfly,* "but it will be necessary to show the daimyos that you are serious people, even though you do customarily float about in free-fall."

Amaya had mercifully avoided making any comment. For which Duncan was grateful. Dealing with colonials taught one to accept the absurd with complete seriousness.

Duncan's attention shifted to Broni. The Voertrekker girl, resplendently arrayed in a skinsuit she imagined would both satisfy Yamatan male-dominant prudery and still impress the visitors with the capabilities of *Glory*'s ancient replicators, had already attracted a substantial cadre of admiring young samurai about her as she led the procession out of the cavernous hangar deck and into one of *Glory*'s more commodious passageways. Buele had joined her, as had Damon, both young men assuming the solemn faces they considered suitable for ambassadors of goodwill. Big, who had been riding with Buele, was briefly seen in free flight as he vanished into the holographic forest Broni had created.

Duncan tongued his com unit and subvocalized to Dietr, who had been instructed to stand by in the carapace compartment nearest the bridge with a full assortment of antivertigo nostrums. It would not take long for the more adventurous Yamatans to slip out of their grav harnesses and try the freedom of moving about unencumbered in the null gravity. Unfortunately, adventurousness was no proof against the nausea free-fall could induce.

"Are you ready for surgery, Cybersurgeon?" he asked with hidden amusement. The notion of Dietr administering to a crowd of motion-sick Yamatan businessmen-samurai elicited a sardonic amusement in Duncan. There was little enough to smile about, he thought. The telescopic images of the last Yamatan MD ship being consumed—there was no better word for it—by the fiery portal that had opened without warning out near Planet Honda chilled the blood. In the mythology of his people, the Thalassans, ice-giants and dragons lived beyond the curve of the world—a vast distance away to a people who earned their keep in skinboats. No one actually believed the myths, of course, but they were part of the culture, brought by the clans from Earth along with the ancient tartan patterns of their weaving and a taste for Scotch whiskey. The fisherfolk of Thalassa lived a harsh life on their rocky islands, but they were not ignorant. They knew the difference between stories and real life.

And now, after so many years and so far from Earth, did the myths became real? Somewhere in the vast literature of the homeworld there was a phrase: *Here there be dragons.* . . . and real, terrifying death. *I am a simple man,* Duncan Kr thought, looking at the high, arching ceiling of the great hold. *But this is my life, and I must defend it.*

"*Duncan?*"

"*Yes, Dietr.*"

"*I asked you if many were coming down with motion sickness.*"

"*Not yet. The grav harnesses are clumsy. They'll start shedding them and then you will have patients.*"

"*I can hardly wait.*"

Dietr, brilliant surgeon that he was, had never lost his Teutonic parochialism. *He will meet his match with these people,* Duncan thought. He glanced at Anya, walking between Kantaro and the Shogun. She was smiling and talking animatedly. Apparently even New Earther feminism had its limits. Perhaps it was the opulence of the brocade kimono she wore. She seemed very different from the image he knew best: the naked Sailing Master floating in the gel of her pod, Wired to *Glory* and guiding a ship as large as a city and populated primarily by ghosts.

Dietr, too, was having fretful thoughts.

When the *Gloria Coelis* broke orbit at Nineveh and began to ride the Coriolis wind back toward Tau Ceti, the Cybersurgeon had been silently dubious about Duncan's hope of finding allies for the coming battle with the Terror. It had been Dietr Krieg's experience that human beings were neither the brave nor the idealistic creatures they believed themselves to be. It had never been a simple matter, the Cybersurgeon believed, to enlist soldiers in an unwinnable war.

But Duncan believed, and therefore so did *Glory*'s other Wired Ones. Dietr had watched developments at Yamato first with doubt, then with amazement, as Japanese colonials, a race of transplants who appeared to imagine themselves players in some centuries-old Noh drama, abandoned their real lives as entrepreneurs and engineers and businessmen, and followed Duncan emotionally into space, where the most horrible enemy ever faced by spacefaring Man waited. It was a revelation of how powerfully Duncan Kr affected those around him, and it was an epiphany of the romantic way the Yamatans saw themselves: as true samurai.

Lieber Gott, Dietr thought, *the universe is a far, far stranger place than I had ever imagined it to be.*

For the first time the practical, prosaic Cybersurgeon felt an approving brush across his mind. It came from near and far, from the hidden vastnesses of *Glory.*

From the cats, *by all that is holy,* Dietr thought.

And from *Glory* herself.

14

THE LORD OF KAI

•

We have been aboard this vast hulk for a hundred hours, Minamoto-sama," the Lord of Kai complained, "and we have done nothing but look at ghastly images of the way in which people died at Nimrud. What is the point?"

Yoshi Eiji was the descendant of "late ones"—meaning colonists who arrived at Yamato aboard the second, and seldom mentioned, Goldenwing, *Musashi*. The latecomers had arrived a mere century of local time after the *Hachiman* colonists, and, as had happened before in other places, their arrival was not met with rejoicing. *Musashi*'s passenger list had been rife with social misfits and low-caste workers from the Home Islands. In a pattern often repeated in the colonization of Near Space, the Jihad on Earth drove away first the able and adventurous and then the less so, the less capable and the burdens on a slowly collapsing Terrestrial economy.

Every colonized world that absorbed more than one shipload of colonists had a similar disadvantaged minority. But if the Japanese of Yamato were parochial to an unpleasant degree, they were also, and above all else, pragmatists. Their history on Earth told of repeated occasions of the lower castes being allowed, in times of great need, into positions of leadership. The Taiko Hideyoshi, one of the founders of Terrestrial Japan, had begun his career as a foot soldier in the ranks of the vassals of Oda Nobunaga. When the Lord Oda made him samurai he had been too poor to own a horse. Yet he, with Oda and Tokugawa Ieyasu, created a nation that lasted for a thousand years.

Some of the *Musashi* latecomers found the new world to their liking. Peasants became entrepreneurs, mechanics became engineers, village lawyers became politicians and sometimes even statesmen. A few of Yamato's great clans were founded by such men. The descendants of the Yoshi, who arrived on Yamato late and penniless, now ruled the domain of Kai and the spaceport on Moon Hideyoshi.

Yoshi lacked the steel of his ancestors, but he had their shrewdness and self-interest. He had come up to Goldenwing *Glory* with misgivings; he remained to suffer the discomfort of zero gravity and the fear of great spaces, both within and without the great ship. But Yoshi was aware that the *gaijin* had experienced something truly remarkable in the Ross Stars, and his politician's instinct told him he could not yet abandon the gathering and return to the planet. First, the Shogun must commit totally to this suicidal fool's errand.

Yoshi did not lack intelligence; his unmet need was breadth of vision. Cupidity told him that if *his* mass-depletion ships were the only, or at least the first, colonial vessels freely to roam Near Space, it would be much to Yoshi Eiji's advantage. But someone must first discover a method of protecting Yamatan ships from the thing that had happened out near Planet Honda. Otherwise crews would soon refuse to launch.

Yoshi was by training an off-planet engineer. He had never worked at his profession, and was in fact not very good at it. But he was a shrewd politician and he understood how important it might be to acquire the technology of whomever or whatever was ravaging MD ships. With such magic in his hands, Yoshi believed, the next shogunate might be his for the taking, for Minamoto no Kami was in his nineties.

The Shogun regarded his visitor dourly. Lord Eiji, he thought, was exactly the sort of man who rose to power among a people isolated from their true roots.

But he listened. Yoshi was a bellwether of discontent, capable of giving an early warning of serious dissent among the daimyos.

At the moment Yoshi was still playing the samurai. He was addicted to the Japanese fixation on acquiring a famous name. As the Lord of Kai, on Earth once the domain of the Mountain

Lord Takeda Shingen, he yearned to be allowed to adopt the Takeda name for his own. There were no real Takedas left and had not been for fifteen hundred years, but a favorable recommendation from the Shogun would make Yoshi Eiji, parvenu, into a descendant of the great Mountain Lord.

So far there was no sign that Minamoto no Kami would even consider such a thing.

"We have weapons," Lord Yoshi declared, puffing his full face into a samurai mask as he had been trained to do, acting "military." "We are aboard an antique whose time has passed. Why can't we simply arm this empty hulk and send it out to do what it should have done in the Ross Stars?"

He imagined the Lord Takeda Shingen might speak so. The samurai lord who had died during a siege because of his wish to listen to the flute playing of an enemy soldier had been a prodigious warrior.

But Shingen's death had brought to the lordship his son, a feckless young man who did not heed his father's dying advice to stay in his mountains. He had marched his splendid army down to the coastal plain, where the combined forces of Oda Nobunaga and Tokugawa Ieyasu had shot it to pieces with imported muskets at a river crossing called Nagashino. The mournful tale had been told with tears for two millennia. It was one of the best-remembered laments of a people who loved laments—the sadder the better.

Yoshi Eiji yearned to be a true Takeda of Kai.

The compartment occupied by Minamoto no Kami was as austere as any other aboard *Glory*. In her larger spaces, the Goldenwing was capable of using holographs and illusions to create an astonishing range of environments from the information in her data bank. But the actual living quarters aboard were plain, without ornamentation, functional. The Goldenwing had been designed by Spartans, Minamoto no Kami thought approvingly.

He said to Yoshi, "Are you suggesting that Wired Starmen do our fighting for us?" He had known the Lord of Kai for forty years and he had never liked him.

"It has yet to be proven, Minamoto-sama, that it is our fight. But if it should be, would it not be better to let the *gaijin* do it?"

The Shogun waited for him to make the next, obvious, statement. That even if there should be fighting and dying to be done that it had become Yamato's business only because the Wired Ones had been followed into the Amaterasu System.

But Yoshi Eiji did not. He was a man who was cautious in all things. Most of the daimyos Minamoto had dragooned into coming aboard the Goldenwing saw themselves as samurai (which they were not), and as a reincarnation of the *bakufu*—the ancient military government of Japan—which had ruled the Home Islands until the formation of the *daibatsu*—the cabal of industrialists who had ruled Japan in peace and war until it was destroyed by the Jihad.

But we are none of those things, Minamoto thought wearily. *We are simply colonists far from Earth, isolated in Near Space, and in danger.*

This enterprise was vital to Yamato and, eventually, to all the colony planets. The evidence the *gaijin* presented was compelling. Everyone aboard now had seen holographic reconstructions of the engagement fought in the Ross Stars. Minamoto no Kami was not a squeamish man, but the sight of a man being consumed by fire from within was not easily forgotten.

But the Lord of Kai found it unpleasant to consider so grave a threat. In this he had companions. The sentiment among the daimyos was shifting away from risking their precious ships in a confrontation with a power they did not understand. Secret meetings had been held, and a consensus was growing. Let the *gaijin* do it. Surely it was they who had brought the danger to Amaterasu space.

Yoshi Eiji was neither a soldier nor a scientist. He hired soldiers and scientists. As many as he required for whatever task needed doing. All this talk of a fleet of ships, manned by samurai—including their daimyos—and led by the strangers, was an absurdity.

Yoshi had opposed welcoming the *gaijin* from the moment Goldenwing *Gloria Coelis* appeared in Yamatan telescopes. He was among the daimyos who contributed to the fund for hiring a ninja to kill the strangers in Yedo. When the attempt failed, Yoshi Eiji was shaken. A ninja failure was a thing that had happened only a dozen times in nearly the last four hundred years.

Though occasionally a fool, Lord Yoshi could also be a realist. *I am no warrior,* he told himself. *I covet Old Takeda Shingen's name and fame, but* not *his battles.* Substituting lazeguns for *katanas* made fighting too dangerous. It was a great pity, for the Lord of Kai was second to no one in his love of the trappings of *bushido.* But he had no intention of confronting any powerful enemy with a weapon in his hand. A man could get killed doing a thing like that.

"I only suggest, Minamoto-sama, that we should arm this ship with laze cannon and distance it from Yamato," he said carefully. "We have the means. We even have the men to fill a proper crew for this ghost ship if they are needed. The *gaijin* want aid. Let us give it to them and send them on their way. A ship or two to collect the mysterious technology of the invaders—that I am prepared to contribute."

The old man frowned, his distaste for the Lord of Kai writ on his lined face. The Shogun's intelligence resources on Planet Yamato were extensive, and Minamoto no Kami was by now reasonably certain that Yoshi was one of the daimyos who had contributed to the shame in Yedo.

A man who would lend himself to such a scheme with so little accurate knowledge concerning what a political murder at this time might precipitate was an undoubted fool—but he was far more than that. He was a menace to the best interests of Yamato.

The Shogun spoke with the full authority of his office. "The people of Kai have historically been calm and thoughtful men, Lord Yoshi. While they are descendants of the people of the *second* Goldenwing, they have almost always conducted themselves with calm wisdom. . . ."

"Almost, Minamoto-sama?" The daimyo's voice grew thin at the slight to his family.

"Almost," Minamoto repeated evenly.

Yoshi Eiji had blundered into the Shogun's presence without serious thought. On the island-continent of Kai, a well-oiled governmental-industrial machine had made the Yoshi family rich. Minamoto no Kami, an aristocrat to his fingertips, thought that was reward enough for a daimyo descended from the people of the Goldenwing *Musashi.* At ninety-some, Minamoto no Kami was unlikely to change his mind. At times, the Shogun thought, it appeared that Yoshi Eiji would never be content until he achieved his own Nagashino.

He motioned impatiently to cut off further discussion. "I don't care to get into a lawyers' argument about ethics and the good of Planet Yamato," Minamoto declared.

"We are envied, Shogun," Yoshi said clumsily, "is for the rewards received because of our service to the state."

"No doubt," Minamoto said wearily. "I would be the last to deny that the domain of Kai has served the *bakufu*." The Shogun used the archaic term deliberately, for its effect on a parvenu. "I will grant that you are serving Yamato now by being here at great inconvenience to your interests." He had difficulty in controlling the irony in his tone. *I am getting too old for this,* he thought. *Soon let it be Kantaro's time.* "But it is unseemly for us to try to entice the Starmen to go in harm's way without support."

"I am only considering the possibilities, Shogun," Yoshi Eiji said stiffly. "What would be best for Yamato."

The old man regarded Yoshi Eiji narrowly. "What other possibilities have you also considered, Yosh?" The sudden use of the familiar diminutive was not an endearment. On Yamato children and inferiors were addressed in that manner. Yoshi retreated swiftly.

He had almost decided that it was worthwhile risking a challenge to the old man's authority. Yoshi rethought that precipitously.

Minamoto no Kami was certainly a very old man. And on the homeworld, a Shogun had been nearly a god. Here in Tau Ceti space, matters were different. The lords of Yamato lived under the rule of the Minamoto Shoguns because to attempt some other way was to risk the internecine strife and bloodshed no Earth colony could afford.

Blood could be shed on Yamato. But there were ways, means and methods that did not risk the destruction of the state. That was why ninjas still existed. Yoshi studied the Shogun guardedly. How much did the old man know? Sometimes it seemed Minamoto no Kami was an aging dodderer. At other times he seemed a dark, ancient demon.

"I only hoped to suggest a course of action, Shogun," Yoshi said. He sat on the tatami-covered fabric deck, and as he spoke he bent deeply from the waist over his spread thighs; his fingertips, extended, touched the floor in a manner customarily used by women and, very occasionally, by samurai wishing to show submission.

Minamoto no Kami inclined his head in acknowledgment. The Lord of Kai knew his proper body language. He should. The Yoshi, lowborn but highly placed, were all experts in the protocol of dealing with their social and political superiors.

But never mistake the gestures for the reality, Minamoto no Kami told himself. *This man spreads trouble wherever he goes. Even here aboard this vast, ancient ship.*

When Eiji had excused himself and made his way hastily out of the shogunal compartment (he was still having great difficulty getting about either in zero-G or in the gravity field generated by the pack he wore under his *hakama*), Minamoto no Kami spoke aloud. "You heard, Kantaro-san?"

Kantaro appeared from a dilating fabric valve leading into the adjoining compartment. On his shoulder rode a small, ruddy cat. One Minamoto no Kami had not seen before. This one lacked the hair-thin wire antenna that many of the others aboard the Goldenwing displayed. Yet it sat firmly anchored to the padding in the shoulder of Kantaro's broad-shouldered surcoat. The small head was very close to Kantaro's ear and it seemed for one curious moment that the cat was speaking to him.

"I see you have found a *neko* to be your companion, nephew," Minamoto no Kami said curiously.

Kantaro ran his knuckles over the small beast's breast. "I believe *she* chose *me*, Shogun," he said.

"She?"

"Definitely she," Kantaro said. His face showed a momentary puzzlement. "I knew it at once. I don't know how I knew it—I am not an expert in feline anatomy."

"And does she speak with you?" Minamoto no Kami asked the question half-smiling. The cats were a peculiar delight aboard the Goldenwing. They moved about the ship like furry birds. Starman Amaya explained that they had all been born in space, and were completely at home in null gravity. She also suggested that if one listened in the right way, the small beasts *would* speak with you. Though what she actually meant by "speak" was not clear to the old Shogun. But their presence pleased. Clearly,

Kantaro was captivated by the graceful creature riding on his shoulder.

Kantaro shrugged. "She speaks, I think, in her way."

"And has she a name, your *neko*?" Minamoto no Kami asked. It was odd, he thought, that he had called Kantaro into the compartment to discuss the matter of Yoshi, but had fallen easily into a discussion of the cat.

"I call her *Hana*, Shogun." He caressed the small, alert head and was rewarded with an almost inaudible purr.

"Flower," the Shogun said. "It suits her."

Kantaro lifted Hana from his shoulder and handed her gently to his uncle, who cradled her against his breast. "But she is not mine, uncle." He smiled. "I suspect no one owns these cats."

Minamoto no Kami, despite the rigidity of his upbringing as a samurai aristocrat, had always been one of the most sensitive and empathic of men. It was a characteristic much desired in the ruling families of Yamato.

The moment he held the cat and looked into her golden eyes, he had the strange feeling of being valued and understood. Was that possible? Or had he simply fallen under the spell of the stories the Starmen told about the cats of the *Gloria Coelis*?

For an unsettling moment he wondered about the wisdom of discussing so Yamatan a problem as the Lord of Kai in the presence of this small, alien being. Then he reined his imagination into control and began to speak to his nephew about how and what might have to be done to keep Yoshi from creating a disaster.

Hana listened attentively, as Mira intended she should.

15

MIRA

•

Under the arching, transparent carapace of the forward skydeck, and tethered to *Glory* by the long cable of the drogue in his skull, Duncan Kr floated facing the planet that filled the sky "above" him. Since his earliest days aboard *Glory,* Duncan had found solace in this ever-varied, never-changing place.

The child of a Class G8 star, Planet Yamato was possessed of an austere environmental purity with its copper-tinged oceans and isolated island-continents. In a four-hundred-kilometer orbit, *Glory* would pass swiftly from day to night and then to day again in its great inverted swing over billions of hectares of empty sea. Nearing the dawn terminator, *Glory* was a brilliant golden morning star in the sky over Kyushu, the westernmost continent. The Yamatan MD spacecraft followed her in line astern, like the units of a fleet. But a fleet operated on discipline and an agreed-upon purpose. Thus far, the orbital congregation had neither.

Planet Yamato was not far in time from its Gondwana period; the island-continents were still drifting away from one another. To Duncan this seemed a metaphor for the conclave of daimyos now aboard *Glory*. From space the islands closely resembled one another: rockbound coasts, links land and timbered mountains, rushing streams and rivers. The islands would have been perfect breeding grounds for a varied fauna, but life had taken another turn on Yamato. Of flora there was plenty, though the parochial colonists had spent nearly a millennium nurturing the plants and agriculture of their distant homeland. But there were no animals of any sort native to Yamato. The native plants were almost all bisexual, and those that were not were pollinated by the cold winds that blew from the frigid sea to the only slightly less frigid land.

The Yamatans saw themselves as austere as their world. They were, Duncan thought, quite wrong. They were an emotional people quick to anger, even quicker to grieve. Men shed tears as readily as did the women. Even more readily, Duncan thought with a bleak smile. But their emotionalism did not lend itself to ready agreements. Their personal code of behavior demanded adherence to the ancient code of *bushido*—the way of the warrior—a set of rules that was a thousand years out of date before the first Japanese left the homeworld. How these folk had managed to build a complex industrial society on Yamato was a source of wonderment to Duncan Kr, and a measure of Yamatan adaptability.

But thus far the daimyos gathered aboard *Glory* had done nothing but "seek consensus." To the Master and Commander of the *Gloria Coelis* the discussions sounded like quarreling and seeking advantage, but he was aware that, empath though he might be, the Yamatans were not yet an open book to him—nor to anyone aboard the Goldenwing.

Except, perhaps, the cats. The Folk seemed to be cultivating the colonists in a rather remarkable way. Yamatans, most particularly those who commanded the mass-depletion ships following *Glory,* were seldom seen now without some member of Mira's pride accompanying them.

Duncan looked again at the planet above. The Goldenwing had already overflown the Inland Sea and the islands of Takeda and Honda. Beyond lay the third island-continent in the group, and then another long transit over megameters of empty, copper-colored sea.

To Duncan Kr, child of dour Scottish clans to whom names were sacred, the Japanese practice of constantly renaming people and places was vaguely irritating. The practice was disorienting for empaths, who often used names as psychic engrams.

But the name-shifting tradition was strong on Yamato. Young colonists had one name until puberty and Boys or Girls Day—at which time they would take a new one. These they would carry until (or if) they performed some service to daimyo or state that made it seemly to honor them with still another name change.

The island-continents went through similar nominative evolutions, though less often. "It is like baptism on a geologic timescale," Broni, fresh from a session with *Glory*'s information retrieval system, declared. "Kyushu was once Kagoshima and Shikoku used to be Akita. Their history is full of things like that."

Only Honshu, the home continent of the daimyos of Minamoto descent and the site of the capital city of Yedo, still carried the names they had been given on Lander's Day.

The constant naming and renaming created a veritable salmagundi of names of persons, clans, domains, and ancient, distant geography that was discomforting to the conservative Master and Commander of the *Gloria Coelis*. Though Duncan revered memories of Earth (a world he had never seen), he believed that man would not succeed in space by making icons of his past. There was only one future, and that lay ahead.

It was a grim truth that if mankind were to participate in that future, some action would have to be taken aboard *Glory,* and very soon. But for now it was restful to float alone in the silence, and think quiet thoughts. He used to do much the same when, as a child, he lay in the pale sunlight of the Wolf sun on the limestone cliffs of the Thalassan coast. Often he would remain on the cliffs until dark to watch the great moon Bothwell rising, and to hear the roar of Bothwell's great tidal surge smashing against the shore.

As on many colonial worlds, the day on Yamato closely matched that of Earth. A twenty-one-hour rotation accommodated human biological clocks. Even after sixty generations, men and women here still remembered Earth. On Planet Yamato the months numbered thirteen to fit the seasons. The planet's cold, heavy air was weather-rich; on every orbit *Glory* overflew cyclonic formations of rain and ice-laden cloud laced with violet flashes of lightning. Duncan thought the Yamatan weather beautiful. The planet appealed to him. To the north lay the edge of Yamato's substantial northern ice cap, a floating continent of frozen ocean seldom visited save by the submarine purse-seiners seeking beneath the ice the colorless kelps the Yamatans had learned to relish.

Glory's size made the presence of the hundred or more Yamatans aboard incidental; a thousand could easily be lost aboard a vessel built to carry whole populations. But the Yamatans were made uneasy by the size and emptiness around them. They were accustomed to human habitations built on a tight scale. In their cities they lived elbow to elbow. There were other problems as well. It was apparent that though good manners precluded complaint, the informal behavior of the Starmen in their own environment upset the Yamatans.

Duncan had cautioned the syndics against nakedness. The Yamatans' ancestors had once enjoyed mixed, nude bathing. But time had made them rather more prudish. It seemed that now the colonials became quite agitated when on-duty syndics travelled about the ship only marginally clothed. These things seemed petty to Duncan, given the purpose of the assembly in orbit.

Duncan wondered that the precocious behavior of Mira and the ship's other cats did not upset the Yamatans. It was almost, Duncan thought, as though the cats had been commanded to ingratiate themselves with the strangers. Was that possible? It was a long time since Duncan, or any of the Wired people, had treated Mira's pride as "pets." But was Mira now instructing her progeny in the fine art of human cultivation? Duncan was prepared to believe it. The *neko,* as the colonists called them, were making ailurophiles of the people from the planet. Were the cats acting under the guidance of *Glory* herself?

The Monkey House had been pressurized and there had been a steady traffic of cats into and out of the place. Dietr was under the impression this was the result of a program he had written for *Glory* to help rehabilitate the skittish and xenophobic monkeys. But as far as Duncan could see, either *Glory* was acting on her own, or the cats were. They were, among other things, teaching the monkeys to plug themselves into the ship's electric-power storage—something no syndic had ever been able to persuade the small cyborgs to do for themselves. Had Mira told the Folk to teach the monkeys to feed themselves? Food was a Terrestrial animal's primary way of comforting itself after a trauma. Mira, who had learned in kittenhood to operate the food replicators, would know that.

Duncan watched the seascape roll above the ship. He found it grimly amusing that Dietr Krieg was obsessed with the desire to become a figure of myth to the enhanced breed of cats he had created. How typical it was, Duncan thought, of the Cybersurgeon to confuse learned scientific skills with godhood. If Dietr imagined his experimental programs could control both *Glory* and her pride of cats so simply, the Cybersurgeon knew less about the animals and the ship than he ought.

I must see what Mira says, Duncan thought, finding it not at all strange that the idea should take such form.

The small matriarch drifted not ten meters from him, a tiny patch of darkness in the compartment lit only by the sunlight reflected from Yamato's planetary ocean.

At this hour, the higher-ranking daimyos were bestirring themselves in their austere compartments. It would be another hour before one of the Shogun's chieftains would appear to ask Duncan to join in one of the interminable consensus-seeking meetings they loved to convene.

The trouble was that no one, not the Yamatans nor any of the syndics, had any idea of where the Outsider would strike next. Even Wired, the Starmen could make only estimates. *Glory's* mainframe was a vast pool of information and deduction, but the ship was, like her people, limited by what she had actually learned from her encounter in the Ross Stars.

Through the thick drogue cable came gigabytes of information generated by *Glory*. She observed the distant stars for navigational information, the thin almost-atmosphere of near-planetary space, the set and condition of the few thousand square meters of skylar spread on the yards to hold her in low orbit. The ship was *waiting*. Duncan could sense it. He could almost feel her impatience.

Duncan closed his eyes and concentrated. *"Mira."*

He was pleased by the response—a warm sending of appreciation and affection. Mira was learning to communicate with humans, but her essential *catness* remained uncontaminated. *If anything,* Duncan thought, *it is we syndics who are changing rather than the Folk.* He half-smiled as he remembered that some writer of ancient Earth had once written that if man and cat were ever able to interbreed, it would ennoble man, but diminish the cat.

In his mind's dream he saw again, misted now by time and stellar distance, the almost feline face of Eliana Ehrengraf

Voerster, Broni's mother. He remembered making love to her here, in this very place, drifting on the air, watching the heavens circle as *Glory* orbited another world. He surrendered momentarily to a grief as pure and bright as the distant stars.

He felt a soft touch. Mira anchored herself on his shoulder. How did she do that without inflicting pain? he wondered.

The cat's eyes were the color of amber.

She issued a single, soft trill and ran the tip of a rough tongue across his cheek.

The projected thought that formed in his mind was roughly: *"Why are we still here? The hunt is out there."* It had sensory overtones that human speech never had. The smell of a jungle night he knew Mira had never actually experienced. The taste of blood from a fresh kill—something else the small cat had never known. A touch of the angry hunger felt by the predator seeking prey. Did these feelings come from *Glory*'s vast database, or from an ancestral memory buried in that small, neat head behind the amber eyes? Who could tell?

Duncan turned his attention once again to the stellar night beyond the rim of the planet. Here the sky closely resembled that seen from Earth. A mere four parsecs scarcely distorted the constellations. Orion the Hunter ran with bright-eyed Sirius. Cassiopeia reclined between Cepheus and Andromeda.

Only Dietr of the syndics had ever actually seen the heavens of Earth, but the Cybersurgeon was too pedestrian to dream about them. Perhaps, Duncan thought, that was the better way. To regard the life around you without an overburden of imagination simplified the daily business of living aboard a starship. In this moment a simple life seemed very desirable to the Master and Commander of the *Gloria Coelis*.

To colonists the Wired Ones seemed immortal, but Duncan knew far better than most how old the lonely years made a man feel. *But the sky, ah the sky,* he thought, *incredibly ancient and forever young . . .*

Mira, too, watched the sky. The distances were far greater than the most prodigious feline leap, but they were ignored by the Folk, because she knew that when the time came, the enemy, the prey (she saw it as a vast, snarling dire wolf creature, part dog, part dragon) could not hide from her. She reached out with her small mind to a distance she did not understand or wish to understand. She knew all that she needed to know about the being that stalked them down the silent dark.

The large ones thought there were many, but there was only one. Speed and anger were what made it so formidable. Mira knew that in the time she could leap from plenum wall to plenum wall, the great wolf could leap across what the syndics called the sky.

While the dominant tom and the queen called Anya had prowled about doing who-knew-what on that brilliant space above, Mira had spent her time more profitably with the great-queen-who-is-not-alive. The great queen did not know everything. There were things about the Folk she still needed to learn, but she knew a great deal about the dark forest where the great killer dog lived. It was shaped like a ribbon of night, twisted once and rejoined to itself so that it had only one surface.

At first this concept had puzzled Mira, but then her feline sensibilities had come to her resuce. For ten thousand generations the Folk had survived by being indifferent to those things that did not concern them. Mira did not care how space was shaped or how large it was. It sufficed her to know that the great dog could dig through the twisted ribbon, ignoring distance. A leap for that furious creature might be the distance from Big's nose to his tail-tip or from this light in the sky to that other whence the young queen had come. Size and distance were limitations the great wolf did not recognize. It made the creature very dangerous.

Though Mira had been loved and appreciated since kittenhood, she understood about cruelty and death. She belonged to a line much closer to its beginning than did the syndics. There were memories imprinted in her DNA that influenced how she regarded her world.

But the small cat knew about danger from experience. She remembered well the horrors and fury of the encounter in the Ross Stars. She had not been shocked to see men die. The large ones belonged to a species that was expert in killing—not for food any longer, but often for joy. It was fitting that the wolf-dragon should hate and fear the people, but they were Mira's people and the great queen's people, and that was all she cared to know.

She released her hold on Duncan and allowed herself to drift away from him in the stark light. They were oddly shaped animals, the syndics. She had always thought so, but recently she had begun to look at them with a less critical eye. The dominant tom had a certain hairless grace to him. There were times in estrus when she found herself wishing that he were a cat.

She stretched and rolled over in the air, exactly as she would have done in a pile of autumn leaves—bright natural coins she had never seen and would never see except as images given her by the great-queen-who-is-not-alive. Once having learned how to access the great queen's database, Mira had set herself to learning everything she could about the place that gave both the syndics and the Folk their original life. Now, often, as she slept, she would dream of that sunlit place of grasses and trees and vast savannahs populated by prey.

She scanned the sky. The great dog was nowhere to be found. Yet she felt a certain sense of unease. Something threatening was moving nearby.

She twisted again so that she could examine the shadows below her. They moved and shifted with each movement of the ship and change in the reflected light streaming in through the eyelike lens of the carapace.

Something moved below that was not accounted for by the shifting of the light. She sensed human excitement, smelled human sweat, threat, danger.

She reacted to the sudden release of aggression far below. A shape moved swiftly through the still air. Mira yowled with fear and anger. She projected herself straight at the dominant tom, struck him with her claws fully extended so that he recoiled in sudden pain.

"Mira! Damn, Mira!"

The shape flew past, spinning with angry precision, hissing in the air. It struck the duralite transparency of the carapace, held for a moment and then fell away. Duncan snatched it out of the air and stared angrily at it.

It was a throwing star, points dark with poison.

Reflexively, Duncan gathered himself and pushed off from the transparent overhead. He flew steeply downward the dozen meters toward the nearest valve. As he changed position to strike the deck with his feet, he heard the soft rustle of the valve recycling. It would take eight seconds for the cycle to complete, another two to reset itself. There had never been a reason for the syndics aboard *Glory* to modify the interface between the skydeck and the twisted fabric tubes that surrounded it and connected the compartment to the rest of the ship.

Duncan reached the valve panel and entered the open code. He might have done better, he thought, frustrated, to give the command through the drogue he had been wearing, but which was now slowly retracting into its spool on the distant far bulkhead.

He was conscious of Mira nearby. She was still highly agitated. The fact was, he thought, that Mira had saved his life. The throwing star remained in his hand. He held it lightly in deference to the shiny black coating of venom on the weapon's points.

The valve began to recycle. His anger was undiminished, but his hope of apprehending the would-be assassin was small and he knew it. Since coming back aboard he had been into the database, studying the exotic subject of ninja, both on the home planet and here on Yamato. What he had learned was not encouraging. Assassination had a long and very nearly honorable tradition in the Asian societies of Earth. Not only was the dark art practiced widely, but it was practiced extremely well, by an assortment of highly skilled villains—among whom the Japanese ninjas were the most adept. With ten seconds in hand, the thrower of the steel death star would be far down one of the empty plena that ran like a circulatory system through the vast body of *Glory*.

The ship herself might be able to locate the would-be killer, but not without a ship-wide alert complete with locked valves and constricted passageways. The visitors would be at best scandalized and at worst driven to take umbrage at what they would see as a racial insult to the lordly daimyos of Planet Yamato.

The valve opened enough for Duncan to slip through into the silent dimness of an empty plenum. He trembled with unused adrenaline. Twice, he thought, they've tried twice. And but for Mira he would be a floating corpse, bloated with swift venom.

The cat appeared at his shoulder. Her coat was raised and her tail brushed to twice its normal size. Her pupils were dilated with fear and anger.

He caught her and held her momentarily against his naked

chest. *"Thank you, small Mira,"* he thought, and was gratified to hear and feel a soft, reassuring trill. The thought was well formed, and though there were no recognizable human words, Mira was saying, *"You are Duncan. You are the dominant tom. No harm will come to you while I am with you."*

Duncan Kr found the message peculiarly reassuring.

But the matter of the assassin aboard *Glory* had to be settled without delay. *We may have brought a killer aboard, and now we have a war on two fronts here,* Duncan thought. Bringing the ninja aboard showed how little the colonists really understood what they faced. The ninja brought the Outsider nearer. Duncan was certain of it. Blood lust drew it, destruction fed it. *Up to now,* he thought, *I have let the Yamatans set the pace. No longer.*

16

WIRED

•

When Duncan summoned the syndics, Anya Amaya was with Minamoto Kantaro in one of the small observation compartments in *Glory*'s ventral country. Kantaro had expressed a desire to see the Amaterasu System from a vantage point undominated by the planetary bulk of Yamato. Since *Glory* orbited inverted relative to Planet Yamato, a view of the outer reaches of the Amaterasu System could only be had from the small observation decks near the Goldenwing's keel.

The two—and Hana—had been *viewing* (a Yamatan expression implying great aesthetic pleasure) the gas giants Toshie and Honda. Toshie and Honda were vast, swiftly spinning planets of extremely low density. When they were, as now, in conjunction with one another and simultaneously with Planet Yamato, their disks were visible or discernible to the naked eye. This was infrequent, and the sight was much praised by Yamatans.

Kantaro was becoming accustomed to moving about in null gravity, and he had left his bulky grav harness in his quarters. It secretly pleased him that he could now move about almost as easily as did Amaya.

His satisfaction amused and touched Anya Amaya. For the days the Yamatans had been aboard she had been observing the Mayor of Yedo with increasing interest, wondering if Duncan would object to her taking the young man as a lover.

Anya was bored with the slow pace of the discussions with the daimyos. It seemed to her that each day the conversations became more elliptical and less likely to produce the help *Glory*'s

Starmen would need in their next encounter with the Outsider. But this was apparently the manner in which Yamatans dealt with problems. Meetings one after another, and a tediously meticulous search for consensus.

She was also somewhat annoyed with the fact that Mira's kittens—grown into adolescent cats now—were choosing humans to be their companions. The small beasts were showing a powerfully developed sense of discernment. Since she had never been an overt ailurophile, she accepted the likelihood that she, Amaya, would be among the last chosen by the persnickety little creatures. But she had not been prepared to have one of the cats choose Kantaro while she still waited to see if one would choose her.

"Her name," Kantaro had told Amaya with infuriating solicitude, "is Hana. Which means 'flower.' "

To her chagrin, the Sailing Master found that she was jealous of Kantaro for having been chosen before her. The pettiness of the feeling shamed her and drove the notion of Minamoto Kantaro as lover out of her thoughts.

Duncan's summons seemed to agitate Hana, who rode, syndic-fashion, on Kantaro's shoulder. Amaya caught an un-Wired sending from *Glory* that made her feel that something was amiss. With a brief explanation, she left Kantaro to be guided back to the more populated areas of the ship by his precious new friend. *"Talk to him if you can, Hana,"* the Sailing Master sent.

She was surprised when a reply sprang full-blown into her mind. The reply was not in words, not human in any way, but the sense of it was crystal clear. *"I shall, old queen,"* Hana almost certainly replied.

Dietr Krieg left his computer program running untended—or rather tended by *Glory*—while he hurried through the various plena that would carry him most swiftly to the bridge. The urgency of Duncan's summons filled him with apprehension.

He had not been delighted to have nearly a hundred colonists aboard, most particularly colonists whose ethnic and social patterns were so vastly different from Dietr's own. He wondered if there had been some sort of contretemps between Duncan and the Yamatans. Duncan was a practiced diplomat at need, but for the Captain to issue so unequivocal a command to *Glory*'s people suggested unexpected trouble.

The Cybersurgeon was being followed—one might almost say tracked—by a young orange tom from Mira's most recent litter, one of the last animals to be surgically fitted with a drogue.

The cat had been "around," spending much time perched on Dietr's workstation, watching the Cybersurgeon with what Dietr regarded as a strangely judgmental stare.

At first Dietr had been pleased by the cat's attention. He had had poor success communicating with his previous veterinary patients. But the marmalade tom, whom he had decided to call Paracelsus (the florid name was quickly shortened to Para, by Dietr or by the cat—the physician could not be sure), appeared to enjoy the Cybersurgeon's company.

From time to time Para's thoughts seemed to come through with startling clarity. For the time being, Dietr Krieg was keeping silent about the exchanges—if exchanges they were. He could not, actually, be certain. Dietr was never at ease with what he could not measure.

He had been tempted to speak of Para to, of all people, Buele. A child, to be sure, but wise in cat lore. Buele had remarked only yesterday that Mira's small Folk were far cleverer than the cheets of his native Planet Voerster. The comment suggested that Buele knew more than he was saying, and waited only for the physician to ask his counsel. The very idea, Dietr thought, was absurd.

He had been rewarded with a strong, almost feral impression of himself seen through other eyes: *"You are powerful. You are he-who-cuts."*

It would take the Cybersurgeon substantially more time before he could admit to himself that the communication he had coveted since the time of his first experiments on Mira had actually taken place.

Meanwhile, Para tracked his syndic, guarding and watching.

Damon Ng had been sleeping in his quarters, dreaming his customary sweat-inducing dreams of endless falling. The young man from Nixon had learned to control his acrophobia, but it was far from conquered. Damon was relieved to receive the order from Duncan. He had been planning a visit to the Monkey House, where the small cyborg deck-apes were being cared for—for the first time, Damon told himself with satisfaction—by the cats.

Cats were rare in the tree-cities of Planet Nixon. But despite his lack of experience with cats, and to his enormous pleasure, he, too, had been adopted by one of the cats, a dun-colored young tom from Mira's second litter. Broni had named him Pronker, after one of the few Earth animals to survive transplantation to her native Voerster. She explained that the animal's name was properly "gemsbok," but that it had a way of leaping straight-legged into the air, apparently for pure joy. In Broni's native Afrikaans, the leap was called a *pronk,* and it was a move that the Damon's young tom joyfully mimicked.

Pronker was reserved with the other syndics, but with Damon he was extraordinarily demonstrative. As a prodigious leaper, Pronker delighted in reaching and perching upon the most precarious projection at the highest point within any compartment. Often this was as much as fifty meters or more from the deck. Even in null gravity, heights were always a problem to the Rigger, but Pronker's example was beginning to give him confidence.

Damon still felt fear each time he found himself outside and at a great height. Climbing the rig was torture for him—a bitter burden considering that his primary duty aboard *Glory* was that of Rigger.

But recently when Damon went EVA, Pronker took to appearing in the suiting-up room, climbing into Damon's space armor ready for adventure outside the ship. Anchored to Damon's padded shoulder, small head inside the suit's roomy helmet, Pronker clearly enjoyed every moment spent outside. Damon was becoming accustomed to Pronker's trills and purrs whenever the two found themselves kilometers above the *Glory*'s decks.

Now as Damon responded to his Captain's command, Pronker kept pace with his movement through the plena by sailing from one claw-hold to the next in soaring leaps, a wingless, furry bird. Damon did not find it at all strange that the young cat led the way as often as he followed. All the cats seemed to know the labyrinth of the Goldenwing better than did the Starmen.

Clavius rode precariously on Broni Ehrengraf's shoulder as she flew down the plenum toward the bridge. The tom had some memories, implanted by the great-queen-who-is-not-alive, of the original Clavius, the black Starman who had spent nearly twenty years grounded on Voerster. Black Clavius had been a different sort of human from those who belonged to the great-queen-who-is-not-alive. Surely it was the music. Clavius was learning to deal with abstract questions, and the puzzle of his naming was such a question. He was pleased that the Starman Clavius had been greatly loved by Broni. The human concept of love was still strange to Clavius, being mingled with so many emotions having little to do with sex and reproduction. Clavius, just reaching maturity, was obsessed by sex. Sex was important. He seethed with hormones and sexual fantasies, and he waited anxiously for some of his female siblings to reach estrus.

But Clavius was, like Black Clavius, a singer. The man had made music on an inanimate thing called a balichord, which Broni also played. Broni's pleasure in the music was profound. She was convinced that no living being had ever, or would ever, make more beautiful sounds than the great black Starman had done. For reasons that Clavius could not fathom, his sweet yowlings did not arouse in Broni the same delight they did in many of the young female Folk.

As the girl moved through the cold air of the plenum, Clavius could hear the metallic sounds of her artificial heart. He did not yet know about medical prosthetics, but he did know that his person had a noisy thing inside her body that held her life hostage.

He also knew, because Broni did, that she was destined never to enjoy an interval on that great bright disk in the sky or any other like it, which Clavius knew were many.

As they flew swiftly toward the place Clavius thought of as the inner lair, the tom could sense his siblings—those who had been matched by Mira to humans of their own—assembling. Outside the great queen was the domain of the Beast. Each of the Folk had his or her own vision of the thing that stalked them. To Clavius it was a great dog with bloody jaws. The blood, he thought with a shiver, smelled and tasted of the Folk. He had never seen a dog, but he knew enough to be afraid. It was part of the wisdom given him before he was weaned.

Tonight Mira was yowling warnings to her pride that there was danger inside. The cats, being young and with little real experience of danger, reacted in their own individual ways.

But Clavius realized that safe play and secret learning were almost at an end. A time of tooth and claw was upon them all.

Big, the cobby tom who had attached himself to Buele, was not the quickest of Mira's pride, nor the most intelligent. But under the influence of the Voersterian boy's extraordinary empathic Talent, Big was far advanced along the path to direct communication with the human syndics.

He had progressed to the point of adopting the habit of using human names. He recognized Big as his own name. He even knew what it meant—though he thought it foolish, since Buele, indeed any of the humans aboard, was far larger and more massive than Big. But that was the way humans thought.

Buele had discussed with him the human view of the other syndics (most particularly the young queen, Broni) and the feline view of the rest of Mira's pride. Between cat and boy a lingua franca had begun to develop. Because of Buele's inability to articulate cat sounds or assume the necessary postures to transmit feline body language, the language they were developing was more human than cat. But the human meanings of words were slurred, elided, and modified by Big's peculiar worldview. For example, to "discuss" did not imply the tedious and tendentious human way of worrying a topic. Instead it suggested an acceptance, and even an understanding, of the way each participant in the exchange viewed the problem. This did not mean that the encounter could not explode into a furious matter of tooth and claw. The cats understood that there were times when nothing less would serve. The humans had apparently once known simple truths, but time had dulled their natural senses.

To Buele, the simple statement "I am hungry" meant a desire to visit a food replicator. To Big the same phrase meant the scent and taste of Mira's breasts, the anger and sorrow of being weaned, the half-joy, half-fury of quarreling with a sibling, and even the possibility of fighting and killing. Only then came the learned memories of the food replicators and the satisfactions they offered.

Both Buele and Big were intensely interested in the phenomenon of the wolf-dog-dragon that flashed with the speed of thought about the night outside the great queen. They feared it. They dreaded summoning it with their anger or pain or sorrow.

But they were steadfast in their knowledge that it must be faced, and killed because it stalked them relentlessly and would until either they or it were dead.

Big understood death better than did Buele. There were few vermin aboard the great queen, but those there were had been used by Mira as prey for her offspring. To show them death taught them the value of life.

It was a terrible, simple lesson, but a profound one.

Anya Amaya watched with some annoyance as her fellow syndics arrived and took their accustomed places in the bridge. She was still shaken by the clarity of the message she had received from Hana. Un-Wired, she had not expected it. Something profound was taking place aboard *Glory*.

The idea of suspecting a *cat* of some kind of human conspiracy was lunacy. But was it, really? Mira and her breed were not ordinary cats. Dietr's meddling had changed them into something quite different than they would have been had they been brought out of cold-sleep as any other mammal aboard *Glory* had been. Now, thought Anya Amaya, here were Buele, Broni, Damon, and Dietr Krieg, all accompanied by cats. It was unsettling, as though she were being excluded from something important taking place just out of her sight and hearing. The Sailing Master was still brooding on this as Duncan and Mira came though the valve.

There was a tear on one arm of Duncan's skinsuit; blood stained the fabric. There was anger in his lean, lined face. Amaya knew that anger. It manifested itself in a darkness that settled on Duncan when he blamed himself for putting his ship and his people at risk.

Without preamble he anchored himself to the control console and addressed himself to the group. "I thought we had left the worst of Yamatan politics behind when we agreed to meet here on *Glory*. I was mistaken." He held aloft an object five centimeters in diameter. "This is a throwing star. In the hands of one who can use it, it can kill. If it were not for Mira, it would have killed me."

Dietr immediately reached for the star. Aboard Goldenwing *Glory* weapons were his concern. None of the other syndics had the experience or the desire to become expert.

"Be careful," Duncan said. "I think the points are poisoned."

Amaya was by his side. She touched the bloodstained tear in his skinsuit. "Mira did this?"

"Yes. She saw the damn thing coming. I don't know how. If she hadn't I'd be floating dead in the dorsal ob-deck."

Mira, clinging to the console beside Duncan, looked inscrutable. The other cats lashed their tails.

"See, Brother Duncan," Buele said, "they all *know*."

"Leave that for a minute, boy," Dietr Krieg said brusquely. To Duncan he said, "Did the star touch you at all?"

"Only my hand. It didn't break the skin."

"I can give you an inoculation to be safe."

Duncan looked at the somber faces around him. "After what happened in Yedo I should have taken better precautions. It could have been any one of you. We will take care now. But first we have a decision to make. We can't go into Deep Space with an unknown assassin aboard."

"We must tell the Shogun," said Broni. Killing had been common on her homeworld, but an attack on a Master and Commander aboard his own ship was a sacrilege. To colonists—and Broni was the descendant of colonists—the Master of a Goldenwing was a mythic, untouchable figure. The ninja attack in the square of Yedo might have been excused as a flash of local political beastliness. But not an attempt aboard *Glory*. That was an outrage. Broni, and all the syndics, had taken it as an article of faith that such barbaric behavior would remain on the planet's surface.

Damon said, "The Shogun must account for it, Master and Commander." As always in times of stress or danger, syndics had a tendency to become archaic in their use of the language of the ancient seas of Planet Earth.

"All in time, Damon," Duncan said. "Wire up, all of you. And never mind considerations of privacy. I want you all to let the cats join in." He smiled ruefully. "Mira paid their dues."

The Starmen socketed their drogues. Instantly perceptions widened. Each member of the crew partook of Duncan's singular memory of the event. What was most remarkable was that they could experience the event through Duncan's perceptions *and* through Mira's. The cats reacted first, arching their backs and bottle-brushing their tails as they experienced Mira's precisely recalled memory of the moment when she sensed the danger in the shadows. Big, and therefore Buele, reacted with alarm and anger. The large young tom's reaction to most challenges was one of aggression. Now he growled and searched imaginary shadows for a perceived threat. He saw a human form, unrecognized, but clearly one of the Yamatan colonists. Each of the animals amplified the impression for the human to whom they had attached themselves. The result was a burst of sensation brimming with warning signals and impressions that would be instantly recognized by any of the Wired Ones on the bridge. The would-be assassin could not hide from the feline senses of Mira and her children. The cats paid no attention to human names because they were without true meaning. But the thrower of the star, regardless of his ability to shed one identity for another, was now a marked being aboard the Goldenwing. He was prey.

Duncan brought the conclave back to a human level. *"Does anyone recognize him?"*

It was Amaya who had spent the most time studying the Yamatans on the inbound journey, she who might best understand them. Duncan, she felt, was darkly angry at the notion of treachery from the Yamatans.

Anya sent, *"If he is a ninja he is totally focused, totally committed. He will have to be killed."*

All received the impression of a man spaced—thrust into the void without armor or breathing gear. It was the traditional way of death for miscreants aboard spacecraft since the days of the first Mars missions in the dawn of the Space Age.

Dietr added his opinion, an odd mélange of academician's equivocation and Teutonic sense of a need for rigid justice and discipline: *"If, Sailing Master. If. We must be certain. We should not offend the Yamatans."*

Duncan felt the spillage of outrage and anger from Anya Amaya. The Sailing Master was easily the most emotional of all the Starmen aboard *Glory,* and her New Earther's anger could be explosive.

The cats responded to her state with anger of their own. What threatened Duncan threatened the great-queen-who-is-not-alive. What threatened her put at risk the cats' whole universe.

"Anya. Control." Duncan's sending was measured and reined. *"Remember what we face out there."* It was too easy to allow anger to build. It was contagious. And the Terror fed on it. Fed?

Duncan wondered. Perhaps strong emotions were only signposts for the stalking death, guiding it across parsecs and centuries. But the strongest impression Duncan had had, even when he had been adrift in the Ross System and filled with the realization that death was very near, had been *fury*.

Buele picked up on Duncan's thought with startling swiftness. *"It is more than that, Brother Captain."* The syndics' attention focused on the Voersterian boy.

"Say more, Buele," Dietr Krieg sent. *"Say more."*

"I felt sadness. Grief. Loneliness."

The syndics recoiled almost physically from what they sensed was a genuine sympathy for the thing that tracked them across space, eager to kill.

"You are an idiot, boy!" The Cybersurgeon snapped aloud. The change from empathic communication to spoken language made the cats uncomfortable. Mira arched her back and bared her teeth at Dietr Krieg.

"Don't threaten me, you saber-toothed little monster. The boy is talking like a fool," he said.

His own companion, Paracelsus, growled softly. Para relished the closeness of the pride, of the Folk, and of the syndics. He was distressed by whatever disturbed it.

Mira's sending, urging patience, calmed him. Para was particularly prone to the feline trait of showing indecision when no defined reason for a quick choice of behavior was indicated by the situation. He nevertheless uttered another, softer, growl. It was the young tom's way of establishing psychological territory, what Buele would call a "yes, but" growl.

"I am sorry, Brother Captain," Buele addressed himself to all, but it was Duncan he wanted most to convince. *"I know it was angry. It wanted you, Brother Captain. But it was sad, too. A deep, deep sadness. It may be lonely."*

"Try that one on *Glory*," Dietr Krieg said, again aloud.

Duncan addressed himself to the entire crew. *"Dietr—all of us—we must remember.* Glory *is a machine. A marvelous one that every year and every kilometer in space makes still more marvelous. But she is still a device. The cats know. See how they treat her. They love her but they seem to understand better than we what she is. The great-queen-who-is-not-alive. She holds terrabytes of knowledge and we can use it, but we cannot expect her to decide questions like this for us. All that* Glory *knows about the Terror is what she—and we—have learned on these voyages. Don't just dismiss what Buele tells us.* Glory *will confirm it. But we need to know much more."*

The fear that Duncan had felt in his own close encounter with the dark stalker still masked the essence of what Buele had declared. In the oceans of Earth, he wondered, did the fleeing prey feel grief for the shark?

An attack by a ninja was a political act on Planet Yamato, bloody-minded, but tolerable. But not aboard a Goldenwing. It broke the covenant between colonists everywhere and the Wired star sailors. Without that covenant man in space became utterly isolated by interstellar distances.

But Buele's statement had shifted the agenda of the meeting, causing a momentary confusion.

Now, to Duncan's surprise, Broni Ehrengraf spoke as one among equals. The girl cradled Black Clavius and said, *"An important decision has to be made."*

Dietr Krieg bridled. The Cybersurgeon, being the least empathic of the Starmen, was the last to realize that something unique was happening to the group. He framed his statement as loftily as he knew how. Broni was, after all, only a girl. The male chauvinism of the homeworld had never been eradicated. The Jihad had seen to that.

The cat Paracelsus regarded the physician intently. He-who-cuts was about to make himself foolish. Para's tail lashed in irritation. Mira disciplined him with the subsonic growl all her kittens knew well.

Dietr Krieg drew heavily on *Glory*'s database. Amaya looked speculatively at the him. As he moved about, his drogue coiled and uncoiled in the null gravity. The Serpent of Eden, Anya Amaya thought, remembering her Bible lessons that marched so strangely with the matriarchal feminism of New Earth.

Dietr addressed Broni formally, and by the title she bore aboard *Glory:* *"What decision, Astroprogrammer? What is there about that thing that needs some new decision from us?"*

The reply, and the manner in which it was given, surprised the Cybersurgeon—surprised them all, save Buele. Broni displayed a polished empathy and situational understanding that made her statement translucently clear. Her sending was precise and to the point: *"Do we kill it, or do we allow it to kill us?"*

She looked from one to another across the bridge deck. *"We don't sail under some mythic prime directive nor are we commanded by God to sacrifice ourselves. We fought it at the Twin Planets, and* Glory *saved us. But the choice of fight or flee—was one that we made. Now we have to decide again."* Her vision was so empathically clear that the moral dilemma she posed touched each syndic deeply and personally. Duncan drew a deep breath, expanding with sudden pride. For the first time since *Glory* had lost the Astroprogrammer Han Soo to old age before Planet Voerster and Supernumerary Jean Marque at Einsamberg, *Glory's* people were one. He looked at the Cybersurgeon and was gratified to see the realization and gratification in his face as well. It was not necessary to probe Dietr's mind. Broni's coming of age as a Starman was as pleasing to the physician as it was to all the others. It was as though each had touched hands with all the others. *I had forgotten the joy and pride of full unity,* Duncan thought. *Since Eliana, I have brooded alone too often. I have not done all that I should have done for* Glory's *people.* It was the second time within moments he had felt justified in using that unique description of the Goldenwing's crew. He indulged himself still again. *In all the Universe,* he thought, *only we are* Glory's *people.*

Eliana Ehrengraf's daughter is a complete syndic at last, he thought, *a creature of Deep Space—as are we all.* In the true meaning of the word, he felt Wired.

Glory announced suddenly: *"Master and Commander, the colonists are convened on the hangar deck. They ask that you and the Sailing Master join them."*

Duncan pulled the drogue from his socket. At once the vast globe of awareness that he had commanded grew small. Parsecs became mere kilometers.

In ancient Rome, Duncan suddenly remembered, a Commander returning in triumph from the wide world to the City was provided with a slave to ride in his chariot through the tight confines of the Forum, whispering so that only the hero could hear: "Remember, you are only a man."

Mira trilled softly in his ear.

Thank you, small queen, he thought. *I will remember.*

17

THE WAR FANS

•

With their customary industry, the Yamatans had transformed the hangar deck into a fantasy simulacrum of their world. The holographic forest Broni and Buele had so proudly put in place for *Glory*'s visitors remained, Earthly pines in the distance, but the hectare where the MD spacecraft had been parked had been changed by the visitors to resemble a clearing in the Shogun's garden on the planet below.

Not to be outdone in holography by their hosts, the Yamatan engineers had installed their own hologenerators to create a clearing on a tableland above the image of an arm of the coppery Yamatan sea. The spacecraft had been formed into a circle around the barge *Dragonfly,* their lazegun ports covered with paper disks decorated with origamis of three inward-pointing hollyhock leaves. These were the leaves found in the *mon* of the Tokugawa clan, which Minamoto no Kami, by right of descent, claimed as his own family crest.

Screens of stretched paper bearing the same ancient device had been assembled in an open circle, and here the Shogun, his generals, and a score of high-ranking daimyos sat on camp stools awaiting the arrival of the *gaijin*. Aligned on either side of the formation stood the lower-ranking members of the Yamatan delegation. It was the first time they had presented themselves to the syndics in this way. The three-man crews of the thirty MD ships stood unarmored, but still dressed in traditional silk. Still lower-ranking members of the daimyos' staffs formed a third, outer circle. All told there were over a hundred Yamatans on hand. These engineers and scientists and businessmen had transformed themselves into a circle of anachronism.

To Duncan and Anya Amaya, the effect of the fantastical scene was of having travelled back in time to feudal Japan. Shogun and daimyos, clearly the centerpieces of the display, were ceremonially dressed in the *hakamas,* kimonos and the lacquered and gilded armor of that distant place and time. They sat like statues, the steel face masks exposing only their mouths and their dark eyes.

Duncan, who had been exploring the Japanese history in *Glory*'s database, noted that Minamoto no Kami wore a steel helmet decorated with large, curving horns of gold. *Glory*'s database held images of Tokugawa Ieyasu, the victor of Sekigahara, wearing such a helmet.

The daimyos held war fans, each with the *mon* of his clan. The exception was Minamoto no Kami's, which bore the sun disk of Amaterasu. Duncan had seen such war fans in the holoprograms *Glory* produced for him. Long ago on Earth they had been used to transmit orders in battle.

Amaya whispered, "What are they trying to say with all this, Duncan?"

Duncan looked about the circle of daimyos. The lords of Domains formed the first seated rank, cross-legged in the tatami matting that had been spread for them. All were dressed in ceremonial armor. Behind each man his retainers stood like statues. The relative affluence of the Domains was reflected in the opulence of the caparisons the Lord and high-ranking retainers wore. The daimyo of Hokkaido, Genji Akagi, though poor, was the Lord with the most exalted lineage, being descended from the rulers of preshogunal Japan. Duncan had seen almost nothing of the Genji during this convocation.

The Lord of Hokkaido was old, even for this company of mostly elderly men. It seemed to Duncan that the mere effort of attending the meeting was exhausting the man. Minamoto Kantaro had, in the most polite tones, remarked that Genji fortunes had declined steadily since Lander's Day. (All colonists seemed to speak of the day of their landing on a colony planet as though it were yesterday, Duncan thought. On Yamato, Lander's Day had been more than a thousand years ago.)

Kantaro's remark about Genji Akagi had been an understatement. Hokkaido was the least favored domain on Yamato, a desolation of ice and snow in the high northern latitudes. The Genji's war fan, like many others, rested facedown on the matting—hardly an indication of warlike resolve.

Duncan looked at the manner in which the other Lords displayed their fans. If the placement of the fans had significance, as *Glory*'s database informed the syndic that it did, the prognosis of this gathering was not encouraging.

To Amaya, Duncan said in a low voice, "The fans were used to signal orders in the wars on Earth. And to indicate intent."

Anya glanced at the circle of daimyos. Facial expressions were hidden behind lacquered steel masks that exposed only the obsidian black eyes. She looked carefully at the two Lords flanking the Shogun. On his right sat Minamoto Kantaro. His fan bore the device of the city of Yedo. On the Shogun's left squatted Lord Yoshi Eiji of Kai. Anya glanced quickly at Duncan. The daimyo of Kai's body language was that of a frightened man.

"Minamoto-sama means to fight," Duncan said quietly. "And so does Kantaro. I don't think the others do."

The daimyo's replicated armor appeared to contain grav devices. The difficulty of producing such apparel, and for merely ceremonial purposes, was enormous. Duncan wondered if these people, isolated for so long, had devoted as much care to the production of new weapons. What would be effective against the Terror? *Glory* had driven it away by quieting a battle with coldsleep. But killing it? Duncan feared that might be a very different task. Perhaps it was an impossible one.

Behind the Shogun stood a double row of archers. The fletching on long arrows showed above the retainers' armored backs. The bow and arrow was a weapon peculiarly adapted for use in space, Duncan thought sadly. Like all of mankind's weapons, they had been designed by men millennia ago to kill other men. *We have always been good at killing one another,* Duncan thought. *We have done it in war, in bloody ceremony, or in drunken rages.* He remembered the Samhain Festival on his native Thalassa. There, at the time of the summer solstice, the antique claymores and spears carried from Earth were unwrapped and the clansmen drank whiskey and danced the sword dances of their ancestors from dusk until sunrise. And often enough, when the liquor set the blood on fire, men of Thalassa fought and killed one another.

An uncle of Duncan's own marriage group had died in a Samhain brawl the year before the old Wired Ones of the *Gloria Coelis* arrived at Thalassa on Search.

Minamoto Kantaro got to his feet and advanced, fan held rigidly at his side. He planted himself, legs apart, before Duncan and Amaya and made a formal bow.

Duncan returned it in kind, and several of the daimyos uttered a grunting bark of approval.

Kantaro was distressed. Both empaths could feel it. A part of his distress had to do with a recent decision. But there was more. Duncan suddenly received a powerful empathic signal. It was not in words, but the meaning was crystalline, and the thought was aimed at Duncan and at no one else. It came from Mira. It could have come from no other: *"He knows that one of his threw death at you."*

The paper screens cut off much of Duncan's view of the huge compartment. But Mira was out there, watching and waiting. For a moment Duncan was almost overwhelmed with angry despair. He had hoped that Kantaro could be counted on. He felt the steel-masked Yamatans around him. They had come to see what force a Goldenwing could deploy to protect their world. They had failed utterly to understand the scope of the challenge and what defeat would surely mean. Duncan's empathic surge was so powerful that it startled Anya Amaya. "Duncan," she whispered. "What just happened?"

He shook his head. *"Later."* He looked coldly at Kantaro. The young man's eyes were wide, startled. Was Hana nearby? Duncan wondered. Of course the Folk could be anywhere they chose aboard *Glory*. If she was nearby, she had passed the information to Mira, who moved instantly to warn him.

He straightened from his formal bow. Kantaro said, in Anglic, a language Duncan had not even known he commanded, "Do you understand the language of the war fans, Kr-san?"

The language of the fans, Duncan thought. *How elegantly archaic.* And how impossible to contest. The time for that was over.

It had come and gone before the Starmen, all of Caucasian-Terrestrial descent, could act.

And if we should act, what would it accomplish? Duncan wondered bitterly. The "language of the fans" was the language of imperatives, of commands. The fans were a signal to act, not an invitation to discuss. *What simple creatures we syndics are,* he thought. *Life seems so straightforward to us. We consider and we convince ourselves of what must be done. But we are too isolated from ordinary men. We forget human self-interest, human ability to be wrong. So we carry our simplicities with us, no matter how many parsecs we travel.*

This ornate, antique ceremonial charade with modern men playing at ancient warriors was simply a way of delivering a verdict that could not be countered. In such a situation, the mere fact of another attempt at Zen murder was irrelevant.

Kantaro signalled to pages standing by. They brought camp stools and a heated flask of sake. Drinking bowls were produced and filled. Minamoto no Kami said through his steel mask, "We are not yet done, Kr-san."

He moved to the center of the semicircle of lords and began to speak in ancient, archaic Japanese. He lifted his bowl and signalled Duncan and Amaya to drink. Then he threw the bowl to the tatami and raised his fan.

For several minutes he spoke in a harsh and strident, even angry, voice. When he had finished he elevated the fan in a kind of salute and counted three emphatic thrusts into the air. The Lords knelt silently, unwilling to move. Again the Shogun shouted at them, emphasizing his words with movements of the fan.

Suddenly Kantaro leaped to his feet and raised his own war fan, echoing the Shogun's cries.

Minamoto no Kami glared at the Lord of Kai over his steel mask. He thrust the fan menacingly at Yoshi Eiji again and again.

Lord Yoshi struggled to his feet as the Shogun held the fan under his chin like an ax blade. Yoshi made the explosive noise Yamatans used to indicate total compliance. He raised his own fan and held it up for all the Lords to see. But his hand was trembling.

The remainder of the council hesitated. Yoshi shouted at them. One after another they laid their fans down on the tatami, rose to their feet, and filed out of the screened circle. When the last of them had gone, leaving only Kantaro, Yoshi and their retainers within the screened-in circle, the Shogun's mask came down. Other pages took Kantaro's and Yoshi's. Duncan was somehow not surprised to see that the Lord of Kai was pale, and grateful when Minamoto no Kami called for more sake and the drinking began.

It had been as stereotyped as a Noh play.

What Minamoto no Kami had done was divide his strength—ordinarily a sin against the rules of warfare. But not here and now. There was a dictum of the teacher of war Sun Tzu that said, "Use your force wisely. If victory is foreclosed, yet protect what you can."

Minamoto no Kami remained at the point of greatest danger. But his homeworld would receive the best protection he could offer it. But why keep Lord Yoshi here? A more unwilling warrior did not exist under the Tau Ceti sun.

In time, Duncan thought. Perhaps in time he would understand the complex old man.

Minamoto Kantaro remained troubled. *Well you should,* Duncan thought. *You have explanations to make.*

He looked back at the Shogun. The man suddenly looked very old and very weary. Duncan asked, "How many ships, Minamoto-sama?" It was not a time to ask, but he had to know.

"Six ships, Kr-san. Two of mine and four of Lord Yoshi's."

"Not what I had hoped for, Shogun."

"Karma, Kr-san."

Duncan appreciated the irony. "If you say so, Minamoto-sama." Duncan hesitated. "But I am concerned for your safety, Lord Shogun."

Minamoto no Kami stood in the center of a circle of abandoned war fans. "That is of no consequence, Starman."

"Your choice, Shogun," Duncan said.

The retainers had fallen back to converse in small groups. Yoshi Eiji looked sick with fear.

Duncan glanced at Kantaro in subdued conversation with Anya Amaya and wondered, *Who will rule on Yamato if the Shogun dies?*

And then: *Will anyone?*

18

CATS

•

Free of his ceremonial armor and silk brocades but not of his other concerns, Minamoto Kantaro stood on the deserted bridge of the barge *Dragonfly* watching the last of the withdrawing mass-depletion craft. It moved carefully down the length of the vast hangar, through the open valve and into space.

The pilot, Baka Ie, a low-ranking member of the Baka clan of Hokkaido, had impressed Lord Genji, his daimyo, with his skill at maneuvering the clumsy little MD ships. Normally, Baka would never have been trusted with so valuable a piece of equipment as an MD craft. Hokkaido could afford only three, and even that had strained Lord Genji's resources. But Yamatan traditions were inflexible. A thousand or more years ago on Earth, Japanese nobles had been forced by their Tokugawa Shoguns to spend lavishly, living at the Court, so that they would have little left to spend on rebellion. There had never been a rebellion on Planet Yamato, but every daimyo was expected to spend money on spacecraft. Lord Genji, old and distinguished though he might be, could not be spared this drain on his meagre resources. Hokkaido had provided four MD craft to the fleet that had risen from the planet for the conference aboard Goldenwing *Gloria Coelis*.

Kantaro had enjoyed viewing the elegant way the Hokkaidan MD had lifted from the hangar deck, rotated while hovering above the fabric floor, and then powered straight for and through the open valve into space. It had been a masterful job of piloting. Kantaro himself was considered a polished pilot of small spacecraft, but he was no match for the natural talents of Baka Ie.

The unhandsome young man from the glacial fields of Hokkaido had been beside himself with joy before departure. He had secretly hoped that his daimyo would allow the three Hokkaidan ships to remain with the Goldenwing and partake of the dangers to come, opening the way to promotions and preferments from the Shogun. But this hope had come to nothing. Lord Genji and his noble retainers had no intention of putting their three MD ships at risk. It was not for lack of fighting spirit, Kantaro realized. Hokkaido, lacking very nearly everything else, was well supplied with the spirit of the *bushi*. The Genji didn't lack for brave men. What they were short of was money.

They claimed descent, like so many Yamatans, from the gods. In actual fact they were descended from nobles defeated at the Battle of Sekigahara on Earth in 1600. Their basic trouble was picking the wrong sides in war; they had sided with the Toyotomi against the Tokugawa fifteen centuries ago and were still paying for it. It was not their courage that was in question, but their judgment.

Baka Ie had hoped to break out of his small circle of poverty by fighting the demons the Wired Ones claimed were ranting about in space. It had been a forlorn hope at best. But much to Baka's surprise, a compliment about his pilotage from Shogun Minamoto no Kami had been noted by the young man's daimyo—and as a reward Baka received the right to change his name. Though this was a frequent thing among the upper classes, Baka was descended from first peasants and then tanners on Earth, and from common laborers on Yamato. Such people had, in antiquity, been given contemptuous names by samurai who tormented them. Baka meant "fool," "idiot," "moron." During the Jihad it had meant even worse. Bakas had followed the Muslim armies as cleaners of latrines and, when needed, as beasts of burden.

The reward cost the daimyo of Hokkaido nothing, but no honor could have pleased Baka—soon to be Ashikaga—more.

The changing of names was a quintessentially Japanese tradition. The great warrior peasant Lord Hideyoshi, who helped to found the Japanese nation, ended his days as the exalted Taiko (he was never given the title of Shogun) Toyotomi.

The honor did not save his family from destruction at the hands of Tokugawa Ieyasu, but at least they died as members of the Clan Toyotomi, rich and cushioned by honors until the day they committed seppuku in their burning castle while the soon-to-be-Shogun Tokugawa watched.

In Baka Ie's case, the name change was promised for the day of arrival back in Hokkaido. Minamoto Kantaro approved whole-heartedly. Kantaro's aristocracy did not prevent him from understanding just how large a triumph this name change was for the unfortunately yclept Baka. And he considered this as he watched the last of the Hokkaidan ships clear the hatch and began his prereentry orbit. The MD would be seen once again on *Glory*'s next orbit, and Kantaro expected Baka to express his happiness as Yamatan pilots often did, with elegant maneuvers.

For a moment the small craft was limned against the ruddy disk of Yamato. *Glory* had not yet begun to move from orbit, and the departing mass-depletion ships were strung out like a neck-lace of silvery beads in the light of the Tau Ceti sun.

The valve through which the ships had departed, an iris five hundred meters across when dilated, began to contract. It closed slowly, like the aperture of a camera. It would take ten minutes for it to secure, and as long again for the hangar to repressurize.

The Shogun, fatigued by the antique formalities of the "*bakufu* camp" war-fan ceremonies, had retired to his quarters. The pageantry with the screens, the fans, the armor and camp stools was all very well, thought Kantaro, but the simple fact was that the colony planted on Yamato by the Goldenwing *Hachiman* was millennia past the true meaning of such ceremonials, and had been even on the day when the First Landers had touched Yamatan soil.

One day, Kantaro thought, *our foolish worship of the old ways will be the death of us.* He shuddered at his own choice of words.

The holographs, both Yamatan and ship-generated, were dark now, leaving one vulnerable to the overpowering size of the nearly empty hold. The forested tableland of the Shogun's garden had been replaced by an vast plain of monofilament skylar-reinforced fabric. The light came from glow disks set into the distant walls and overhead. The effect was one of sere emptiness.

Kantaro wondered what it would be like to live for years

aboard a vessel larger than a planetesimal, and as empty of life. Surely these Wired Starmen were far stranger than they appeared to be.

Kantaro's original involvement in the conspiracy to meet the syndics with a ninja lazegun in the city square of Yedo was now open to serious question. The presence in the Amaterasu System of *Glory* and her syndics created a situation unlike any he had ever experienced. He would have to confess his complicity to Kr-san. And to his uncle as well. That might mean a slit belly. There was no way of knowing until the situation was faced. The first ninja had paid for his mistake with his life in a spectacular act of suicide. Not, Kantaro's orderly mind admonished, strictly seppuku. The word referred to a ceremonial opening of the abdomen, not the head.

And what method will you use, Lord Mayor of Yedo? The thought formed, sharp as a swordblade—sharp as a claw—in Kantaro's head. For that matter, what amends to his ancestors was Tsunetomo going to make for *his* failure to kill the Captain of the Goldenwing? He looked about him in the stillness of the unmanned control room. Only Hana sat, inscrutable as an amber carving, atop a navigational holograph generator.

Kantaro studied the small beast intently. Had those thoughts come from her? Surely not. But who could ever be sure with these strange spacefaring cats who flew like wingless birds in zero gravity and communed with the Goldenwing's vast mainframe computer seemingly at will?

He turned again to look down the empty venue toward the slowly contracting iris. Yamato proper was no longer visible, though its ruddy reflections could be seen repeated over and over again in the shining, golden skylar of the sails now slowly emerging from the masts and yards.

Beyond, Kantaro could make out the full disk of Moon Tokugawa, a gas planetesimal 2,900,000 kilometers from Yamato. Tokugawa would be short-lived, as natural satellites go. He lacked the mass to retain the methane of which he was made. In a mere million of the local years, Moon Tokugawa would be a wizened, dark, and frigid iron core. When that time came, the history-conscious Yamatans would have to rename him.

It would not do to have the most commanding figure out of the Japanese past represented by an iron cinder.

Kantaro again looked at Hana. In spite of his anxieties, he smiled at the cat. "Was that your comment or mine?" he asked aloud.

For answer Hana leaped from the projector into Kantaro's willing arms. Together they stood by the port, watching the hatch close and snuff out the stars, one by one.

Pronker sat alertly in the special bubble Damon Ng had added to his space armor. From this vantage point he could see the monkeys moving through the lower reaches of the rig, clearing halyards and unfurling sails, setting them to reflect the light of the red sun.

Pronker understood what it was the half-living creatures were doing because his person, the human tom known as Damon, had such an open mind that he had learned to regard it as his own. He surmised that all the scurrying activity of the half-critters in the rig had to do with the wish of the great-queen-who-is-not-alive to move from where she presently was to where she preferred to be.

Mira had taught all the Folk that the desires of the great queen were important and that they were to be fulfilled at once, even at the risk of injury or death.

The idea of injury, let alone death, was alien to Pronker. In his young life there had been scuffles with his littermates, but these small battles were never allowed to escalate into serious catfights. A small scratch or bite customarily received soothing attention from the mother, or, recently, from his own human tom.

Pronker, like all the Folk, had been encouraged by Mira to visit the newly modified Monkey House and to spend time with the dull and timid creatures who lived there. The cats were instructed to reassure the half-alive chimp-machines that they were not in danger any longer.

The "any longer" was because at a place where the sky had been very different, some humans who did not belong on the great queen had come aboard with their ugly auras and killing instruments. For reasons totally incomprehensible to Pronker, they had blundered in amongst the monkeys and killed one, terrifying the others so that they were afraid to leave their lair.

The monkeys were not the work of he-who-cuts and so could not be modified. The cats were commanded by the mother to re-

assure the foolish creatures that they were once again safe. Visits to the Monkey House had bored Pronker, but they improved after the young tabby bonded with Damon, who could explain (with exasperating tedium and difficulty) what it was the monkeys were required to do. Or rather to resume doing.

The young human tom had fears not unlike those of the monkeys, but he managed to control them. Pronker found this remarkable. When he, Pronker, was frightened, he either fought or took flight. The mother explained that these were not always the only options, and she instructed Pronker to learn from Damon. This Pronker did. None of the Folk ever failed to do what the mother demanded of them. Some did it well, some poorly. But Mira's command was the law of the pride.

Reassuring the foolish monkeys had not been difficult. The duty had been divided among Pronker, Big, and Paracelsus (who behaved loftily because he was bonding with he-who-cuts). And the critters were remarkably adept at picking up signals from the Folk and the great-queen-who-is-not-alive. No one of the Folk dared to ask Mira why the boring monkeys had to be reassured, and no one did. But now, watching from within Damon's metal skin, Pronker realized that the monkeys had a place in the great queen's scheme of things. Approvingly, he watched them darting about in the golden web of the rigging. They appeared to be playing, but Damon said no, that they were doing things that must be done.

The concept "must be done" was not an easy one for Pronker or any of his siblings to grasp. The human idea of work was quite absurd. Why should any creature do what he or she had no desire to do? A cuff and a growl from Mira warned that certain behavior might result in punishment. But this "work" was something quite different.

Damon conveyed to Pronker that work was something one did without compulsion because it was necessary. Pronker pondered this odd idea and concluded that it might have something to do with subsistence, or at least with the process of obtaining food.

But since the great queen had taught all the Folk to operate the food dispensers as soon as they opened their eyes, and the task was simple and undemanding, the concept of work remained unimpressive.

Still, his human tom seemed tediously devoted to it and

Pronker did not object. It gave him an opportunity few of the Folk had to see the great-queen-who-is-not-alive from a new and interesting perspective.

He put his cold nose in Damon's ear as a gesture of appreciation.

The Rigger mouthed the antivertigo caplet he had tongued out of his first-aid kit. Pronker's chill kiss made him smile, although he still felt somewhat nauseated at being high in the rig again. It was the first time in more than a month of shiptime.

But he was delighted to see how well the monkeys were performing. For a Monkey House crew that a short while ago had been in complete revolt, refusing absolutely to stir into the sailplan, the swarming enthusiasm of the small cyberorganisms was a great relief to Damon Ng.

He had always found it difficult to understand how and why it was that when he left Planet Nixon to join the Wired Ones aboard *Glory* he had been given the job of Rigger. It was the one task that required a Wired One to be outside the ship for long periods of time and on frequent occasions.

It seemed a long while ago that Damon had left the tree-cities of Nixon for cybersurgery and a life in space. He knew that his Talent was adequate, but no more than that. Duncan, who was conducting the Search himself, had taken a liking to the awkward and fearful boy Damon had been.

His first years aboard the Goldenwing had been made difficult by Jean Marque, the Supernumerary who had been driven to madness by memories of a killing on Earth. Jean had been a difficult and frequently cruel man. But then there had also been Han Soo, the ancient Astroprogrammer who had actually been born on the home planet, and who had died in space on the journey to Voerster, an aged man in ship-years, and a veritable immortal in down-years. Han Soo had been kind to Damon.

So, too, had Anya. Her ways were rough and joking, but in the way of Wired Starmen, she had instructed Damon in sexual matters and had defended him against Marque.

But nothing had cured his aching acrophobia. He had coped with it, but just barely. Until now. Somehow (and despite the vertiginous nausea to which he remained vulnerable) he was now so nearly free of his phobia as to hope that he was cured.

Duncan and Amaya were delighted. Dietr (who had rather taken Jean Marque's place as Damon Ng's personal harpy) remained unconvinced and insisted on a full protocol of medications—which Damon accepted. But Damon knew Dietr's medications were not the reason for his improvement.

It was Pronker. Damon had not the slightest doubt. Since Pronker had taken to riding inside Damon's space armor, the dozen-kilometer-tall spars and *Glory*'s sails were no longer a golden purgatory. He often wondered what he would do when he had to go out alone, wearing only a helmet and skinsuit, relying only on Pronker's remote Talent, his own, and the interface provided by Pronker himself.

From his location high on the port-side mainmast Damon watched the monkeys attentively assisting the servomechanisms that extruded the skylar courses from the spars. As the gleaming sails caught the light of ruddy Tau Ceti, great shafts of golden light slashed through the spidery webbing of the rig. Each stroke of brilliance left a cometlike trail through the haze of monofilaments, and the light-retention quality of the material from which the stays and braces were made glowed for several seconds after the reflections had passed. The effect was stunning, and Damon was filled with a sense of amazement that he had never really noticed these beautiful effects before now. Without fear of falling clutching at him, he looked at his environment very differently than before.

Pronker, he observed, had no particular interest in the light show. He looked, and then looked away, out there, beyond the long reach of the spars and yards, past the slowly deploying sails, parsecs beyond the planet still filling three-quarters of the dark sky. Damon derived a dividend of satisfaction from Pronker's scrutiny of the dark and distant sky.

Diligently guarding his young queen, the human girl Broni, Black Clavius sat like a carving on the curve of the Astroprogrammer's pod. His tail was wrapped neatly against his body, but the tip twitched and lashed with each sending from Broni.

She was responding to the feel of tachyons on her bare skin, which was as sensitive as Black Clavius's own. Broni was Wired, totally at one with the great-queen-who-is-not-alive. This brought her into a tight rapport with the cat, who sat unblink-

ing, staring through the girl's senses and the great queen's at the gas-giant planet the Yamatans called Handar, barely detectable near the limb of the red sun.

It was near that bright point of light that the Hunter had struck last. The imprint left in the fabric of space by the creature's raping entrance was still discernable to Black Clavius. He saw it as the still partially open mouth of a black lair, within which were the half-consumed remains of strange life-forms that neither Clavius nor the great-queen-who-is-not-alive had ever seen, bits of life neither cat nor ship would ever truly see.

They had originated in a place far beyond the Folk's ability to leap, past the limits of Glory's humans' ability to travel. Only the Hunter, the Terror, the Outsider—each being aboard the great queen had a secret name for it—could reach so far or so swiftly. The disturbing thoughts made Clavius draw his black lips back to expose his formidable fangs in a reflexive challenge.

Broni squirmed under the increasing rain of tachyons on her naked skin. Clavius, now reaching his full tomhood, felt the tingling, piercing sensations, too. He growled as if to frighten away a competitor. Inside the pod, where Broni lay blank-eyed and Wired to the ship, the odd mixture of human and feline sexuality made her well-defined nipples rise.

Broni had calculated the maneuvers needed to free Glory from her low orbit around Yamato, and she used her surrogate eyes in the dozens of cameras scattered throughout the sailplan to watch the spreading skylar. She was aware of Damon and Pronker out there in the rig, and of the monkeys swarming along the spars, ready to intervene should any of the millennium-old system fail and cause a jam.

Broni was also aware of Anya Amaya in the pod next to her. The Sailing Master was programming the computer subsystems to hoist the sails in a predetermined and efficient order—a task she had performed a thousand times before.

Broni sensed an almost sullen dissatisfaction in the Sailing Master, but she was too young and inexperienced to understand the cause.

Black Clavius, however, understood perfectly.

Duncan, also Wired, but not on the bridge, was with Mira in his favorite place within the carapace, where he could watch the last of the retreating daimyos' MD ships dropping out of orbit and disappearing below the limb of Planet Yamato. The last vessel, the one piloted by the samurai Baka, would be seen once again before *Glory* left orbit on a course for the space around Toshie.

The syndics had been unanimous in their objection to Duncan going anywhere alone. They were convinced—and with good reason, Duncan conceded—that the ninja must still be aboard. It was improbable that his employers would have taken their failed assassin with them back to Yamato.

But Duncan refused to be escorted everywhere, in fact anywhere, aboard his own ship. "Mira will be with me," he said. "She will watch over me better than any of you could do."

Duncan Kr being Duncan Kr, the discussion ended there.

In several lower compartments below the bridge deck, the Yamatans waited uneasily. Even those who had been in space before were awed by the idea of moving so large an object as the *Gloria Coelis* out of orbit and out into the ever more threatening dark.

19

THE RED SPRITES

·

*T*he evolutions of a Goldenwing leaving low planetary orbit are unlike any other maneuver in space. Though Glory is constructed of the lightest materials available at the time of her building, a mass of several million metric tons of inertia is being set in motion solely by the pressure of light from the local stellar primary and by the millennial wind of tachyons streaming out of the vast black hole at the galactic center.

For Glory this evolution requires the setting of all her eighty million square meters of gossamer golden skylar, from main courses to the third- and fourth-level skys'ls and tops'ls and a full suit of spankers, jibs and stays'ls.

With majestic deliberation, the Goldenwing's delta-V begins to increase. From orbital velocity she slowly accelerates, and her separation from the planet below grows. Light flashes from her yards and sails. St. Elmo's fire dances through the rigging in the attenuated atmosphere. Her syndics and their helpers guide the great shimmering arcs of skylar as they unroll from within the thousands of yards. To observers on the planet below the sight is breathtaking. Every meter of sail is being spread to the light and wind. It is near to miraculous, the Yamatans say, that they can spread such a golden field of light-capturing, tachyon-taming skylar in the time it takes to complete one orbit of Yamato. In the short time of Goldenwing Gloria Coelis's stay at Yamato, the colonists have become knowledgeable. Were the gaijin ship in orbit around Toshie or Honda, Tau Ceti's gas giants, the Yamatans tell one another, the deep-gravity wells would *hold the Goldenwing captive for several ship-days.*

But Glory *is under weigh and accelerating, and to those aboard, the aspect of the planet they are leaving changes. The sun angle shifts, becoming steeper, so that the coppery light burns into a coppery sea. The storms that hide the southern ice cap turn brighter, like silvery swirls of liquid metal.*

Most of the MD spacecraft that had sheltered within the starship's vast interior have completed their reentry.

All save one, the last Hokkaidan vessel, piloted by Baka Ie.

The efficiency of the monkeys, who recently had been cowering fearfully in the Monkey House, was an improvement on monkey performance measurable in orders of magnitude. Somehow, Damon Ng realized, Mira's pride had hugely reinforced the half-living cyborgs' resistance to fear of strangers. The fact that there were still a substantial number of Yamatan colonists aboard the great-queen-who-is-not-alive was being ignored by the monkeys, who swarmed almost joyously through the intricate maze of the *Gloria Coelis*'s rig.

Damon was in his pod between Broni and Amaya, aware that ordinarily during this maneuver he would be high in the rig, watching to prevent any one of ten thousand possible glitches to which sailing craft were susceptible. He was even slightly regretful that for this particular departure Duncan had instructed him to stand his watch at his post on the bridge with his fellow syndics.

Damon was Wired, deeply into psychic symbiosis with the ship, all his perceptions enhanced. He began to feel the tingling excitement of tachyons on his skin, and the mental expansion of his senses reaching far out from *Glory*. He was grateful that this manner of standing Rigger's Watch was intended to test the recovery of the monkeys, rather than a concession to his phobia. Pronker had grown to enjoy his extravehicular adventures and would have much preferred the mastheads to the pod in which they lay. But he understood.

The cat reclined beside him in the warm gel. An observer might have thought him asleep. He was not. Duncan was receiving a steady stream of impressions from Pronker, whose senses were Outside with those of others of his kind: Big, Black

Clavius, and Para—all empathically ranging the volume of space around *Glory.*

Damon's hand touched the cat gently. Pronker's tail twitched in acknowledgment. His attention was Outside with his litter-mates. This was the first time a team of the Folk had participated directly in a move of the great-queen-who-is-not-alive. All were intent on the search they were conducting. They could sense the presence of Mira and the dominant tom ranging about the great queen. There was a strangeness out there. They could all feel it. But it was not the signature of the great wolf, though it had the same electric charge that made the fur stand on end. The cats' excitement was pronounced, but unfocused.

Para's syndic, he-who-cuts, is also Wired. He is lying in his own pod inside the slowly pulsing fabric walls of Glory's *sick bay and surgery. Dietr Krieg's task at departure times is to monitor the life signs of the syndics on the bridge. It is recorded that at times in the far past, the empathic control of millions of square meters of sail and thousands of kilometers of stays, braces and halyards had become too much for certain unfortunate star sailors and there had been hysterical outbreaks and even bloody murders on starship bridges.*

It is Cybersurgeon Krieg's belief that such emotional explosions may explain the disappearance of several of the earliest Goldenwings, though recent events suggest darker causes. But whatever the reasons for past disasters, Dietr does not intend that any mental or psychic collapses should overtake the syndics of his ship. He has already lost one Starman to madness on Voerster. He does not intend to lose another.

Paracelsus, whose empathic prowess is far superior to that of he-who-cuts, lies across the foot of the medical pod, one eye lazily open to observe the Wired Cybersurgeon within, while the remainder of his attention prowls through dark space ahead of Goldenwing Glory, *ahead of Black Clavius and Big and Pronker. Mira would not approve of this sort of freelance prowling, but for the moment the mother is otherwise occupied and the young tom is deliciously on his own.*

Para is adventurous, but not foolhardy. He controls his quest-ing carefully, never allowing the essence of his mind to roam out of sight of the enormous glittering bird that is the great-queen-

who-is-not-alive. Instinct tells Para that what he is experiencing is being shared, though on a far lower level of sensitivity, by he-who-cuts. If Para ventures too far off, he-who-cuts might grow alarmed. The human is an odd, tangled ball of heroic desires, sexual repressions, tender affections and a powerful, overall need to be loved by his fellow syndics. By the Folk, as well, though this particular hunger lies very deep, hidden under the many layers of a multiphasic personality.

Para sees it all, but in simple, feline terms. He-who-cuts should simply present his pheromones and allow all aboard to accept him or fight him.

But the great-queen-who-is-not-alive has already made Para far too sophisticated to believe that this will ever happen. It is a pity. He-who-cuts might be a formidable fighter, capable of winning status for himself and his companion. But no.

Para rises, stretches, turns through a 360-degree circle, and lies down again to resume his watch.

In the streets of Yedo, and on the flat rooftops of the villages surrounding the city, colonists are watching the night sky. *Glory* is a naked-eye object resembling a golden dragonfly moving ever more swiftly across the distant starfields. The returning mass-depletion ships are like bright beads dropping from the hand of the Archer, the brightest constellation in the Yamatan sky. The eye of the Archer is the star Alpha Carinae, which the Yamatans call Ryukotsu. The Archer is a spring constellation, and his presence in the sky is regarded as a good omen for enterprises begun at this time of year.

But there is something else in the Yamatan sky, something resembling a visitation of the infrequent aurora borealis. On Yamato the auroras, north and south, paint the sky with faint curtains of violet light that dance and ripple across the polar latitudes. This is something different, and the people viewing *Glory*'s departure ask one another if it is somehow related to the presence of the Goldenwing.

With increasing frequency, millisecond bursts of bloodred light flash above a bank of the familiar thunderhead clouds that populate the sky over the Yamatan ocean. To observers on land and on ships at sea, the red bursts appear to be hardly higher than the anvilheads of the cumulonimbus cloud formations. But in the observatories on Hokkaido, alert for a glimpse of their returning MD craft, measurements show that the bursts are taking place at a much greater height, well past the troposphere and actually deep into the ionosphere. Polar observers can make out a further phenomenon: The subliminal bursts of ruby light spawn purple tentacles that appear to dangle for an instant toward the ground, then vanish.

Yamatan astronomers and meteorologists turn immediately to the database available to their computers. No such phenomenon as this has ever occurred in the skies of Planet Yamato. But a continuing search produces accounts of a phenomenon known, long, long ago—on Earth.

What the Yamatan scientists are watching are "Red Sprites." These manifestations, brilliant red bodies trailing purple "tentacles" reaching down into the planetary atmosphere, were seen and reported in space about the homeworld two thousand years ago. They were described as natural phenomena, cause undiscovered.

The Red Sprites vanished from Earth in the years before the Jihad, leaving only the accounts filed in the ancient databases.

One unusually persistent and energetic Yamatan astrophysical intern at the State Observatory in Hokkaido set in motion a search for recent similar anomalies. He found none. The destruction of a space station in the Earth year 2022 had been documented in detail, but records of the event were lost in the Luddite turmoil of the Jihad.

The Red Sprites are hidden from observers aboard Goldenwing *Gloria Coelis* by the limb of the planet they are leaving. But not for long.

MD pilot Baka Ie's departure from the Goldenwing, accomplished with such panache, such *bushido,* had filled the young man with a soaring delight in his own skill and his good fortune. His brief conversation with his overlord, Genji Akagi, and the promise of a new and more exalted name for himself and all his family, had filled Baka with more sheer happiness than he had ever, in his short life, experienced.

The people of Hokkaido lived a cold and austere life, always trapped and struggling between extremes of weather and penury. For the Baka family, as with others of their social caste, the bitter conditions of existence on the northernmost island-continent of Yamato had been made more bitter still by the innate degradation of the name they bore. Like most Japanese, they had an ingrained respect, even reverence, for social approval. It was this reverence that had caused four generations of Bakas to seek the most difficult and dangerous duties in the service of the Lords of Hokkaido in the hope that opportunities for advancement would present themselves.

Such opportunities never had. Until now. The promised change of name was richly symbolic on Planet Yamato. It was a key in the lock of the door leading to affluence, respect and, above all, a deep and joyous satisfaction.

Such was Baka Ie's joy that he found himself actually singing aloud as he tapped the required commands into the burn sequencer. His two crewmen, also Hokkaidans, regarded one another, grinning. They had, of course, heard of their pilot's good fortune. It was conceivable that some of it might spill over onto them. Poor Lord Genji Akagi might be, but so noble was his ancestry that any evidence of friendship or appreciation bestowed upon a Hokkaidan might well be shared out among the fortunate clansman's associates.

"Friend Baka." Izu Matsushira, the small craft's Navigator, spoke with mock solemnity. "Will you still remember us when your name is Akagi or some such noble thing?"

The Engineer, a reedy and malnourished twenty-year-old from the most northern reaches of Hokkaido, far above the arctic circle, made the slurping noises that were, he and his mates believed, the mark of high-breeding at the great banquets he was certain took place daily in the mansion of the Lord Genji. "Hear me, Baka? I am practicing my good manners so that I may be a credit to you as you rise among the mighty."

"I hear you and can say that no one makes better eating-noises than you do, Tokichiro."

The three men shouted with delighted laughter.

Their small spacecraft, shedding velocity, began to drop toward the coppery planet below. The onboard computer presented line after line of code, confirming the polished skill with which their ship was being handled.

The Goldenwing, which had been accelerating ever since Baka Ie's MD craft had left the hangar-ramp, had vanished over the rim of Yamato a third of an hour ago. Baka activated the rearward-facing imagers. *Glory* would soon be reappearing over the horizon behind them, having completed an orbit while the Hokkaidan vessel slowed to reentry speed.

Baka's fingers raced nimbly over the control console. It seemed to him that he had never flown better, had never taken more delight in his skill. He realized that it was immodest and probably impolite to be so ecstatic about his own abilities. His mother would surely caution him about the dangers of hubris, but it was impossible to curb himself. There may be other times, he told himself, other joys. But this day, this moment, was surely unique. His joy and sense of good fortune surrounded him like a cloud.

The truth was that he was even reluctant to continue with the reentry, reluctant to consign himself to the darkness of the high-latitudes storm he could see covering most of Hokkaido. Another orbit, surely? But no, one of the most appealing things about this moment was that Lord Genji Akagi and the members of his court, all far more gently born than Baka, would be waiting for him on the frozen landing-ground. His family had been notified by radio that they were to be there to greet their kinsman, and there was no doubt but that they would be. He doubted that they had been warned of the auspiciousness of the occasion. That was the way things were done on the frozen island. But once the MD was down, steaming in the ice, everyone would know that the Baka name was no more.

The rearward imagers began to pick up the shimmering streaks of ionic disturbance that almost always preceded the appearance of a vessel in orbit. Goldenwing *Gloria Coelis* was so enormous that she disturbed the planet's ionosphere with a bow-wave extending fifty kilometers along the ship's intended track. Baka Ie could see the first signs of it, a distortion of the starfields far beyond, and a subtle change of color in the individual stars. *Glory* had made almost one full orbit while Baka's ship shed delta-V.

Tokichiro, the Engineer, flashed the attention light above Baka's pilot's console.

"Ie-san. Look at that. What is it? Look ahead."

Baka changed views on his screen.

Ahead and above he could see a flattened reddish area of light against the dark sky. Not what preceded the Goldenwing. Not at all.

It was difficult to estimate the size of the phenomenon. There was nothing against which one could measure scale. But it was large, very large. And at first it appeared to ripple and flicker, as though it were trying to stabilize itself in the ionosphere above the arctic storm raging over Hokkaido. As he watched, the image grew more distinct. It was still insubstantial, electric, but clear and growing clearer with each passing moment.

"What is it, Ie-san?" The Navigator laughed, but nervously. "The way it moves—the thing seems to be searching, Ie-san."

"Or hunting," the Engineer said.

As they watched, odd electric tentacles of bright lavender formed and were hanging—Baka Ie had no other way of expressing the situation—were hanging from the shimmering disk. Stranger still, they appeared to be alive, writhing like the limbs of some insubstantial sea creature.

"Look. There's another," the Engineer said.

The forward imaging cameras had caught another of the things rising from the cyclonic clouds over the planet's polar cap.

"Maybe we should evade," the Navigator said uneasily.

"It's too big," Baka Ie said, his throat suddenly dry. And it was too big. It was enormous. Both of the manifestations were gargantuan. Together the two objects reached from horizon to horizon.

Baka's ecstasy of moments ago translated with terrifying swiftness to alarm. *Another orbit,* he thought, *one more while we take steps—*

To do what? He did not know.

The MD's speed had carried it almost to the edge of the thing. The sky reddened as light from the stars and from the distant moons, shone through it.

Great Buddha, Baka thought, *what can it be?*

The MD slipped lower and more pointedly *under* the vast apparition.

Was this the Terror of whom the Starmen spoke?

But it was nothing at all like the thing in the Deep Space encounters they had described. They had said nothing of any monstrous red shapes materializing inside the ionosphere.

Baka's hand was descending on the reaction engine's firing controls when the first of the hanging tentacles brushed his ship. The air inside crackled with electricity. Paper tapes were magnetized and drawn in wild, scrolling streams from the ship's recording computer. The smell of ozone burned in the crew's nostrils.

Baka Ie no longer thought about his joy or his good fortune. He thought only that he wanted, most desperately, to live.

As *Glory*, now at an altitude of 430 kilometers, cleared the eastern limb of the planet, the Wired syndics in the bridge and the Cybersurgeon in the sick bay were struck by a tidal wave of emotion and fear originating ahead and below.

The cats probing ahead of the ship were the first affected and the most disturbed. Para, unwisely questing ahead of the others, was overwhelmed with a primal terror of the vast red disk hovering just over the highest cloud-tops of the cyclonic storm over Yamato's polar region. Physically near to the Wired Cybersurgeon, Para had stiffened into an attitude of extreme fear and rage. His back arched, his coat rose to make him look twice his normal size. His tail stood erect and brushed out to its very limit.

Dietr Krieg felt the psychic blow from the Red Sprite, followed swiftly and sharply by the pain of Para's claws digging into his flesh. The cat was trying to merge with his syndic, instinctively seeking to pool the inner terror that fuelled his fight-or-flee instinct, young Para's immature response to the wave of rage that engulfed the ship.

Dietr Krieg felt Para's claws strike into his shoulder. He reacted to that before he could react to the other, somehow dreadfully familiar, assault.

With an effort he projected himself into the closed circle of the *Gloria Coelis*'s Starmen, all of whom were reeling with the impact of the attack.

On the bridge, Broni and Amaya cried out in agony before *Glory* could act to shield them from the worst of the dark anger flowing around the ship.

Duncan's response was the most controlled. Mira had warned him microseconds before the blast of rage and hatred smashed through the ship. Instantly, Duncan was ranging through the bridge-crew stations, testing responses and resistance to the attack.

"Glory, *give me a holograph!*"

Duncan's command was harsh and comforting. *Glory*'s people responded to his authority instinctively.

"*Broni, Buele, Damon! Bring them back inside,* now!"

There was no question who was meant. Clavius, Big and Pronker had been mind-probing Outside, ahead of the ship. Two of the three cats were wildly agitated, and Pronker lay next to Damon, stiff with shock and terror.

Mira released her hold on Duncan and leaped across the bridge to Damon's pod, where Pronker lay shivering in the gel. Damon seemed more frightened by what had happened to his feline companion than by what was happening Outside. He offered a stunned hand to Mira, who snarled and cuffed it aside as she crouched to groom and comfort Pronker, who responded by uttering a piteous howl.

The broad-spectrum holo materialized in the bridge. Seen from above, the red disk looked menacing. Lightning played through the clouds below it. Purple, searching tendrils were questing.

Duncan saw to his dismay that a small spacecraft, the last mass-depletion ship to leave *Glory,* was being savagely torn apart. Between the lashing, electrically charged tentacles of the red object Duncan could catch glimpses of a blackness so deep it seemed infinite.

This was the familiar Terror at work; Duncan's own savaged instincts confirmed it. But the great red disk, kilometers across, and the questing tendrils of purple light reaching down into the storm, were things he had never seen—or even imagined.

Amaya made contact. "*Duncan, what* is *that?*"

"Glory. *Search.*" Duncan ignored the Sailing Master's question and made his sending as brief and as urgent as he could manage. "*A red disk, fifty to one hundred kilometers in diameter. Mean altitude, one-fifty to two hundred kilometers. Multiple discharges from the ventral surface resembling tentacles. These extend into the lower atmosphere. It appears that they, or some other force, have produced structural failures in a penetrating spacecraft.*" He paused, dry-mouthed. *Glory* was now passing over the edge of the red disk. The purple discharges from the underside of the phenomenon were invisible.

"Oh, God," Amaya said aloud. The fragments of the Hokkaidan MD vessel were reentering the atmosphere in a display like a meteor shower.

"Duncan, what can we do?" That was Broni, still child enough to seek hope where there was none. The crew of the mass-depletion ship were burning to cinders as the fragments of their craft fell through the curtain of light the color of rotting blood.

The tension in the bridge deck was raw, a palpable presence. From time to time one of the cats, overcome by anxiety, would raise a yowling cry of protest. *Glory*'s search of the database was under way. *If only we could do more,* Duncan thought. But *Glory* was rapidly picking up delta now; the tachyon pressure on the mains and courses was adding speed enough to be felt as gravity aboard the ship. The fabric walls bowed and throbbed as the air aboard was moved as if by a tide.

Duncan sent a brief message to Dietr in the sick bay a half-kilometer from the bridge. The response was slow, and when it came Duncan had a swift impression of a huge dog or wolf looking up at *Glory* from within the shimmering auroral construct below. Dietr came through less sharply than did Para's fearsome images.

"Duncan . . . it's the Outsider again . . . did you see it?"

What Duncan had seen, or rather sensed, was Paracelsus's interpretation of the ultimate enemy. Duncan received a jumble of images from the cats. Mira saw a thing of fire, tooth and claw. Big and Black Clavius snarled at a leaping dogpack, all felt the Outsider's rage as *Glory* swept over and beyond the red apparition.

Broni sent, *"It's bound to the red thing, whatever it is. It can't rise above it."*

Duncan gave an order to Damon: *"Make more sail."*

More skylar appeared on the yards, bowed to the tachyon wind. Duncan swivelled the mast-mounted imaging cameras to keep the Red Sprite in view and duplicated in miniature inside the bridge.

At once he reacted to the term *Red Sprite*. It had come through the drogue from *Glory*'s data bank. Swiftly, the mainframe filled in the sending.

"Red Sprites were first observed on Earth in the last decade of the Twentieth Century by geophysical researchers at Stanford

University. The fanciful name was given them by Professor Umran S. Inan and his assistants, Victor Pasko and Timothy Bell. Sprites appeared intermittently in and over Earth's atmosphere with increasing frequency over the next two hundred years. The phenomenon reaching a peak in the middle years of the Jihad."

Glory's sending reached each syndic simultaneously.

The implications of *Glory*'s statement were stunning. If, as Broni sensed, the red construct was bound in some way to the Terror, the Jihad must have drawn the horror to Earth. Who could guess how many of the reputed atrocities committed in those years were the work of the Outsider?

"Specifics, Glory," Duncan commanded.

"The disk is a plasma, as are the tentacles that appear to descend into the planetary atmosphere," Glory complied. *"There is no confirmed information in the database, but the observed evidence suggests that the Sprite is used to draw energy from powerful planetary storm systems.*

"Hypothesis: While the Outsider is absorbing energy from planetary weather systems, it is unable to disengage until the transfer is complete or until an unspecified percentage of capacity is reached. The degree of local cosmic-ray bombardment is probably a factor in the planetary-Outsider exchange. What this means in terms of actual elapsed time is unknown, and given my resources, probably unknowable. It is a valid supposition that the presence of a Red Sprite is a sure indication of the intimate proximity of an Outsider, and it is also a valid supposition that given the assumed purpose of the Outsider-Sprite relationship, Red Sprites are a creation of the Outsider and can exist only in the low stratosphere of an atmosphere-bearing planet.

"I suggest, Duncan, that we put as much distance as possible between ourselves and Planet Yamato."

Mira snarled in agreement.

Buele asked aloud, "How are the Yamatans taking all this, Brother Captain?"

Glory made the calm reply: *"I have confined them to their quarters. I could not risk the damage they might inflict on me if they should panic and take it into their heads to leave."*

Ever practical Glory, Duncan thought. But how were Minamoto no Kami and his people facing the waves of angry emotion that had moments ago penetrated the ship?

"Duncan?" It was Broni. *"I am puzzled."*

"Yes, Broni?"

"Why did it kill Baka Ie? He wasn't angry. He was happy at the honor done him by his daimyo."

Duncan sent, *"We have assumed that only rage and fear draw the Outsider. It may be that pleasurable emotions do as well."*

Amaya: *"That's horrifying, Duncan."*

"It's a possibility we can't ignore. A second is that Baka's mass-depletion engine interfered in some way with the energy transfer that was under way through the Red Sprite."

"How much grace do you think we have, Duncan?" the Cybersurgeon sent from the surgery.

"There's no way of knowing until the Sprite begins to dissipate," Duncan replied.

"Then may I suggest more sail still, Master and Commander?"

Duncan was grateful for Dietr's irony. Men didn't indulge in irony when they were in the grip of panic.

"Anya," Duncan sent, *"I think we are safe for the moment. Un-Wire and go down to the Yamatans. Do what you can to calm them."*

The Sailing Master emerged from the pod still gleaming with gel, and, without a word, launched herself into the plenum beyond the valve.

The holoimage in the center of the bridge deck glowed with ruddy malevolence. It seemed as bright as ever, but Duncan had no way of judging how long it might last. When it vanished, the Terror would be free again; *Glory's* people were only too aware what that meant to them and to their ship.

The cats on the bridge moved away from their partners and began to prowl across the deck around the holo of the Red Sprite. Big, more adventurous than most of the cats, rose slowly onto his hind legs and cuffed speculatively at the projected image. Its insubstantial nature seemed to puzzle him and he dropped back onto all fours and circled the holograph still again, ears laid back, eyes wide and pupils dilated. Black Clavius, still under the influence of Broni's sexual reaction to the storm of tachyons now passing through the ship, dropped to the deck and snarled at the diminishing Sprite. Mira, who had remained at Duncan's shoulder, trilled commandingly at the young toms.

The animals' reaction to the image of the Red Sprite was not what any of the syndics would have expected. Clearly the cats' understanding was imperfect, but just as clearly they chose to treat the holograph as something more than a natural phenomenon.

Mira's mind brushed hard against Duncan's. The import of her sending was crystal clear.

"There are times for fighting and times for flight. Run, dominant tom, run far and run fast."

20

FLIGHT

•

Anya Amaya arrived at the section of compartments assigned to the Yamatans still sensitized from her Wired session on the bridge. Through the woven monofilament walls of the plenum she could feel the agitation of the confined colonists.

She opened a wall storage, withdrew a drogue and settled it in the socket in her skull. Immediately the raw emotion of the men on the other side of the plenum wall was amplified into a turmoil of fear and anger. Amaya had noticed, ever since arriving at Planet Yamato, that the Yamatans had unique emotional valences. Her experience, other than that acquired on feminist New Earth, had been with a dour and often melancholy Duncan Kr, with the Teutonic Cybersurgeon Dietr Krieg, and with the tensely controlled Damon Ng.

The readiness of the Yamatans to express their emotions under stress unsettled the Sailing Master. She had learned, from her study of *Glory*'s data bank, that ethnic Japanese could be extreme stoics under some circumstances and extravagantly emotional under others. It was noted in the data bank that many of the folktales of Terrestrial Japan had been prized for a unique combination of heroism and blatant sentimentality. A favorite legend—and one that Minamoto Kantaro seemed to treasure—was the tale of the Forty-Seven *Ronin,* the classic story of forty-seven samurai whose master was forced to commit seppuku for having attacked—within the grounds of the imperial palace—a nobleman who had diminished his dignity. For this offense, his clan was disbanded and his followers, the forty-seven among them, reduced to penury as *ronin*—masterless samurai. These same men banded together, attacked the nobleman who had caused the misfortune, killed him—and then surrendered to the Shogun's justice. Which consisted of an order to slit their bellies at once.

Kantaro had recounted this 2,500-year-old story to Amaya with tears flowing down his cheeks. "It is, Amaya-san," he said, "a tragic tale." Anya had been amazed to realize that the young man was genuinely moved.

Now as Anya prepared to release the Yamatans from *Glory*'s temporary confinement, she recalled Kantaro's reaction to the gory end of the ninja in Yedo and his stoic acceptance of the fact that his uncle might require him to apologize to the *gaijin* by emulating the Forty-Seven *Ronin* and committing suicide.

It was difficult for a woman, a product of so politically correct a world as New Earth, to reconcile Kantaro's tears and his acceptance of suicide as a means of apology with Kantaro's obvious modernity of outlook and his courage.

She gave *Glory* instructions to unlock and open the valve confining the Yamatans. As it dilated she was struck by the emotional blast of fear and suspicion *Glory* had caused by locking the colonists in place.

The section containing the quarters assigned to the colonists consisted of a large compartment (once, long ago, filled with titanium racks and cold-sleep gear, but now stripped and empty) and a concentric ring of smaller and more livable spaces where the individual daimyos might conduct their own private affairs.

The complex was near—that is, within a kilometer of—the hangar deck where *Dragonfly* and the seven MD ships remaining on board were secured. It was the proximity of the Yamatans' spacecraft that had decided *Glory* to restrain the guests. The Goldenwing had made a computer decision that the colonists were safer and less troublesome confined during the encounter with the Intruder and the Red Sprite. Anya did not expect them to be pleased about *Glory*'s arbitrary decision, and they were not. Inside the dilating valve Amaya found a rank of colonists, not wearing antique armor now, but space armor of obviously sophisticated design, and carrying energy weapons—heavy lazeguns.

Only the typically Japanese clan crests on the space armor recalled the pageantry of several hours before. At the head of the first angry rank stood Kantaro, his titanium armor blazoned with the *mon* containing the three inward-growing hollyhock leaves that had blazoned all that belonged to descendants of Ieyasu Tokugawa.

The cold air of the compartment was rank with the smell of angry, desperate men. Still Wired, Amaya reacted to the Yamatans' battle-pheromones as Mira might have done, with a mix of her own anger and the sort of desperate sexuality mammals feel when faced with danger of death.

She pulled the drogue from her socket, and the raw emotions subsided but did not dissipate completely. She moved easily in the near-null gravity, positioning herself squarely in the open valve.

"Honorable guests," she said more calmly than she felt. "Accept the Goldenwing *Gloria Coelis* syndics' apology for your having been temporarily inconvenienced here in the guest area." Would Duncan be pleased with her slippery manner? Anya wondered. For all the years she had been aboard *Gloria Coelis* she had tried to avoid being the diplomat. But this duty was not avoidable. The Yamatans were seething with outrage. And with fear, she told herself. Even un-Wired, she could smell and taste it. If she had had any doubt that the Terror had been close to the Red Sprite, the rank battle-smell of the Yamatans would convince anyone who had ever encountered the dark Intruder.

The first rank of space-armored daimyo shoved forward. The artificial gravity of their suits gave their movements a brutish, mechanical quality. Did they fight their wars in the same way? If so, this sortie against the killer was doomed.

"Again, honorable sirs," she said. "You have our apologies. But there was no chance to prepare you for the encounter we have unexpectedly just been through. Our enemy has appeared without warning. We have overflown it and are leaving it behind. For the time being, all is well."

She wished she were as certain of that last statement as she sounded. She longed to re-Wire and stay in intimate touch with the swiftly changing situation.

Duncan had foreseen her dilemma. The sound systems in the vast compartment came to life. "Minamoto no Kami, this is Kr-san speaking to you. We have only moments ago had a close encounter with the thing we call the Terror. We believe it is temporarily immobilized and we are using this opportunity to open some space between us. Understand that it may not be possible. In the past, the concept of 'space' has not been meaningful as regards the Terror. But we shall see. We are leaving orbit as I speak. If we are pursued, I will notify you so that you can board your ships and act as you see fit. If we are not taken immediately under attack, I will meet with you and your daimyos on the bridge in one hour of standard time.

"Obey Sailing Master Amaya-san. She is an experienced and competent officer."

Anya took advantage of the cessation of Duncan's voice to select Minamoto Kantaro from the crowd of daimyos. "Take me to the Shogun, Kantaro-sama," she said, ignoring the jostling daimyos.

Kantaro opened his face mask. His cheeks were shiny with sweat. Amaya felt a twinge of sympathy for the Yamatan. She well knew what the first encounter with the dark Outsider did to one's emotions and confidence. The Terror sucked life and warmth and courage out of one's very soul. She had been through it. She knew the vast, destroying *fear* that the Terror imposed on inhabitants of normal space.

"Anya-san," Kantaro said. "I saw Baka Ie and his crew die. Or I think I did. It was as though the life was sucked from their souls. Am I going insane?"

Amaya shook her head. "No, Kantaro-san."

Kantaro's eyes were black, shining, featureless—the eyes of a terrified man. "But Baka wasn't afraid," he protested. "He was filled with joy. Your people said it is fear and anger that calls it. How could Baka's people die like that?"

Anya felt a sagging despair. "We have a great deal to learn about—it—whatever it is. We can't even decide how we should speak of it." She heard her voice go slightly shrill and she brought herself hard under control. "Daimyo," she said formally. "Take me to your uncle."

Kantaro, too, took refuge in formality. He bowed slightly and turned to lead the way.

The Shogun was armored for space like the others, but his helmet stood on a camp stool beside him. Kantaro's cat companion, Hana, lay alertly in his arms. Minamoto's delicate fingers caressed the cat's ears.

"I have been expecting one of you, Anya-san," he said. "My people insisted that we arm and make ready to be expelled into space." He made a grimace. "A trifle melodramatic, given the circumstances, but we are a race of Noh actors."

Anya was amazed to discover that she could discern no fear in the man, nothing to match the discordant suppression of human terror she felt all around her. Hana regarded her calmly out of eyes the color of turquoises.

"Remarkable, isn't she?" Minamoto no Kami said. "While we were all in a near panic arming for space and thinking we were betrayed, she remained as you see her." He regarded Anya steadily. "I must have one of her siblings, Anya-san. There is much they can teach us. As I am certain you know."

Anya Amaya wondered, *Shall I say that I, of all the syndics, remain unchosen?*

Minamoto no Kami said, "Tell me what has just happened. Something cold and black swept through the heart of this ship like an executioner's sword. Kantaro swears he saw Baka Ie and his people die. Saw it or dreamed it." He cupped Hana's small chin and looked into her eyes. "Perhaps it was she who saw Baka and shared the vision with Kantaro. There are legends about far-seeing beasts in our history. But Baka is dead, is that not so?"

"It is so, Shogun," Anya said. "Our bridge recorders made tapes of what could be seen. You will be shown."

"Why were we confined?"

"It was the Goldenwing's decision, Shogun. There was no time to do anything else."

"Do you know what we experienced while we were arming?" The old man seemed suddenly angry.

"I can almost imagine," Anya said.

"The worst thing in the world," Minamoto said.

"Shogun?"

"For each man. His worst imagining. For some death by swordcut. For others by drowning. Asphyxiation. By fire. For me it was a stroke. I was paralyzed, dying very slowly, unable to move, to speak, to feel. Only to die moment by eternal moment." The dark eyes raged. "It all took place in an instant. Or a lifetime. Now that it is past, who can say? But we have each been shown the worst thing, the very worst. Did that happen to you?"

Anya felt a deep pang of guilt. "We were Wired, Shogun. The ship protected us. But we have had the experience you describe. In the Ross Stars. We each had our private death."

The old man's expression softened. "Forgive me, Anya-san. We were angry and frightened. I should have realized that the syndics have been through all this before. We doubted you. Even when we were told of our lost ship out in Honda space we imagined nothing like this. Now we have looked, with you, into the black pit of hell. We understand."

21

THERE IS A DEVIL

•

Anya Amaya guided the Yamatans through the plena back to the hangar deck. It was there, Duncan told her by drogue, that he wanted most of them to stay now, aboard their ships.

"Where is it?" Amaya asked.

"Eight thousand klicks back. At Loss of Signal the Sprite was beginning to fade," Duncan said through her radio-link.

"Is that significant?"

"It may be. But distance won't save us from another encounter. I am convinced it doesn't conform to Einsteinian limits."

"How is that possible?"

"I wish I knew," Duncan said. *"When you have the Yamatans aboard their ships, bring Minamoto no Kami and Kantaro to me."*

"Aye, Captain."

At the valve to the hangar deck, Kantaro asked, "To whom do you speak?"

"To Duncan-san," Anya said. "He wants your people to go aboard their ships and wait."

"Wait? For what? Isn't the enemy just outside?" His unwilling fear made his voice tight.

"The enemy is behind us. We have lost his signal."

"But he is faster than we."

"Far faster, Daimyo," Amaya said.

Kantaro seemed about to make some protest, but Minamoto no Kami ordered him to silence.

"We have chosen to follow Duncan-sama," the Shogun said. "We will do it without complaints."

He spoke to Kantaro, but his words were meant for the daimyos gathered about him in the plenum, Yoshi Eiji of Kai among them. Amaya estimated that he was the most senior of the daimyos who had been commanded by the Shogun to remain behind when the others retreated to Planet Yamato.

The Lord of Kai was not pleased about it. Anya caught strong empathic signals of apprehension and displeasure from him. Anya wondered what he intended to do about it. To her sorrow, however, she was empathic and not clairvoyant.

The crowd of clansmen and samurai pressed around her. As they did she caught another empathic signal. This one from a person unknown, but very nearby. It was a dark sending, filled with a kind of black arrogance. She searched the faces of the Yamatans. But her Centauri background did not serve her well. New Earth was a world without ethnic Mongoloid people. There were ethnic characteristics behind which a trained mind could hide from a Caucasian, core beliefs that shut out Anya's probings. The ninja was in this crowd of jostling, angry warriors. There was no doubt of it. Did Kantaro know? Did Minamoto no Kami? There was no way of knowing.

If I had a cat partner, Anya Amaya thought bitterly, *I would not now fail in my duty to my ship and my Master and Commander.*

She opened the valve to the hangar deck and stepped aside. To Minamoto no Kami she said, more brusquely than she intended, "Instruct your people to get aboard their ships and be ready for new orders. Then you and Kantaro-sama must return with me to the bridge. Be quick. There is very little time, Shogun."

Minamoto Kantaro found himself responding peculiarly to the firm orders he was receiving from the Sailing Master. His first response was compliance—such was the strength of Anya-san's character. He had found himself reacting to the power of the outworlder's personality as long ago as their flight with Kr-san to the Shogun's garden, when the threat they faced was theoretical and seemed subject to a considered, dispassionate solution. Even then, it was not the Yamatan way to permit women to command. True, on occasion, Minamoto no Kami had shown signs of a willingness to countenance change in the age-old Japanese tradition of female subservience. But, Kantaro thought, any true recasting of the social order of Planet Yamato was a fantasy.

Still, on Anya-san's own ground matters were different. She willingly subordinated herself to Kr-san, but that was because of his rank rather than the biological fact of his being male. As Kantaro trailed Anya and his uncle, the Shogun, he felt out of his depth, as though he were losing contact with the verities he had known since childhood.

Worse still was the secret guilt he felt at having been involved, before the syndics appeared in the Tau Ceti System, in the business of hiring ninjas as a defense against the changes the Starmen would surely bring to Planet Yamato.

In a matter of a day and some few hours things had changed. Kantaro's fear was no longer of changes, but of the killer he had been instrumental in bringing aboard the Goldenwing. *I must do something,* he thought. But what? A ninja was adept at subtle violence as well as a master of disguise. To unmask Tsunetomo was beyond the capabilities of an ordinary man. So what then? Rely on the Starmen to apprehend a Master of Ninjas? Minamoto Kantaro's very genes seemed to cry out against such a betrayal of his essential Yamatan nature.

I thank the Goddess, he thought, *that the attacks on Kr-san's life have failed. But what now? Where will we be if the next attempt succeeds?*

Kantaro was discovering that even for a Yamatan aristocrat absolution for attempted murder was not easily come by. One simply did not extricate oneself easily from treachery on so grand a scale. The ninja had not disappeared, nor, Kantaro suspected, had he meekly retreated back to Planet Yamato with the daimyos the Shogun had dismissed. The Mayor of Yedo remembered the encounter in the grove in the Shogun's garden. *Men like Tsunetomo vanish like smoke,* he thought, *but never before their task is done.*

What would Amaya-san think if she knew? More to the point, what would she recommend that the Master of this great vessel do? Opening the hangar deck and ejecting the colonists into space naked as newborns was not an outlandish notion to a man born and raised on Yamato.

He felt a soft touch on his shoulder. It was Hana. She had materialized from somewhere, gripping the padding of his armor with imperceptible gentleness. She thrust her temple against his ear and trilled softly.

Without his volition, his spirits rose, and as they did so Anya Amaya turned to glance at him. Sometimes between the syndics and ordinary men flashed some extraordinarily powerful connections. He had had the strong and urgent feeling that Anya-san responded to him as a man. She still did. But suddenly he felt a spike of envy from her.

For a moment that confused him, and then he realized that she envied him *Hana.* For a second moment he experienced an almost childish satisfaction that this woman who so attracted him sexually while simultaneously intimidating him could wish for anything that he possessed.

He was admonished for that thought with an almost inaudible growl from the small cat on his shoulder. The statement was not in human words, but its meaning was unmistakable: *"I am not owned. I am not possessed. I am Hana."*

Thinking to avoid shocking the Yamatans with the sight of near naked syndics in pods, Wired to the ship, Duncan had considered conducting his war council with the Shogun and his people on the skydeck under the carapace. But he decided against that because it had become necessary (as it was inevitable that it should be) that the Yamatans see the people with whom they had decided to cast their lots *as they were.*

Until now there had been neither necessity nor opportunity to allow the colonists the sight of Goldenwing *Gloria Coelis's* bridge-crew at their proper stations. Duncan knew from experience that it could be a daunting sight. As a boy recruit, he had been stunned by the sight of the near immortal Starmen naked in the gel of their pods, their heads sprouting the grotesque segmented cable of the drogue that connected them to their vessel.

Duncan had mentioned this in passing to Minamoto Kantaro, who had replied with the expected disclaimer about how any sophisticated person would realize that a ship as vast as a Goldenwing could not be sailed in any ordinary fashion. But many a promising relationship had foundered on the reefs of good intentions and well-meaning tolerance.

Now, however, there was no time for a leisurely indoctrination. First Minamoto no Kami and Kantaro, then all of the daimyos and MD crewmen aboard, must see, and have confidence in, the age-old techniques by which the great, silent ship was operated.

There was the additional consideration that the view from the transparent carapace was calculated to affect the instinctively isolationist colonials adversely as they watched their Yamato recede astern at an ever faster pace as *Glory*'s delta increased.

Some concession to the real situation was required, however. Duncan had surrendered the con to Buele and assigned the task of sail trim to Damon Ng so that he could meet the Shogun and his people looking somewhat more normal than he did when he was connected to *Glory*'s mainframe.

The holograph of the space within a five-hundred-kilometer radius of *Glory* still hovered in air between the crew pods and the interface wall with its peculiarly out-of-date potpourri of analog, digital and empathic gauges and manual controls—all the seldom-used instruments of human physical control. The Yamatans were technically literate enough to understand the purpose of the isolation pods.

The holo's version of Yamato was nearly complete, save for the slice of planet that lay outside of the exterior imaging cameras' field of vision. From *Glory*'s viewing angle the main feature of the planet they were leaving was the vast cyclonic disturbance that raged with demonic intensity over the planet's north pole.

Violent flashes of light betrayed the intensity of the storm. Yamato's northern hemisphere was into its spring, approaching the vernal equinox. At precisely this time of year were the storms most fully charged with energy. The thing was feeding, Duncan thought. Somehow it was draining energy from the aurora and the storm. In another man it would have been a guess. In an empath of Duncan's quality it was an epiphany.

Duncan wondered: *How does it know? Does it perceive reality as we do?* No Red Sprite was visible from this viewing angle, but oddly prehensile columns of purplish light probed the northern aurora from a point beyond the limb of the planet.

We have gained a little time, Duncan thought. And then, bitterly: *What does that really mean? The Terror seems simply to ignore the Einsteinian conditions that frame existence for human beings.* What, after all, did time mean to a thing that could move with the speed of thought?

"Duncan?" It was Anya Amaya on the voice com-link.

"Yes, Anya."

"We are on our way. What is happening outside?"

"So far, nothing. We are outward bound from Yamato. The monkeys appear to have resolved their psychological reluctance to work. They are still in the tops watching the sail-set." Duncan essayed a thin smile. *"They will never replace your fine touch, Sailing Master."*

There was a momentary hesitation, and then Anya said, *"Thank you, Duncan,"* and broke the link.

Duncan made a temporary connection. *"Broni,"* he sent, *"set a course to keep Hideyoshi and Nobunaga between us and Yamato."* Once again he warned himself against a surfeit of hope. If the Intruder remained content to stay in Yamatan space gorging on the planetary plasmas of Yamato's northern lights for as much as a single day, the odds would increase enormously in *Glory's* favor. But what did distance mean to the Terror?

A day ago it had killed an MD ship 120,000,000 kilometers away near the gas giant Honda. And only hours ago it had killed the Hokkaidans. Were such attacks senseless expenditures of energy rather than a form of feeding? If so, why would so powerful an entity do such things? What benefits could it derive?

Pleasure? Simple pleasure? Was that possible? The idea was so revolting that Duncan was sickened. If that were the why of it, then the priests and sages had always been right, he thought.

There *is* a Devil.

22

WARRIORS OF DARKNESS

•

Under the stumpy delta wing of their largest mass-depletion spacecraft, the retainers chosen from the Kai contingent stood uncertainly with their daimyo. Yoshi Eiji had no wish still to be on board the Goldenwing, most particularly not now, when whatever it was that the Yamatans had come to fight lay an unknown distance behind them.

It was in exactly situations like this one that daimyos were traditionally expected to earn their privileges and rank. Since the days of medieval Japan on Earth, daimyos in extremis had gathered their samurai around them and prepared for battle, sometimes in merely practical ways but often in the meditative way of the ancient Zen warriors who sought victory but were always prepared for death.

But Yoshi was samurai in name only. He was a "latecomer," a descendant of the second wave of colonists who arrived aboard the Goldenwing *Musashi*. He was no warrior and he had no wish to be. He was an engineer by training, a rich man by inheritance and an entrepreneur by inclination. He understood quite well that the Shogun, Minamoto no Kami, had ordered him to remain aboard not as a mark of favor, but in order to keep him under surveillance. He knew that the Shogun suspected him of being involved in the ninja affair, and so he was. But what Minamoto no Kami did not know was that Yoshi's cautiousness had kept him untainted by any *direct* contact with the Order of Ninjas. Now that it was rumored that the Order had put another assassin aboard the Goldenwing to redress the first assassin's failure, the Lord of Kai was at a loss. He looked about him at the faces of his retainers. Being naturally penurious, he did not maintain an army of clansmen in Kai. When he had been selected to join the conference aboard Goldenwing *Gloria Coelis* he had made up the numbers required to enhance his station from the many *ronin* who roamed from Domain to Domain on Yamato upholding the age-old tradition of the wandering warriors of Japan.

Planet Yamato was a fertile ground for resurrection of the ancient ways, and though the planet's history was not appreciably different from that of other colonial worlds, the nature of its people encouraged a wistful replication of their storied past.

For Yoshi Eiji, however, the situation encouraged no wistfulness. He had no wish to be here. It was clearly dangerous. There was no profit in it. And worst of all, outraging his entrepreneurial instincts was the fact that he now stood in the hangar deck beside one of his hideously expensive spacecraft, surrounded by strangers. He looked suspiciously at his "retainers" and wondered which of them was the substitute assassin put aboard by the Order of Ninjas. There were twenty clansmen, and one was surely what the others would call a warrior of darkness.

The clansmen of Honshu and Kyushu who had remained at the Shogun's command had dispersed to their own MD craft, and the barge crew was already aboard *Dragonfly,* preparing that ship for flight. No one on the hangar deck had any notion of what would happen next, but all expected a swift encounter with whatever it was that had destroyed the Hokkaidan MD as it attempted reentry over Yamato's northern ice.

"Daimyo." The speaker was one of the new retainers, a middle-aged man named Ishida Minoru. "We should be preparing ourselves for battle."

Yoshi regarded the man disdainfully. Many of the other lords of domains employed masters-at-arms or chief retainers who were able to marshal the clansmen into some semblance of order. But Yoshi Eiji had never done that. The pay of a chief retainer was high because most men holding that rank were swordmasters, archers, adept in the art of the traditional weapons.

Occasionally one might hire an ex-soldier, but these were uncommon on Yamato. The planetary wars had ended generations ago, and former soldiers were rare on the islands. Now, for the daimyo of Kai to be accosted by a recently hired nonentity seeking, one supposed, to distinguish himself enough to justify permanent employment, irritated the distraught Yoshi.

"Oh, should we be?" Yoshi said coldly. "How do you suggest we do that?"

"I noted aboard the *Dragonfly* the Shogun has *shinai* and *bokken,* Yoshi-sama. I am skilled at *kendo.*"

"Are you, indeed?" The man's confident manner irritated Yoshi Eiji more and more. "And you think that a fencing demonstration would stiffen the backbones of my employees?"

The man's face seemed suddenly to lose much of its plasticity and harden into a mask. "The battle may soon be within this ship, Daimyo. Some strengthening of spines would not be amiss."

Yoshi looked more carefully at the *ronin.* It seemed he was seeing him for the first time. A cold chill moved into the pit of the daimyo's stomach. *By the Goddess,* he thought, *how could I have missed it?* Here, in plain view, was the ninja. He had no doubt of it. Darkness seemed suddenly to gather around the stranger.

"It is time to take command, Daimyo," Ishida said.

Yoshi felt a flash of cold panic. Take charge and do what? Fulfill his ninja contract? Kill the Starman Kr-san? And then what? Yoshi had heard that ninjas were single-minded to the point of madness. The possible consequences of having this man discovered to be part of the Kai contingent aboard the Goldenwing were suddenly terrifying. Minamoto no Kami would not hesitate for an instant to order a seppuku. And failure to comply would bring the strangler's garrotte or a swordsman's thrust. The old man was capable of ordering it with scarcely a second thought.

"Come with me, Ishida-san," Yoshi said. "The rest of you stay here where you are and await word from the bridge." He led the way around the spacecraft and stopped well out of the other's hearing.

"I think I know you," he said, hoping his voice did not tremble.

"I am Ishida, Daimyo."

"I do not think so, ninja-san." Yoshi met the flat, black eyes with difficulty. Instinct told him that to admit fear of the man was to risk setting him in motion. "I know why you are here. I approve of it. You must know that I was one of the first to subscribe to the idea that a member of the Order was the only response to the outworlders. Now, however . . ."

The face remained expressionless and craggy, like a skull *kami* at the head of a sand garden.

Yoshi's voice failed him as his throat went dry. He began again. "Understand me. I know why you are here. I see no alternative to what you must do. But not *now*, Ishida-san. Out here we are totally at the Starmen's mercy. Have you any idea of what we can expect from them if Kr-san is—injured?" He could not bring himself to say "killed."

Yoshi had seen holofilms of a great beast of the homeworld, the great white shark. For three million years it had swum the seas of Earth. For three million more it would continue as before, a creature totally without fear, striking where and when it chose. Ishida's eyes were like those of a great white, Yoshi thought.

I must manage the murder of this madman, the Lord of Kai thought. *I must manage it before he fulfills the task for which he has come aboard.*

"Wait," he whispered. "Wait until we are free of the danger *out there*, Ishida-sama. When that time comes I will offer you all the resources of the Domain of Kai."

The flat, blank shark's eyes looked at him unblinking. "I will not need the resources of Kai, Daimyo," the ninja said. "Only these." He held up his brown, callused hands for the Lord of Kai to see.

"I had hoped for more time, Shogun," Duncan said. "But that hope is denied. We have encountered our nemesis again—and in a form unfamiliar to us." He manipulated the holograph controls until an image of the Red Sprite hovered over the polar storm on Planet Yamato. "You must let yourself imagine the proper scale. Take note of how the red disk is situated directly over the planetary pole. We think that the Sprite is a manifestation of the phenomenon we have taken to calling, for obvious reasons, the Terror. Have you ever seen a display like this in the polar sky of Yamato?"

Minamoto no Kami and Kantaro were reeling from the impact of the strangeness on the bridge. Both had heard, had been told, and understood that Goldenwing syndics sailed their great ships from isolation pods that strengthened the connection between the Starman's brain and the ship's systems. But it was one thing to be told, another to see at first hand members of a Goldenwing bridge-crew lying nearly naked in the conductive gel within the pods, long cables seemingly sprouting from their skulls to join them to the banked consoles on the bulkheads.

To the Yamatans, a highly innovative technical race, the surroundings here on *Glory*'s bridge seemed at once archaic and like a scene drawn from some slightly mad futurist's imagination. Many of the banks of instruments on the consoles were of analog design—a thing not seen on Planet Yamato for two hundred or more years. The pods themselves were of metal with permanently transparent closures. Yamatans were accustomed to enclosures that reacted to ambient conditions in their homes and workplaces and in their spacecraft.

However, the holograph image that *Glory* had reconstructed was of a clarity and intensity that far exceeded the ability of Yamatan engineers to duplicate. The storm raging over the Yamatan polar region lay beneath the thing Kr-san had called the Red Sprite. It was impossible not to suspect that there was a connection among the storm, the Sprite and the high combs of light of the aurora borealis.

"You cannot see the intruder, Shogun," Kr-san said. "But it is there. This image is constructed from data gathered only moments after the Hokkaidan mass-depletion ship was consumed."

Kantaro looked at the display with dread. The image radiated menace.

"Consumed, Kr-san?"

"Yes, Kantaro-san. We are so accustomed to the thing that we forget others are not. We believe that it consumes whatever it attacks."

Two of the Goldenwing cats, Mira and Damon's Pronker, crouched on the pod holding the Rigger, uttered low growls. Hana leaped from Kantaro's shoulder to the pod and touched her nose, in silent exchange, to Mira's. Pronker hissed softly at his sibling. Anya watched the exchange. Was the expression of displeasure because Hana now carried Kantaro's alien scent? Or were the cats simply behaving as animals? For months Anya had, with repressed resentment, disregarded Mira's Folk, but now it seemed fitting that she should look carefully and try to understand what was happening.

The Shogun and Kantaro stared fixedly at the holograph. The aurora was a common sight on Planet Yamato, but neither man had ever seen it from above. Nor had they ever seen anything remotely resembling the Red Sprite.

"I don't understand you, Kr-san," Kantaro said. "This manifestation is a part of the threat?"

"We believe so, Kantaro-san," Duncan said. "There was nothing like it during our encounter in the Ross Stars, or before that in Deep Space. There may *be* nothing to see. Or at least nothing that we can see. We believe it comes from outside our space-time from some reality where, perhaps, light does not exist. We have reason to believe that in its own medium it travels unlimited distances instantaneously."

The syndics' empathic Talent warned them that Kantaro was finding this hard to believe.

"Nothing can exceed lightspeed, Kr-san. Nothing," the Yamatan declared.

"Not in the universe as *we* know it, nephew," the Shogun said softly.

Amaya whispered, as if to herself, "The sound of one hand clapping."

"Just so, Sailing Master," the Shogun said. "A follower of the Buddha has less trouble than most accepting such a life principle. In precolonial times didn't some Terrestrial cosmologists hypothesize about an infinity of multiple universes? If universes are infinite in number, is the idea of a universe without space or time so impossible then?"

Duncan said, "On Planet Armstrong of Barnard's Star there is a school of physics taught that states time and space form a Klein bottle. Others say no, that is too complex and inelegant, the universe must be shaped like a Moebius strip, finite and one-sided."

"Intellectual games," Kantaro protested.

"Perhaps so," Duncan said. "But our adversary is no intellectual game—it is real, and it can intrude into our space-time. Each time it does it comes to destroy. We don't know why. But we must try to stop it, or this is as far into Deep Space as Mankind is ever likely to go."

"What action do you intend to take, Kr-san?" the Shogun asked.

"I had hoped we would have more time to plan," Duncan said. "But that's unlikely now. Our first concern is to lure the Intruder away from Yamato. Our last experiences with it suggest to me that it has learned most of what it finds necessary about human beings. It isn't complimentary to us, Shogun. In spite of how well we have fared in the business of predation and fighting, we are not formidable by comparison with the threat. That leaves us guile."

"Can we deceive it?" Kantaro demanded.

"We believe it to be intelligent and sentient. So it can be deceived. If we are subtle enough," Anya Amaya said.

Duncan broke off to address *Glory* by spoken word. "Any change in position of the Sprite?"

"A change in intensity only, Master and Commander."

"That may mean it is surfeited," Duncan said. "We have to assume so."

From the wall com-units came Dietr Krieg's voice from the surgery. "We must keep the thing's movements from the colonists, Captain."

"That is not acceptable, Kr-san," Kantaro said sharply.

"Not even possible, Kantaro-san," Duncan said. "There is no way we can disguise our emotional sendings. I feel certain that we are leaving a wake of psychic disturbances behind us. If we could be found in Deep Space, there is no way we can hide here." He turned to Minamoto no Kami. "I intend to use one of your ships and crew to trail behind *Glory*, between the ship and the intruder."

"With such members of my contingent as I choose to send, Kr-san."

"Not you, Shogun."

"No," Minamoto no Kami said sadly. "I am too old to be of use in a battle." He turned to his nephew. "But you, Kantaro. If the Minamoto are to survive, a Minamoto must have a part in the battle for survival."

Amaya was looking aghast at Duncan. "You, Duncan? Bait?"

"If need be, Anya."

"Glory won't permit it," she said desperately.

"It is *Glory* who commands it, Sailing Master."

The Shogun looked thoughtfully at the holograph. "Out of a universe without time or light," he murmured, lifting his gaze to the two syndics standing before him. "We Yamatans have our own cruel version of the principle. The intruder comes to take lives like a ninja. There comes a time when we are all warriors of darkness. Say what you require, Kr-san. If it is within Yamato's power, you shall have it."

PART II

•

When the time comes, there is no moment for reasoning.
                    —Yamamoto Tsunetomo, *Hagakure*

23

"YOU MAY BECOME THE LAST
SAILING MASTER"

•

From a distance of 150,000 kilometers the ruddy surface of Yamato's planetary ocean glistens like a sheet of burnished copper. The cyclonic storm systems of the Yamatan spring mottle the surface of the planet with light and shadow. Yamato has completed one full revolution since Glory broke orbit. The Gold-enwing's present course is a translunar injection aimed at sling-shotting around Moon Hideyoshi and then on to Tokugawa, the methane satellite Yamatan scientists believe is the smaller of an early two-planet system with Yamato itself. From Tokugawa, the plan is to leave the plane of Amaterasu's ecliptic in the hope that the intruder will be distracted from populated Planet Yamato and Moon Hideyoshi. From the command pilot's seat aboard the mass-depletion vessel chosen by Shogun Minamoto no Kami and his daimyos for the first hazardous probe at the intruder, Duncan can see the western hemisphere of Planet Yamato from pole to pole. He is concerned that the Red Sprite is no longer visible. The lack makes the conditions of a possible encounter even more uncertain than Buele had calculated.

The Supernumerary, having assimilated almost the entire canon of knowledge about the Terror possessed by *Glory,* had warned that if the Sprite was, as Duncan suspected, a manifestation of the Intruder's manner of ingesting planetary plasmas, its disappearance could only mean that its task was completed and the Terror was charged with what must surely be trillions of gigawatts of electrical energy generated by the vast dynamo of Planet Yamato's aurora borealis.

Because the syndics had never actually seen the Terror, only its horrifying effects and manifestations, Duncan had hoped that the Sprite would remain in place above Yamato's pole. He desperately needed a semifixed manifestation of the intruder in an environment of light, time and space. But this had not happened.

The Terror might be temporarily inert, but it was not far away. Duncan could feel its presence, as could Mira, Hana, and Pronker, who prowled the small bridge of the MD ship, investigating nooks and corners, all the while lashing their tails, meowing and growling.

Amaya had protested Duncan's decision to take Damon as the second syndic in the MD probe. She insisted that the task was rightly hers and that Damon and Pronker were needed aboard *Glory* to handle the monkeys and be available for sudden changes in the sailplan. Duncan rejected her contention, leaving her no room for discussion or recourse. "You are the Sailing Master, Anya," he said. "You remain to command in my absence. That's the end of it. No more argument."

Before boarding the MD craft in the hangar deck, Duncan had instructed *Glory*'s computer to record his personal recommendations for the future operation of Goldenwing *Gloria Coelis*.

Buele would be surprised, Duncan knew, if he survived the coming encounter and managed a return, that Amaya would be *Glory*'s Master only until Buele was ready to assume command. Knowing Anya's pride and her drive for excellence, it had not been an easy message to convey.

"A Talent of such dimensions as Buele's can't be wasted, Anya," Duncan recorded in his *Sailing Instructions*. *"It has been my intention to groom the boy for command. His Talent is greater than any of ours. Eventually, he must be Master and Commander of* Glory.*"* In his Personal Log, intended to be heard only by Anya, he said, *"I leave it to you, dear Anya, to know when it is time to relinquish command to Buele. Until then, keep the syndicate together. You may become the last Sailing Master of the last Goldenwing. It is a task I would demand of no one else."*

For a long and painful moment Duncan had wished he had someone upon whom he could lean, someone with whom he could share the responsibility for the gamble he was taking. But there was only *Glory*, and in the final analysis *Glory* was a machine—a wondrous construct, but still a device. Computers were marvels of calculation and organization, but original thought came only from living beings. He absently caressed Mira's small head as he reminded himself that all he, all *anyone*, knew of the Terror came from encounters in the Ross Stars and in Deep Space. *We have never even* seen *the Intruder,* Duncan thought bleakly. *All we know is what it has done—what it has destroyed as we watched. And all that* Glory *knows is what her computer has filed away in her vast data bank. Lines of code, no more.*

The theory that the Red Sprites were subsets of the Terror in a gravity well, feeding on the immense manifestations of the belts of cosmic energy surrounding planets, was only that, he told himself. A theory.

His thoughts were too disturbing to dwell upon. Better to concentrate upon the second tier of problems his leaving *Glory* to fight independently created. Better to convince himself that he was not abdicating too great a responsibility to Anya Amaya.

Duncan understood what he was asking of the New Earther, but he was clear in his mind that only she, of the present syndics of Goldenwing *Gloria Coelis,* could protect his beloved ship against an uncertain future.

I have, in effect, written a will, Duncan thought grimly. A bitter necessity. In other times and circumstance, aboard vessels crewed by hundreds, as were the clipper ships of ancient Earth, command would devolve, upon the death or loss of a vessel's Master, to the next in rank.

But sailing the tachyon trades aboard a Goldenwing crewed by six Starmen made it imperative that command fall to the syndic with the greatest abilities. The paucity of Talent had historically made it necessary to sail the Goldenwings with as few as four and seldom more than a dozen empathic crew members. There was no question of command following the archaic notion of rank.

Buele would not be ready to command for years, but eventually he would take over *Glory* because his was the ability—no, perhaps even the destiny—to become *Glory*'s Master and Commander. He had the Talent without which the great ship simply could not be sailed.

As the MD pilot, Yamaguchi Kendo, a Kaian boy of not more than nineteen planetary years, let the small spacecraft fall astern of *Glory,* the others aboard—Duncan, Damon, Kantaro, and Ishida, the sullen retainer of the Lord of Kai put aboard by Yoshi Eiji's specific demand—searched the sky for some sign of unusual menace. They could discern none.

But the Intruder *was* nearby. The cats remained tense and quarrelsome, crouching, gathered as if to attack, with ears flattened and warning mutters for anyone approaching them.

Mira's response to the retainer Ishida was particularly hostile. Duncan studied him intently. The man's hooded eyes were blank, almost without sheen. Was this the man who had attacked him in the carapace? Duncan wondered. If he were, Mira would tell Duncan in a dozen different ways. But at the moment the new surroundings and the growing separation between Mira and her Folk seemed to have silenced the small cat.

"It is all right, queen," Duncan sent carefully, *"we are safe together."*

Does she believe that? he wondered. *Do I believe it?*

Duncan watched Kantaro Minamoto carefully. The young Mayor of Yedo was staring intently at Lord Kai's retainer. The ruler of Kai had insisted that Ishida was the best of his warriors, and highly trained in the art of spaceship handling. Whether this was true remained to be seen. Duncan lived with the suspicion that Ishida's talents lay in a vastly different direction. But only when Mira became less distrait would she be able to tell him.

24

ANYA'S FAMILIAR

•

Distraught by Duncan's decision to occupy what the Yamatans called the fighting chair aboard the MD craft, Anya Amaya fled down the plena toward the carapace deck where she and Duncan had so many times made love.

On the bridge Broni and Buele lay Wired and naked in their pods. Their enhanced personas ranged far on either side of *Glory*'s track.

On the hangar deck the Shogun and his people waited aboard the barge *Dragonfly* while Kantaro and the retainer Ishida joined Duncan on the MD ship.

As Anya flew through the fabric tubes she could sense the unseen presence of Mira's Folk—some, but not all, cats who had been enhanced by Dietr's experimental surgeries.

By this time the Starmen of *Glory* had lost track of the number of still unnamed felines belonging to Mira's pride who roamed the vast empty compartments of the ship. Dietr contended that he had not artificially inseminated any of the last generation of cats, that they had been reproducing in the normal, feline way. Which Anya had no reason to doubt, but she still found it difficult to believe that the recently born no longer required Dietr's surgical interventions in order to Wire to *Glory*'s computer. All she had ever learned about genetics (and genetics was a subject of surpassing interest on New Earth) told her that what Dietr reported could not be so.

Yet Duncan had cautioned her against closing her mind to any possibilities. He loved to quote Twentieth-Century Terrestrials, the last thinkers, he said, before the nightfall of the Jihad. One of these men, with the strange name of Eden Phillpotts, once wrote that the universe was "full of magical things, patiently waiting for our wits to grow sharper."

How like the Master and Commander that was, Anya thought. She felt *Glory*'s interior winds drying the tears on her cheeks. *Damn you, Duncan,* she thought bitterly. *I am weeping for you already, mourning you even as we fly to our own destruction.*

There was no chance, she told herself, no chance at all that Duncan could survive an encounter with the Intruder in so flimsy a shell as a Yamatan mass-depletion ship. Space would open up unseen, the Terror would slip through, raging, and consume all it could reach.

If we had enough time, the New Earther thought. *If we had hours and days to put distance between us and the darkness, its powers might be diminished.* But it was nearby. She could feel its presence, stirring, pressing, questing. What was Minamoto Kantaro thinking now? No longer could the young man take refuge in ancient samurai traditions. No armor, no war fans. Only the thin shell of a flimsy, experimental relativistic spaceship.

Was the Terror watching? She wondered why it had not already swept Goldenwing *Gloria Coelis* and her people into hell. Duncan must have been right when he guessed that the Red Sprite somehow held it immobile as it drank in the power of Yamato's aurora borealis. But now the Sprite had vanished. Was the Terror waking?

The Sailing Master reached the carapace deck and dove through the barely open valve into the familiar, starlit cavern. She hastily opened a drogue compartment and, pulling the drogue cable after her, leaped upward toward the transparent overhead fifty meters above. She spanned the silent distance, settling the drogue into her skull socket. She hungered for privacy to face her grief, yet she ached for the comfort of the Wired state.

As *Glory* expanded her Talent, reality exploded around her. The enhancement suffused her consciousness. The gestalt provided by the ship and by her shipmates was warm and familiar. Each time it happened, it seemed to be happening for the first time. Every time the drogue locked into her skull it was the rebirth of the raw girl from New Earth. The universe pinwheeled into wonder all around her.

She projected her anima past the carapace, beyond the glowing net of the rig, away from the gleaming gold of the hectares of skylar *Glory* flew. It seemed that the tachyon wind's particles penetrated her flesh to tingle against her blood and bones. She felt as airy as one of the meter-long dragonflies of New Earth's narrow floral jungle. It was said that the short-lived creatures were so finely made that mere light kept them aloft in the still air of equatorial New Earth.

It had been months since Duncan and Anya had floated in the starshot darkness of this vast space. Yet the very fabric of the bulkheads seemed to have absorbed the psychic memories of all that had transpired here. She closed her eyes and remembered the slow floating lovemaking here in the time before the planetfall at Voerster, where Duncan fell in love with Eliana Voerster, Broni's mother, and then lost her to some stern sense of duty she had felt she must obey.

Her friend and Captain had turned inward, sustained by his own sense of duty to *Glory* and to all who sailed in her. But Anya thought, *My simple love was something he could always accept, even after you, Eliana of Voerster.*

It was here, too, that Anya the Sailing Master instructed the children of the ship, Broni and Buele, who had never truly seen the stars until they emerged from Dietr's surgery as Wired Starmen.

At this very moment the animas of the two young Voersterians were out beyond *Glory*'s bow-wave, accompanied by their feline familiars, guarding the ship from ahead as Duncan guarded her from behind, where the Terror prowled.

Dietr, Wired in his surgery, greeted her wordlessly. He had been concerned about her from the moment Duncan announced that he was taking the fighting chair in the trailing MD craft. The Cybersurgeon did not delude himself that he was an expert on the psychology of human interactions, but he had made a study of wars and weapons and he was not impressed with Yamatan military preparedness. Their armament was capable, the Cybersurgeon thought, of pyrotechnics and not much else. The combination of Yamatan arms and Duncan's stern sense of duty had all the syndics concerned, Anya Amaya most of all.

"Anya, everyone aboard is nominal," Dietr sent. *"Even the colonials are reasonably calm."*

Amaya was not so certain of that. The Yamatans were more sophisticated than Dietr Krieg credited. They lived an interior life, deeply affected by their admixture of Zen and animist religions. This was a mind-set that Dietr was incapable of penetrating. They could be on the verge of an emotional outbreak and the Cybersurgeon would know nothing of it until the storm broke.

Anya felt the disapproval of Dietr's familiar, Paracelsus, reacting to her reservations about the Cybersurgeon. It was astonishing, Amaya thought, how well matched to his or her human associate each cat had become. One could almost imagine Para meowing with a Terrestrial German accent.

The notion brought a near-smile. She wiped at her eyes with the heels of her hands, as she had long ago as a child on New Earth.

She felt a distant sending from Duncan. She could not decipher it fully, but she felt his concern for her and the caress of his unique mind. How she envied the other syndics with their feline familiars. She had seen at once how the cats facilitated the empathic bond among the Starmen. It was not fair that only she should still be isolated.

A year ago, she thought, the idea of describing her state as "isolated" would never have occurred to her. But much had changed aboard *Glory* since Mira's first litter began to mature. Now, with the prowling felines everywhere in the ship, a whole new level of empathic interdependence was standard. What more it was, Amaya did not know. She knew only that she was less a part of life aboard *Glory* than she had been.

She twisted so that she lay in the air with her face upward, painted golden by the sunlight reflected from the great shining sails of skylar above her. Beyond lay the hard, methane yellow disk of Tokugawa, presently framed between the starboard foremast and its supporting shrouds. Farther beyond still lay the dusting of stars that formed the eternal background for a Goldenwing's celestial hemisphere. To port lay the star nearest Tau Ceti, Epsilon Eridani, which the Yamatans called *Eridanusu*, five light-years away. So near, in fact, that one could almost see the sixteen points of light that were Epsilon Eridani's solar system of gas giants.

The light of Amaterasu played on the concave surface of *Glory*'s sails from astern. Anya tried to make out the reflection of the MD ship, but she could not. The reddish light of Amaterasu was too bright on the stacked courses, stays'ls and mains.

Broni and Buele were doing a creditable job of sail-handling, she thought. Their feline familiars were making it easier for them to deal with the temperamental monkeys, whom Anya could see, in brief flashes, as they moved through the rig.

The cats were sharpening everyone's reactions and responses. Every syndic was performing at a steadily higher level. *Except me,* Anya thought bitterly. *Damn them.*

Duncan, even though he was kilometers astern, must have caught her momentary anger. She could feel his swift disapproval, followed by his empathic sending of support and control.

She was tempted to remove the drogue from her socket, and the temptation appalled her. She had never, ever, considered hiding from her shipmates.

She felt a soft thump on her breast and a tingle of pinpricks. She found herself looking closely into the face of a tiny black-and-white kitten whose eyes were the color of topazes. The small face was an inch from hers. The tiny needle-claws were fixed in her skinsuit.

Her first reaction was instinctive. She caught the small cat and pushed it away so that it spun helplessly in the near-zero gravity. The result was a twisting recovery and an angry mew of protest.

Before she could retreat, Anya felt the claws in her shoulder. The kitten had swiftly returned and fixed itself once more to Anya's skinsuit. It lowered its head and butted Anya's cheek. The Sailing Master was shocked at the clarity of the sending. Before she could disengage the tiny critter, she heard an explosive command in her mind.

"Don't!"

Anya was stunned to realize that she had received the command so clearly. It had even been delivered with a New Earth arrogance Anya had not heard in years.

"You are mine," the kitten sent.

It isn't possible, the Sailing Master thought. *Cats have no human language.*

The little beast was female. That came through with great clarity.

"Where have you come from?" Amaya asked.

Was it a kind of madness to address a creature that could not be more than two months old as though it were an intelligent human being?

Amaya was rewarded with a sending of confused images.

The Sailing Master saw a long flight through familiar plena. The view was from behind, and she felt in her own muscles the determination of a small creature working very hard to catch up. From this perspective the Amaya ahead was a fleeing giantess. There followed a swift leap though a closing valve. And at last, satisfaction. Huntress's claws firmly fixed in . . . Anya Amaya.

Anya cupped the kitten in her two hands and looked into the topaz eyes. *Artemis,* the Sailing Master thought. *What else?*

Despite the fears and concerns of the moment, Anya Amaya, syndic and native of New Earth, felt a great warming in her breast. *At last,* she thought, *at last.*

The kitten squirmed in her hands, struggling to be free. Amaya sensed her outrage at being restrained. The message was crystal clear: *"I am not a pet."*

"You have much to discover that will delight you, Sailing Master."

The sending came from Duncan. It was miraculous in its clarity, swift and distinct. It had come from Duncan to Mira to *Glory* to Artemis to Anya.

Anya released the small cat and remained very still until Artemis anchored herself again firmly to the skinsuit.

Anya Amaya sent, *"I hope I have time to learn, Master and Commander."*

Anya felt a soft tattoo on her shoulder. The little cat was kneading her, doing what Broni called making bread, by pressing first one small paw and then the other on Anya's flesh.

Unwilling to disturb Artemis's gesture of trust, Anya Amaya floated silent and unmoving in the still air of the carapace deck. The stars overhead slowly rotated through the glowing rig as *Glory* changed attitude. Long spears of red sunlight strobed through the mist of spars and monofilament. Anya closed her eyes and listened to the soft, whispering purr of the small creature on her shoulder.

A warm contentment totally unsuited to the moment and to the hazards stalking the ship suffused Anya.

We are being robbed, she thought. *We have a* right *to feel at rest, to feel united to our ship and our shipmates. So stay alert, syndic, lest the darkness know and attack you for anger or for joy. Control your animus, lest that bring the Terror through invisible Gateways.*

She had to cradle the kitten. She could feel the rumble of the tiny throat with her fingertips. The little cat's eyes were closed. Amaya brushed her lips across the kitten's small round head. The eyes did not open. In the baffling way of cats, Artemis had fallen asleep.

25

I AM WITH YOU

•

The Master Ninja Tsunetomo, deeply set in his impersonation of the low-ranking samurai Ishida Minoru of Kai, sat in the lotus position on the vanadium-steel deck of the MD craft and studied the syndic in the fighting chair.

The *gaijin* had long bones, and he was thin, with a melancholy face and deeply set eyes the color of the snow lakes of Hokkaido. None of these things announced a formidable warrior, yet the round-eye had escaped two ninja attacks—one delivered by the Master Killer of all the Order. That made him formidable. And he was even more to be feared if his people were anything at all like he was. Did they really speak to animals? Sometimes it seemed so. And did they have the skill to teach ordinary men to do the same? Ishida glanced at Minamoto Kantaro at the navigation station. A *neko* perched familiarly on the Minamoto's shoulder. Was it truly a cat, or was it some alien being masquerading as a household pet? Much remained to be learned before another attack was made on the *gaijin* Captain.

Lord Yoshi Eiji had at least solved a part of the problem. By delivering Kr-san alone and separated from his people into the ninja's hands he had made the Order's task simple, if not easy.

They were a strange lot, these Wired Ones, Tsunetomo thought. It was said that when they Wired themselves to their ship through those hideous sockets in their heads they became what passed for warriors of darkness in their worlds. How else to explain their mysteries? They seemed to speak with their machines as well as animals. Tsunetomo had seen them do it. There was a weird quality of all-knowingness about them and their precocious cats.

There were telepathic exchanges among them. Even though excluded, one could *feel* it. Tsunetomo was certain that the *neko* with the long *gaijin* had somehow warned him of the attack in the huge, empty dark of the Goldenwing's carapace.

The challenge of assassinating a man so protected filled Tsunetomo with excitement. The killing of his animal familiar was only slightly less appealing. Yamatan ninjas might wait generations before the Sun Goddess Amaterasu again offered them so pure a challenge.

All the talk about the mysterious force outside the ship and the hideous way it killed made no impression on the Master Ninja. Though they themselves were shadow warriors and unseen killers, ninjas had no inclination to create any demons more formidable than those whose rice they had eaten and whose sake they had drunk in the secret conclaves of the Order.

Tsunetomo watched the man in the fighting chair intently. The foreigner was a worthy challenge to the greatest ninja of the age. He was the only man Tsunetomo had attacked and failed to kill. A ninja could not live long with such shame.

"Kantaro-san." Duncan spoke aloud.

"Hai, Kr-san?" The Lord Mayor of Yedo was transfixed by the images sweeping past the exterior imaging cameras on the MD ship's hull. It had been a very long time since Kantaro had piloted a spacecraft. He had been a novice pilot when his uncle, the Shogun, plucked him from Orbital School for training in the life of a Yamatan politician.

He drew his eyes away from the displays with an effort and swivelled his chair to face Duncan. Hana trilled softly and leaped the distance between Kantaro's station and Duncan's. She landed on Duncan's lap and leaned against his chest, purring loudly. Mira, atop the fighting chair's exterior imager, regarded her second-generation offspring with aloof but watchful interest.

"There's been no chance to speak of tactics," Duncan said.

"No, Kr-san. None," the Yamatan replied.

Duncan sketched a mirthless smile. "That is because we have no tactics. You should understand that—I regret there was no time to tell you so."

"Perhaps there is no need," Kantaro said. "Perhaps it has gone far away." Even as he said this, he knew it to be untrue. He was receiving a somewhat muddled sending from Hana. Something about a pack of black dogs stalking her through the dry grass of some alien equatorial plain. He knew it was equatorial because Hana had seen a distant sky, harsh with the summer of a GO sun. And the white summer light was *Earth*. The impression was dreamlike and filled with contained fear. Hana had never seen Earth. Hana had seen only the massed and woven plena and compartments of the Goldenwing *Gloria Coelis*. But she knew Earth. She knew Earth as Kantaro himself knew it. It lived in racial memory.

Duncan said, "They can do that, Kantaro-san. I don't know how. You will see more clearly when you become accustomed to her. And better still when she matures."

Kantaro should have shown delight. But instead he shivered and returned to watching the images of Near Space on his console screens.

From the stern *Glory* was slender-flanked and spiky with masts and yards that seemed to Kantaro like the spokes of a wheel. He had not noticed this manifestation when first he saw *Glory* from the Shogun's lounge aboard *Dragonfly*. With the masts and spars all laden with vast hectares of golden skylar, the Goldenwing had grown perceptibly smaller in the last few minutes. Running before both the solar wind and the Coriolis trade circling out of the galaxy's center, *Glory* was gaining speed from a storm of photons and tachyons against the gleaming golden skylar.

This, Duncan had told him, was *Glory*'s finest point of sail. The rest of the syndic crew, Duncan had said, did have a tactic—a simple one. He had told them to open as great a distance as possible between themselves and Planet Yamato.

The appearance of the Red Sprite and some research and calculation with *Glory*'s powerful mainframe had alarmed Duncan. It was not a certainty, but possible, that the Sprite could not only drain the plasmas of the aurora, but also life from a planetary populace as well. It might be far-fetched, Duncan had said, but it was not to be considered impossible that the Red Sprite could be used to make a direct attack on the people of Yamato.

If that were so, Kantaro's world was in deadly peril. He had seen images of men dying under attack by the Terror. The thought of such flaming deaths taking place by the tens of thousands on the streets of his Yedo filled the Yamatan with dread.

Yet even this is denied me, Kantaro thought bitterly. *If I do not rein my emotions, I may call the horrid thing down upon us.*

He glanced covertly at Duncan. But wasn't that exactly what Kr-san wished to do? Hadn't Kantaro heard Anya-san's cry of anger and anguish as she accused Kr-san of baiting a trap with the MD ship and its people?

Duncan sensed the surge of conflicts in the younger man. Hana had felt them most profoundly and complained to Mira, who passed the conflict on to Duncan. In effect, she said, *"I will stand with you, fight beside you, help you. But the solution is yours, dominant tom."*

How like the matriarch that was, Duncan thought. Mira and her kind were as complex as any human, but their instincts remained as straightforward as they had been before *Felis libyca* became a god in Egypt. The Folk were creatures of infinite variability, but their core belief was simple. Mira was informing Duncan, *"Challenge me, and I will fight or flee. If there are other choices you must make them."*

Duncan was by now well aware of how Mira and her get responded when faced with the unthinkable. The blurred image that came from Kantaro's Hana was charged with feline imagery and tension. Duncan received it only incompletely, but he smelled the dry grasses and heard the black dogs barking under the African sun.

He projected an empathic sending at the small cat, making himself large and protective. She responded with a trill and a tiny growl. Duncan was pleased to sense that Kantaro was comforting her, offering protection. The exact form of the Yamatan's sending was indistinct because he was untrained, unpracticed and clumsy in the method. But Hana was reassured and for the moment that was enough.

On the sunward side of the two ships' track, their changing attitude unmasked the ring that circled Moon Tokugawa. The thin cut of a line it had displayed while *Glory* was in orbit around Yamato broadened like a wound opening. Duncan had suggested to Minamoto no Kami that all the people on Tokugawa should be evacuated. But there had not been sufficient time. Duncan hoped that he, the MD ship, and *Glory* would be enough to distract the stalking Terror. He had the chest-tightening feeling that they were all on the edge of a massacre. The unpredictability of the situation was unnerving. But this was a moment for patience. Each second of shiptime that passed was a second plus a fraction of downtime that increased Planet Yamato's slight margin of safety. *For the moment let that be enough,* Duncan thought, willing time to pass.

Four hours later, in the exterior image screen Duncan's finely tuned perceptions could detect the first slight reddening of the stars astern. The percentage of the speed of light attained at this point was infinitesimal, but it was detectable. Details of the Goldenwing could no longer be discerned without magnification of the image. To starboard and astern, the half-disk of Planet Yamato occupied an eighth of the dark sky. Moon Tokugawa stood high and large in the holographic image, its methane atmosphere bright yellow against the blue-black of space.

At the mass-depletion-engine console, the Kaian crewman sat in a state of what was plainly high tension. Duncan would have wished for an older man in that position, but the Lord of Kai had insisted on "giving the *gaijin-san* the very best pilot among his retainers." Whether this was so or not, Duncan had no way of knowing. He had not been favorably impressed with Yoshi Eiji, but it was obvious that the Shogun had had his particular reasons for holding the contingent from Kai aboard *Glory* when with the ceremony of the war fans he had contemptuously dismissed the rest of the company of samurai. It plainly stated that this small ship, Kantaro, the dark-visaged warrior Ishida, and young Yamaguchi at the pilot's station were the best aid Minamoto no Kami could offer in the shadow war to come.

"Yamaguchi-san," Duncan said. "What percentage of lightspeed have we reached?"

The young pilot, conscious of his low status, used the ancient designation for the Captain of a vessel. "One point three percent, *Kaigun taisa.*"

As the lightspeed percentage rose, Duncan knew, a spaceship's mass would normally increase. But the Yamatan engineers had devised an engine that reversed the expected effects and caused mass to deplete, leaving the ship on the very cusp of Einsteinian reality, able to open a Gateway into an adjoining universe—if a state of being without true space or time could be called a universe.

In such a state the MD could, in effect, *jump* to another locus and instantly return to normal space—vast distances from where the first locus had been opened. It was an achievement of enormous potential: instantaneous movement unaffected by relativistic limits.

But this effect was attained, the Yamatan scientists had explained to the syndics, by a huge consumption of energy. If an MD "outjumped" its energy reserve by more than fifty percent, it would return to normal space to become a derelict, unreachably far from its point of origin.

Duncan intended to use the MD's capabilities not as a means of far travelling, but as an intrusion on the Terror's own space-not-space.

The chances for disaster were too large to compute. The MD's weapon was not very formidable; no one knew with certainty how long Terrestrial animals could survive in the blankness beyond the mass-depletion portals. And worst of all was the inability to know with certainty that the Terror would be there—rather than in one of uncounted similar contiguities of the known universe.

"*Kaigun taisa-sama.*"

"What is it, Yamaguchi-san?"

"I am getting fluctuations in our energy reserves."

It was far more than that, Duncan thought. Mira had leapt across the console to be physically near him. Hana returned to Kantaro, and as she did so she uttered a yowl of mingled anger and fear. Duncan felt a psychic buildup that seemed about to swamp his empathic sense. It was an effect he remembered with dread from his encounter with the stalking Outsider in the Ross Stars. One's physical senses became overloaded. Skin, sensitized by the tingling bombardment of tachyons, grew painful to the most ordinary touch. Mira was growling and yowling with her own discomfort. Duncan could feel her seeking refuge in his mind, and he could "see" the image she had of the encounter. Long ago, and often enough to remember, he recalled that Mira—the first of the enhanced cats—would sense the threat at a vast distance, dire wolves prowling through a dark, primeval night. *"We are the prey":* The thought was clear and urgent. Duncan reacted to a kind of spillage from some unknown, unknowable place. Raw emotion, not human, not animal, but more clearly alien than it had been during the battle aboard *Glory* near Ross 248. His talent supercharged by fear, Duncan recognized the difference in the two occasions. In the Ross Stars encounter, the Terror had been drawn by the chaotic emotions of contingents of two warlike people.

This time, the thing that drove it was self-created, a thick, dark mingling of loneliness and fury.

A kilometer from *Glory*'s quarter, very near the englobature that Broni and Clavius were guarding, a black rent in space began to form.

Damon Ng, who had been tense and silent ever since boarding the MD ship, cradled Pronker and studied the ominous, growing distortion of space shown in the imaging screens.

Damon was both proud and terrified that Duncan had chosen him to accompany him on this desperate thrust at the Terror. Ever since his childhood in the tree-cities of Planet Nixon, he had been cursed with an assortment of psychological challenges he must face.

He had no sooner begun to control his rampant acrophobia than he now found himself serving as a casualty replacement for a man whose courage and skills were untouchably above his own. Duncan had meant well when he explained that he would be expected to bring the Yamatans and their small craft back if Duncan himself should be unable to do so.

The very idea of such a responsibility chilled Damon Ng to the marrow. Pronker put his forepaws on Damon's chest and raised his head so that his amber eyes were on a level with Damon's brown ones. The message was clear: *"Do not fear. I am with you."*

26

TO THE NEAR AWAY

•

Buele, lying in his control pod in *Glory*'s bridge with Big twitching beside him, had an astral-eye's view of the first contact.

Using a dozen of the imaging cameras scattered throughout the Goldenwing's rig to localize his view, he had placed himself, in effect, a half-dozen kilometers off *Glory*'s port quarter and facing forward along *Glory*'s track. The Voersterian boy had learned to enjoy these EVA-by-proxy affairs. He had heard the Sailing Master discussing his skill with the Cybersurgeon a number of times, and her opinion seemed to be that Buele was showing a greater Talent at these out-of-body tasks than had anyone ever before in *Glory*'s history.

Duncan had told him that even though he himself had learned to enjoy the business of projecting his anima (a Jungian term, Buele learned from *Glory*'s computer) out of the ship and into Near Space, he had never found the task easy. Even Mira's assistance did little to reduce the cold, chilled loneliness the procedure brought about. Yet Buele found it a simple matter to project his awareness almost anywhere within a hundred-kilometer englobature of the ship. The presence of his friend Big made the task more pleasant rather than easier. Buele had begun to wonder if it might not be possible to extend his anima much farther into space than he had so far done. The boy often wondered how his early mentor, Mynheer Osbertus Kloster, the Astronomer Select of Voerster, with whom Buele had lived much of his early life on the Grassersee, would respond to his potboy's developing gifts.

Buele remembered the old scientist with genuine affection; it saddened him to know that the laws of relativity had already forever separated him from those early years at Sternheim in the company of the ancient one-meter refracting telescope that had been brought so lovingly and at such great expense from Earth.

I would have become Brother Osbertus's heir, Buele thought, *although I never guessed it then.*

Differences of class and status had made an adoption appear impossible. But it had never been as far out of reach as it had seemed before Goldenwing *Gloria Coelis* had appeared in Planet Voerster's sky. Buele had come to realize that old Osbertus had truly loved him. So much so that an orphan *lumpen* boy might actually have turned Voersterian society on its head and become a part of the Mynheerenshaft. Eliana, Broni's mother, the rebellious Voertrekkerschatz who became the Elmi, would have sanctioned it. Buele had no doubt of that.

These thoughts brought Buele a certain sadness for what might have been. He was, after all, a son of Planet Voerster, and life at Starhome had been gentle and rewarding.

But the paths to the future are obscure and unforeseen. In those days Buele could not have known that his future lay *in* the sky, not peering at it as the stars wheeled over the Sea of Grass. The ways of Brother God, he told himself often, are strange, indeed.

Buele felt Big beside him, large paws twitching as the cat visualized the sky in his own terms: a dark savannah, redolent of menace and thick with the spoor of a great dire wolf.

"Speak to Clavius, Big," Buele sent. *"Let him calm you."*

For reply, the large young tom extended his foreclaws to grasp Buele's naked flank. Buele bore it stoically. Big was an excitable personality. Most particularly when he felt himself *Outside* the ship and vulnerable.

"What is it? What do you sense? What do you feel?"

Buele dealt gently with his partner. It was better to soothe Big than it was to challenge him. The latter could be a painful experience, whether it was in space, among the Folk, or simply at the food replicator. Big had a tom's fighting spirit, an active imagination and an enormous appetite for the fish-flavored concoctions *Glory* had taught him to select from the feeding consoles.

These, and other thoughts very like them, were never far out of Buele's mind. Life aboard *Gloria Coelis* was a forever-fermenting challenge, and *Glory* herself was a never-flagging source of facts, theories, expatiations, suggestions, pointers, discourses and elaborations on tens upon tens of thousands of subjects Buele found fascinating. Save for Duncan himself, who had a very special sort of relationship with Mira, Buele's relations with the Folk were farther advanced than anyone's aboard, even Broni's, whose bonding with Clavius was deeper and more powerful than anyone, even Broni herself, knew.

The result was that the boy, listed in *Glory*'s computer only as "Supernumerary" (*Glory* declined to limit Buele's usefulness), had a more focused grasp of the environment *Glory* inhabited and the ambience she created for her people than any of the older syndics—perhaps even including Duncan Kr.

None of this bestowed upon Buele an attractive physique nor a charming personality. In this respect he remained what he had always been, a *lumpen* potboy, largely self-schooled, untactful, and a human being of enormous courage.

It was this last trait that was required now as, lying in his bridge-pod and accompanied by the anima of the large comatose tomcat beside him, he seemed to float off *Glory*'s stern quarter as the very fabric of space formed a dark vortex, a construct that resembled an accretion disk and a swiftly deepening whirlpool of fuliginous blackness that began as a single microscopic point and expanded rapidly into a ravening tower of spinning dark shot through with a fine network of ultraviolet electrical discharges.

From invisibility the manifestation grew into an abominable spinning rent in the sky that towered far above the tall spars of the speeding Goldenwing.

The com circuits aboard both *Glory* and the MD ship came alive with crackling urgency. But the nearness of the electrical disturbances in the black vortex scrambled all electronic communications. For the moment, each Starman, each familiar, and each ship was isolated by the intensity of the disturbances.

In the image-world inhabited by Buele and Big, the image that most expressed the cat's vision of the world was a wolf shape of grotesque proportions. Big's anima appeared, expanded, larger and larger still, a silhouette of remarkable menace, back arched, tail brushed, claws extended, fangs threatening in a mouth framed by black lips drawn back in a snarl of violent, outraged anger.

This image appeared to Buele in an interval so short that it was unmeasurable. There was no sound in space, but Buele heard Big's raging, howling challenge—a scream that pierced the high registers and became a supersonic wail of rage.

For just one moment Buele felt the Terror's response. A cold heat, a sullen fury, confusion and that bitter emotional streak of loneliness. It seemed to Buele that he lay at the bottom of an enormous spinning vortex while unseen, far above him, Big—grown into an enormous image through which the Near Stars shone only dimly—crouched, snarling and holding at bay the darker creature.

Buele had a flash of childhood memory.

He was an abandoned child on the night roads of Planet Voerster and he had stumbled upon a kraal of Kaffirs sacrificing to the Six Giants—the bright planets of Voerster's winter sky. There were chants and wails, and the child Buele shivered as he remembered the talk heard of Kaffirs sacrificing Voertrekker babies in their search for nature's few bounties.

The seekers appeared in the starlit night, an old Kaffir shaman and his mud-masked apprentices. They were using rods in rhabdomancy, searching for edible wild roots in the clay soil of the plain below the Shieldwall.

The shaman found him and Buele tranced into his first remembered exercise of what syndics would one day call his "Talent." For an instant, the boy was that shaman. He felt the caked mud on his cheeks, the dirt beneath his feet, the pull of a penis-sheath decorated with stones, the pain of a broken molar, the hunger that drove him.

In that remembered moment, Buele was many things.

What he was *not* was afraid.

Broni Ehrengraf, lying with Clavius in her bridge-pod, experienced many things at once. She heard Big's yowl of feline rage and fear even through the thick walls of Buele's pod and her own. It was a cry that Clavius amplified with his own feral cry of anger. Broni experienced the cat's fury as well as his terror, and she experienced it as a free anima in space on *Glory*'s port bow. Moments before she had been in psychic free-flight beside *Glory*;

despite the general apprehension that dominated the Golden-wing and all aboard her, the girl had been unable to reject totally the pleasure her present empathic state gave her.

She knew that she trailed Buele in the process of learning to control and command her own Talent, but her skills had grown in the months since leaving the Ross Stars. She had allowed herself a touch of arrogance in recent days.

Amaya, who had become Broni's primary mentor aboard *Glory,* had been less critical since the encounter in the Ross Stars. And even Duncan, who could regard self-satisfaction with great suspicion, seemed to be pleased with Broni's progress as a syndic.

But though the Voersterian girl had learned something of the techniques of psychic battle at Ross 248, this new encounter was of a different order of magnitude.

What her anima perceived was the same rent in space that Buele and Big had seen. She saw it less clearly, and consequently more uncertainly. The very concept of space itself having sufficient physical reality to be ripped like a piece of cloth was alien to any and all the science to which she had been exposed during her life on Planet Voerster. The discussions with her fellow syndics aboard *Glory* had been intellectual exercises of the sort difficult to translate into actual events.

Yet against all reason the rift in space existed and was swiftly growing larger. Broni felt the demanding presence of Anya Amaya.

"Back to the ship, Broni."

"But Duncan is out there!" Broni's protest was as firm and as resolute as she could make it. *Duncan is my exemplar, my true father, my lover. And I am Voertrekker,* the girl thought, *I cannot desert him.*

She could feel Duncan at a distance, Duncan and Mira together making ready to take some desperate action. Anya seemed to know what it was. Why did the Sailing Master know and not she?

Anya Amaya commanded: *"Broni! Obey me!"*

All that the girl felt for Duncan, all the imaginings and the sexual dreams, all the fear of losing his protection, turned her ordinarily orderly mind into that of a frightened child.

Again, Amaya: *"Back to Glory, Broni! Back!"*

Broni wanted desperately keep her fear at bay, but her skill was insufficient. The stygian rent loomed and the Near Stars vanished. The edges of the spatial tear grew veined with dancing violet plasmas.

Broni sensed the full threat of the Terror. It was overpowering. At this distance it filled the sky. But the image was real, not hers. It came from Clavius—an unreal half bird, half dragon. A basilisk. But Clavius kept it at bay.

Broni watched in horror as the Yamatan MD ship began to react to the forces of the Gateway. It seemed suddenly to be veined with ultraviolet light, and it was no longer firmly shaped. Its outlines melted and flowed with the plasmas in the Gateway. What had been a spaceship was transforming itself into a fluorescent stain in black water, no longer a solid thing, but a liquid image, an object in transition from an objective reality into a metaphor. It flowed ever more swiftly out of a universe Broni knew and into one that neither she nor anyone within a million light-years would recognize.

And Broni remembered a thing the original Black Clavius would often say when he appealed to his God: "Yea, though I walk through the valley of the shadow of death, I will fear no evil: for thou art with me; thy rod and thy staff they comfort me."

As a sick child she had taken comfort from the black Starman's words. Her failing heart had often taken her close to the valley of the shadow. But now her courage faltered.

The mass-depletion ship elongated as it passed the event horizon, spilled into a spinning maelstrom of other-space, attenuated into a streak of fading light that could have been a dozen meters or a thousand kilometers long—and vanished.

PART III

If one will *do it, it can be done.*
> —Yamamoto Tsunetomo, *Hagakure*

If it can be done, it will *be done.*
> —Western dictum

27

ARE THEY DEAD?

•

Anya Amaya thought she was prepared for what she had witnessed, but a stab of deep grief and terrible fear told her that she was not. In the instant the Yamatan spacecraft flowed through the Gateway and disappeared—in that instant Anya knew that all Duncan's oblique attempts at preparing her for what might come had failed.

It seemed almost as though *Glory* herself were mourning. A cybernetic spasm spread like a cold wave through the empty holds and passageways of the Goldenwing.

Every mind and heart aboard the great-queen-who-is-not-alive was shaken by it. Anya was first aware of Broni's cri de coeur, accompanied by a frightened yowl from Black Clavius. The sense of both cries was: *"Are they dead?"*

The fear expressed by Broni and her partner was a true measure of how dependent on Duncan Kr were Goldenwing *Gloria Coelis* and her people.

Anya felt a thickening of emotion in her throat. For a decade of uptime years she had been Duncan's second-in-command, disciple, quondam lover and faithful friend. Now, in this one terrible moment for which she had only imagined herself prepared, she became his mourner, as did the ship and every living thing on her.

Anya held Artemis too tightly and struggled to contain her near panic. Gallantly, the little cat did not struggle to be free.

In their control pod, Buele and Big experienced the disappearance of the MD ship as a sudden vanishing. Their loss focused upon Damon and Pronker, with whom they had been spending much time recently. Buele felt the loss of the Rigger acutely; since arriving at Tau Ceti the two young men had developed a genuine fondness for one another. Now both Damon and the Captain were swiftly, shockingly, gone. To make a bad situation worse, Pronker and Mira, the matriarch of all the Folk aboard, were also gone. Overwhelmed with fear and grief, Big emitted a shrill and anguished yowl that filled the pod.

Buele's breath expanded under his ribs until it seemed he must suffocate. His bare legs and arms extended, jerked, drummed against the padded sides of the metal pod. The inexperienced but combative Big reacted as his kind had responded to the unknown for millennia. Everything nearby became an enemy. Cornered, the young tom prepared to fight or flee. He leaped onto Buele's naked breast, claws extended, back humped, fur bristling.

It was *Glory* who saved the boy from serious injury. The great-queen-who-is-not-alive took command and suppressed Big's desperate response. Buele's sense of loss was less easily banished. He felt suddenly lost in emptiness and grief-stricken.

Big released his bloody grip on the young man's smooth chest and began to lick away the blood, grooming him apologetically.

In the hangar deck, where the Yamatans had gathered around their Shogun aboard the *Dragonfly*, a link from the external imagers in the Goldenwing's rig showed them what had happened to their MD ship.

Reactions were varied. To Lord Yoshi, the would-be samurai, the sight of the spacecraft flowing like water into a crevasse was terrifying. He had been toying with a grand dream of becoming a hero to the *bakufu* lords of Yamato, but the disappearance—so swift, so easily accomplished, as though Man and his works were nothing—squelched what little fighting spirit he had been able to muster. All mysterious things were frightening to Lord Yoshi.

But the event was real. It had happened. And to the point, it had happened to *others*. There was a lesson in that, Yoshi thought shakily. And like the natural entrepreneur he was, the Lord of Kai began to search for an advantage in this sudden turn of fate.

Yoshi Eiji imagined that the disappearance now eliminated the troublesome ninja. And, as a bonus, it also wiped from the political slate the person of Minamoto no Kami's nephew and heir apparent.

The nonagenarian Shogun was grief-stricken, though his iron personal discipline kept his feelings hidden from his retainers. Yet he had been prepared. The master of the Goldenwing had made it clear that a battle *must* be fought, and that he intended that it should be fought as far as possible from both his ship and from the millions of colonial descendants living on the continental islands of Yamato.

The colonials made a prodigious effort to remain as outwardly calm as their Shogun. None were calm. They had seen the imagers' visual report of what had taken place a very few kilometers from the ship in which they were contained. They had seen the rustling terror of the ship's monkeys as they tumbled from the rig, falling in nightmare slowness to the vast, empty deck, and from there crawling and scrambling for the imagined safety of the Monkey House.

Others, retainers and attendants with closer personal ties to the Shogun and his family, reacted to the loss of the Lord Mayor of Yedo according to how highly they esteemed him. Since Minamoto Kantaro was a highly visible member of Planet Yamato's ruling class, there were loud lamentations.

Funereal grief and ceremonial death were traditions imported from Earth, and such traditions were matters of enormous importance to all colonists, wherever they might have settled among the Near Stars. For the Yamatans, the forms of communal grief were described in detail in the *Monogatari no Hachiman*. Each daimyo and dependent, down to the most rustic Lord, had in his library ancient scrolls depicting the ten thousand ways of samurai death and the rituals surrounding each.

Dragonfly was filled with members of a social class to whom death was not an enemy, but a demanding master. The shogunal barge's salon was filled with emotional sounds, practiced often and uttered now as signs of respect for Minamoto no Kami and, indirectly, all the Yamatan descendants of the ancient Tokugawa clan.

But of all the lamentations voiced aboard *Dragonfly*, those softly uttered by the ninety-year-old Shogun were the most sincere.

* * *

Clavius perceived the disappearance as a scene upon some dark savannah, lighted by a thin crescent of yellow moon and a few stars dimmed by the oppressive atmosphere. Clavius had reluctantly been constrained by his duty to the pride to stay with his human female. She rested fitfully in a low dish of dusty ground, her naked body trembling with each silent shower of the tachyons that fell upon both girl and cat out of the distant night.

Clavius had sensed the presence of the Other. He had sensed it looming behind the first swirl of force that indicated space was about to change character. The black cat bottled his tail and made himself large, showing long teeth in a saber-toothed snarl. Whenever danger approached, Clavius saw himself as a massive black smilodon, but still dwarfed and made small by the enormity of the Other.

For the first time Clavius had the disconcerting perception that the menace approaching was not a living being in the sense that the Folk understood the idea of living.

Among the Folk one was alive until one was killed or became dead. When that happened, there was a short period of investigation as each of the Folk used the acute senses of touch and smell and hearing to reassure himself that something that once lived no longer did.

If the dead were prey, there would be ritual play, then an offering to the Matriarch, sometimes even to the humans. But this was pro forma. Next came the decision whether or not to eat the recently living prey. Such was the normal pattern among the Folk; such it had always been.

The rip in the sky began to open, and Clavius danced sideways beside the sweating, fearful girl. He snarled and growled at the sky. Somewhere out there were Mira, the mother, and Hana, a kitten too new to face what was suddenly racing down out of the dark sky.

Clavius saw the sky's mouth open. Black lips were laced with electric violet spittle. A great howling deafened him and he very nearly turned to run.

But he could not leave the girl. He could not.

He did not see, except with his mind. There was the vast, black, empty savannah. The thin yellow moon had never really existed except in some chained ancestral memory that survived an eon and more since remembered by that smilodon who lived on Earth a million years ago.

Where the moon had been, there was the mouth of the sky. And into that mouth bounded the animas of Mira and little Hana, and with them their human partners.

Clavius roared a challenge, but the Other ignored him. Instead the mouth of the sky closed like the jaws of a predator far greater than Black Clavius.

The cat struggled against the urge to shriek in fear. Instead he burrowed against the thrashing girl's sweat-damp breasts, never taking his wide eyes from the darkness where the sky had been.

Deep within *Glory* where Dietr Krieg had his surgery and infirmary, the psychic shock of the MD's disappearance was muted by the Goldenwing's protective mechanisms. It was not to *Glory*'s advantage that her crew of Wired Starmen should be incapacitated by the loss of any one or two of their number. But syndics were often more vulnerable than they imagined themselves to be.

Krieg, of all aboard *Glory*, considered himself an unsentimental man. He had never been particularly tolerant of young Damon Ng, and over the uptime years he had taught himself to deal with the Rigger in a peculiarly severe and inflexible manner. He had, in fact, always thought of Damon as a kind of Cybersurgeon's copybook exercise in practical psychiatry.

I am immune to grief, he thought. *I do not feel loss or loneliness. A Cybersurgeon must be stronger than ordinary men.*

He sat at his workstation erect and still, stunned by his bereavement. *Damon,* he thought, *and Duncan—good God, Duncan.* For the first time in many years, Dietr Krieg, physician of Earth, wept like a woman.

28

EPIPHANIES

•

For the occupants of the MD ship there was first a flash of blue-shifted light as the plunge toward the singularity steepened. Duncan was overwhelmed with the strangeness of the fall. It happened with no consciousness of time passing, no sense of space changing, even as the ship and all it contained assumed the threadlike proportions demanded by the Einsteinian hypothesis.

Duncan was aware of the stretching of space as the ship passed through the singularity, but there was no visual indication within of what his Talent told him was actually taking place Outside. In theory, they should all be dead, stretched into singular chains of atomic constituents by the massive gravity of the Gateway. But it was not happening that way. He was swept by a terrified anxiety. Was anything happening? Or were they all dead, experiencing an undreamed-of reality of pure perception?

Duncan grasped the padded arms of the fighting chair. The sensations were real enough. He felt disembodied, but the action of the mass-depletion coils girdling the ship could explain that. The others in the ship, Kantaro, the Kaian retainer Ishida, Damon and the cats looked real enough, though Damon seemed stupefied by the fall.

No, if this was death, then what was it *out there*? The screens of the external imagers were blank washes of shifted light, fading even as Duncan watched. What replaced the light was not the expected darkness. It was an emptiness, a blankness, beyond the Thalassan's experience. The experience, he thought, was as though he were trying to see without the organs of sight. It was, to his human senses, *nothing*.

How was it possible that within the ship no shapes changed, no spatial or temporal relationships were transformed?

"Higashi-san," Duncan said. "Does this happen when the MD coils open a Gateway?"

The young Yamatan was pale and wide-eyed. "No, Kr-sama. A mass-depletion gate opens into another space. But not like this one. I have never seen *that*." He indicated the blankness of the imaging screens.

"Rotate the ship through three hundred sixty degrees," Duncan ordered. "Enable all scanners."

The instruments on the console before Duncan reacted sluggishly. That was to be expected, because the mass-depletion engine reduced the inertia of the ship and all it contained nearly to zero. But the scanners remained as blank as before.

Duncan guessed that the ship and what it contained were locked in a bubble of reality held together by the output of the MD engine. The bubble was maintained by a voracious consumption of energy in the mass-depletion coils. What would happen when the craft's inertia dropped to zero? When an MD moved through a gate of its own creation and then consumed all the inertia it had carried through, it would run out of power and fall back into normal space—though often at a vast distance from the site of the original gate. Duncan suspected that this was a very different reality. He had serious doubts that the MD coils would be able to generate enough force to create another singularity. *We may have crossed a barrier through which we cannot return,* Duncan thought. And meanwhile, the Terror, the Outsider, was still nearby. The reality within the bubble was thick with threat.

Mira cast herself adrift in the near-null gravity; she floated with claws extended, teeth bared, ears flattened against her skull. Duncan saw that small Hana had assumed an almost identical posture of aggression. He probed empathically, seeking to co-opt Mira's mental images. He could not. The sensory equipment of the Folk was more sensitive than humans' by orders of magnitude.

Duncan reacted to the proximity of the old enemy with self-discipline. Fear was unacceptable, as was hatred or anger. Those emotions attracted the Terror as blood in the water attracted the sharks of Earth's oceans. He shut away his dread and despair. *I came here to find you,* he thought. *Show yourself.* The challenge created an angry wave that washed over and through the MD ship. So the content of null space and the reality within the bubble were interactive, Duncan thought. That meant *It* could reach them. Perhaps it also meant that *they* could reach *It.*

Duncan remembered well the feel of the encounter in the Ross Stars. But this time perhaps the adversary was not totally the aggressor. It had been surprised by the pursuit of the MD ship. It was likely that it had never been surprised before. There was the familiar burning rage, and even the streaks of angry loneliness Buele had once claimed to discern. But the sullen fury was less than the killing force Duncan had expected to encounter.

Mira's images seemed to come with incredible speed. She called furiously. Duncan had a flash memory of the images Mira sensed. Once they had lurked out there at great distances. But no longer. The man was certain that Mira—and possibly Hana and Pronker, as well—could see the adversary clearly.

For the first time since the fall through the singularity, Damon Ng stirred out of his frightened torpor.

"Calm, Damon," Duncan said. "Calm." To Kantaro he called, "What does Hana see?"

"I cannot tell, Kr-san. It is indistinct."

It was too soon for the mental bridge between Kantaro and Hana to carry much useful information. It was even possible that the link would never really form. *It will take time,* Duncan thought, *and have we time?*

It came to him that in this null space where they found themselves, the familiar parameters did not exist. If there was no true space, then could there be time? For many months aboard *Glory* Duncan had considered and hypothesized about the Terror's ability to ignore all the Einsteinian limitations. Was this the true answer? Did the Klein bottle of Creation contain universes where neither time nor distance had any reality?

Mira growled and bared her teeth. The cat sensed the Terror nearby. Whether the image was accurate Duncan had no way of knowing. But Mira was tracking the enemy. Why was it that the lack of time or space failed to deter her? It had never inhibited her ability to see and feel the enemy at a distance that in her native universe might be extragalactic. What the Folk ignored, Duncan thought, did not inhibit them. It was the first of many epiphanies.

The second epiphany, and not a pleasant one, was that the Yamatans might suddenly have been pushed beyond their ability to respond. If this were true, the mistake was Duncan's, whose dour and melancholy disposition had prepared him, almost from birth, to cope with the unbelievable.

Kantaro was shaken, but still in command of himself. How much of that was due to small Hana? Had *Glory* and, through her, Mira, prepared Hana for what might come? Kantaro had lived thirty standard years in preparation for this trial. Hana had lived six weeks. Broni might say it was a wonderment. And it was.

The Kaian retainer Ishida presented a divergent set of problems. Mira despised him on sight. Even before passing through the singularity, she had avoided him, hissing at him if he drew near.

The man himself seemed befuddled by their situation. As well he might be, thought Duncan. A Yamatan samurai retainer, more than most men, would require the assurance of an orderly world and of his place in it. Not a peaceful world, far from it, for Ishida was not a peaceful man. That was evident in his every word and action.

But was he capable of clinging to his rationality in this *place* where they found themselves? That would remain to be seen.

Kantaro's voice seemed thin, attenuated. "Kr-sama—what is happening to us?"

Duncan's own voice sounded strange, as though the bubble containing the ship were fragile, allowing the reality within to leach away slowly. "We are in a kind of null space, a place beyond the singularity we passed. So far we have a small initiative. The Terror is startled. Can't you feel it? Mira does, and so do the other cats."

The MD pilot, Yamaguchi, spoke hoarsely. He was pallid, like a man slipping into shock. "It has never happened like this before, Kr-sama, never. An ordinary jump for a ship like this is short, almost instantaneous. No one has ever found a place like this one." The "and returned" was not spoken, but it was there.

His tone had the shrill component of one who stood on the edge of an abyss.

"We passed through *Its* singularity," Duncan said. "The MD coils are probably what is keeping us alive. Look at the imagers. What do you see?"

"Nothing, Kr-sama," the pilot said. "Nothing at all." He sounded on the verge of hysteria.

"There is nothing to see, Yamaguchi-san," Duncan said. "There is no space, no time outside our own perception." It was not courage the MD pilot lacked. It was belief. Yamaguchi simply found it near to impossible to find himself—here.

Duncan sympathized. He was struck by the stunning thought that even if a return should be possible, the MD ship might pass again through the singularity into a universe or a reality—the words were interchangeable in this situation—in which a year or ten thousand years had passed.

We must retain a link with our own actuality, he thought. It was vital. To relinquish that link meant madness.

Damon Ng was succumbing to the stress. His eyes widened, tried to roll back in his skull. Pronker sought him out and fastened himself to his skinsuit. Pronker's sending—a cry for help—was so powerful that Mira and Hana reacted by seeking close physical contact with the young tom. Somehow the group sending created an image Damon could interpret. He said hollowly, "It is running from us, Captain. We must follow."

It was what Duncan had hoped for, yet had dared not expect, the smallest weakening in the Outsider's merciless behavior. But he had to be certain. "How do you know?" Duncan demanded.

Damon put his arms around the cats in his lap who were struggling to be understood. Pronker and Mira yowled with a mixture of fright and anger. Hana, young and with powers not fully developed, sought comfort by attempting to burrow through the slick skinsuit and touch Damon's flesh.

"*I* don't know. *They* do." His eyes were glazing. He looked Wired. Without *Glory*'s massive computing power sustaining their psychic Talents that should be impossible, Duncan thought. Yet what did "should be" and "impossible" mean in this place—if place it was?

Ishida spoke in a flat, uninflected voice. "The pilot is faint-
ing, Kr-san. Shall I take over?" In fact, the Kaian retainer was
right. The pilot was sinking more and more deeply into shock.

Duncan lifted the weightless Yamatan from his seat and took
his place. His knowledge of colonial vessels was almost primitive. But plainly this nameless mass-depletion spacecraft was of
the first generation of things to come. *If we live,* Duncan thought.
If we survive and return . . .

That was Duncan's third epiphany.

Mira launched herself at Duncan, eyes wild and tail brushed.
It was a pose Duncan knew well. She assumed it often when, in
the privacy of the Captain's quarters aboard *Glory,* they played
with crumpled balls of paper and lengths of cord. But Mira was
not playing now. With her ears flat against her skull and her small
but formidable teeth bared, she had the look of a predator making a sudden, final rush at her prey.

I do not know if we humans are ready, Duncan thought. *But
Mira is ready. Mira, in fact, is ready for war.*

Was the Terror weaker than Duncan remembered it from the
Ross encounter? There might be unsuspected reasons. How long
had it lived in this null space that might be native to it? A hundred centuries? A thousand? Once again his humanity betrayed
him. Human beings lived by the clock and calendar, but Time
had no meaning here. Had never had meaning. There was no past,
no future, only a null-dimensional . . . *what*?

Duncan reined himself. He could feel the deep and terrible
loneliness of this place without sun, stars, without light or sound
or time or distance. Few humans had ever been so divided from
their own kind.

Duncan treated his momentary weakness with self-contempt.
Surely a man who spent a solitary boyhood in the open skiffs of
Chalkmeer, one who, before he could walk or swim, learned from
the adults of his marriage group how to face the toothed, fur-
bearing fishes alone under the great red glow of Moon Bothwell,
could face this raging emptiness?

He had actually stalked the Terror hoping to find some weakness. Had he done so? Its use of the Red Sprite to feed from the
Yamatan aurora was an activity none of the syndics had seen before. How efficient was the energy transfer? How much life must

the entity consume to perform the miracle of the Gateway, so like a black hole in miniature? But though it ate life, it consumed energy in many forms. The transfer of power from the Yamatan aurora had been a dazzling, daunting, *intimidating* event.

There is so much we do not know, Duncan thought. *What weapons might one use against such an entity? And where was the monstrous thing?* Outside the ship, his human eyes could see nothing.

How large was the Terror? No human had ever seen it fully materialized and lived. The Collective of Nimrud's soldiers had discovered that. They, at least, were granted the mercy of dying under their own sun.

Possibilities were racing across the landscape of Duncan's mind. He broke through the blindness and glimpsed the rocky coast of Thalassa in a driving rain. Lost in the mist and distance, a furred leviathan was thrashing furiously in the tumultuous sea. Was it wounded? Old? Surrounded by enemies? Dying?

Or was it not there at all?

His intimacy with Mira and the Folk aboard *Glory* had taught him that reality had an infinity of faces. *Glory*'s syndics most particularly knew this to be so because their Talent made it possible for them to create mental surrogates for what their feeble eyes and ears failed to detect. It was this ability that formed the core, the very heart, of the link between the human beings of the *Gloria Coelis* and the new and strange cats who populated their world.

Duncan thought, *When familiar reason abandons us to the irrational, then we must do as the Folk do—create an alternate reality in which we can effectively live, and fight, and if need be, die, for we are Wired Starmen.*

That was Duncan's fourth epiphany.

29

SYNDICS

•

They are gone and we don't know where," Anya Amaya said to the group gathered on the bridge deck. "It was Duncan's intention to take the battle to the Terror rather than run from it. He did that. Now he and the others are gone. And so, I think, is the Terror. None of the Folk can sense it nearby, and neither can *Glory.*" Amaya was too straightforward a person not to go on. "It is almost certain that we will not see any of them again. Duncan warned me the price of driving the intruder off could be high. He and Damon were willing to pay it." She looked at the colonists clinging to the fabric bulkheads. "I hope your people were as willing," she said.

Her eyes were red, but there were no more tears. She had received all of Duncan's behests from *Glory* and she was now the acting Master and Commander. A single hour had passed since the sky had opened and swallowed the MD vessel. In that awful moment there had been a surge in the empathic signature of fear, genuine fear, and anxiety aboard the Goldenwing, but there was no corresponding counterattack from the Terror. Quite the contrary. The cats aboard had lost interest in the chase, and the humans felt only their personal grief. Their friends and fellow syndics had vanished, and with them the devil that had stalked *Glory* half across the sky.

The Sailing Master had ordered sail taken off the spars the moment the level of tension began to fall. Duncan had left instructions that *Gloria Coelis* come about "immediately we are engaged" and return with all haste to Planet Yamato.

Anya had seen no reason why all aboard should not hear, in Duncan's own words, what he had left for them to do.

"No matter if a fight begins," he said in *Glory*'s voice, "and assuming we are not immediately consumed or destroyed, *Glory* must return to synchronous orbit at Yamato, which is the only place, so far as we know, in Near Space where the relativistic-speed problem is even being addressed. This means that if we fail to incapacitate, or at least discourage, the phenomenon we have been referring to as the Terror, another attempt must be made. I leave it to you, Anya, and you, Minamoto no Kami, to assume this duty. It must be done, or Mankind's time among the stars is at an end."

The Yamatans, wearing funereal white, responded to Duncan's words with formal bows. The Shogun's face was etched with the loss of his nephew, and Anya was touched with the memory of a thought she had had only yesterday, and that now seemed a whisper from the distant past.

We were never lovers, Minamoto Kantaro. Perhaps it is as well. Grief should be pure.

It was a thought worthy of the grim-faced women who had raised and then rejected her on New Earth.

Despite this, and despite the love and respect Anya had for Duncan, her inbred feminism rose in a surge of anger and grief. Duncan had performed an act that was typically a *man* thing, heroism fuelled with testosterone. *And now I am alone to deal with what comes after,* Anya thought bitterly.

The Shogun wore a *hachimaki,* a cloth headband bearing the sun disk of Amaterasu and a calligraphic prayer for the "happy rebirth" of the Yamatans who had died, as the colonists put it, "in the Near Away."

The old man's grief was evident. A lifetime of stoicism did not ease the pain of the loss of his nephew and heir. Yet only now could he allow himself to consider whether or not Kantaro had been as blameless as he, Minamoto no Kami, would have preferred him to be.

Before the dismissal of the war fans and the return to Yamato by most of the daimyos, Minamoto had struggled against the suspicion that Kantaro knew more about the attempts on Duncan's life than was honorable. The young man had shown a reticence to speak of the ninja attacks that Minamoto had found disturbing.

Well, he thought bleakly, it was unimportant now. But had Kantaro's complicity in some plot against the Goldenwing syndics and even—may the Gods forbid—against the legitimate order on Planet Yamato made it easy for the young man to volunteer so insistently for the MD mission to the Near Away?

Minamoto no Kami put such thoughts out of his mind. If what the woman syndic declared was the way things actually were, his duty as Lord of Honshu and Shogun of Yamato was to return and suppress any unrest or even insurrection that the loss of Kantaro and the others might encourage.

The thing these Wired people called the Terror was apparently gone, attacked and possibly even destroyed by the starship Captain's reckless thrust into the unknown. The cost was high and the unknown and unknowable nature of the battle, if battle there was, left a Yamatan samurai unsatisfied. But Minamoto no Kami, a feudal Japanese to his fingertips, understood where his own duty lay.

"Is there any service we can render, Sailing Master?" he asked formally. "We are few, but you are fewer."

"I thank Minamoto-sama," Anya Amaya replied as formally. "But this Goldenwing is self-sufficient. However, it will take some time and distance for us to change course. We shall have to swing around Moon Hideyoshi to turn *Glory*. I have ordered the monkeys and the computer to use the light pressure of Tau Ceti." A New Earther under all and any circumstances, she disregarded the discomfort among the Yamatans at the use of the Terrestrial name for Amaterasu—who was, after all, the astronomical aspect of the Sun Goddess. Already, Amaya was disengaging herself from the colonists. It was a defense ingrained in the syndic psyche. Only by such separation could the "immortal" Starman survive his or her life of continuing personal loss.

Amaya recognized what she was doing and was of no mind to change it, even if she could. *A Starman once, a Starman always.* It was an axiom aboard Goldenwings. Amaya herself had never truly needed—until now—to accept terrible losses without complaint. Duncan had shown her that it was possible when he left Eliana Ehrengraf on Voerster. Now the crew of Goldenwing *Gloria Coelis* must all do the same. Leave Yamato and leave Duncan Kr and Damon Ng, relegating them to the log and legend of the ship.

"We are still within range of Yamato, Amaya-san," the Shogun said. "Since you have no further need of us, we will make preparations to depart at once. Our MD ships can shed their inertia and make an almost instantaneous turnaround by using the mass-depletion engines. So we will go in the MD ships and leave *Dragonfly* aboard to reclaim when you reestablish orbit. If that is acceptable, Master and Commander."

Broni, defiantly floating in air above a control console and holding Clavius as though he were a kitten, bridled visibly at the use of Duncan's title. Buele, close enough to her to touch, squeezed her wrist in warning, displaying a social sophistication he had not heretofore been known to possess.

"Your plan is acceptable, Lord Shogun," Anya said. "Our speed is dropping swiftly. What inertial overload can your engines handle?"

The Shogun looked to one of his companions, a mass-depletion engineer. "Point zero zero five lightspeed, Minamoto-sama."

The Shogun looked to Anya for confirmation. "Is it possible, Amaya-san?"

"We will be down to that speed within an hour, Shogun."

Minamoto steadied himself with a hand on the flexing bulkhead and inclined his head. "We will prepare, Master and Commander."

Once again Buele's short-fingered *lumpen*'s hand closed on Broni's wrist. Still far from being in command of herself, the Voertrekker girl snatched her arm away. Big, perched on Buele's shoulder, raised his hackles and hissed at Broni. Buele silenced him with an unspoken interspecies caution. Anya Amaya shot a stern look at Buele and Broni. It would not do, particularly at this time, to give the Yamatans the impression that the syndics of Goldenwing *Gloria Coelis* were at odds.

Minamoto no Kami and his people left the bridge. Most had come to terms with the business of moving about in the almost nonexistent gravity aboard *Glory*. Those who had not still wore the grav units. Yoshi Eiji, the Lord of Kai, was one of these.

When the colonists had cleared the bridge, Amaya rounded on her crewmates.

"I do not want to see a display like that one ever again," she said. "We are syndics. I expect us all to act like syndics." She glared at Broni. "Without exception."

Broni, a Voertrekker aristocrat unaccustomed to being disciplined, responded furiously. *"He called you Master and Commander."*

"He did, and I am," Anya said in a voice steely with command. "You heard Duncan's instructions to *Glory.* Unless there is a miracle, there is no more to say. *Is that clear, Astroprogrammer?"*

For a syndic to use a Starman's shipboard title was a clear warning given that discipline was being enforced. Life aboard a Goldenwing was seldom strict and not often formal. But on any vessel crewed by so few individuals, a direct appeal to ship's discipline was not to be challenged. That had been true on the clipper ships of old Earth, and it was true now, near the limits of Near Space.

Broni bit her lip and held back the tears. Buele reverted to type and said gently, "We all miss them, Sister Broni. But there is the ship to care for."

Broni clung to Clavius, holding him against her breast. He remonstrated with her as gently as one of the Folk may do. *"I am not a pet,"* the cat sent. The Folk were never pets.

Everyone on the bridge read the sending. Tragedy had sharpened and enhanced their empathic Talents. The more sensitive among them, Buele and Broni, could "hear" the reassurances being offered them from all the unknown number of cats throughout the ship.

Buele said, "See, Sister Broni? We are not alone."

A strong pulse came from *Glory* herself. It was a nurturing touch from a machine that had nurtured the men and women who had served her for a thousand years. Broni caught the swift thought from Buele: *"What is being alive compared to that?"*

Cybersurgeon Dietr Krieg, who had been silent throughout the interview with the Yamatans, said, "Paracelsus is young. He grieves for Mira." Despite the situation, he could not restrain himself from announcing, in this anonymous way, that he, the cold and cerebral man of old Earth, was no longer alone.

"So do they all, Brother Physician," Buele said. "Can't you hear them?" He glanced at Anya, a woman newly decorated with a new kitten on her shoulder. Anya was comforting her small familiar, cupping the small head in a hand and touching an ear with her lips.

Broni regarded Buele with a regard she had never known she felt for him. She noted that he had reverted to the "Brother This" and "Sister That" form of address. He had not done that for weeks, but it seemed just right now.

One day Buele will command us, Broni thought. *Duncan as much as told us that many times.*

"All right, then," Amaya spoke with authority. "Let's get the ship into a slingshot around Hideyoshi and back to Yamato as quickly as we can. Buele, can you replace Damon with the monkeys?"

"Aye, Captain."

"See to it the Yamatans stay on the hangar deck. We can't afford to have the monkeys frightened." They were all only too aware of how the small cyborgs had gone into fugue when soldiers of the Collective had blundered among them and murdered a few.

Amaya looked at Broni steadily. Her amber eyes held steady on Broni Ehrengraf Voerster's blue ones.

"Is there anything more you want to ask?" Amaya said.

"No, Captain," Broni said in a low voice. "Nothing more."

Within six uptime hours, *Glory*'s delta had dropped sufficiently for the computer to align the ship with the pass, awkward for a vessel of the Goldenwing's size, needed to make for a slingshot maneuver around Moon Hideyoshi.

Seven hours of backing sails to the solar wind of Amaterasu had also reduced *Glory*'s speed enough to allow a launch of the remaining mass-depletion-engined ships still aboard. With their mass neutralized, the MD craft would begin their fall back to their homeworld from a point of neutral gravity. Their voyage back to Yamato would be swift and undemanding.

Yoshi Eiji, the second-wave daimyo of Kai who was now the senior retainer present in the retinue of the Shogun Minamoto no Kami, was finishing the business of getting all the Shogun's people who had come in the barge *Dragonfly* into the more crowded accommodations aboard the MD ships. He had already been heard to complain about the lack of amenities aboard the

Shogun's experimentals. His own, he made it known, were superior in every way.

Minamoto no Kami, dressed now in a contemporary manner for space, stood with Anya Amaya in the shadow of *Dragonfly*'s stubby atmospheric foils. His distaste for the Lord of Kai was evident in his manner, but it would have been out of character for the old man to discuss Yamatan politics with a *gaijin*.

"There is a thing I should say to you, Captain-san," he said quietly. "My most skilled MD engineer was watching our vessel penetrate the Gateway into the Near Away. . . ." He hesitated, as though unsure of how, precisely, to say this to the new Master and Commander of the Goldenwing *Gloria Coelis*. This venture had not gone well, and he did not now wish to make it worse. "He watched carefully. The Gateway was not what one customarily sees when an MD coil is activated. It was very different, Anya-san."

"Tell me, Lord Shogun."

"It did not resemble a Gateway at all. What it appeared to be was a black hole. That, of course, is impossible. But nevertheless, Akaga-san is seldom in error."

Anya felt a stab of further grief. If what the Yamatan said was true, then those aboard the missing mass-depletion ship were truly and forever gone, torn apart by the powerful gravitic interplay of the hole. "I have read papers on the possibility of miniature black holes, Minamoto-sama, but everywhere *Glory* has sailed such things are intellectual constructs, not actual things."

The old man regarded her sadly. "I devoutly hope that you are right and my engineer is wrong." He essayed a melancholy smile. "But whatever you must face, you will face it well. As will I, Master and Commander. We are born and trained to our respective tasks. It is," he finished gently, "our karma." He bowed. "I bid you good journey back to Yamato."

30

AN INCAUTIOUS PURSUIT

•

For Duncan it was a plunge into emptiness. He sat in the unfamiliar chair of the MD pilot, his hands on controls he understood imperfectly. But Kantaro, with Hana on his shoulder, had moved to Duncan's side and stood ready to intervene if assistance was required. Damon, closely attended by Pronker, was engaged in whispered, intense conversation with the young Yamaguchi Kendo, who seemed dazed by all that had happened to the vessel entrusted to his care by the Shogun.

That left the odd-man-out character of Ishida, whose presence aboard the MD ship was unexplained. The man sat on the deck, motionless, as though lost in some deep meditation. His heavy-lidded eyes were veiled. From Mira came the warning that the man was dangerous. Duncan was certain that it had been Ishida who had thrown the star in the carapace deck aboard *Glory*. Minamoto no Kami had done Duncan no favor by assigning the silent man to the mission into the Near Away.

But there was no time to unravel all the twisted strings of feudal plotting, political maneuvering, and Yamatan motivations. Kantaro had warned Duncan that politics was a dark tangle in the colony and that because of it Duncan and the syndics might find themselves at risk. The time was now, Duncan thought. If he had been able to develop his original plan of isolating Yamato's ruling daimyos aboard *Glory* and well out into space where in isolation and utilizing the obligation with which Wired Starmen were regarded, a true alliance might have taken form. But the Terror had preempted any hope of that, and Duncan was forced now to pass political concerns on to another, to Kantaro, who knew his people and why they behaved as they did—but whose motives were as obscure as any of Planet Yamato's ruling class.

Thank God, Duncan thought, for Mira and Pronker and small Hana, without whom the humans aboard the MD craft were deaf, dumb and blind in this limbo of the Near Away.

Mira sent Duncan visions:

She was in pursuit of a shadowy enemy. It was dark night, a night without moon or stars, the footing was damp and had the smell of rank growing things—

Yes, yes, Duncan thought. That is how it was in deep space. Mira always knew where the threats were; time and distance meant nothing to her when she hunted.

In a response to a command from Mira, Pronker left Damon and attached himself to Duncan's other shoulder, gripping hard enough to drive the tips of his claws through the monomolecular fabric of the skinsuit.

Duncan felt the small, hard head press against his own. He could feel, too, the wispy touch of the drogue wire Dietr had planted in Mira's skull, unwittingly beginning all that had happened to *Glory*'s cats. Duncan abandoned himself to the powerful empathic sendings.

Two cats now stalked the dark grassland, searching, testing the scent of the air, tasting the feast of wild odors on the wind. A third cat appeared. A young female, still weeks from her first estrus. These were one with the saber-tooth and the smilodon who prowled this vast savannah. A hunting pride was forming, purposeful, dangerous.

Somewhere, not nearby, but within the globe of his awareness, Duncan sensed his own forebears. Not yet true men. What was happening to time? Duncan saw small, hungry creatures with heavy brow-ridges and fearful eyes. He remembered them. On summer nights, he huddled with them around a sparking, smoking fire while the cats watched from the shadows.

I will not crouch tonight, *he thought.* I am not *Homo habilis.* I am something else entirely. *Something that was never born, yet here it is. He felt the grasses brushing his belly as he crept forward toward the prey. He smelled its fear. His hunger burned like fire. . . .*

Duncan opened his eyes. The reality within the ship was indistinct, fading. He had to concentrate his effort to keep from drifting back to the empty savannah with Mira and Pronker and young Hana. His hands on the helm console seemed to be appendages of another being, too civilized to prowl the black night of interstellar space.

He was aware that he had recklessly fed mass into the grid within the MD coils girdling the ship. Without points of reference, it was not possible to know how fast the ship was moving—or if it was moving at all. But the outsider left a spoor of fear behind it.

Is it truly afraid of us*?* Duncan wondered. All living beings could feel fear. Wasn't it possible that the intruder had never before been threatened with extinction? *In the Ross Stars we fought its* aspects, Duncan thought. *We saw how it killed and we were terrified. We sought escape. We never considered retaliation.*

Had Man finally become too civilized to survive in the savannahs of Deep Space?

Hana squeezed between Mira and Pronker, so that Duncan wore a living necklace of cats. All of them were uttering deep, soft growls. Their eyes were wide open, the pupils dilated. The lights of the control console reflected in the black mirrors of those far-seeing eyes.

What could they see? Was it the scene that became ever more real in Duncan's mind? A world of their creation built of species memories reaching back a thousand centuries and a dozen light-years.

Duncan was struck by a thought that left him shaken. If there was no time in the Near Away, then there could be no true space. Were the cats getting sendings from the others still aboard *Glory,* as near or as far as one's perceptions allowed? But was it what he truly wanted? Didn't the empty savannah whisper a more powerful call? To hunt, to stalk the dark enemy, to find and to kill . . .

He resisted the empathic coma. *I cannot live as they do,* he thought. He struggled to control his anima. *Mira,* he thought, *I honor you, but I cannot* become *you.* He reached blindly to touch his familiar.

I am a man, he thought. *Only a man.* But was that really true? That was only one reality.

There was another.

With a rush of desire, he reached for it, embraced it, and abandoned himself once again to the hunt.

Minamoto Kantaro, crouched beside the pilot's chair, looked disbelievingly at the chronometers in the console. They were a blur that could not be read.

In normal space there was always a sense of time passing.

In the Near Away there was none.

There was a void where the human sense of temporal awareness should be. The ship could have passed through the singularity moments ago. Or years.

Damon Ng was receiving the empathic spillage of the sendings being exchanged among Duncan and the Folk. Damon had actually seen, heard, experienced, if only for an instant, the same incredible savannah that Duncan and the cats were experiencing. But Damon's Talent was too small, too weak, to stabilize the visions.

To Kantaro he whispered, "I saw something for a moment. Did you?"

"Was it real?" Kantaro's voice was even lower than the young syndic's. His was a native Talent, too late to be recruited and schooled. But his vision had been powerful enough to make him, for a moment, slightly more than human.

He had glimpsed an endless plain he did not know, a night without stars he did not understand, and he sensed the deep anger of dire beasts resolved at last to turn and fight. *Four great cats. Not three* . . .

Damon said, *"Everything is real here."*

The Near Away was not a place where time did not exist. It was a location where *all* time existed. Everything that ever was, ever had been, ever would be, was here, somewhere imbedded in the topology of the Near Away.

The thought was terrifying.

The fourth cat raised his head and tasted the night. The enemy—he thought of it as prey—lay just ahead. The chase had been long, very long. Yet the great cat and his companions felt no physical fatigue. On the contrary, the depth of the night and the emotion of the chase made them stronger, angrier.

He knew the three others relied on him to lead the attack when it must be led. There would be death. That was understood. The fear that accompanied the understanding was familiar. All of life was laced with fear. It made life precious.

The savannah was changing. There was still no light in the sky, but the cats together sensed that they were penetrating into the territory of others. Their spoor was faint, but it was there, and growing more powerful.

The young female raised her voice to utter a challenge and was cuffed to silence by the queen. She subsided, belly to the black Earth, and crept forward flanked by the dominant tom and the young male.

The hunting pride slowed and advanced with ever more caution. The spoor of the others who shared this region of night grew ever stronger. None of the great cats had ever tasted life quite like it.

The dominant tom stopped, stood frozen, one forepaw lifted as he extended his senses into the space ahead. The intruder, the destroyer—a thing of enormous powers and primitive intelligence—fled, spreading a tsunami of fear as he fled down the night. The dominant tom uttered a guttural cry of fury. The others out there had visions of a kill. Driven by their own fear they intended to attack, to steal the pride's prey. The dominant tom opened his throat and gave a cry of rage that reverberated across the vast spaces, shattering the silence with a challenge.

The hunters rose out of concealment, and plunged forward in a furious charge. . . .

31

SENDINGS

•

Buele, relieved on watch by Anya Amaya, lay thoughtfully on air in his quarters. He was sad and depressed, a state of being that was uncommon for him. But he was mature enough by now to know that a syndic should rest when he could. He also understood that the acting Captain was using him with care, groping, as inexperienced people will, for the proper mix of discipline and concern that was the mark of a good Commander.

The Supernumerary had been shown parts of Duncan's standing orders, particularly those pertaining to himself and his future. He chose not to dwell on a possible career as the Master and Commander of Goldenwing *Gloria Coelis*. The others would do enough of that. They must have doubts, as he did himself. But Duncan's word was still the law aboard *Glory,* as it had been for years.

He squinted at Big, who crouched atop a fabric ledge where, by choice, he usually slept while in quarters. Big was growing into an enormous tomcat with an impressive head and great amber eyes. The cat was regarding the Supernumerary with an unblinking stare.

How Dietr Krieg could say that the Folk had no true sense of interspecies hierarchy was beyond imagining. Big—and in fact all the Folk aboard *Glory*—tended to test the people on board constantly with an unlimited book of feline quirks and gestures. The unblinking stare was a common ploy, as were the silent meow and—a favorite of Big's—the turning of the back as a sign of shunning or displeasure.

Broni said the Folk did these things to make certain that their influence over the possessors of hands and opposed thumbs remained unchallenged. Broni was probably right. *Glory*'s cats were achieving a social and intellectual development that made Buele wonder which was to be the dominant life-form aboard Goldenwing *Gloria Coelis*.

The Folk were not revolutionaries, of course. They were conservative to the claw-tips. Sudden changes upset them almost as much as did attempts to discipline them (which they almost loftily ignored). What they expected was comfort and successes. The species, even in its unenhanced form, was dismayed by failure.

"I do not suppose you would tell me honestly what you feel right now," Buele said aloud in Voertrekker Afrikaans. He often spoke to Big in the Voertrekker tongue. Images were clear to Buele in the language of his birth world.

He anchored himself with a fingertip to the softly undulating fabric wall. "Are they truly lost?" he asked.

Big blinked his eyes deliberately. The cat had a way of constantly conducting communications drills. A slow opening and closing of the great amber eyes was a signal of thoughtful attention. Attention was not given cheaply. The mature Folk aboard, like all obligate carnivores, were only conditionally social. Much of their inner life lay far beyond man's ability to comprehend. But from time to time, and in times of great need, they deigned to share their concerns.

Big was a tom who preferred to respond to challenges with direct actions. Fight or flee. Big understood such choices excellently well—as did Buele.

Big responded instinctively. Buele had learned *his* responses as an abandoned child in the alleys of the sad kraals of the Grassersee on Voerster. Boy and cat shared oddly similar psychological gestalts.

The terrible events of the last day and a half had plainly depressed Big. His ropy tail lashed irritably. Big did not take defeats gracefully. Even the thought of a visit to the food replicators did not improve Big's outlook. Big liked to eat. But he was not hungry now. The tail thumped the fabric wall like a drum.

Big had recently become fond of Pronker, allowing him to trail along on Big's personal explorations of the kilometers of plenum and empty hold in *Glory.*

Cats always mourned their dead; they were capable of deep feelings. But sensitivity to the feelings of other species had never been a human strength. Life aboard *Glory* was different, though, more so with each passing day. *Glory*'s cats brought to bear on *Glory*'s syndics an arsenal of sensitivities. But all aboard understood that the Folk were pragmatic. Though they grieved deeply, they would not grieve long.

Big, however, was a special case. He had been the largest kitten of Mira's original litter, and he was unquestionably a leader of the Folk. When Buele first had realized that Big was a chosen one among the Folk, he wondered if the large tom was ready for such a station in life. Big could be, in many ways, something of a clown. He was, in fact, rather like Buele himself.

Buele knew what his partner was feeling. Big was wounded by his losses, and he was angry with a fate that dealt such blows to those who deserved better. The cats had an innate sense of the fitness of things. Buele, having come from a low station in life on a rigidly hierarchically structured planet, understood the cats well.

He regarded his companion with deep affection and empathy. *You are luckier than I,* he thought. *Perhaps because your lives are short, you will not be burdened with long sorrows.*

"*Mira,*" Big sent back. He was in no mood for an interspecies philosophical discussion. "*Where is Mira?*" he demanded.

Buele felt hot tears in his eyes. What could he say to his bereaved friend and companion? He wanted to say, "Find her, Big, if you can."

Exercising the electromechanical skills he had developed as observatory assistant to the Astronomer Select of Voerster, Buele had filled his compartment with racks of electronic devices. He had constructed a bank of sensitive holographic connections to the starship's exterior imagers, and it was his habit to keep the holos working and recording for hours at a time. What transpired Outside the ship was a source of never-ending interest and delight to Buele. In less stressful times, Big, too, seemed to enjoy studying the recordings Buele's scavenged devices accumulated and stored. He wondered if Big simply enjoyed the displays—or did he know what it was he was seeing? Buele, like Duncan, had already learned that the Folk had the ability to create inner images more suited to their nature than did the human beings of Goldenwing *Gloria Coelis*. Buele had no difficulty accepting this seeming anomaly. Even at Starhome he used to drive Osbertus Voerster to distraction by repeatedly asking the old astronomer to describe precisely what he saw at any given time, and then asking him if there was any way in which true perceptions could be shared. How else could one person ever know another? Buele wondered. His favorite question was a demand to know if what Osbertus saw as, say, "green," was also what he, Buele, saw as green. Or was it something else entirely, forever hidden within each person, unreachable—even unsuspected?

Buele had never received a satisfactory answer from Osbertus, or from any man. But within the environment of a brotherhood of empaths he had become hopeful that one time, somehow, he would see a thing *exactly* as Big saw it—and then he would know.

Buele stared thoughtfully at the holographs his breadboarded instruments were producing. *Glory* was rounding Moon Hideyoshi, in the slingshot maneuver that would put the Goldenwing on a return course to Planet Yamato. The holo showed the airless, inhospitable surface of the moon where one could make out the gantries and construction cradles, the hangars and worker billets of the Kaian enterprise on the smallest of Yamato's three natural satellites. There was no activity discernable on the surface. The Shogun's arrival at Kai Island, Yamato, where the spaceport was located, had been followed with an announcement on the Planetary News Net by Minamoto no Kami. A national period of funerary ceremonies for Lord Minamoto Kantaro was declared, and all spacecraft in the jurisdiction of the planetary government were grounded until the mourning period was completed. Business was at a standstill, and white death-flags flew all over Planet Yamato, and some even hung in the airless dark of Moon Hideyoshi.

Buele addressed himself to Big: *"No one is very hopeful. The bad news has hit the Yamatans very hard, I think."*

The reply was a formless longing for Mira, the matriarch. Buele could feel Big's comforting memory of being groomed as a kitten by Mira. The warm, wet rasp of her tongue brought deep feelings of security and relief. Followed by the realization that Mira was no longer available to form the beating heart of the Folk.

There were often times when Big would have chosen not to enter into exchanges like these. Buele realized that like most of the Folk, Big had a tendency to be single-minded. Big might easily think Buele's commiseration frivolous and ignore it. Big considered life as an enhanced cat aboard Goldenwing *Gloria Coelis* a serious business.

But he offered a reply. He did not deign to frame it in human words, which he thought a clumsy instrument for self-expression. Instead he allowed Buele to feel a small part of his grief for his prowling mate and even for little Hana, of whom he had only recently become aware. And referring to Mira, the mother and matriarch, he sent plainly that *Glory*'s Folk did not think things had gone well. Not at all. He unsheathed his foreclaws and bared his long canines to show Buele in feline body language how he thought the dark enemy should have been dealt with. *"We will have to hunt again,"* he sent distinctly.

Buele did not want Big disappointed. *"We shall have to see about that,"* he sent.

"Mira," Big sent back, still grief-stricken and angry. *"Mira! I want Mira!"*

In the emptiness of the carapace deck, lighted by the coppery sunlight reflected from the harsh, pocked globe of Moon Hideyoshi, Broni Ehrengraf gyrated through a melancholy dance with Clavius.

The black tom had a remarkable skill in low-gravity movements. Broni often had the impression that Clavius heard some inner, private music when he moved. She could almost hear the sweet countermelodies she loved so when they were played on the balichord by the tom's namesake, the beached Starman Black Clavius, and sometimes it seemed to the girl that Clavius was an odd reincarnation of the wanderer she had loved so on Voerster.

It was quite absurd, her Voertrekker aristocracy declared. Reincarnation was an ancient fraud from Earth, and the notion that a man could be reborn as a cat smacked of Buddhist mysticism. Planet Voerster had its mysteries, particularly among the

Kaffirs, but the idea of man into cat was too absurd to take seriously.

Yet as Broni watched her feline partner move through the slow and graceful evolutions of his inner-driven dance, she felt hot tears in her eyes. Poor Clavius was grieving, as were all the cats aboard. This was a thing said to be impossible by the legions of veterinary medics and zoologists whose wisdom was contained in the vast data bank of *Glory*'s computer. Cats felt loss and bereavement, the authorities said, but not for long. Opinions varied, but a consensus suggested that a week of mourning was all that *Felis catus* was likely to experience.

"So much for what they know," she thought, addressing the sending directly to the ship. In the last few days, since Duncan and Damon disappeared into the Near Away, her own emotional bruising appeared to have increased her empathic sensibility. From time to time she was finding it possible to address *Glory* directly, without needing to seat a drogue in her skull socket.

Clavius uttered a plaintive, singing cry and returned to settle against her naked breasts. Like Anya Amaya, Broni had begun to discard her clothing much of the time. She derived a sensual comfort from the tingling touch of tachyons penetrating her bare, golden skin.

Broni rolled onto her back so that she could look at the play of light on the rig, the flash of sun off the hectares of shining skylar. Beyond the mist of stays and halyards Broni could see the grayish, sterile surface of Moon Hideyoshi. At this distance the works of the Yamatans were invisible. Black Clavius used to quote the Earth Ecumenical Bible. One of his favorite lines was from the book of Hebrews: *"What is man that thou art mindful of him?"*

What, indeed? Broni wondered. Her youthful spirit had been badly wounded in the last few days. Black Clavius had often warned that man was only one of many vulnerable creatures inhabiting the Increate's vast universe. *And yet*, Broni thought, *and yet God offers to let us touch small miracles now and again*. She cupped Clavius's round head in her hand. "Glory *goes on, Clavius,"* she sent, *"even if Duncan and Damon and Mira and Hana, and Pronker die."*

Clavius twisted to look directly into her eyes. *"They are gone, not dead."*

Broni's artificial heart beat on methodically, but her breath caught in her throat. *Gone* but not *dead?* What could that possibly mean? She had seen their ship swallowed up by the singularity that should not have been in the Gateway.

"Clavius," she sent severely. *"Clavius. Listen to me."*

The cat turned his back on her and departed. She had used the wrong approach. The Folk hated to be probed and queried. The things they knew they assumed everyone knew. There was no need to experience again and again things that were unpleasant. Clavius felt gloomy, sad. Like Big, in another part of the ship, he longed for Mira to come back and make life aboard the great-queen-who-is-not-alive right again.

But no one had died. Not yet.

Broni turned and swam swiftly downward through the reflections toward a drogue in the wall near the valve into the outer plenum. She needed to talk with the others—the others of her own kind: Anya, Buele and Dietr. Above all with Dietr, who was, aboard *Gloria Coelis,* a master of hard knowledge.

32

ACROSS THE VAULT OF HEAVEN

·

The man calling himself Ishida was confused. He had imagined, when Lord Yoshi contrived to obtain a place for him aboard the MD craft that would penetrate the Near Away, that the voyage would be short and the murder of the *gaijin* simple. Now he told himself that he had not only been mistaken, but that he had been manipulated into a situation from which there would be no escape.

In his persona of Tsunetomo, the Master Ninja of Yamato, Ishida was a man to be feared and respected. He was skilled in the one thousand and one ways of killing, with sword, knife, star, dart and bare hands, that all ninjas were expected to master, and he had taken command of this particular assassination when his first messenger had floated away headless from the city of Yedo in a grav harness.

To Master Tsunetomo (which was the way he thought of himself) there was no more demanding duty than the killing of the foreign Starman. Once it was known on the home planet that the Order of Ninjas had been hired to put the Goldenwing's commander to death and had failed to do so, a millennium of tradition and power would come to nothing. This could not be.

In the cramped quarters of the mass-depletion spaceship, where consoles, racks of equipment and five men had to share a few square meters of space, it was difficult to compose one's mind for the burst of killing activity needed to eliminate the *gaijin*.

It did not even occur to the ninja that with every moment that passed, it became more and more likely that no one, certainly no Yamatan, would ever know what transpired in the small ship while it traversed the Near Away for meters or light-years. Ishida was not a scientist, nor was he an engineer. He did not understand the principles of mass-depletion spaceflight, nor did he care to speculate. Since earliest childhood, in fact since the moment his nameless and impoverished mother had delivered him as an infant to the dark mansion of the Order, Ishida had learned only the old ways, the ancient skills and traditions. He had been in space only once before, on a training mission aboard an antique shuttle—the vessel dedicated to the purpose of teaching novice ninjas the skills needed to kill in null gravity.

He was discovering now, to his dismay, that he disliked spaceflight. That it unsettled him and made it difficult to maintain the draconian discipline to which he had dedicated his life.

He had no duties aboard the MD ship. The suggestion from the Lord of Kai to the Shogun was that he could assist in the serving of the MD's one, hastily mounted weapon—a low-power lazegun—a weapon no one was certain would be of any value whatever against the thing they were pursuing.

The plunge through the Gateway, and through the singularity that should never have been where it was, had shaken Ishida. For a man with a profound respect for fantasy and hallucinations, the timeless, dimensionless void that all the outer imaging cameras returned was frightening. Worse still was the behavior of the *gaijin,* blank-eyed and necklaced with the three cats that had been brought aboard. Ishida had seen men in the grasp of the spirit world before. During the Order's prayers to Hachiman, the God of War and Death, men often drifted into dream states during which they sweated and foamed and even bled. All from exertions and battles fought and wounds taken in wars of the Inner World.

It had never happened to him, and so he had doubted. Yet there, before his eyes, the towering man from the Goldenwing had experienced *something.* Ishida had been shocked to see that Duncan's hands and feet were scratched and bleeding, as though he had moved on all fours through some unseen field of razor grass.

The ninja rose from his seated position and considered striking the death blow now, while the others on board seemed riveted to the imaging screens. But he was unable to touch the hilt of the *wakizashi* thrust into his belt.

He stared unbelieving at his own hands. They were unchanged, familiar. Yet it seemed that he had never really seen them before. The weapons work of a lifetime had hardened them. They were as strong as a raptor's claws, and as deadly.

"Ishida! What is the matter with you, man? Lend a hand here!" The shogun's nephew, Minamoto, spoke sharply and commandingly. He and the second *gaijin* were struggling, awkwardly in the absence of gravity, to move the dazed Kr-san out of the pilot's chair and onto a cleared area on the deck. The tall *gaijin*'s eyes were still unfocused, but his lips were drawn back in a snarling gesture that made him look terrifyingly like a hunting animal. The impression was so strong that Ishida had to recite a sutra to calm himself sufficiently to touch the foreigner.

His skin was hot, as though his body temperature were degrees higher than normal. His respiration made growling noises in his throat. And the cats hovered over him, furiously protective, teeth bared, ears flattened, fur on end. One of them, the older female, uttered a taut, challenging wail of rage as he touched the foreigner.

"All right!" Minamoto Kantaro said. "Leave it, then. Don't anger them."

The ninja retreated, watching in disbelief. He had never seen a living leopard or tiger. He knew them only from the books and films brought long ago from Earth aboard the *Hachiman*. Yet for one insane instant it seemed to him that the *gaijin* had not been a man at all, but a long, pale-skinned cat.

Duncan, near to shock from the swiftly changing states, opened his eyes. The first image that registered on his brain was the intense cat face of Mira, her gaze fixed upon him. He instantly translated her expression with a clarity never possible to him before. Mira regarded him with a mixture of fear, concern, and a hunger to continue the chase. She was communicating, urgently, but in images that were far from the human referents he had been using all his life. He became aware that for the first time he had shared the feline mystery in a way no man had ever done before. The experience had changed both cat and man profoundly. He shifted his gaze to Pronker. (He knew of course that Pronker was not his name; it was not even an approximation of the gestalt that identified *this* cat and made it possible for Duncan to know him in a population of millions.) Little Hana uttered a soft meow and ran her raspy tongue across his cheek. *I know you, small sister,* Duncan thought. *We shared a dark savannah.* Instantly, from Mira, whose true name was a symphonic cascade of sensations and sounds and smells and tastes, came a sending that was received with a clarity as powerful as hot sunlight.

"The cruel one is out there. We are very near. I want to kill it."

No adult human being would communicate so basic a desire with such singleness of purpose. A brilliant child might put it in such terms, but human adults spent their lives unlearning such directness.

Duncan struggled to sit erect. His heart still raced. The breath was thick in his throat with the smells of the savannah that Mira's and Hana's and Pronker's distant forebears had known and passed on across tens of thousands of generations to these three. The miracle was stunning in its implications.

Damon and Kantaro supported Duncan as he steadied his overloaded senses.

Damon looked closely at Duncan and whispered, "Thank God you're alive, Captain."

Before Duncan could reply, the confined space rang with a cry of mingled terror, astonishment and disbelief.

"Minamoto-sama! Look! Oh, God, look at the sky!"

Duncan pushed aside Damon and Kantaro and steadied himself on the holographic screen of an imager. What he saw took his breath away.

Duncan Kr had become a creature of Deep Space. When he departed the majestic coasts of his homeworld where the mists fell but could never quite obscure the sky-filling grandeur of the great Moon Bothwell—the commanding object that dominated the heavens above Thalassa's endless, turbid seas—he had never expected to see anything so grand again.

But this . . .

He flew to the closed port that opened directly into space. "Draw back the shutters," he shouted. "Draw them back!"

The young pilot looked at Kantaro. The shutters of the direct ports were never opened aboard a mass-depletion ship. It was the opinion of the physicians, those few who had been in the Near Away, that prolonged exposure to the blank emptiness of the medium through which the small ships moved was a temptation to mental instabilities.

"Do what Kr-san orders!" Kantaro said in a voice he did not recognize as his own. He, too, had caught a glimpse of the image in the holo projector.

The shutters slid back into their sheaths and the port opened like a diaphragm so that only crystal glass separated the men at the port from what lay beyond.

Duncan felt a hand close around his heart. He had seen much, but not this. Never anything like this.

The ambiguity of the Near Away was gone. The Terror had opened another Gateway and the MD ship had plunged through it in pursuit.

To what appeared to be the celestial north the sky was ablaze, thickly populated with young stars scintillating in flaming colors against the obsidian darkness of space.

Duncan gripped the frame of the port with both hands. Blood from his injuries oozed between his fingers. He searched the overarching vault of the alien heaven. In this region of the sky, the stars were colder, older, less exuberant. Duncan looked across an unpopulated gulf of darkness. It was as though he stood naked on the edge of infinity.

The ship lay near the edge of an elliptical cloud of suns, and beyond, across the dark southern sky, lay the most gorgeous object he had ever seen.

Spread across a third of the great starry vault lay a nebula, an immense galaxy with spiral arms alive with colors. At the center of the great disk rose a cloudy mountain of stars that resembled the tumbled silvery mists of Thalassa.

I know that mountain of star-mist, Duncan thought. *I know the Great Nebula, too, though I have never seen it from this angle. The stellar cloud where I stand is also something I have seen— from an enormous distance.*

And beyond the nebula lay another star cloud, diamond bright against the clear dark of Deep Space. *Even if I could not see it ablaze with stars beyond the vast, perfect spiral,* Duncan thought, *I would recognize it.*

He closed his eyes against the tears that formed unbidden

under his lids. He thought, *I do know this place. I have dreamed of it all my years in space.*

We stand on the edge of the Lesser Magellanic Cloud, Duncan thought. *The distant star cloud is the Greater Magellanic Cloud. And that is M31—so near one might almost reach out and touch it. Oh, Black Clavius,* Duncan thought. *How you would delight to be in this place.* The old Starman would surely stand here, and in his resonant voice he would proclaim the words of the Psalmist:

"The heavens declare the glory of God; and the firmament sheweth his handiwork."

Filled with the wonder of it, Duncan said, "We are two million light-years from home."

Though he should not have been, he was amazed by the reaction of his human companions. Have we become so dulled, Duncan thought, so accustomed to the safety of the familiar, that we cannot see what has happened to us? We are the children of Earth, he thought, a small planet lost in a great and now distant galaxy. Yet here we stand amid the suns of the Lesser Magellanic Cloud.

He looked at his human companions in surprise. *All that I see,* he thought, *is fear. Desolation. Isolation. The glory of what we have done means nothing to them. Damon, at least, should share my joy,* Duncan thought. *He is a Starman.* But fear and shock robbed one of the exaltation that was due.

Duncan looked from Damon to Kantaro to the MD pilot and finally to the brooding Ishida. "We have done what no one has ever done," he said. "We have turned the Einsteinian laws upside down. Does that mean nothing to you?"

The men looked at him with dumb fear in their eyes. The cats sat in the pilot's chair, indifferent, now that the moment had passed, to the meaning of their impossible journey. The Folk only waited impatiently to carry on the chase, to find the dark enemy, to kill it.

"Mira," Duncan thought. *"Can you explain it?"*

Mira showed no interest whatever in explaining anything. Her tail lashed the cushions of the pilot's chair, announcing that she was interested only in getting on with the chase—finishing it with the kill. The cats had enormous Talents and abilities, but they were simply not interested in any distance that could not be covered in a leap.

Damon Ng lowered his head and spoke in a strained, low voice. "We are ordinary men, Master and Commander. We do not see things as you do. It takes us more time."

"There is no more time," Minamoto Kantaro said. "Look."

Approaching from the direction of the celestial pole at a speed that shifted their images to blue, a fleet of ships was drawing near. Duncan studied the vessels intently. Who could know, he thought, what beings were contained in those nearly relativistic hulls?

For the first time since penetrating this space, the Kaian Ishida Minoru spoke. His voice was ragged with tension. Duncan recognized the signs of impending emotional cascade. "Those ships," Ishida said, "look at them. They are warships." He flexed his hands as though to draw the *katana*—which he did not carry—from a scabbard. He glared at Duncan. "You brought us here, Starman. You brought us to this spirit place to die without the comfort of our gods or the honor of our clan—"

Kantaro got a grip on his own fears and said sharply, "Since when did a ninja fear dying?"

Duncan reacted automatically, but it was still too late. A short blade materialized in Ishida's hand and he leapt at Kantaro.

"Nooo!" wailed Damon. "You'll draw the thing to us!"

But it was already too late. The young pilot, acting on his own secret instructions from Minamoto no Kami, produced a laze pistol and raised it in the direction of Ishida.

Ishida switched his attack from Kantaro instantly and struck with the short-bladed *wakizashi,* drawing the blade through the young man's neck as tidily as a surgeon. Blood from a severed carotid artery fountained in the near-zero gravity.

Kantaro had also drawn a weapon, but Duncan stepped between him and Ishida. He delivered a single blow with a rock-hard fist and the Kaian was lifted from the deck to rebound like a rubber man from the blood-drenched pilot's console. Duncan caught him by an arm and twisted it behind him with such violence that he felt it break in his grip. *"Enough!"* he commanded, shaken by his own anger.

But it was already far more than enough. Between the distant alien ships and the MD craft, a darkness had formed, a vast, dark shape laced with streaks of angry fire. Duncan felt the unreasoning rage of the thing. It was no different here, two million light-years from home, than it had been in the Ross Stars: lonely fury, killing rage. And fear. Fear of the creatures that had coursed it across the miles and light-years and parsecs without pause or caution.

The beings in the warships were empaths. Whatever their intent, they forewarned the Terror with the waves of emotion that preceded them. The Dark Intruder had come this way before, Duncan guessed.

Duncan took the fighting chair and initialized the lazegun. Kantaro took the pilot's place. The cats yowled their fighting cries as the MD, under Kantaro's guidance, came to life and moved, with shocking acceleration, in the direction of the coming battle.

33

A WAR ABOVE THE SKY

•

Minamoto Kantaro, sweat-streaked and disheveled, took command of the MD ship as it accelerated toward the swirling dark that blotted out the strange, bright stars. The mass-depletion coils had converted most of the ship's mass to energy in the passage through the Near Away. How much remained was unknown. The MDs were experimental craft, not intended for violent and lengthy adventures in the Near Away or wherever else outside normal space they might find themselves.

For over a thousand years it had been assumed by all Terrestrial colonists that fighting in space was next to impossible. As far as Earth's colonial children were concerned, a space-warship was an oxymoron. Or had been, until now.

"We have almost no maneuvering mass, Kr-san," Kantaro reported. "I will have to make the shortest, most direct approach."

Duncan charged the laze rifle mounted in the nose section of the MD. "Do it," he said. He glanced at the proximity radar screen. The Terror was off the inner range scale. The targets beyond, more than a thousand of them, formed an encircling pattern at ranges of from one to two hundred kilometers. Their delta had fallen from nearly ten thousand kilometers per hour at approach to less than a thousand as they closed.

"Those ships are *big*," Duncan said. The size of the alien craft shocked him. They were larger than *Glory* and bristling with sinister projections that Duncan suspected were weapons. But the fleet was primitive, even by Goldenwing standards. Ships such as these would be useless in the space Duncan knew, even for planetary exploration, unless the beings who owned them were physically enormous and lived long, very slow lives. Duncan did not get that impression. What he sensed was anger and fear that were almost Terrestrial in character.

What could have persuaded a spacefaring culture to devote the resources necessary to build such an armada as this? The answer emanated empathically from the alien fleet. What the aliens aboard their great slow battleships sought was *revenge*. Duncan had guessed that the Terror had passed this way before. This confrontation confirmed it. But how long ago had all this taken place? The elapsed time-span was staggering. If these people were as bound by their temporal frame of reference as were Terrestrials, the probability was that they had been preparing for *this engagement* for whatever interval passed for millennia in this place. They were ready at a moment's notice to swarm into the sky and defend their civilization. The concept of such fear and hatred was staggering—even to one with Duncan's record of struggle with the Terror. These creatures must have detected the Terror's approach, and over a span of time that had lasted moments to those aboard the MD ship but must have lasted—here and now for these beings—months, years, even millennia, or whatever units of time they used to organize their lives.

Damon, closely attended by an excited, tail-lashing Pronker, crouched by the fighting chair. "What happens if we attack the Terror and *they*"—he indicated the cluttered radar screen—"decide to attack us?"

"During the Jihad, our ancestors learned a simple reality from the Muslims. 'The enemy of my enemy is my friend,' " Duncan replied.

Damon was silent, his eyes fixed on the enlarging images on the screens. Then he asked quietly, "Will we ever get back, Master and Commander?"

"I don't know, Damon," Duncan said. "At the moment I see no way we can return. I'm sorry."

The alien ships were sparks of colored light in the screens. The Terror was a mass of darkness and threads of fire. Duncan drew in a slow, deep breath. If the killer's attention were not already heavily engaged, Duncan was sure that it would by now have made an attempt to engulf the MD ship. There was nothing whatever about the Yamatan technology that inhibited attack. Perhaps a Gateway and a retreat into the Near Away might forestall the Terror. But that path seemed foreclosed. Ahead was where duty lay for *Glory*'s syndics.

Duncan spared a glance for Ishida, who lay, still dazed and cradling a broken arm, against a bulkhead. The young pilot lay dead in a veritable lake of blood. There were still englobed droplets in the air. When they struck the imaging screens they adhered and smeared the surface of the cathode-ray tubes.

"Kantaro-san," Duncan said. "Can you give me a clear holograph?"

In the well of the flightdeck an image formed. Tiny spacecraft closed on a star-killing darkness. As Duncan watched, one of the first wave of alien craft loosed what appeared to be a spread of torpedoes. They left golden trails as they vanished into the fire-shot cloud. Two flashed with a brightness that was unmistakably nuclear. Two hot globes appeared within the darkness and were swiftly engulfed. A crooked bolt of electric-violet light snaked across the intervening distance between the Terror and the leading ships of the attacking fleet.

Two of the vast vessels that had fired missiles began to dissolve into dazzling fountains of light. How many lives aboard those ships? Duncan wondered. Judging from the size of the vessels, there were probably thousands. They imploded, collapsed into corroding fire. Within seconds, two of the mammoth ships were reduced to white-hot debris tumbling away from the heart of the destruction.

How long had it taken the Terror to learn such combat? The scope of the puzzle was mind-numbing, Duncan thought. *When it fought us in the Ross Stars it was an* elemental—*a force of nature, violent, but devoid of destructive sophistication.* Yet now it attacked the alien ships as though it were itself a vehicle of war. It took years, perhaps centuries, to change so radically. That left a daunting question: How many years, centuries, aeons, had passed since the battle at Ross 248?

We are disadvantaged by our need for linear time, Duncan thought. *We can accept* intellectually *that we have passed through a space, a dimension (what should one call it?) in which time, like space itself, either did not exist or existed in forms corporeal entities such as we could not conceive.*

Yet the battle developing now was real enough. Those beings aboard the destroyed ships, whatever and whoever they might be, were beyond question dead, destroyed, reduced to their constituent atoms.

The injured ninja began to stir.

"Keep him under control, Damon," Duncan ordered.

"Aye, Captain." Damon stepped over the body of the MD pilot and stationed himself over the reviving Ishida. The man's broken arm, bent in the wrong place and wrong direction, made Damon feel queasy. The only violence Damon had ever experienced were the earlier encounters with the Terror. He considered binding Ishida, but decided against it. He did not wish to inflict pain.

Kantaro, in the pilot's chair, said over his shoulder, "Two more ships are coming in to attack, Kr-san. With five more behind them."

"Get us closer," Duncan said, raising the power of the lazegun to the maximum setting. He suspected that the laser would have no effect. So far the weapons used by the alien spaceships had been ineffective, and they were clearly more powerful than what the Yamatan craft deployed.

But we have not come all this way to surrender, Duncan thought, and Mira yowled angry agreement.

The spark representing the MD ship within the holograph moved in a tightening curve as it approached the dark shadow. Duncan put his forehead against the sight and directed a hot beam of coherent light into the center of the target. The beam penetrated the darkness and vanished. No damage had been inflicted. None at all. But the laze had provided a distraction, and the alien vessels closed to exploit it. Whoever or whatever fought the ships of that alien fleet were being strained and trained again for battle. Whatever else the Terror might have done in the distant past of this space, it had impressed upon this race the absolute need for an ability to wage war.

This time the aliens attacked with energy weapons. Jagged beams of violet light formed on forward projections of the lead craft and then flung themselves at the enemy. It was as though the beams themselves were intelligent and sought their target with a malevolence to match the Terror's own.

At the point within the darkness where the beams intersected, a coruscating fireball formed, extended fiery, questing tendrils of light. For a moment the Terror seemed in danger of being overwhelmed by the power of the weapon, then it recovered, smothering the inner fire with its darkness.

"Again!" Damon shouted empathically. *"Shoot again!"*

As though the alien warriors heard the empathic command, a rank of the huge warships repeated the attack with the beams of violet light. Duncan counted an attack by a dozen ships before the Terror's movement blotted out half the ships and left the others gutted and in expanding masses of ruin. The environment resonated with the death agonies of thousands.

The cats screamed and Duncan fought off the avalanche of pain and death that radiated from the destroyed ships. Damon had slumped to the deck, his anima outraged by the terrible dying of the alien thousands.

Even Kantaro, who was only a partial empath and totally untrained, was staggered by the tsunami of death. He fought to keep the MD pointed at the swirling, furious darkness.

Duncan felt its anger. He felt, too, its fear. It was orders of magnitude greater than that of the quarry he remembered from the dark savannah of their passage to this place. He fired a second bolt of light into the sooty cloud. Again the tiny attack distracted, and Duncan felt its attention focus on him at last.

There was a flash of recognition. *"The thing remembers us, Mira,"* he sent. He fired the laser still again. Mira sent back, *"Kill it, dominant tom."*

"If only I could," Duncan lamented.

But he had drawn its attention, and the warriors aboard the ships of the alien fleet had millennia of battle knowledge to guide them. The violet weapon formed on the projectors of the entire fleet, held there for one long moment, and then converged upon the Terror.

The darkness was shot through with light and fire. Duncan wondered what the accumulated power of those weapons might be. Millions of gigawatts? Billions? Without *Glory*'s computer banks and sensors he had no way of knowing. But the effect on the Terror was vast. Duncan felt Mira's triumphant surge of pleasure. Small Hana gripped the top of a console and trilled with satisfaction.

Have they killed it? Duncan wondered. *Is it truly ending now?*

Will we see it die here and know Glory's *people are safe at last?*

The fire spread through the cloud like a cancer. Second and third discharges from the alien fleet struck the Terror again and again.

Surely it is dying now, Duncan thought savagely. *Die, damn you. Die!*

"They have done it, Kr-san!" Kantaro shouted.

The Terror swirled, diminished. The fires within burned hot and white. Duncan remembered how men had died in the Ross Stars, consumed by fire from within.

Between the MD and the Terror a point of light appeared. Duncan stared, appalled.

"What is it, Duncan?" Damon shouted. "What's happening?"

"A singularity," Duncan said, aghast. "It is opening a Gateway!"

The point opened into a double fan of light. Beyond the light lay the indeterminate space of the Near Away.

"Kantaro!" Duncan called desperately. *"Follow it!"* He heard Mira's scream of rage and fear.

Damon Ng's voice was shrill as he screamed, "No! Duncan, look out!"

That was the last thing Duncan Kr heard before the point of a throwing knife struck him in the back and began to drain the life out of him.

34

SCHRÖDINGER'S CAT

•

Anya Amaya, exhausted by the undesired responsibility of commanding Goldenwing *Gloria Coelis,* lay lightly tethered to her bunk in her austere quarters. Her eyelids twitched in Rapid Eye Movement sleep. The feminist from New Earth was dreaming.

Duncan lay bleeding from a wound that would kill him, yet his eyes were open and filled with some urgent message that she, Amaya, could not grasp. And while she failed in her task, Duncan slipped farther from life, drowning in a lake of blood.

She could see Artemis stepping daintily through Duncan's blood, sniffing at his face, running her rasp of a tongue across his pallid lips, then lifting her head and yowling mournfully. Somehow the other syndics' cats were also in Amaya's dream. Buele's Big twisted and darted across the frozen lake where Duncan now, miraculously, lay facing a white sky in which a white sun held motionless. Now Buele and Broni, together with their cats, shouted across the empty ice at Anya, who could not hear them. Dietr Krieg, wearing Paracelsus like a fur collar, loomed before Anya and said scornfully, "No woman is fit for command of a Goldenwing. No woman has the gifts. No woman has the imagination. Duncan made a mistake when he chose you, Amaya. Can't you hear him, Anya? We can hear him, why can't you?" Anya heard herself protesting, "Why doesn't he speak to me, Dietr? Tell me why." And suddenly she was a small girl again, a failure at Leadership School, soon to be cast out of her clone. The other Amaya 6 Clone girls materialized around her and

threatened to beat her—and all the while Buele and Broni Ehren-
graf were calling her name, again and again. . . .

She opened her eyes in shock. The syndics had all gathered
in her room. Their cats clung like bats to the fabric walls and uttered wailing, frightened calls.

Dietr Krieg, his customarily pale face dead white, said, "You
were dreaming, too."

Anya looked from one to another. Buele was Wired; his eyes
had the glazed look of one undergoing an information overload.

"I dreamed Duncan is dying," Broni said. "Did you?"

"Yes, yes, I . . ."

"Listen," Dietr said.

From beyond the fabric walls, beyond and down the tangled
plena, came a howling tumult.

Amaya's eyes widened. "The cats?"

"All of them," Broni sent. *"All."*

Dietr said, "Do you have any idea how many cats there are
aboard *Glory?*"

Amaya shook her head in bewilderment. She had never asked,
never investigated. Until Artemis appeared to choose her as partner, she had deliberately avoided thinking about how many of
Mira's descendants, natural, in vitros, or clones, there might be
in the kilometers of internal passageways and holds of the ship.
Duncan knew, but he had never actually said.

"There are dozens, Anya," Broni sent. *"Ours are only the*
cleverest ones. Clavius told me tonight."

Dietr broke in brusquely. *"They are hearing from Mira and*
Pronker and Hana—the little cat that chose Kantaro."

"Hearing? How can you know that?"

"We were all dreaming. You dreamed that Duncan was dying,
didn't you? Artemis says you did."

It was the first time Dietr had ever communicated with Anya
empathically.

Anya felt a surge of joy that immediately became a plunge of
grief.

"But they died. We saw them follow that thing through a sin-
gularity."

"No!" It was Buele's powerful sending. *"Find drogues. Wire*
up! Hurry!"

"Get to the bridge. Leave me here. Hurry." Anya realized that

the syndics were all communicating without *Glory*'s help. Only Buele was Wired, and he was using *Glory* to amplify his Talent by orders of magnitude. The force of his sendings was enormous. *"Go!"*

The syndics flew through the plena toward the bridge. When they tumbled into their accustomed pods and Wired, they realized that *Glory*, acting on her own, had reduced her delta to a minimum. This was both a difficult and a dangerous evolution. Sails had to be trimmed, some had to be furled, still others reefed. The holographs showed tiny monkeys swarming through the rig in a flurry of activity. Anya was shocked to receive sendings from the small critters. The empathic messages were primitive, but they were self-directed in a way that had never happened before. It was as if all the living things aboard *Glory*, even *Glory* herself, were combining into a superorganism intent on retrieving a part of itself.

This is insanity, Anya Amaya thought. The great-queen-who-is-not-alive was what the cats called the ship. How could a non-living being acquiesce in the recombination of all the life-forms within and without to form this—*cyborg*? What mind controlled the transformation?

Artemis clawed indelicately at Amaya's naked shoulder. *"Wire!"* the cat demanded. *"Anya, Wire!"*

Anya seated the drogue in her skull socket. Instantly there came the familiar broadening of perceptions, the expanding awareness and vision. She soared momentarily above the ship, needing a moment of solitude to integrate the changes that were taking place in her capabilities.

She "heard" a rustling background of tiny empathic voices calling plaintively for *"Damon. Damon. Damon."* It was the monkeys whispering as they scrambled through the kilometers of the glowing skylar rig. Anya felt a twinge of pity for the half-living beings, and a discovered warmth. Neither she nor any of the other syndics (except, perhaps Damon?) had ever been aware of the monkeys as entities with wants and loyalties.

Yet why not? Hadn't the small critters shown that they had fears and wants after the fight in the Ross Stars? Hadn't they, in effect, gone on strike because they were afraid? What was happening to *Glory*?

She returned her anima to the bridge and was immediately bombarded with sendings from Broni.

"Did you hear the cats?"

"Clavius is forcing them to stop shouting."

Then Buele, floating on the end of a drogue tether in Anya's quarters: *"I can't get* Glory *to respond, Sister Anya. Help me."*

"Glory—what is happening?" Anya made the query as forceful as she dared. The truth was that she doubted her ability to command *Glory* in any sort of emergency without Duncan to back her.

"The cats are receiving a message from Pronker."

"But Pronker must be dead."

"There is no 'must be,' Sailing Master."

The communications were short, abrupt. As though *Glory's* enormous computing capacity were being strained.

"Explain," Anya demanded.

"Not possible."

Anya fought an upsurging of desperation. Over the years one came to expect *human* responses from *Glory*. One tended to forget that she was not human, not even, as the cats so succinctly put it, alive.

Broni interrupted, *"But Clavius says—"*

"Broni," Anya sent firmly. *"Be silent."*

The girl subsided and Anya heard Clavius's growl of complaint. *"Glory,"* Anya sent again. *"What do you mean, 'there is no must be?' "*

That question the ancient computer handled firmly. *"There are many theories about an infinitely variable universe. If any one of them is true, then there is nothing that 'must be.' All things are."*

Amaya suppressed an outburst of exasperated anger. This was no time for abstruse theories. But she had asked and had been answered.

"Is there a message from the Near Away?"

"The cats hear one."

Hope exploded in Amaya's chest. *"From where? How far away?"*

"From here. There is no 'away.' All possibilities are part of one reality."

Amaya's eyes burned with tears of frustration. *"I do not understand that,* Glory."

"It cannot be stated more simply. The language does not permit it."

"I haven't time for mathematics!" Anya Amaya shouted aloud. Then she controlled herself and sent, *"Who do the cats hear?"*

Artemis yowled in a frustration that matched Amaya's own.

"I know you are trying to tell me something," Amaya sent to her partner. *"But I am only a human being."*

Glory sent cryptically, *"I am only a machine."*

Oh, God, Amaya thought. *Help me.*

Buele pushed his way into the rapport. *"I think I hear Pronker and Mira. Support me,* Glory. *Help me to hear them."*

Amaya caught the overspillage of the empathic exchange. It was being conducted on a plane she could not reach, and at a speed that burned the empathic environment as a speeding bullet might burn the air.

Broni was listening. Amaya and Artemis could feel Clavius intervening from moment to moment.

Glory sent to all, *"There have been, will be, may be, two deaths."*

Dietr Krieg interrupted heavy-handedly, *"None of this makes sense. What does 'have been, will be, may be'—mean? Are our people alive or dead?"*

Maddeningly, *Glory* responded, *"There was a Twentieth-Century physicist, Erwin Schrödinger, who won a Nobel Prize for Physics in nineteen thirty-three. He propounded this question: 'If my cat is confined in a box for an unspecified length of time, he may be alive or dead when the box is opened. But until it is, the cat is both alive and dead—' "*

"Glory! We have no time for parables!" Amaya's sending was an empathic scream of desperation.

"Sailing Master," Dietr Krieg sent, *"calm yourself. You are speaking to a machine!"*

Amaya reined in her surging emotions and sent to all, *"Artemis hears them. Can any other partners do the same?"*

Buele sent, *"Big hears them."*

"So does Clavius," Broni sent.

"Para, too!" This from the Cybersurgeon.

Artemis trilled desperately and not-so-gently bit Amaya on the hand.

The Sailing Master had a flashing insight. *Guidance,* she thought. *Guidance is what they must have to live.* "Everyone! Glory! *Buele, Broni, Dietr! I want every living thing aboard this starship—people, cats, monkeys, too—trying to lead them home.*"

35

HOW LONG IS FOREVER?

•

Through the single small port facing to starboard, Minamoto Kantaro watched the shoulder of the ship's mass-depletion coil glow first red, then yellow, shading to white, until it began to radiate in the blue end of the spectrum. The Mayor of Yedo looked desperately at the sprawled body of the young pilot. *Be alive, damn you,* he thought. *Open your eyes and tell me what to do next.*

But the young man lay still, sullenly buoyant as a log in swamp water in the almost nonexistent gravity within the ship. The fresh-faced would-be samurai had flown his last adventure aboard his beloved faster-than-light ship. Near him floated his murderer, the dreaded Master Tsunetomo, half his head burned away by the heat of the laze pistol he, Minamoto Kantaro, had fired with intent to kill.

The fact was that Minamoto Kantaro had never killed a fellow human being before, no matter the provocation. It made him feel sick. It did not make him regard the future—that is, those few moments between now and extinction—with any equanimity. The inexorable approach of certain death tended, as some ancient American had once said, to organize the mind splendidly. It was not a soothing thought to carry with one into the next world.

If there was a next world. In truth, Minamoto had never seen or conversed with anyone who had died. Religious faith was expected of the rulers of Planet Yamato; he had never admitted his doubts to anyone, not even to his uncle, the Shogun. But here and now he had begun to doubt his doubts.

It was a fact that he had stood by a crystal port and looked out at a universe he had never truly believed existed. It was all very well to be taught from earliest childhood that the universe was a profusion of exploding galaxies, millions of them, fleeing one another as though fearing contamination. Red shifts and blue shifts told their stories, but who *really* believed them? One was taught, from the time one learned the *kanji* and began to absorb human wisdom, that nothing could *ever* exceed *C,* the speed of light, a universal constant.

That being so, all those lights in the sky might as well have been illusions.

A Shinto priest once lectured a young Kantaro: "Do you remember where you were and what you did the day before you were conceived in your mother's womb? No? Then how dare you imagine what exists beyond the most distant stars?"

The logic had seemed flawed, but the confidence of the deliverer had been monumental. All of nature had seemed encompassed by the priest, the forest, the copper-colored sea and the torii gate under which student and *sensei* sat.

But certainties crumbled. The glowing coil around the small spaceship's middle was radiating away what remained of the ship's mass. When it was gone, the ship and all it contained would either dissipate into its constituent particles or it would simply implode, like a black hole, to drift forever in an alien space.

Either result of the end of mass depletion was acceptable for Kantaro. Life, even one without a guaranteed passage to the next, was without value now. Living two million light-years from home, in a solar system owned by who knew what sort of beings, did not appeal to Kantaro.

On Earth, the Japanese people had been among the most parochial on the homeworld. Yamatans were no different. Their rice grew on Yamato, their temples had been built there, the hemp garlands on their toriis lifted to the winds from Yamato's planetary sea.

For a moment Kantaro was tempted to abandon his post at the pilot's chair. The Terror had vanished, none knew where. It had been badly hurt by the headlong attack of its Magellanic enemies. Perhaps it, too, yearned for a peaceful place to die, Kantaro thought.

He glanced across the compartment. The port was still open, but beyond the glass there was nothing. On the deck, the young syndic Damon Ng was gripping Kr-san's wrists with all his concentration. His head pressed hard against Duncan's pallid brow. He had made no visible effort to staunch the flow of blood from the wound in Duncan's back, which was badly placed and deep. Yet the bleeding had nearly stopped. Kantaro did not know whether this was because the senior syndic was dead, or nearly so, or because Damon, in some mysterious Starman's way, had taken control of Duncan Kr's bleeding, holding it in check with the empathic power of his remarkable Starman's mind. Did Damon Ng suffer guilt as a Yamatan surely would, for having failed to guard the ninja as he should?

Then there were the cats. Kantaro tried hard to understand what was happening that involved Mira, Pronker and small Hana. He could not. They were crouched atop the instrument consoles staring fixedly in that strange way of the breed at . . . nothing. Or what seemed nothing. Their eyes seemed focused on a point in the blank Near Away. Kantaro, with his merely human senses, tried to imagine whatever it was they seemed to observe.

What could be so near to be of interest to the beasts? They were, after all, children of Planet Earth, as he was. They, too, had seen the alien splendor of M31 spread across the vault of the sky. And they, too were two million light-years from home.

The weight of such a distance overbore him. He longed for seppuku. If he could only now sit on the deck, make his peace with Amaterasu, and draw a knife across his abdomen in acceptance of honorable death . . .

Hana uttered an angry screech: *"No! Help us!"*

Help? To do what? And how?

Mira turned her head and stared straight into his eyes. *"You are a man. Do what men do."*

Kantaro was stunned. None of the syndic's cats had ever bespoken him so clearly and forcefully.

"Tell me."

Again she bespoke him clearly, powerfully.

"Call to Glory. Reach out to the great-queen-who-is-not-alive. You seem a man like the dominant tom. Be one. Make the great queen respond to you."

*   *   *

Broni Ehrengraf lay in the warm gel of her pod, Wired to *Glory* and closely bonded empathically to Clavius. The cat had been with her inside the pod until a few moments ago, but the hours that had passed since Big had heard the first sending from Duncan and Damon were difficult for a young tom to endure, and he had leapt up out of the pod to sit erect on the metal shoulder of the device.

Clavius was having difficulty with his attention span. One of the characteristics of all cats was an inability to remain concentrated on any thing or subject that did not regularly produce attention-demanding bursts of activity. Broni was aware that Mira had recently been concentrating her schooling efforts on the young cats, especially the males, whose attention was most apt to wander inopportunely.

Not that Broni objected to another, even Clavius's mother, schooling her partner without her present. Yet Mira, who could be arrogant to a fault, ignored her wishes and had continued to train Clavius in the art of concentration.

Broni, lurking about near the scene of the exercises, had distinctly heard Mira's sending to the effect that not every object of required attention was going to bound like a rabbit or smell like a field mouse. (Both of which objects Broni was certain neither Mira nor any of the cats, natural and enhanced, aboard *Glory* had ever actually seen.)

Now it remained to be seen how well Mira had taught her partner his lesson. Since congregating in the bridge, none of the syndics, human or feline, had heard so much as a subetheric whisper from the missing shipmates.

Was it possible that they had imagined hearing an appeal from the absent ones? Had they wanted to hear one so much that, in the event, they did?

That cannot be, Broni Ehrengraf thought. *"Stay alert, Clavius. Stay alert and listen."*

"I listen," the cat sent shortly. Long concentration made Clavius even more short tempered than it did the others.

The Goldenwing was moving slowly, adjusting its course accordingly. Moon Hideyoshi still lay under the stern of Goldenwing *Gloria Coelis*. The great ship seemed to be drifting, though of course that was pure illusion. But *Glory* was travelling far below her usual speed in space, the conning being done by sail trim, with *Glory* attending to most of that herself, while the monkeys provided the marginal requirement for the constant, small adjustments needed to keep the Goldenwing on a return track to Planet Yamato.

Buele remained in the Sailing Master's quarters, where he had chanced to Wire up after Big informed him that Mira was calling for help.

For help, he thought. Was it possible or were they all in a hallucination created by Big's powerful and effective mind? Brilliant he was, but still a *cat*, Buele thought. On his own homeworld of Voerster, women kept cheets as pets and men trained the larger varieties as hunters. But cheets were only *like* cats. The Terrestrial felines were a very different matter. Their small brains were as active as were human brains. Perhaps more active. The beasts were organized along certain clean design lines that the latent engineer in Buele approved. Instead of creating a being with a large brain that could use only a small percentage of its volume, the Increate had instead designed a small, efficient and, alas, short-lived animal whose autonomous nervous system could perform the necessary housekeeping in sleep with all—or nearly all—the brain cells available. A cat's years raced by in comparison to a man's. But a cat's waking life, though short by human standards, had a breadth of experience and empathic skill no human could duplicate.

Man, *Glory*'s database had instructed Buele, was gifted with a brain that was inventive, creative, and yet almost totally lacking in the ability to comprehend the nature of the surrounding universe.

A cat's brain was swift, feral, incapable of long periods of single-minded study and purpose, yet brilliantly endowed to perceive, and to receive signals from anywhere in the true universe. *It is as though,* Buele thought, *we humans look at reality through a gauze curtain.* They *see it all.*

Buele glanced at Big lying in Amaya's bunk. He thought, *You see reality as it is. Multiplex. Layered. Interactive. Can we ever learn that?*

Big's sending was brief and to the point. *"I don't understand you. Be silent and listen."* The cat repeated, almost verbatim, what old Osbertus Kloster, the Astronomer Select of Voerster who had adopted Buele and raised him, often said. And, as such memories tended to do, even in times of great stress, they brought melancholy.

He looked at Big with affection.

To roam the Near Stars I left the old man without a backward look, he thought. Big purred as Buele stroked his broad head. *Don't do to me what I did to Brother Osbertus,* he thought.

But Big only sent again, *"Listen!"*

It was *Glory* who sounded the true alarm. Since the first tentative signal out of the Near Away, *Glory* had been at work to modify and amplify her own capability to receive empathic calls. Since she was not truly alive, she received Mira's call as a series of ones and zeros, a language *Glory* understood well.

She began relaying the translations instantly.

Paracelsus merged from a trance state with a trilling cry and laid-back ears. Dietr Krieg received the call with stunning clarity. Of all the people aboard *Glory,* he was the last to expect to be chosen. But the cry out of the Near Away seemed guided to him and to his feline partner specifically from Damon Ng.

The torrent of images tumbling through the empathic gap was frightening. A deep, primitive wound. Much blood. Failing life signs. Damon using a level of empathic skills he had never been known to possess to keep a dying man alive.

"Help me, Dietr! Help me. I can't manage alone."

The others aboard *Glory* closed ranks immediately. Dietr felt his fellow syndics supporting him, aided by all life aboard the great ship. Even the chittering cyborgs in the rig were offering their empathic pittances.

Paracelsus scrambled into Dietr Krieg's open pod, and the Cybersurgeon felt it all.

He closed his eyes and sent, *"Hear me, Damon, hear me."*

Clearly, he received, *"Duncan is dying."*

A wave of grief crashed over Broni and Anya.

Dietr sent angrily, *"No time for that. Help Damon!"*

Amaya sent, *"Who is piloting the ship?"*

"Kantaro."

Before the tenuous rapport could break, Buele sent, *"Mira and Pronker are helping Damon keep Duncan alive. Can't you feel that? Who else is there?"*

Amaya sent, *"Kantaro has a kitten with him. He calls her Hana."*

Buele sent, *"You help Kantaro to find us, Sailing Master. The rest of us support the doctor."* And then in an unmistakable tone of command he sent, *"And you, Physician, Help Damon. Guide him. And—God help you—DON'T LET DUNCAN DIE!"*

36

OUT OF THE NEAR AWAY

•

This, then, thought Duncan, *is how it feels to die. There is some pain, though less as time passes. What have I said—'as time passes'? But there is no time; there is only perception of time. A human invention? Are other lives conscious of time passing, like the water in a river? Mira, does time pass for you, or do you only tolerate my fantasy of minutes, hours, days and years? Yet I can feel my time running out, and even if it is an illusion, I am grateful that there will be an ending.* He had spent years pretending to be a stoic, but pain had always daunted him. Pain and failure. Perhaps failure even more than pain.

I was given Glory to care for, Glory and her people. I was rash. I risked them all to hunt the Terror. Now I will not see the ending.

He could feel Damon's hold on his hands. *He is keeping me from shock,* Duncan thought. *No one taught him that. Somehow it was simply there when he needed it.*

I am not breathing, Duncan thought. *Damon is doing that for me. The air is shallow in my lungs, but it is enough to hold death at bay for a time. We have all become symbionts,* Duncan thought. *At need we can share all that we are with one another. Did Glory do this?* Did other syndics aboard other Goldenwings become partners in life-sharing?

Sharing. Could it be that this intertwined creature called Goldenwing *Gloria Coelis* was the next stage of man? He could hear Glendora, the matriarch of the marriage group that bore him all those parsecs and uptime years ago, speaking in a crofter's longhouse by the turbulent Thalassan sea. She addressed Duncan now as clearly as she had on the day he stepped aboard *Glory*'s shuttle with the aged syndic who had come to claim him. Glendora had kissed him, which was strange, because Thalassan Scots were not a demonstrative people, and she said, "Live honorably. Die well."

It was a farewell suited to the people who hunted the great furred fishes of the Thalassan Planetary Sea from coracles of bone and leather.

It suited Duncan's situation now.

I will, Mother, he thought. *And it will not be long.* The void of death lay very near.

He resisted Damon's entreaty to lie still and allow a fellow empath-symbiont to breathe and circulate the blood for him. *What little blood I have left,* Duncan thought sardonically. He could feel it, thick and cooling, puddled on the deck beneath him. Damon had stopped the worst of the bleeding. That was a remarkable achievement when the patient could help so little.

Duncan closed his eyes and found himself a child, straddling a spearpine bough and looking fearfully down at a forest floor dappled by the golden light of a GO sun. He was terrified, and urine ran down his slender leg and fell to the ground a quarter-kilometer below. It grieved him that the height frightened him so. The spearpine was the one allotted his peer group for their season in the forest canopy. All the boys of Planet Nixon were expected to have lost their fear of heights by the time of the season in the leaves. How else could they become the environmentalists they were meant to be on Nixon?

But Damon's fear of heights was as strong as it had ever been. The boys in the lodge taunted him for it, and his parents were ashamed. He had heard that a syndic had come downworld from the Goldenwing in orbit. The old syndic, it was rumored, was on Search, looking for the next generation of Wired Starmen for Goldenwing *Gloria Coelis*. The boys of his group said that he would be offered to the Ancient One, and good riddance.

To live in the sky! What would that be like? Would it be terrifying? How high was the sky? How long was the fall? Was it fraud to give Wired Starmen a child flawed by phobia? Fear rose like an acid tide. *No, Damon,* Duncan thought. *Don't be afraid. Think only of the joy. . . .*

I am not Damon Ng, Duncan thought. *We are intermingled, and empath though I am, this is the first time I can feel his dread of the phobia that has dominated his life. Yet he shares his life with me as an empath must. I have a need like his now. With every shallow breath, the ninja's wound brings me closer to the point of no return.*

He felt the soft touch of a paw on his cheek. Mira. *"Mira, my little queen. You will miss me. And I you if there is a heaven."* He closed his eyes and yet could see, in the dark colors of the feline spectrum, his own still face, and Damon's, tear-streaked with effort and grief. The image was slightly doubled and Duncan could not think why, until he realized that he was sharing Pronker's view as well.

He sent to the Folk in a weary, mental whisper: *"Guide them home. Guide them home."*

Kantaro gripped the guide-sticks that controlled the MD's attitude and heading. He was unwilling to allow the ship's automatic systems to do what they were designed to do. How could they, he asked himself fearfully, when there is no direction, no time, no space in this dreadful place those without imagination had dubbed so off-handedly the Near Away?

The truth was that neither he, nor any other scientist or pilot who had preceded him into the Near Away, had the slightest notion of whether or not it was near or far, or even whether it existed at all.

His imagination still reeled from the shock of emerging into true space and seeing the stars of the Magellanic Cloud and the overwhelming sight of the Great Andromeda Nebula dominating the vault of heaven with its immense beauty.

I did not see that, Kantaro thought. *None of us saw that. It was a dream. A hallucination. A projection of all Man's imaginings.*

Yet it had been there. *As we were,* he thought. And if it had not been for the resumption of the chase of the Terror, the Magellanic stars and the Great Nebula would still dominate the crystalline port that he, himself, had closed to make his grip on reality strong enough to pilot the small spacecraft on, in search of the vanished Terror, or, far better still, back home.

On the back of the pilot's chair, Hana crouched, claws fixed in the fabric upholstery. Her coat resembled that of a porcupine; her tail, thick as a bottle brush, she held straight up at ninety degrees from her twitching back. Kantaro found it hard to believe, but he was receiving a series of powerful sendings from the half-grown kitten. At first he made an effort to translate them into the Yamatan tongue, but soon he found that this was hopeless. The sendings from the small cat were garbled with indications of anger, of fear, and of anxious appeal.

Kantaro could also sense that they came through Hana rather than from her. The impressions he was getting were directional—though under the circumstances, and without any frame of reference within which to place the MD he now piloted, the directionality of the feline demands were beyond his level of empathy.

The mass indicators on his console warned that the ship had consumed most of its mass. What would happen when the mass was totally depleted, he could only guess. And the guesses did not include one that saw them bursting out of the Near Away in close low orbit with Planet Yamato.

Hana howled with exhaustion and anxiety. The empathic signals wavered and became unreadable by Kantaro. He swept the cat from the chair-back and cradled her against his chest. She whimpered and tried to purr. "Dear Hana," Minamoto Kantaro murmured, "are we killing you?"

Kantaro looked at Mira and Pronker. The two mature Folk looked intent on what seemed to be their first priority: doing something to assist Damon Ng in the rapidly complicating task of keeping Duncan Kr alive.

That is my fault, Kantaro thought bitterly. *To my everlasting shame, it is I who acquiesced in the hiring of the Order of Ninjas, and so it is I who bears the responsibility for Tsunemoto being here on board, and for the repeated attempts to kill Duncan Kr. If, by some miracle, I survive this adventure, it will be my honorable task to ask the Shogun for permission to commit seppuku.*

Thoughts of death did not affect the cats. They ignored death, as they had when they were wildcats in the dawn of Earth's lifetime. When they became excited and assumed fighting stances, backs arched and ears flattened, one forgot that they were complex creatures of surprising depth.

These were not lost animals. Kantaro reminded himself that on the ancient homeworld they had been known, when lost or abandoned, to find their owners over ranges of thousands of kilometers. So was it possible that they *were* receiving calls from the animals populating the Goldenwing?

Hana squirmed free and took an excited fighting stance. Pronker and Mira seemed torn between their duty to Duncan and their instinct to survive. Kantaro's anxieties peaked as the temperature inside the MD began to climb.

The fleeing Terror had turned on its small tormentor and reached out to crush and burn it.

On *Glory*'s bridge the first indication of the Terror's presence was from the untrained cats spread throughout the nearly empty ship. For the second time in memory, *Glory* howled with the fury of the Folk. Artemis, snarling at the air, sent a clear and unambiguous message to Anya Amaya: *"The black dog is back!"*

Instead of rising panic, Amaya felt a stir of furious hope. When it had vanished, Duncan and the people aboard the Yamatan ship had plunged headlong after it. In a typically male, testosterone-driven attack mode, Amaya, child of New Earth, thought bitterly. Well, if they were still alive, the men aboard the MD would follow the killer back into normal space. The war was not yet over.

She concentrated on interpreting Artemis's sendings accurately. She could sense Buele and Big crowding close behind her. If there was to be any disagreement on a plan of battle, Amaya thought, her support would have to come from Broni—who was young, often foolish, but well partnered by Clavius, and *a woman.*

We have no weapons to speak of, Amaya thought. *Only the ship.* Could the million metric tons of *Glory*'s mass injure the Terror? Duncan had never tried it, but Duncan would never deliberately put the ship herself at risk. The syndics, yes. But not the Goldenwing *Gloria Coelis.* Never.

"Broni," she sent. *"Where is It?"*

"Clavius sees It, I think. A spatial distortion a hundred kilometers off our port bow."

"Dietr, what does Para see?"

"Nothing, Sailing Master."

"Buele?"

"Big sees the anomaly. It looks like a Gateway opening."

Amaya weighed the options of command. A man would not divide his forces. But a woman might disperse her battle assets. "It is all in the perception, Duncan," she whispered aloud.

"Buele, Broni. Suit up and take a shuttle out. Dietr, we are going to fight. Be ready for casualties."

"Aye, Acting Captain," the Cybersurgeon sent.

In the surgery, Dietr Krieg initiated the healing pods. These devices had not been used since Broni Ehrengraf had come aboard with her leaking, rheumatic heart. Paracelsus watched from his position clinging onto the surgery wall.

"Yes, Para," Dietr sent. *"If any of the Folk are hurt there is room for them."*

The lean tabby trilled at him and looked wise.

You are a fraud, my friend, Dietr Krieg thought. *So are we all.*

Here, in the Amaterasu Sun's gravity well, time was real, moving, as time often did, with precise intent.

Monkeys raced through the rig; the skylar sails of the great Goldenwing shifted and retrimmed to a port tack and filled to the tachyon wind. *Glory*'s change of course was dignified, majestic. Nearly three thousand years ago the great, wind-driven wooden warships of Earth had performed just such ponderous evolutions to close with their enemies.

Glory, child of that harsh tradition, sailed toward the spatial anomaly.

Duncan struggled to make himself understood. His powers were fading. When he opened his eyes it seemed he looked through a long, darkening tunnel. But Mira's warning was still clear. Damon and Pronker were too engaged with the effort to keep Duncan breathing to react to the warning Mira sensed.

But Damon, not understanding, sent angrily, *"Mira, your partner is dying. Don't abandon us. We need your help."*

Mira snarled and cuffed at him. *"Look. Look where we are and where we are going!"*

Hana, her attention fixed, with Kantaro's, on the empty-seeming space ahead, uttered a cry of fright.

With a burst of light and radiation, space ahead of the MD ship changed character. In a microsecond a brilliant singularity appeared, followed by an involuted spatial construct with dark, lip-like boundaries. Fans of light in the near ultraviolet flashed, and beyond could be seen a dark sky shot with dim stars.

Duncan took control of his own respiratory system and sucked air painfully into his punctured lung. The pain was like a blade of fire piercing him from the inside out.

"Kantaro!"

There was not enough trained Talent in the Yamatan to receive Duncan's command. He cried aloud, "Kantaro! Block the opening! It must not enter normal space again! Use the ship and block the Gateway!" *"Help him, Mira! Guide him!"*

The effort brought Duncan back to the edge of death. Damon caught him as he slumped back to the bloody deck.

Kantaro glimpsed the shoulder of the mass-depletion coil encircling the ship. It glowed deep violet. The ship's maneuvering was consuming the last of the mass-depletion energy.

37

OUT OF THE NEAR AWAY

•

Buele and Broni Ehrengraf, armored for space and seated side by side in the strongest of *Glory*'s wedge-shaped shuttles—the nearest thing to a gunship *Glory* could boast—saw the first gleam that warned of the imminence of an opening Gateway. It appeared as a point of light only microns in diameter, but potent with the energy of a collapsing sun. Big and Clavius gave shrill warning cries and Broni, acting as pilot, swung the shuttle so that the point of the wedge, heavily coated with heat-and-radiation-proof ceramic, faced the event horizon that was in the process of materializing around the singularity.

The event, as an astronomical phenomenon, violated all the laws of astrophysics the young syndics knew, but on this voyage they had been forced to confront many similar events.

Duncan had once passed on to Broni and Buele a dictum learned from Han Soo, once *Glory*'s Astroprogrammer, who had died in space a shiptime month from planetfall at Planet Voerster. "Know what you believe," the ancient Earthman had often said, "but believe what you can see."

Duncan had passed a number of Han Soo's homilies on to the younger syndics. Han claimed to have been born in the Yangtze Valley of China the year the Jihad began. He counted his 120 shiptime years as more than a thousand of the swift downworld kind.

Since neither Broni nor Buele had ever known Han Soo, they allowed themselves to be a bit skeptical about his age. But about his wisdom they had no doubt.

The singularity, the heart of a tiny black hole, was *there*. They had seen it before. And if it challenged the Einsteinian dogma spacefaring people lived by, so be it. Their own elongated lifetimes were just such a challenge.

Buele used the com unit in his suit helmet. "Can you see it, Sister Anya?" It was a measure of his stress that he had fallen back into his early habit of addressing his shipmates as "Sister" and "Brother."

Anya Amaya's reply was loud and clear in Buele's helmet. Anya said, "Stay clear but stay near. That thing will have *Glory* to deal with now." The headset also produced a trilling growl that Big acknowledged as Artemis's signature.

Those syndics aboard *Glory* who had partnered with cats had modified their helmets so that they would protect the partner riding on a shoulder. Broni settled Clavius on her shoulder and closed the helmet of her suit. She and Buele had already discussed and decided upon a move through the Gateway to see if the Yamatan mass-depletion ship had remained close to the swirling black of the Terror. How they would present this plan to the Acting Captain was an unresolved argument between them. Broni, ever more impulsive than her companion, favored a straightforward rush through the Gateway as soon as it was fully open. Buele, with his greater respect for rules, insisted that they must get Anya Amaya's approval before attempting so hazardous an action.

The shuttle's track lay below and to the right of the spreading Gateway. From their vantage point the two syndics could see nothing beyond the puffy black lips of the spatial opening.

As sometimes happened to Buele, he received a sudden sending that came from he knew not where.

"Kantaro . . . follow it . . . use the lazegun."

"Broni!" Buele sent. *"Did you get that? Did you, Big? Clavius? Anyone?"*

No human responded. But Clavius did. It was an ever-recurring mystery that the ability to send and receive empathic messages varied from cat to cat, and from cat to cat hour to hour.

Clavius, greatly agitated, projected a garbled image of a man, badly injured by one of his own kind, down and close to death. The personal signal that identified every living thing capable of empathic exchange was so faint Clavius could not read it.

It was followed by another identifier: *"Damon!"*

"Sailing Master! They are there, on the other side of the singularity," Buele sent.

Broni demanded, *"Are you sure?"*

Buele ignored her. He had his plan of action complete now. He took the controls from Broni, intending to plunge through the Gateway.

But the black, shapeless threat they had come to know had materialized in the throat of the anomaly. Long ago, Buele had sensed primitive emotions from the Terror. Then it had been loneliness. Now it was anxiety. It was trying to run away. Into Near Space, Buele guessed. He fired thrusters and accelerated the spear-pointed shuttle directly at the Gateway.

The Terror was forming on the near side of the Gateway. Broni said, "Wait, Buele! Look!"

Even as she spoke, a beam of laser fire pierced the center of the darkness and drove off into space.

"Sailing Master, did you see that? Stay clear. Stay clear." Broni's sending was sharp and as authoritative as a pubescent Voertrekker empath could make it.

The laser seemed more an annoyance than a threat to the Terror. It folded in upon itself like a great Klein bottle, and sent a streamer of fire-threaded black back into the singularity.

Buele intercepted another sending.

"Drive into it! Into it, Kantaro!"

This time the sending was unmistakably Damon Ng's. With Big's help, Buele began to send, filling Near Space with empathic signals, trying to pierce the open Gateway.

"We are here! We are here, Brother Damon!"

Simultaneously from Amaya and Dietr: *"Duncan?"*

So they could hear Damon now. But nothing from Duncan. Buele wondered with sinking heart: Was the dying man in his empathic images Duncan Kr?

Sensitive to all that concerned Duncan, Broni had picked up his thought and began an emotional torrent. *"It can't be. I won't have it. Not now that he is so nearby."* Then, *"Duncan! Duncan! Please answer!"*

The Klein-bottle shape of the Terror seemed to be convulsing. It protruded from the anomaly, sending unaimed bolts of violent lightning fifty kilometers into normal space.

Then with breathtaking suddenness, a ball of yellow fire exploded inside the Terror. All the empaths within range were staggered with a burst of fear, surprise and rage from the Terror.

Debris tumbled out of the Gateway. Metal, ceramics, small bits and large, all tumbling out of the singularity. The Gateway began instantly to close around the Terror. Tighter and tighter, until it became once again a brilliant point of light. Which imploded into total darkness, leaving shuttle and Goldenwing alone, ten thousand kilometers from Moon Hideyoshi.

Near Space was glittering with debris.

Broni and Buele stared at one another. The debris had the shiny, polished look of Yamatan metalwork.

"No, oh no," whispered Broni.

"Kantaro was piloting," Buele said in a low voice. "I have heard that the ancestors of the Yamatans sometimes committed suicide by diving their craft into their enemies. . . ."

Broni stared, aghast.

But the cats were purring. *Purring.* The young syndics turned bitter, their grief suddenly renewed and their anger frustrated.

Then from *Glory* came a simple radio signal:

"Shuttle. There is an escape pod in the debris. Recover it and return."

EPILOGUE: GLORY'S PEOPLE

•

It is the end of Duncan's fourteenth day in a recovery pod. Dietr Krieg, the Cybersurgeon, is proud of the results he has had with healing Duncan's injuries. It also delights his Germanic soul that he has complete charge of the Master and Commander.

Glory is about to leave orbit around Planet Yamato and the physician has decreed that the Master and Commander is not required for so simple an evolution. The junior syndics, under the supervision of the Sailing Master, will conduct the departure.

Minamoto Kantaro, about to descend to the planet, has come to bid Duncan Kr farewell. He carries Hana in a special pocket in his travelling clothes.

He stands beside the gel-filled pod and grasps Duncan's hand in friendship.

"Will you be Shogun?" Duncan asks.

"Perhaps. There are careers I would rather follow."

Duncan smiles.

Kantaro says thoughtfully, "We did not learn how it is done. We had no time. But we found that it could be done. That means it will be done."

"Not in my lifetime," Duncan says.

"Do not be so certain, Kr-san. We are an inventive people."

Duncan, still weak, regards the Yamatan steadily. "Have you told them?"

Kantaro runs a hand thoughtfully across his smooth cheek. He shakes his head. "Not yet. Have you?"

"Not yet," Duncan replies.

They discuss changes on the planet. The Shogun has stripped Yoshi Eiji of his Domain and ordered him to trade with the Genji Lord: Kai for frigid Hokkaido. And he has been ordered to war with the Order of Ninja. "The fright has nearly killed him," Kantaro says.

As they speak, cats have been coming into the surgery. Kantaro recognizes only a few of them. Mira is there. Big. Clavius. Artemis. Paracelsus. A dozen others.

They sit in silence watching him.

He hears a soft mew. Hana has climbed from his pocket and sits on Duncan's pod, regarding Kantaro sombrely. "Hana," he sends. "You are not coming with me?"

From the others he gets only a question: "What would her life be?"

His eyes dampen. He feels a fool. To Duncan, he says, "She wouldn't be the same on the planet, would she?"

"No," Duncan says.

Kantaro cups Hana's small head gently. There is a lump in his throat. "A long life, sweet Hana," he sends.

The cats weave about his legs for a moment and then depart. Hana follows them.

Broni Ehrengraf, who will fly the shuttle to Honshu, appears to announce that it is time for departure.

"Good-bye, Master and Commander," Kantaro says. "I will regret all my life that I was not chosen on Search to be a Starman."

"Good-bye, my friend. Remember. You have seen Andromeda."

It is a sending Minamoto Kantaro will remember for a long lifetime.